KILLING FLOOR

'Great style and careful plotting . . . Depicted with the
kind of detail that builds dread and suspense'
New York Times

At least as good as any of Grisham's'
Cork Examiner

THE VISITOR

'Compulsive reading right up to the last page'
The Times

'A thumping good read . . . This is an excellent thriller
of the Patricia Cornwell variety. Gripping and well
constructed . . . Impossible to put down'
Frances Fyfield, *The Express*

TRIPWIRE

'A slickly effective thriller that confirms Child's ability
to keep the reader guessing – and sweating'
The Times

'Fast-moving, violent and gripping'
Daily Telegraph

DIE TRYING

'Cunning and explosive . . . A thumping good read'
Time Out

'A skilled, smart, violent page-turner'
The Express

Also by Lee Child

DIE TRYING

TRIP WIRE

THE VISITOR

ECHO BURNING

and available from Bantam Books

KILLING FLOOR

Lee Child

BANTAM BOOKS

LONDON • NEW YORK • TORONTO • SYDNEY • AUCKLAND

KILLING FLOOR
A BANTAM BOOK : 0 553 50540 8

Originally published in Great Britain by Bantam Press,
a division of Transworld Publishers

PRINTING HISTORY
Bantam Press edition published 1998
Bantam Books edition published 1999

7 9 10 8

Set in 11/11½pt Plantin by
Falcon Oast Graphic Art.

Bantam Books are published by Transworld Publishers,
61–63 Uxbridge Road, London W5 5SA,
a division of The Random House Group Ltd,
in Australia by Random House Australia (Pty) Ltd,
20 Alfred Street, Milsons Point, Sydney, NSW 2061, Australia,
in New Zealand by Random House New Zealand Ltd,
18 Poland Road, Glenfield, Auckland 10, New Zealand
and in South Africa by Random House (Pty) Ltd,
Endulini, 5a Jubilee Road, Parktown 2193, South Africa.

Printed and bound in Great Britain by
Cox & Wyman Ltd, Reading, Berkshire.

My agent is Darley Anderson in London; my editors are David Highfill in New York and Marianne Velmans in London. They worked hard to get this writer his break. This book is dedicated to the three of them, in appreciation of all their efforts, which went way beyond the call of duty.

KILLING FLOOR

ONE

I was arrested in Eno's diner. At twelve o'clock. I was eating eggs and drinking coffee. A late breakfast, not lunch. I was wet and tired after a long walk in heavy rain. All the way from the highway to the edge of town.

The diner was small, but bright and clean. Brand-new, built to resemble a converted railroad car. Narrow, with a long lunch counter on one side and a kitchen bumped out back. Booths lining the opposite wall. A doorway where the centre booth would be.

I was in a booth, at a window, reading somebody's abandoned newspaper about the campaign for a President I didn't vote for last time and wasn't going to vote for this time. Outside, the rain had stopped but the glass was still pebbled with bright drops. I saw the police cruisers pull into the gravel lot. They were moving fast and crunched to a stop. Light bars flashing and popping. Red and blue light in the raindrops on my window. Doors burst open, policemen jumped out. Two from each car, weapons ready. Two revolvers, two shotguns. This was heavy stuff. One revolver and one shotgun ran to the back. One of each rushed the door.

I just sat and watched them. I knew who was in the diner. A cook in back. Two waitresses. Two old men. And me. This operation was for me. I had been in town less than a half-hour. The other five had probably been here all their lives. Any problem with any of them and an embarrassed sergeant would have shuffled in. He would be apologetic. He would mumble to them. He would ask them to come down to the station house. So the heavy weapons and the rush weren't for any of them. They were for me. I crammed egg into my mouth and trapped a five under the plate. Folded the abandoned newspaper into a square and shoved it into my coat pocket. Kept my hands above the table and drained my cup.

The guy with the revolver stayed at the door. He went into a crouch and pointed the weapon two-handed. At my head. The guy with the shotgun approached close. These were fit lean boys. Neat and tidy. Textbook moves. The revolver at the door could cover the room with a degree of accuracy. The shotgun up close could splatter me all over the window. The other way around would be a mistake. The revolver could miss in a close-quarters struggle and a long-range shotgun blast from the door would kill the arresting officer and the old guy in the rear booth as well as me. So far, they were doing it right. No doubt about that. They had the advantage. No doubt about that, either. The tight booth trapped me. I was too hemmed in to do much. I spread my hands on the table. The officer with the shotgun came near.

'Freeze! Police!' he screamed.

He was screaming as loud as he could. Blowing off his tension and trying to scare me. Textbook moves. Plenty of sound and fury to soften the target. I raised my hands. The guy with the revolver started in from the door. The guy with the shotgun came closer. Too close. Their first error. If I had to, I might have lunged for the shotgun barrel and forced it up. A blast into the ceiling perhaps and an elbow into the policeman's face and the shotgun could have been mine. The guy with the revolver had narrowed his angle and couldn't risk hitting his partner. It could have ended badly for them. But I just sat there, hands raised. The guy with the shotgun was still screaming and jumping.

'Out here on the floor!' he yelled.

I slid slowly out of the booth and extended my wrists to the officer with the revolver. I wasn't going to lie on the floor. Not for these country boys. Not if they brought along their whole police department with howitzers.

The guy with the revolver was a sergeant. He was pretty calm. The shotgun covered me as the sergeant holstered his revolver and unclipped the handcuffs from his belt and clicked them on my wrists. The backup team came in through the kitchen. They walked around the lunch counter. Took up position behind me. They patted me down. Very thorough. I saw the sergeant acknowledge the shakes of the heads. No weapon.

The backup guys each took an elbow. The shotgun still covered me. The sergeant stepped up in front. He was a compact, athletic white man. Lean and tanned. My age. The acetate nameplate above his shirt pocket said: Baker. He looked up at me.

'You are under arrest for murder,' he said. 'You have the right to remain silent. Anything you say

11

may be used as evidence against you. You have the right to representation by an attorney. Should you be unable to afford an attorney, one will be appointed for you by the State of Georgia free of charge. Do you understand these rights?'

It was a fine rendition of Miranda. He spoke clearly. He didn't read it from a card. He spoke like he knew what it meant and why it was important. To him and to me. I didn't respond.

'Do you understand your rights?' he said again.

Again I didn't respond. Long experience had taught me that absolute silence is the best way. Say something, and it can be misheard. Misunderstood. Misinterpreted. It can get you convicted. It can get you killed. Silence upsets the arresting officer. He has to tell you silence is your right but he hates it if you exercise that right. I was being arrested for murder. But I said nothing.

'Do you understand your rights?' the guy called Baker asked me again. 'Do you speak English?'

He was calm. I said nothing. He remained calm. He had the calm of a man whose moment of danger had passed. He would just drive me to the station house and then I would become someone else's problem. He glanced round his three fellow officers.

'OK, make a note, he's said nothing,' he grunted. 'Let's go.'

I was walked towards the door. At the door we formed a single file. First Baker. Then the guy with the shotgun, walking backward, still with the big black barrel pointing at me. His nameplate said: Stevenson. He too was a medium white man in good shape. His weapon looked like a drainpipe. Pointing at my gut. Behind me were the backup guys. I was pushed through the door with a hand flat on my back.

Outside in the gravel lot the heat was up. It must have rained all night and most of the morning. Now the sun was blasting away and the ground was steaming. Normally this would be a dusty hot place. Today it was steaming with that wonderful heady aroma of drenched pavement under a hot noon sun. I stood face up to the sun and inhaled as the officers regrouped. One at each elbow for the short walk to the patrol cars. Stevenson still on the ball with the pump-action. At the first car he skipped backward a step as Baker opened the rear door. My head was pushed down. I was nudged into the car with a neat hip-to-hip contact from the left-hand backup. Good moves. In a town this far from anywhere, surely the result of a lot of training rather than a lot of experience.

I was alone in the back of the car. A thick glass partition divided the space. The front doors were still open. Baker and Stevenson got in. Baker drove. Stevenson was twisted around keeping me under observation. Nobody talked. The backup car followed. The cars were new. Quiet and smooth riding. Clean and cool inside. No ingrained traces of desperate and pathetic people riding where I was riding.

I looked out of the window. Georgia. I saw rich land. Heavy, damp red earth. Very long and straight rows of low bushes in the fields. Peanuts, maybe. Belly crops, but valuable to the grower. Or to the owner. Did people own their land here? Or did giant corporations? I didn't know.

The drive to town was short. The car hissed over the smooth soaked tarmac. After maybe a half-mile I saw two neat buildings, both new, both with tidy landscaping. The police station and the fire house. They stood alone together, behind a wide lawn with

13

a statue, north edge of town. Attractive county architecture on a generous budget. Roads were smooth tarmac, sidewalks were red blocks. Three hundred yards south, I could see a blinding white church steeple behind a small huddle of buildings. I could see flagpoles, awnings, crisp paint, green lawns. Everything refreshed by the heavy rain. Now steaming and somehow intense in the heat. A prosperous community. Built, I guessed, on prosperous farm incomes and high taxes on the commuters who worked up in Atlanta.

Stevenson still stared at me as the car slowed to yaw into the approach to the station house. A wide semicircle of driveway. I read on a low masonry sign: Margrave Police Headquarters. I thought: should I be worried? I was under arrest. In a town where I'd never been before. Apparently for murder. But I knew two things. First, they couldn't prove something had happened if it hadn't happened. And second, I hadn't killed anybody.

Not in their town, and not for a long time, anyway.

TWO

We pulled up at the doors of the long low building. Baker got out of the car and looked up and down along the frontage. The backup guys stood by. Stevenson walked around the back of our car. Took up a position opposite Baker. Pointed the shotgun at me. This was a good team. Baker opened my door.

'OK, let's go, let's go,' he said. Almost a whisper.

He was bouncing on the balls of his feet, scanning the area. I pivoted slowly and twisted out of the car. The handcuffs didn't help. Even hotter now. I stepped forward and waited. The backup fell in behind me. Ahead of me was the station house entrance. There was a long marble lintel crisply engraved: Town of Margrave Police Headquarters. Below it were plate-glass doors. Baker pulled one open. It sucked against rubber seals. The backup pushed me through. The door sucked shut behind me.

Inside it was cool again. Everything was white and chrome. Lights were fluorescent. It looked like a bank or an insurance office. There was carpet. A desk sergeant stood behind a long reception counter. The way the place looked, he should have said: how may I help you, sir? But he said nothing. He just looked at me. Behind him was a huge open-plan space. A dark-haired woman in uniform was sitting at a wide, low desk. She had been doing paperwork on a keyboard. Now she was looking at me. I stood there, an officer on each elbow. Stevenson was backed up against the reception counter. His shotgun was pointed at me. Baker stood there, looking at me. The desk sergeant and the woman in uniform were looking at me. I looked back at them.

Then I was walked to the left. They stopped me in front of a door. Baker swung it open and I was pushed into a room. It was an interview facility. No windows. A white table and three chairs. Carpet. In the top corner of the room, a camera. The air in the room was set very cold. I was still wet from the rain.

I stood there and Baker ferreted into every pocket. My belongings made a small pile on the table. A roll of cash. Some coins. Receipts, tickets, scraps. Baker checked the newspaper and left it in my pocket. Glanced at my watch and left it on my wrist. He wasn't interested in those things. Everything else was swept into a large Ziplock bag. A bag made for people with more in their pockets than I carry. The bag had a white panel printed on it. Stevenson wrote some kind of a number on the panel.

Baker told me to sit down. Then they all left the room. Stevenson carried the bag with my stuff in it. They went out and closed the door and I heard the lock turning. It had a heavy, well-greased sound.

The sound of precision. The sound of a big steel lock. Sounded like a lock that would keep me in.

I figured they would leave me isolated for a while. It usually happens that way. Isolation causes an urge to talk. An urge to talk can become an urge to confess. A brutal arrest followed by an hour's isolation is pretty good strategy.

But I figured wrong. They hadn't planned an hour's isolation. Maybe their second slight tactical mistake. Baker unlocked the door and stepped back in. He carried a plastic cup of coffee. Then he signalled the uniformed woman into the room. The one I'd seen at her desk in the open area. The heavy lock clicked behind her. She carried a metal flight case which she set on the table. She clicked it open and took out a long black number holder. In it were white plastic numbers.

She handed it to me with that brusque apologetic sympathy that dental nurses use. I took it in my cuffed hands. Squinted down to make sure it was the right way up and held it under my chin. The woman took an ugly camera out of the case and sat opposite me. She rested her elbows on the table to brace the camera. Sitting forward. Her breasts rested on the edge of the table. This was a good-looking woman. Dark hair, great eyes. I stared at her and smiled. The camera clicked and flashed. Before she could ask I turned sideways on the chair for the profile. Held the long number against my shoulder and stared at the wall. The camera clicked and flashed again. I turned back and held out the number. Two-handed, because of the cuffs. She took it from me with that pursed grin which says: yes, it's unpleasant, but it's necessary. Like the dental nurse.

17

Then she took out the fingerprint gear. A crisp ten-card, already labelled with a number. The thumb spaces are always too small. This one had a reverse side with two squares for palm prints. The handcuffs made the process difficult. Baker didn't offer to remove them. The woman inked my hands. Her fingers were smooth and cool. No wedding band. Afterwards she handed me a wad of tissues. The ink came off very easily. Some kind of new stuff I hadn't seen before.

The woman unloaded the camera and put the film with the prints card on the table. She repacked the camera into the flight case. Baker rapped on the door. The lock clicked again. The woman picked up her stuff. Nobody spoke. The woman left the room. Baker stayed in there with me. He shut the door and it locked with the same greased click. Then he leaned on the door and looked at me.

'My chief's coming on down,' he said. 'You're going to have to talk to him. We got a situation here. Got to be cleared up.'

I said nothing back to him. Talking to me wasn't going to clear any situation up for anybody. But the guy was acting civilized. Respectful. So I set him a test. Held out my hands toward him. An unspoken request to unlock the cuffs. He stood still for a moment then took out the key and unlocked them. Clipped them back on his belt. Looked at me. I looked back and dropped my arms to my sides. No grateful exhalation. No rueful rubbing of my wrists. I didn't want a relationship with this guy. But I did speak.

'OK,' I said. 'Let's go meet your chief.'

It was the first time I'd spoken since ordering breakfast. Now Baker was the one who looked grateful. He rapped twice on the door and it was unlocked from the outside. He opened it up and signalled me through. Stevenson was waiting with his back to the large open area. The shotgun was gone. The backup crew was gone. Things were calming down. They formed up, one on each side. Baker gripped my elbow, lightly. We walked down the side of the open area and came to a door at the back. Stevenson pushed it open and we walked through into a large office. Lots of rosewood all over it.

A fat guy sat at a big rosewood desk. Behind him were a couple of big flags. There was a Stars and Stripes with a gold fringe on the left and what I guessed was the Georgia state flag on the right. On the wall between the flags was a clock. It was a big old round thing framed in mahogany. Looked like it had decades of polish on it. I figured it must be the clock from whatever old station house they bulldozed to build this new place. I figured the architect had used it to give a sense of history to the new building. It was showing nearly twelve-thirty.

The fat guy at the big desk looked up at me as I was pushed in towards him. I saw him look blank, like he was trying to place me. He looked again, harder. Then he sneered at me and spoke in a wheezing gasp which would have been a shout if it hadn't been strangled by bad lungs.

'Get your ass in that chair and keep your filthy mouth shut,' he said.

This fat guy was a surprise. He looked like a real asshole. Opposite to what I'd seen so far. Baker and his arrest team were the business. Professional and efficient. The fingerprint woman had been decent. But this fat police chief was a waste of space. Thin dirty hair. Sweating, despite the chilly air. The blotchy red and grey complexion of an

19

unfit, overweight mess. Blood pressure sky-high. Arteries hard as rocks. He didn't look halfway competent.

'My name is Morrison,' he wheezed. As if I cared. 'I am chief of the police department down here in Margrave. And you are a murdering outsider bastard. You've come down here to my town and you've messed up right there on Mr Kliner's private property. So now you're going to make a full confession to my chief of detectives.'

He stopped and looked up at me. Like he was still trying to place me. Or like he was waiting for a response. He didn't get one. So he jabbed his fat finger at me.

'And then you're going to jail,' he said. 'And then you're going to the chair. And then I'm going to take a dump on your shitty little pauper's grave.'

He hauled his bulk out of the chair and looked away from me.

'I'd deal with this myself,' he said. 'But I'm a busy man.'

He waddled out from behind his desk. I was standing there between his desk and the door. As he crabbed by, he stopped. His fat nose was about level with the middle button on my coat. He was still looking up at me like he was puzzled by something.

'I've seen you before,' he said. 'Where was it?'

He glanced at Baker and then at Stevenson. Like he was expecting them to note what he was saying and when he was saying it.

'I've seen this guy before,' he told them.

He slammed the office door and I was left waiting with the two cops until the chief of detectives swung in. A tall black guy, not old, but greying and

20

balding. Just enough to give him a patrician air. Brisk and confident. Well-dressed, in an old-fashioned tweed suit. Moleskin vest. Shined shoes. This guy looked like a chief should look. He signalled Baker and Stevenson out of the office. Closed the door behind them. Sat down at the desk and waved me to the opposite chair.

He rattled open a drawer and pulled out a cassette recorder. Raised it high, arm's length, to pull out the tangle of cords. Plugged in the power and the microphone. Inserted a tape. Pressed record and flicked the microphone with his fingernail. Stopped the tape and wound it back. Pressed play. Heard the thunk of his nail. Nodded. Wound back again and pressed record. I sat and watched him.

For a moment there was silence. Just a faint hum, the air, the lights, or the computer. Or the recorder whirring slowly. I could hear the slow tick of the old clock. It made a patient sound, like it was prepared to tick on for ever, no matter what I chose to do. Then the guy sat right back in his chair and looked hard at me. Did the steepled fingers thing, like tall elegant people can.

'Right,' he said. 'We got a few questions, don't we?'

The voice was deep. Like a rumble. Not a southern accent. He looked and sounded like a Boston banker, except he was black.

'My name is Finlay,' he said. 'My rank is captain. I am chief of this department's detective bureau. I understand you have been apprised of your rights. You have not yet confirmed that you understood them. Before we go any further we must pursue that preliminary matter.'

Not a Boston banker. More like a Harvard guy.

'I understand my rights,' I said.

He nodded.

'Good,' he said. 'I'm glad about that. Where's your lawyer?'

'I don't need a lawyer,' I said.

'You're charged with murder,' he said. 'You need a lawyer. We'll provide one, you know. Free of charge. Do you want us to provide one, free of charge?'

'No, I don't need a lawyer,' I said.

The guy called Finlay stared at me over his fingers for a long moment.

'OK,' he said. 'But you're going to have to sign a release. You know, you've been advised you may have a lawyer, and we'll provide one, at no cost to yourself, but you absolutely don't want one.'

'OK,' I said.

He shuffled a form from another drawer and checked his watch to enter date and time. He slid the form across to me. A large printed cross marked the line where I was supposed to sign. He slid me a pen. I signed and slid the form back. He studied it. Placed it in a buff folder.

'I can't read that signature,' he said. 'So for the record we'll start with your name, your address and your date of birth.'

There was silence again. I looked at him. This was a stubborn guy. Probably forty-five. You don't get to be chief of detectives in a Georgia jurisdiction if you're forty-five and black except if you're a stubborn guy. No percentage in jerking him around. I drew a breath.

'My name is Jack Reacher,' I said. 'No middle name. No address.'

He wrote it down. Not much to write. I told him my date of birth.

'OK, Mr Reacher,' Finlay said. 'As I said, we have a lot of questions. I've glanced through your personal effects. You were carrying no ID at all. No driver's licence, no credit cards, no nothing. You have no address, you say. So I'm asking myself, who is this guy?'

He didn't wait for any kind of a comment on that from me.

'Who was the guy with the shaved head?' he asked me.

I didn't answer. I was watching the big clock, waiting for the minute hand to move.

'Tell me what happened,' he said.

I had no idea what had happened. No idea at all. Something had happened to somebody, but not to me. I sat there. Didn't answer.

'What is Pluribus?' Finlay asked.

I looked at him and shrugged.

'The United States motto?' I said. 'E Pluribus Unum? Adopted in 1776 by the second Continental Congress, right?'

He just grunted at me. I carried on looking straight at him. I figured this was the type of a guy who might answer a question.

'What is this about?' I asked him.

Silence again. His turn to look at me. I could see him thinking about whether to answer, and how.

'What is this about?' I asked him again.

He sat back and steepled his fingers.

'You know what this is about,' he said. 'Homicide. With some very disturbing features. Victim was found this morning up at the Kliner warehouse. North end of the county road, up at the highway cloverleaf. Witness has reported a man seen walking away from that location. Shortly after eight o'clock this morning. Description given was

23

that of a white man, very tall, wearing a long black overcoat, fair hair, no hat, no baggage.'

Silence again. I am a white man. I am very tall. My hair is fair. I was sitting there wearing a long black overcoat. I didn't have a hat. Or a bag. I had been walking on the county road for the best part of four hours this morning. From eight until about eleven forty-five.

'How long is the county road?' I said. 'From the highway all the way down to here?'

Finlay thought about it.

'Maybe fourteen miles, I guess,' he said.

'Right,' I said. 'I walked all the way down from the highway into town. Fourteen miles, maybe. Plenty of people must have seen me. Doesn't mean I did anything to anybody.'

He didn't respond. I was getting curious about this situation.

'Is that your neighbourhood?' I asked him. 'All the way over at the highway?'

'Yes, it is,' he said. 'Jurisdiction issue is clear. No way out for you there, Mr Reacher. The town limit extends fourteen miles, right up to the highway. The warehousing out there is mine, no doubt about that.'

He waited. I nodded. He carried on.

'Kliner built the place, five years ago,' he said. 'You heard of him?'

I shook my head.

'How should I have heard of him?' I said. 'I've never been here before.'

'He's a big deal around here,' Finlay said. 'His operation out there pays us a lot of taxes, does us a lot of good. A lot of revenue and a lot of benefit for the town without a lot of mess, because it's so far away, right? So we try to take care of it for him. But

24

now it's a homicide scene, and you've got explaining to do.'

The guy was doing his job, but he was wasting my time.

'OK, Finlay,' I said. 'I'll make a statement describing every little thing I did since I entered your lousy town limits until I got hauled in here in the middle of my damn breakfast. If you can make anything out of it, I'll give you a damn medal. Because all I did was to place one foot in front of the other for nearly four hours in the pouring rain all the way through your precious fourteen damn miles.'

That was the longest speech I had made for six months. Finlay sat and gazed at me. I watched him struggling with any detective's basic dilemma. His gut told him I might not be his man. But I was sitting right there in front of him. So what should a detective do? I let him ponder. Tried to time it right with a nudge in the right direction. I was going to say something about the real guy still running around out there while he was wasting time in here with me. That would feed his insecurity. But he jumped first. In the wrong direction.

'No statements,' he said. 'I'll ask the questions and you'll answer them. You're Jack-none-Reacher. No address. No ID. What are you, a vagrant?'

I sighed. Today was Friday. The big clock showed it was already more than half over. This guy Finlay was going to go through all the hoops with this. I was going to spend the weekend in a cell. Probably get out Monday.

'I'm not a vagrant, Finlay,' I said. 'I'm a hobo. Big difference.'

He shook his head, slowly.

'Don't get smart with me, Reacher,' he said.

'You're in deep shit. Bad things happened up there. Our witness saw you leaving the scene. You're a stranger with no ID and no story. So don't get smart with me.'

He was still just doing his job, but he was still wasting my time.

'I wasn't leaving a homicide scene,' I said. 'I was walking down a damn road. There's a difference, right? People leaving homicide scenes run and hide. They don't walk straight down the road. What's wrong about walking down a road? People walk down roads all the damn time, don't they?'

Finlay leaned forward and shook his head.

'No,' he said. 'Nobody has walked the length of that road since the invention of the automobile. So why no address? Where are you from? Answer the questions. Let's get this done.'

'OK, Finlay, let's get it done,' I said. 'I don't have an address because I don't live anywhere. Maybe one day I'll live somewhere and then I'll have an address and I'll send you a picture postcard and you can put it in your damn address book, since you seem so damn concerned about it.'

Finlay gazed at me and reviewed his options. Elected to go the patient route. Patient, but stubborn. Like he couldn't be deflected.

'Where are you from?' he asked. 'What was your last address?'

'What exactly do you mean when you say where am I from?' I asked.

His lips were clamped. I was getting him bad-tempered, too. But he stayed patient. Laced the patience with an icy sarcasm.

'OK,' he said. 'You don't understand my question, so let me try to make it quite clear. What I mean is, where were you born, or where have you

26

lived for that majority period of your life which you instinctively regard as predominant in a social or cultural context?'

I just looked at him.

'I'll give you an example,' he said. 'I myself was born in Boston, was educated in Boston and subsequently worked for twenty years in Boston, so I would say, and I think you would agree, that I come from Boston.'

I was right. A Harvard guy. A Harvard guy, running out of patience.

'OK,' I said. 'You've asked the questions. I'll answer them. But let me tell you something. I'm not your guy. By Monday you'll know I'm not your guy. So do yourself a favour. Don't stop looking.'

Finlay was fighting a smile. He nodded gravely.

'I appreciate your advice,' he said. 'And your concern for my career.'

'You're welcome,' I said.

'Go on,' he said.

'OK,' I said. 'According to your fancy definition, I don't come from anywhere. I come from a place called Military. I was born on a US Army base in West Berlin. My old man was Marine Corps and my mother was a French civilian he met in Holland. They got married in Korea.'

Finlay nodded. Made a note.

'I was a military kid,' I said. 'Show me a list of US bases all around the world and that's a list of where I lived. I did high school in two dozen different countries and I did four years up at West Point.'

'Go on,' Finlay said.

'I stayed in the army,' I said. 'Military Police. I served and lived in all those bases all over again. Then, Finlay, after thirty-six years of first being an officer's kid and then being an officer myself, suddenly there's no need for a great big army any more because the Soviets have gone belly up. So hooray, we get the peace dividend. Which for you means your taxes get spent on something else, but for me means I'm a thirty-six year old unemployed ex-military policeman getting called a vagrant by smug civilian bastards who wouldn't last five minutes in the world I survived.'

He thought for a moment. Wasn't impressed.

'Continue,' he said.

I shrugged at him.

'So right now I'm just enjoying myself,' I said. 'Maybe eventually I'll find something to do, maybe I won't. Maybe I'll settle somewhere, maybe I won't. But right now, I'm not looking to.'

He nodded. Jotted some more notes.

'When did you leave the army?' he asked.

'Six months ago,' I said. 'April.'

'Have you worked at all since then?' he asked.

'You're joking,' I said. 'When was the last time you looked for work?'

'April,' he mimicked. 'Six months ago. I got this job.'

'Well, good for you, Finlay,' I said.

I couldn't think of anything else to say. Finlay gazed at me for a moment.

'What have you been living on?' he asked. 'What rank did you hold?'

'Major,' I said. 'They give you severance pay when they kick you out. Still got most of it. Trying to make it last, you know?'

A long silence. Finlay drummed a rhythm with the wrong end of his pen.

* * *

'So let's talk about the last twenty-four hours,' he said.

I sighed. Now I was heading for trouble.

'I came up on the Greyhound bus,' I said. 'Got off at the county road. Eight o'clock this morning. Walked down into town, reached that diner, ordered breakfast and I was eating it when your guys came by and hauled me in.'

'You got business here?' he asked.

I shook my head.

'I'm out of work,' I said. 'I haven't got any business anywhere.'

He wrote that down.

'Where did you get on the bus?' he asked me.

'In Tampa,' I said. 'Left at midnight last night.'

'Tampa in Florida?' he asked.

I nodded. He rattled open another drawer. Pulled out a Greyhound schedule. Riffed it open and ran a long brown finger down a page. This was a very thorough guy. He looked across at me.

'That's an express bus,' he said. 'Runs straight through north to Atlanta. Arrives there nine o'clock in the morning. Doesn't stop here at eight.'

I shook my head.

'I asked the driver to stop,' I said. 'He said he shouldn't, but he did. Stopped specially, let me off.'

'You been around here before?' he asked.

I shook my head again.

'Got family down here?' he asked.

'Not down here,' I said.

'You got family anywhere?' he asked.

'A brother up in DC,' I said. 'Works for the Treasury Department.'

'You got friends down here in Georgia?' he asked.

'No,' I said.

Finlay wrote it all down. Then there was a long silence. I knew for sure what the next question was going to be.

'So why?' he asked. 'Why get off the bus at an unscheduled stop and walk fourteen miles in the rain to a place you had absolutely no reason to go to?'

That was the killer question. Finlay had picked it out right away. So would a prosecutor. And I had no real answer.

'What can I tell you?' I said. 'It was an arbitrary decision. I was restless. I have to be somewhere, right?'

'But why here?' he said.

'I don't know,' I said. 'Guy next to me had a map, and I picked this place out. I wanted to get off the main drags. Thought I could loop back down toward the Gulf, further west, maybe.'

'You picked this place out?' Finlay said. 'Don't give me that shit. How could you pick this place out? It's just a name. It's just a dot on the map. You must have had a reason.'

I nodded.

'I thought I'd come and look for Blind Blake,' I said.

'Who the hell is Blind Blake?' he said.

I watched him evaluating scenarios like a chess computer evaluates moves. Was Blind Blake my friend, my enemy, my accomplice, conspirator, mentor, creditor, debtor, my next victim?

'Blind Blake was a guitar player,' I said. 'Died sixty years ago, maybe murdered. My brother bought a record, sleeve note said it happened in Margrave. He wrote me about it. Said he was through here a couple of times in the spring, some kind of business. I thought I'd come down and check the story out.'

Finlay looked blank. It must have sounded pretty thin to him. It would have sounded pretty thin to me too, in his position.

'You came here looking for a guitar player?' he said. 'A guitar player who died sixty years ago? Why? Are you a guitar player?'

'No,' I said.

'How did your brother write you?' he asked. 'When you got no address?'

'He wrote my old unit,' I said. 'They forward my mail to my bank, where I put my severance pay. They send it on when I wire them for cash.'

He shook his head. Made a note.

'The midnight Greyhound out of Tampa, right?' he said.

I nodded.

'Got your bus ticket?' he asked.

'In the property bag, I guess,' I said. I remembered Baker bagging up all my pocket junk. Stevenson tagging it.

'Would the bus driver remember?' Finlay said.

'Maybe,' I said. 'It was a special stop. I had to ask him.'

I became like a spectator. The situation became abstract. My job had been not that different from Finlay's. I had an odd feeling of conferring with him about somebody else's case. Like we were colleagues discussing a knotty problem.

'Why aren't you working?' Finlay asked.

I shrugged. Tried to explain.

'Because I don't want to work,' I said. 'I worked thirteen years, got me nowhere. I feel like I tried it their way, and to hell with them. Now I'm going to try it my way.'

Finlay sat and gazed at me.

'Did you have any trouble in the army?' he said.

'No more than you did in Boston,' I said.

He was surprised.

'What do you mean by that?' he said.

'You did twenty years in Boston,' I said. 'That's what you told me, Finlay. So why are you down here in this no-account little place? You should be taking your pension, going out fishing. Cape Cod or wherever. What's your story?'

'That's my business, Mr Reacher,' he said. 'Answer my question.'

I shrugged.

'Ask the army,' I said.

'I will,' he said. 'You can be damn sure of that. Did you get an honourable discharge?'

'Would they give me severance if I didn't?' I said.

'Why should I believe they gave you a dime?' he said. 'You live like a damn vagrant. Honourable discharge? Yes or no?'

'Yes,' I said. 'Of course.'

He made another note. Thought for a while.

'How did it make you feel, being let go?' he asked.

I thought about it. Shrugged at him.

'Didn't make me feel like anything,' I said. 'Made me feel like I was in the army, and now I'm not in the army.'

'Do you feel bitter?' he said. 'Let down?'

'No,' I said. 'Should I?'

'No problems at all?' he asked. Like there had to be something.

I felt like I had to give him some kind of an answer. But I couldn't think of anything. I had been in the service since the day I was born. Now I was out. Being out felt great. Felt like freedom. Like all my life I'd had a slight headache. Not noticing until it was gone. My only problem was making a living. How to make a living without giving up the freedom was not an easy trick. I hadn't earned a cent in six months. That was my only problem. But I wasn't about to tell Finlay that. He'd see it as a motive. He'd think I had decided to bankroll my vagrant lifestyle by robbing people. At warehouses. And then killing them.

'I guess the transition is hard to manage,' I said. 'Especially since I had the life as a kid, too.'

Finlay nodded. Considered my answer.

'Why you in particular?' he said. 'Did you volunteer to muster out?'

'I never volunteer for anything,' I said. 'Soldier's basic rule.'

Another silence.

'Did you specialize?' he asked. 'In the service?'

'General duties, initially,' I said. 'That's the system. Then I handled secrets security for five years. Then the last six years, I handled something else.'

Let him ask.

'What was that?' he asked.

'Homicide investigation,' I said.

Finlay leaned right back. Grunted. Did the steepled fingers thing again. He gazed at me and exhaled. Sat forward. Pointed a finger at me.

'Right,' he said. 'I'm going to check you out. We've got your prints. Those should be on file with the army. We'll get your service record. All of it. All the details. We'll check with the bus company. Check your ticket. Find the driver, find the passengers. If what you say is right, we'll know soon enough. And if it's true, it may let you off the hook. Obviously, certain details of timing and methodology will determine the matter. Those details are as yet unclear.'

He paused and exhaled again. Looked right at me.

'In the meantime, I'm a cautious man,' he said. 'On the face of it, you look bad. A drifter. A vagrant. No address, no history. Your story may be bullshit. You may be a fugitive. You may have been murdering people left and right in a dozen states. I just don't know. I can't be expected to give you the benefit of the doubt. Right now, why should I even have any doubt? You stay locked up until we know for sure, OK?'

It was what I had expected. It was exactly what I would have said. But I just looked at him and shook my head.

'You're a cautious guy?' I said. 'That's for damn sure.'

He looked back at me.

'If I'm wrong, I'll buy you lunch on Monday,' he said. 'At Eno's place, to make up for today.'

I shook my head again.

'I'm not looking for a buddy down here,' I said.

Finlay just shrugged. Clicked off the tape recorder. Rewound. Took out the tape. Wrote on it. He buzzed the intercom on the big rosewood desk. Asked Baker to come back in. I waited. It was still cold. But I had finally dried out. The rain had fallen out of the Georgia sky and had soaked into me. Now it had been sucked out again by the dried office air. A dehumidifier had sucked it out and piped it away.

Baker knocked and entered. Finlay told him to escort me to the cells. Then he nodded to me. It was a nod which said: if you turn out not to be the guy, remember I was just doing my job. I nodded back. Mine was a nod which said: while you're covering your ass, there's a killer running about outside.

* ★ *

The cell block was really just a wide alcove off the main open-plan squad room. It was divided into three separate cells with vertical bars. The front wall was all bars. A gate section hinged into each cell. The metalwork had a fabulous dull glitter. Looked like titanium. Each cell was carpeted. But totally empty. No furniture or bed ledge. Just a high-budget version of the old-fashioned holding pens you used to see.

'No overnight accommodation here?' I asked Baker.

'No way,' he replied. 'You'll be moved to the state facility later. Bus comes by at six. Bus brings you back Monday.'

He clanged the gate shut and turned his key. I heard bolts socket home all around the rim. Electric. I took the newspaper out of my pocket. Took off my coat and rolled it up. Lay flat on the floor and crammed the coat under my head.

Now I was truly pissed off. I was going to prison for the weekend. I wasn't staying in a station house cell. Not that I had any other plans. But I knew about civilian prisons. A lot of army deserters end up in civilian prisons. For one thing or another. The system notifies the army. Military policeman gets sent to bring them back. So I'd seen civilian prisons. They didn't make me wild with enthusiasm. I lay angrily listening to the hum of the squad room. Phones rang. Keyboards pattered. The tempo rose and fell. Officers moved about, talking low.

Then I tried to finish reading the borrowed newspaper. It was full of shit about the President and his campaign to get himself elected again for a second term. The old guy was down in Pensacola on the Gulf Coast. He was aiming to get the budget balanced before his grandchildren's hair turned white. He was cutting things like a guy with a machete blasting his way through the jungle. Down in Pensacola, he was sticking it to the Coast Guard. They'd been running an initiative for the last twelve months. They'd been out in force like a curved shield off Florida's coast every day for a year, boarding and searching all the marine traffic they didn't like the smell of. It had been announced with an enormous fanfare. And it had been successful beyond their wildest dreams. They'd seized all kinds of stuff. Drugs, mostly, but guns as well, illegal migrants from Haiti and Cuba. The interdiction was reducing crime all over the States months later and thousands of miles further down the line. A big success.

So it was being abandoned. It was very expensive to run. The Coast Guard's budget was into serious deficit. The President said he couldn't increase it. In fact, he'd have to cut it. The economy was in a mess. Nothing else he could do. So the interdiction initiative would be cancelled in seven days' time. The President was trying to come across like a statesman. Law enforcement big shots were angry, because they figured prevention was better than cure. Washington insiders were happy, because fifty cents spent on beat cops was much more visible than two bucks spent out on the ocean two thousand miles away from the voters. The arguments flew back and forth. And in the smudgy photographs, the President was just beaming away like a statesman saying there was nothing he could do. I stopped reading, because it was just making me angrier.

To calm down, I ran music through my head.

The chorus in 'Smokestack Lightning'. The Howling Wolf version puts a wonderful strangled cry on the end of the first line. They say you need to ride the rails for a while to understand the travelling blues. They're wrong. To understand the travelling blues you need to be locked down somewhere. In a cell. Or in the army. Someplace where you're caged. Someplace where smokestack lightning looks like a far-away beacon of impossible freedom. I lay there with my coat as a pillow and listened to the music in my head. At the end of the third chorus, I fell asleep.

I woke up again when Baker started kicking the bars. They made a dull ringing sound. Like a funeral bell. Baker stood there with Finlay. They looked down at me. I stayed on the floor. I was comfortable down there.

'Where did you say you were at midnight last night?' Finlay asked me.

'Getting on the bus in Tampa,' I said.

'We've got a new witness,' Finlay said. 'He saw you at the warehouse facility. Last night. Hanging around. At midnight.'

'Total crap, Finlay,' I said. 'Impossible. Who the hell is this new witness?'

'The witness is Chief Morrison,' Finlay said. 'The chief of police. He says he was sure he had seen you before. Now he has remembered where.'

THREE

They took me back to the rosewood office in handcuffs. Finlay sat at the big desk, in front of the flags, under the old clock. Baker set a chair at the end of the desk. I sat opposite Finlay. He took out the tape machine. Dragged out the cords. Positioned the microphone between us. Tested it with his fingernail. Rolled the tape back. Ready.

'The last twenty-four hours, Reacher,' he said. 'In detail.'

The two policemen were crackling with repressed excitement. A weak case had suddenly grown strong. The thrill of winning was beginning to grip them. I recognized the signs.

'I was in Tampa last night,' I said. 'Got on the bus at midnight. Witnesses can confirm that. I got off the bus at eight this morning where the county road meets the highway. If Chief Morrison says he saw me at midnight, he's mistaken. At that time I was about four hundred miles away. I can't add anything more. Check it out.'

Finlay stared at me. Then he nodded to Baker who opened a buff file.

'Victim is unidentified,' Baker said. 'No ID. No wallet. No distinguishing marks. White male, maybe forty, very tall, shaved head. Body was found up there at eight this morning on the ground against the perimeter fence close to the main gate. It was partially covered with cardboard. We were able to fingerprint the body. Negative result. No match anywhere in the database.'

'Who was he, Reacher?' Finlay asked.

Baker waited for some sort of reaction from me. He didn't get one. I just sat there and listened to the quiet tick of the old clock. The hands crawled around to two-thirty. I didn't speak. Baker riffed through the file and selected another sheet. He glanced up again and continued.

'Victim received two shots to the head,' he said. 'Probably a small-calibre automatic with a silencer. First shot was close range, left temple, second was a contact shot behind the left ear. Obviously soft-nosed slugs, because the exit wounds removed the guy's face. Rain has washed away the powder deposits but the burn patterns suggest the silencer. Fatal shot must have been the first. No bullets remained in the skull. No shell cases were found.'

'Where's the gun, Reacher?' Finlay said.

I looked at him and made a face. Didn't speak.

'Victim died between eleven-thirty and one o'clock last night,' Baker said. 'Body wasn't there at eleven-thirty when the evening gateman went off duty. He confirms that. It was found when the day man came in to open the gate. About eight o'clock. He saw you leaving the scene and phoned it in.'

'Who was he, Reacher?' Finlay said again.

I ignored him and looked at Baker.

'Why before one o'clock?' I asked him.

'The heavy rain last night began at one o'clock,' he said. 'The pavement underneath the body was bone dry. So, the body was on the ground before one o'clock when the rain started. Medical opinion is he was shot at midnight.'

I nodded. Smiled at them. The time of death was going to let me out.

'Tell us what happened next,' Finlay said, quietly.

I shrugged at him.

'You tell me,' I said. 'I wasn't there. I was in Tampa at midnight.'

Baker leaned forward and pulled another sheet out of the file.

'What happened next is you got weird,' he said. 'You went crazy.'

I shook my head at him.

'I wasn't there at midnight,' I said again. 'I was getting on the bus in Tampa. Nothing too weird about that.'

The two cops didn't react. They looked pretty grim.

'Your first shot killed him,' Baker said. 'Then you shot him again, and then you went berserk and kicked the shit out of the body. There are massive postmortem injuries. You shot him and then you tried to kick him apart. You kicked that corpse all over the damn place. You were in a frenzy. Then you calmed down and tried to hide the body under the cardboard.'

I was quiet for a long moment.

'Postmortem injuries?' I said.

Baker nodded.

'Like a frenzy,' he said. 'The guy looks like he was run over by a truck. Just about every bone is smashed. But the doctor says it happened after the guy was already dead. You're a weird guy, Reacher, that's for damn sure.'

'Who was he?' Finlay asked for the third time.

I just looked at him. Baker was right. It had got weird. Very weird. Homicidal frenzy is bad enough. But postmortem frenzy is worse. I'd come across it a few times. Didn't want to come across it any more. But the way they'd described it to me, it didn't make any sense.

'How did you meet the guy?' Finlay asked.

I carried on just looking at him. Didn't answer.

'What does Pluribus mean?' he asked.

I shrugged. Kept quiet.

'Who was he, Reacher?' Finlay asked again.

'I wasn't there,' I said. 'I don't know anything.'

Finlay was silent.

'What's your phone number?' he said. Suddenly.

I looked at him like he was crazy.

'Finlay, what the hell are you talking about?' I said. 'I haven't got a phone. Don't you listen? I don't live anywhere.'

'I mean your mobile phone,' he said.

'What mobile phone?' I said. 'I haven't got a mobile phone.'

A clang of fear hit me. They figured me for an assassin. A weird rootless mercenary with a mobile phone who went from place to place killing people. Kicking their dead bodies to pieces. Checking in with an underground organization for my next target. Always on the move.

Finlay leaned forward. He slid a piece of paper toward me. It was a torn-off section of computer paper. Not old. A greasy gloss of wear on it. The patina paper gets from a month in a pocket. On it was printed an underlined heading. It said:

Pluribus. Under the heading was a telephone number. I looked at it. Didn't touch it. Didn't want any confusion over fingerprints.

'Is that your number?' Finlay asked.

'I don't have a telephone,' I said again. 'I wasn't here last night. The more you hassle me, the more time you're wasting, Finlay.'

'It's a mobile phone number,' he said. 'That we know. Operated by an Atlanta airtime supplier. But we can't trace the number until Monday. So we're asking you. You should co-operate, Reacher.'

I looked at the scrap of paper again.

'Where was this?' I asked him.

Finlay considered the question. Decided to answer it.

'It was in your victim's shoe,' he said. 'Folded up and hidden.'

I sat in silence for a long time. I was worried. I felt like somebody in a kid's book who falls down a hole. Finds himself in a strange world where everything is different and weird. Like Alice in Wonderland. Did she fall down a hole? Or did she get off a Greyhound in the wrong place?

I was in a plush and opulent office. I had seen worse offices in Swiss banks. I was in the company of two policemen. Intelligent and professional. Probably had more than thirty years' experience between them. A mature and competent department. Properly staffed and well funded. A weak point with the asshole Morrison at the top, but as good an organization as I had seen for a while. But they were all disappearing up a dead end as fast as they could run. They seemed convinced the earth was flat. That the huge Georgia sky was a bowl

42

fitting snugly over the top. I was the only one who knew the earth was round.

'Two things,' I said. 'The guy is shot in the head close up with a silenced automatic weapon. First shot drops him. Second shot is insurance. The shell cases are missing. What does that say to you? Professionally?'

Finlay said nothing. His prime suspect was discussing the case with him like a colleague. As the investigator, he shouldn't allow that. He should cut me down. But he wanted to hear me out. I could see him arguing with himself. He was totally still, but his mind was struggling like kittens in a sack.

'Go on,' he said eventually. Gravely, like it was a big deal.

'That's an execution, Finlay,' I said. 'Not a robbery or a squabble. That's a cold and clinical hit. No evidence left behind. That's a smart guy with a flashlight scrabbling around afterward for two small-calibre shell cases.'

'Go on,' Finlay said again.

'Close range shot into the left temple,' I said. 'Could be the victim was in a car. Shooter is talking to him through the window and raises his gun. Bang. He leans in and fires the second shot. Then he picks up his shell cases and he leaves.'

'He leaves?' Finlay said. 'What about the rest of the stuff that went down? You're suggesting a second man?'

I shook my head.

'There were three men,' I said. 'That's clear, right?'

'Why three?' he said.

'Practical minimum of two, right?' I said. 'How did the victim get out there to the warehouses? He drove, right? Too far from anywhere to walk. So

43

where's his car now? The shooter didn't walk there, either. So the practical minimum would be a team of two. They drove up there together and they drove away separately, one of them in the victim's car.'

'But?' Finlay said.

'But the actual evidence points to a minimum of three,' I said. 'Think about it psychologically. That's the key to this thing. A guy who uses a silenced small-calibre automatic for a neat head shot and an insurance shot is not the type of guy who then suddenly goes berserk and kicks the shit out of a corpse, right? And the type of guy who does get in a frenzy like that doesn't then suddenly calm down and hide the body under some old cardboard. You're looking at three completely separate things there, Finlay. So there were three guys involved.'

Finlay shrugged at me.

'Two, maybe,' he said. 'Shooter could have tidied up afterward.'

'No way,' I said. 'He wouldn't have waited around. He wouldn't like that kind of frenzy. It would embarrass him. And it would worry him because it adds visibility and danger to the whole thing. And a guy like that, if he had tidied up afterward, he'd have done it right. He wouldn't have left the body where the first guy who came along was going to find it. So you're looking at three guys.'

Finlay thought hard.

'So?' he said.

'So which one am I supposed to be?' I said. 'The shooter, the maniac or the idiot who hid the body?'

Finlay and Baker looked at each other. Didn't answer me.

'So whichever one, what are you saying?' I asked

them. 'I drive up there with my two buddies and we hit this guy at midnight, and then my two buddies drive away and I choose to stay there? Why would I do that? It's crap, Finlay.'

He didn't reply. He was thinking.

'I haven't got two buddies,' I said. 'Or a car. So the very best you can do is to say the victim walked there, and I walked there. I met him, and I very carefully shot him, like a pro, then recovered my shell cases and took his wallet and emptied his pockets, but forgot to search his shoes. Then I stashed my weapon, silencer, flashlight, mobile phone, the shell cases, the wallet and all. Then I completely changed my whole personality and kicked the corpse to pieces like a maniac. Then I completely changed my whole personality again and made a useless attempt to hide the body. And then I waited eight hours in the rain and then I walked down into town. That's the very best you can do. And it's total crap, Finlay. Because why the hell would I wait eight hours, in the rain, until daylight, to walk away from a homicide?'

He looked at me for a long moment.

'I don't know why,' he said.

A guy like Finlay doesn't say a thing like that unless he's struggling. He looked deflated. His case was crap and he knew it. But he had a severe problem with the chief's new evidence. He couldn't walk up to his boss and say: you're full of shit, Morrison. He couldn't actively pursue an alternative when his boss had handed him a suspect on a plate. He could follow up my alibi. That he could do. Nobody would criticize him for being thorough. Then he could start again on Monday. So he was miserable because seventy-two hours were going to

45

get wasted. And he could foresee a big problem. He had to tell his boss that actually I could not have been there at midnight. He would have to politely coax a retraction out of the guy. Difficult to do when you're a new subordinate who's been there six months. And when the person you're dealing with is a complete asshole. And your boss. Difficulties were all over him, and the guy was miserable as hell about it. He sat there, breathing hard. In trouble. Time to help him out.

'The phone number,' I said. 'You've identified it as a mobile?'

'By the code,' he said. 'Instead of an area code, they have a prefix which accesses the mobile network.'

'OK,' I said. 'But you can't identify who it belongs to because you have no reverse directories for mobiles and their office won't tell you, right?'

'They want a warrant,' he said.

'But you need to know whose number it is, right?' I said.

'You know some way of doing that without a warrant?' he asked.

'Maybe,' I said. 'Why don't you just call it up and see who answers?'

They hadn't thought of that. There was another silence. They were embarrassed. They didn't want to look at each other. Or me. Silence.

Baker bailed out of the situation. Left Finlay holding the ball. He collected up the files and mimed going outside to work on them. Finlay nodded and waved him away. Baker got up and went out. Closed the door very quietly indeed. Finlay opened his mouth. And closed it. He needed to save some face. Badly.

'It's a mobile,' he said. 'If I call it up I can't tell whose it is or where it is.'

'Listen, Finlay,' I said. 'I don't care whose it is. All I care is whose it isn't. Understand? It isn't my phone. So you call it up and John Doe in Atlanta or Jane Doe in Charleston answers it. Then you know it isn't mine.'

Finlay gazed at me. Drummed his fingers on the desk. Kept quiet.

'You know how to do this,' I said. 'Call the number, some bullshit story about a technical fault or an unpaid bill, some computer thing, get the person to confirm name and address. Do it, Finlay, you're supposed to be a damn detective.'

He leaned forward to where he had left the number. Slid the paper back with his long brown fingers. Reversed it so he could read it and picked up the phone. Dialled the number. Hit the speakerphone button. The ring tone filled the air. Not a sonorous long tone like a home phone. A high, urgent electronic sound. It stopped. The phone was answered.

'Paul Hubble,' a voice said. 'How may I help you?'

A southern accent. A confident manner. Accustomed to telephones.

'Mr Hubble?' Finlay said. He was looking at the desk, writing down the name. 'Good afternoon. This is the phone company, mobile division. Engineering manager. We've had a fault reported on your number.'

'A fault?' the voice said. 'Seems OK to me. I didn't report a fault.'

'Calling out should be OK,' Finlay said. 'It's reaching you that may have been a problem, sir. I've got our signal-strength meter connected

47

right now, and actually, sir, it's reading a bit low.'

'I can hear you OK,' the voice said.

'Hello?' Finlay said. 'You're fading a bit, Mr Hubble. Hello? It would help me to know the exact geographic location of your phone, sir, you know, right now, in relation to our transmitting stations.'

'I'm right here at home,' said the voice.

'OK,' Finlay said. He picked up his pen again. 'Could you just confirm that exact address for me?'

'Don't you have my address?' the voice said. Man-to-man jocular stuff. 'You seem to manage to send me a bill every month.'

Finlay glanced at me. I was smiling at him. He made a face.

'I'm here in engineering right now, sir,' he said. Also jocular. Just two regular guys battling technology. 'Customer details are in a different department. I could access that data, but it would take a minute, you know how it is. Also, sir, you've got to keep talking anyway while this meter is connected to give me an exact strength reading, you know? You may as well recite your address, unless you've got a favourite poem or anything.'

The tinny speakerphone relayed a laugh from the guy called Hubble.

'OK, here goes, testing, testing,' his voice said. 'This is Paul Hubble, right here at home, that's number twenty-five Beckman Drive, I say again, zero-two-five Beckman Drive, down here in little old Margrave, that's M-A-R-G-R-A-V-E, in the State of Georgia, USA. How am I doing on my signal strength?'

Finlay didn't respond. He was looking very worried.

'Hello?' the voice said. 'Are you still there?'

'Yes, Mr Hubble,' Finlay said. 'I'm right here.

48

Can't find any problem at all, sir. Just a false alarm, I guess. Thank you for your help.'

'OK,' said the guy called Hubble. 'You're welcome.'

The connection broke and dial tone filled the room. Finlay replaced the phone. Leaned back and looked up at the ceiling. Spoke to himself.

'Shit,' he said. 'Right here in town. Who the hell is this Paul Hubble?'

'You don't know the guy?' I said.

He looked at me. A bit rueful. Like he'd forgotten I was there.

'I've only been here six months,' he said. 'I don't know everybody.'

He leaned forward and buzzed the intercom button on the rosewood desk. Called Baker back in.

'Ever heard of some guy called Hubble?' Finlay asked him. 'Paul Hubble, lives here in town, twenty-five Beckman Drive?'

'Paul Hubble?' Baker said. 'Sure. He lives here, like you say, always has. Family man. Stevenson knows him, some kind of an in-law or something. They're friendly, I think. Go bowling together. Hubble's a banker. Some kind of a financial guy, you know, a big shot executive type, works up in Atlanta. Some big bank up there. I see him around, time to time.'

Finlay looked at him.

'He's the guy on the other end of this number,' he said.

'Hubble?' Baker said. 'Right here in Margrave? That's a hell of a thing.'

Finlay turned back to me.

'I suppose you're going to say you never heard of this guy?' he asked me.

49

'Never heard of him,' I said.

He glared at me briefly. Turned back to Baker.

'You better go on out and bring this Hubble guy in,' he said. 'Twenty-five Beckman Drive. God knows what he's got to do with anything, but we better talk to him. Go easy on him, you know, he's probably a respectable guy.'

He glared at me again and left the room. Banged the heavy door. Baker reached over and stopped the recording machine. Walked me out of the office. Back to the cell. I went in. He followed and removed the handcuffs. Put them back on his belt. Stepped back out and closed the gate. Operated the lock. The electric bolts snicked home. He walked away.

'Hey, Baker,' I called.

He turned and walked back. A level gaze. Not friendly.

'I want something to eat,' I said. 'And coffee.'

'You'll eat up at the state facility,' he said. 'Bus comes by at six.'

He walked away. He had to go and fetch the Hubble guy. He would shuffle up to him apologetically. Ask him to come down to the station house, where Finlay would be polite to him. While I stood in a cell, Finlay would politely ask Hubble why his phone number had been found in a dead man's shoe.

My coat was still balled up on the cell floor. I shook it out and put it on. I was cold again. Thrust my hands into the pockets. Leaned on the bars and tried to read through the newspaper again, just to pass the time. But I wasn't taking anything in. I was thinking about somebody who had watched his partner shoot a guy in the head. Who had seized the twitching body and kicked it around the floor. Who had used enough furious force to smash all the dead inert bones. I was standing there thinking about stuff I'd thought I was through with. Stuff I didn't want to think about anymore. So I dropped the paper on the carpet and tried to think about something else.

I found that if I leaned up in the front far corner of the cell I could see the whole of the open-plan area. I could see over the reception counter and out through the glass doors. Outside, the afternoon sun looked bright and hot. It looked like a dry and dusty place again. The heavy rain had moved on out. Inside was cool and fluorescent. The desk sergeant sat up on a stool. He worked on his keyboard. Probably filing. I could see behind his counter. Underneath were spaces designed not to be seen from the front. Neat compartments contained papers and hardback folders. There were sections with Mace sprays. A shotgun. Panic buttons. Behind the desk sergeant the uniformed woman who'd printed me was busy. Keyboard work. The large room was quiet but it hummed with the energy of investigation.

FOUR

People spend thousands of dollars on stereos, sometimes tens of thousands. There is a specialist industry right here in the States which builds stereo gear to a standard you wouldn't believe. Tubed amplifiers which cost more than a house. Speakers taller than me. Cables thicker than a garden hose. Some army guys had that stuff. I'd heard it on bases around the world. Wonderful. But they were wasting their money. Because the best stereo in the world is free. Inside your head. It sounds as good as you want it to. As loud as you want it to be.

I was leaning up in my corner running a Bobby Bland number through my head. An old favourite. It was cranked up real loud. 'Further On up the Road'. Bobby Bland sings it in G major. That key gives it a strange, sunny, cheerful cast. Takes out the spiteful sting from the lyric. Makes it a lament, a prediction, a consolation. Makes it do what the blues is supposed to do. The relaxed G major misting it almost into sweetness. Not vicious.

But then I saw the fat police chief walk by.

Morrison, on his way past the cells, toward the big office in back. Just in time for the start of the third verse. I crunched the song down into E flat. A dark and menacing key. The real blues key. I deleted the amiable Bobby Bland. I needed a harder voice. Something much more vicious. Musical, but a real cigarettes-and-whisky rasp. Maybe Wild Child Butler. Someone you wouldn't want to mess with. I wound the level in my head up higher, for the part about reaping what you sow, further on up the road.

Morrison was lying about last night. I hadn't been there at midnight. For a while I had been prepared to accept the possibility of a mistake. Maybe he had seen someone who looked like me. But that was giving him the benefit of the doubt. Right now I wanted to give him a forearm smash to the face. Burst his fat nose all over the place. I closed my eyes. Wild Child Butler and I promised ourselves it would happen. Further on up the road.

I opened my eyes and switched off the music in my head. Standing in front of me on the other side of the bars was the fingerprint officer. She was on her way back from the coffee hotplate.

'Can I get you a cup of coffee?' she asked me.

'Sure,' I said. 'Great. No cream, no sugar.'

She put her own cup down on the nearest desk and went back to the machine. Poured me a cup from the flask and walked back. This was a good-looking woman. About thirty, dark, not tall. But to call her medium would be unfair to her. She had a kind of vitality. It had come across as a sympathetic briskness in that first interview room. A professional bustle. Now she seemed unofficial. Probably was. Probably against the fat chief's rules to bring coffee to the condemned man. It made me like her.

She passed the cup in through the bars. Up close she looked good. Smelled good. I didn't recall that from earlier. I remembered thinking of her like a dentist's nurse. If dentist's nurses all looked that good, I'd have gone more often. I took the cup. I was glad of it. I was thirsty and I love coffee. Give me the chance and I drink coffee like an alcoholic drinks vodka. I took a sip. Good coffee. I raised the Styrofoam cup like a toast.

'Thank you,' I said.

'You're welcome,' she said, and she smiled, with her eyes too. I smiled back. Her eyes were like a welcome blast of sunshine on a rotten afternoon.

'So you think I didn't do it?' I asked her.

She picked up her own cup from where she'd put it down.

'You think I don't bring coffee to the guilty ones?' she said.

'Maybe you don't even talk to the guilty ones,' I said.

'I know you're not guilty of much,' she said.

'How can you tell?' I said. 'Because my eyes aren't too close together?'

'No, fool,' she laughed. 'Because we haven't heard from Washington yet.'

Her laugh was great. I wanted to look at her nameplate over her shirt pocket. But I didn't want her to think I was looking at her breasts. I remembered them resting on the edge of the table when she took my photograph. I looked. Nice breasts. Her name was Roscoe. She glanced around quickly and moved closer to the bars. I sipped coffee.

'I sent your prints to Washington over the computer link,' she said. 'That was at twelve-thirty-six.

Big database there, you know, FBI? Millions of prints in their computer. Prints that get sent in are checked. There's a priority order. You get checked first of all against the top-ten wanted list, then the top hundred, then the top thousand, you understand? If you'd been near the top, you know, active and unsolved, we'd have heard almost right away. It's automatic. They don't want any big fugitive to slip away, so the system gets right back. But you've been in there almost three hours and we haven't heard. So I can tell you're not on record for anything very bad.'

The desk sergeant was looking over. Disapproving. She was going to have to go. I drained the coffee and handed her the cup back through the bars.

'I'm not on record for anything at all,' I said.

'No,' she said. 'You don't match the deviance profile.'

'I don't?' I said.

'I could tell right away,' she smiled. 'You got nice eyes.'

She winked and walked away. Trashed the cups and moved over to her work station. She sat down. All I could see was the back of her head. I moved into my corner and leaned up against the hard bars. I'd been a lonely wanderer for six months. I'd learned something. Like Blanche in that old movie, a wanderer depends on the kindness of strangers. Not for anything specific or material. For morale. I gazed at the back of Roscoe's head and smiled. I liked her.

Baker had been gone maybe twenty minutes. Long enough to get back from Hubble's place, wherever it was. I figured you could walk there and back in twenty minutes. This was a small town, right? A dot on the map. I figured you could walk anywhere and back in twenty minutes. On your hands. Although the town limits were pretty weird. Depended whether Hubble lived in town, or somewhere else within the outer boundaries. According to my experience, you were in town even when you were fourteen miles away. If that fourteen miles extended in all directions, then Margrave was about as big as New York City.

Baker had said Hubble was a family man. A banker who worked in Atlanta. That meant a family house somewhere near town. Near schools and friends for the kids. Near shops and the country club for the wife. An easy drive for him up the county road to the highway. Convenient commute up the highway to the office in the big city. The address sounded like a town address. Twenty-five Beckman Drive. Not too close to Main Street. Probably Beckman Drive ran from the centre of town out into the countryside. Hubble was a financial guy. Probably rich. Probably had a big white place on a big lot. Shade trees. Maybe a pool. Call it four acres. A square lot covering four acres was about a hundred and forty yards on a side. Homes on the left and the right of the street put number twenty-five about twelve lots out from town. About a mile, maybe.

Outside the big plate-glass doors the sun was falling away into afternoon. The light was redder. Shadows were longer. I saw Baker's patrol car yaw and bounce into the driveway. No flashing lights. It came slowly around the semicircle and eased to a stop. Bounced once on its springs. Its length filled the view through the plate glass. Baker got out on the far side and walked out of sight as he rounded the car. He reappeared as he approached his passenger's door. He opened it like a chauffeur. He looked all twisted up with conflicting body language. Part deferential, because this was an Atlanta banker. Part friendly, because this was his partner's bowling buddy. Part official, because this was a man whose phone number had been hidden in a corpse's shoe.

Paul Hubble got out of the car. Baker shut the door. Hubble waited. Baker skipped around him and pulled open the big plate-glass door of the station house. It sucked against the rubber seal. Hubble stepped inside.

He was a tall white man. He looked like a page from a magazine. An advertisement. The sort that uses a grainy photograph of money at play. He was in his early thirties. Trim but not strong. Sandy hair, tousled, receding just enough to show an intelligent brow. Just enough to say: yes, I was a preppie, but hey, I'm a man now. He wore gold-rimmed round eyeglasses. He had a square jaw. A decent tan. Very white teeth. Many of them were on show as he smiled at the desk sergeant.

He wore a faded polo shirt with a small logo and washed chino pants. The sort of clothes that look old when you buy them for five hundred bucks. He had a thick white sweater draped over his back. The arms were loosely tied in front. I couldn't see his feet because the reception desk was in the way. I was certain he would be wearing tan boat shoes. I made a substantial bet with myself he was wearing them without socks. This was a man who wallowed in the yuppie dream like a pig in shit.

He was in a state of some agitation. He placed his palms on the reception desk and then turned and dropped his hands to his sides. I saw sandy forearms and the flash of a heavy gold watch. I could see his natural approach would be to act like a friendly rich guy. Visiting the station house like our campaigning President would visit a factory. But he was distracted. Uptight. I didn't know what Baker had said to him. How much he had revealed. Probably nothing. A good sergeant like Baker would leave the bombshells to Finlay. So Hubble didn't know why he was here. But he knew something. I was a policeman of sorts for thirteen years and I can smell a worried man a mile away. Hubble was a worried man.

I stayed leaning up on the bars, motionless. Baker signalled Hubble to walk with him around the far side of the squad room. Towards the rosewood office in back. As Hubble rounded the end of the reception desk, I saw his feet. Tan boat shoes. No socks. The two men walked out of sight into the office. The door closed. The desk sergeant left his post and went outside to park Baker's cruiser.

He came back in with Finlay at his side. Finlay walked straight back toward the rosewood office where Hubble waited for him. Ignored me as he crossed the squad room. Opened the office door and went inside. I waited in my corner for Baker to come out. Baker couldn't stay in there. Not while his partner's bowling buddy entered the orbit of a homicide investigation. That would not be ethical. Not ethical at all. Finlay struck me as a guy who would go big on ethics. Any guy with a tweed suit like that and a moleskin vest and a Harvard education would go big on ethics. After a moment the door opened and Baker came out. He walked into the big open room and headed for his desk.

'Hey, Baker,' I called. He changed course and

walked over to the cells. Stood in front of the bars. Where Roscoe had stood.

'I need to go to the bathroom,' I said. 'Unless I got to wait until I get up to the big house for that, too?'

He cracked a grin. Grudging, but a grin. He had a gold tooth way back. Gave him a rakish air. A bit more human. He shouted something to the desk guy. Probably a code for a procedure. He took out his keys and activated the electric lock. The bolts popped back. I wondered briefly how they did it if there was a power outage. Could they unlock these gates without electricity? I hoped so. Probably lots of thunderstorms down here. Lots of power lines crashing down.

He pushed the heavy gate inward. We walked to the back of the squad room. Opposite corner to the rosewood office. There was a lobby. Off the lobby were two bathrooms. He reached past me and pushed open the men's room door.

They knew I wasn't their guy. They weren't taking care. No care at all. Out there in the lobby I could have decked Baker and taken his revolver. No problem at all. I could have had his weapon off his belt before he hit the floor. I could have shot my way out of the station house and into a patrol car. They were all parked right out front. Keys in, for sure. I could have got out toward Atlanta before they organized effective opposition. Then I could have disappeared. No problem at all. But I just went into their bathroom.

'Don't lock it,' Baker said.

I didn't lock it. They were underestimating me in a big way. I had told them I had been a military policeman. Maybe they believed me, maybe they didn't. Maybe it didn't mean much to them either way. But it should. A military policeman deals with military lawbreakers. Those lawbreakers are service guys. Highly trained in weapons, sabotage, unarmed combat. Rangers, Green Berets, marines. Not just killers. Trained killers. Extremely well trained, at huge public expense. So the military policeman is trained even better. Better with weapons. Better unarmed. Baker had to be ignorant of all that. Hadn't thought about it. Otherwise he would have had a couple of shotguns aimed at me for the trip to the bathroom. If he thought I was their guy.

I zipped up and came back into the lobby. Baker was waiting. We walked back to the cell area. I stepped inside my cell. Leaned up in my corner. Baker pulled the heavy gate shut. Operated the electric lock with his key. The bolts snicked in. He walked away into the squad room.

There was silence for the next twenty minutes. Baker worked at a desk. So did Roscoe. The desk sergeant sat up on his stool. Finlay was in the big office with Hubble. There was a modern clock over the front doors. Not as elegant as the antique in the office, but it ticked around just as slowly. Silence. Four-thirty. I leaned up against the titanium bars and waited. Silence. Quarter of five.

Time restarted just before five o'clock. I heard a commotion coming out of the big rosewood office in back. Shouting, yelling, things banging. Somebody getting really stirred up. A buzzer sounded on Baker's desk and the intercom crackled. I heard Finlay's voice. Stressed. Asking Baker to get in there. Baker got up and walked over. Knocked and went in.

The big plate-glass door at the entrance sucked

open and the fat guy came in. Chief Morrison. He headed straight back to the rosewood office. Baker came out as Morrison went in. Baker hurried over to the reception desk. Whispered a long excited sentence to the desk sergeant. Roscoe joined them. There was a huddle. Some big news. I couldn't hear what. Too far away.

The intercom on Baker's desk crackled again. He headed back to the office. The big front door opened again. The afternoon sun was blazing low in the sky. Stevenson walked into the station house. First time I'd seen him since my arrest. It was like the excitement was sucking people in.

Stevenson spoke to the desk sergeant. He became agitated. The desk sergeant put a hand on Stevenson's arm. Stevenson shook it off and ran toward the rosewood office. He dodged desks like a football player. As he got to the office door it opened. A crowd came out. Chief Morrison. Finlay. And Baker, holding Hubble by the elbow. A light but efficient grip, the same as he'd used on me. Stevenson stared blankly at Hubble and then grabbed Finlay by the arm. Pulled him back into the office. Morrison swivelled his sweating bulk and followed them in. The door slammed. Baker walked Hubble over toward me.

Hubble looked like a different guy. He was grey and sweating. The tan had gone. He looked smaller. He looked like someone had let the air out and deflated him. He was bent up like a man racked with pain. His eyes behind the gold rims were blank and staring with panic and fear. He stood shaking as Baker unlocked the cell next to mine. He didn't move. He was trembling. Baker caught his arm and levered him inside. He pulled the gate shut and locked it. The electric bolts snicked in. Baker walked back towards the rosewood office.

Hubble just stood where Baker had left him. Staring blankly into space. Then he slowly walked backward until he reached the rear wall of the cell. He pressed his back against it and slid to the floor. Dropped his head to his knees. Dropped his hands to the floor. I could hear the rattle of his thumb trembling on the stiff nylon carpet. Roscoe stared in at him from her desk. The sergeant at the reception counter gazed across. They were watching a man fall apart.

I heard raised voices in the rosewood office in back. The tenor of argument. The slap of a palm on a desk. The door opened and Stevenson walked out with Chief Morrison. Stevenson looked mad. He strode down the side of the open area. His neck was rigid with fury. His eyes were fixed on the front doors. He was ignoring the fat police chief. He walked straight past the reception counter and out through the heavy door into the bright afternoon. Morrison followed him.

Baker came out of the office and walked over to my cell. Didn't speak. Just unlocked the cage and gestured me out. I shrugged my coat tighter and left the newspaper with the big photographs of the President in Pensacola on the cell floor. Stepped out and followed Baker back into the rosewood office.

Finlay was at the desk. The tape recorder was there. The stiff cords trailed. The air was still and cool. Finlay looked harassed. His tie was pulled down. He blew out a big lungful of air in a rueful hiss. I sat down in the chair and Finlay waved Baker out of the room. The door closed softly behind him.

'We got us a situation here, Mr Reacher,' Finlay said. 'A real situation.'

He lapsed into a distracted silence. I had less than a half-hour before the prison bus came by. I wanted some conclusions pretty soon. Finlay looked up and focused again. Started talking, rapidly, the elegant Harvard syntax under pressure.

'We bring this Hubble guy in, right?' he said. 'You maybe saw him. Banker, from Atlanta, right? Thousand-dollar Calvin Klein outfit. Gold Rolex. Very uptight guy. At first I thought he was just annoyed. Soon as I started talking he recognized my voice. From the phone call on his mobile. Accuses me of deceitful behaviour. Says I shouldn't impersonate phone company people. He's right, of course.'

Another lapse into silence. He was struggling with his ethics problem.

'Come on, Finlay, move along,' I said. I had less than a half-hour.

'OK, so he's uptight and annoyed,' Finlay said. 'I ask him if he knows you. Jack Reacher, ex-army. He says no. Never heard of you. I believe him. He starts to relax. Like all this is about some guy called Jack Reacher. He's never heard of any guy called Jack Reacher, so he's here for nothing. He's cool, right?'

'Go on,' I said.

'Then I ask him if he knows a tall guy with a shaved head,' he said. 'And I ask him about Pluribus. Well, my God! It's like I stuck a poker up his ass. He went rigid. Like with shock. Totally rigid. Won't answer. So I tell him we know the tall guy is dead. Shot to death. Well, that's like another poker up the ass. He practically fell off the chair.'

'Go on,' I said. Twenty-five minutes before the prison bus was due.

'He's shaking all over the place,' Finlay said. 'Then I tell him we know about the phone number in the shoe. His phone number printed on a piece of paper, with the word "Pluribus" printed above it. That's another poker up the ass.'

He stopped again. He was patting his pockets, each one in turn.

'He wouldn't say anything,' he went on. 'Not a word. He was rigid with shock. All grey in the face. I thought he was having a heart attack. His mouth was opening and closing like a fish. But he wasn't talking. So I told him we knew about the corpse getting beaten up. I asked him who else was involved. I told him we knew about hiding the body under the cardboard. He wouldn't say a damn word. He just kept looking around. After a while I realized he was thinking like crazy. Trying to decide what to tell me. He just kept silent, thinking like mad, must have been forty minutes. The tape was running the whole time. Recorded forty minutes of silence.'

Finlay stopped again. This time for effect. He looked at me.

'Then he confessed,' he said. 'I did it, he said. I shot him, he said. The guy is confessing, right? On the tape.'

'Go on,' I said.

'I ask him, do you want a lawyer?' he said. 'He says no, keeps repeating he killed the guy. So I Mirandize him, loud and clear, on the tape. Then I think to myself maybe he's crazy or something, you know? So I ask him, who did you kill? He says the tall guy with the shaved head. I ask him, how? He says, shot him in the head. I ask him, when? He says last night, about midnight. I ask him who kicked the body around? Who was the guy? What does Pluribus mean? He doesn't answer. Goes rigid with fright all over again. Refuses to say a damn word. I say to him, I'm not sure you did anything at all. He jumps up and grabs me. He's screaming I confess, I confess, I shot him, I shot him. I shove him back. He goes quiet.'

Finlay sat back. Folded his hands behind his head. Looked a question at me. Hubble as the shooter? I didn't believe it. Because of his agitation. Guys who shoot somebody with an old pistol, in a fight or in a temper, a messy shot to the chest, they get agitated afterwards. Guys who put two bullets in the head, with a silencer, then collect up the shell cases, they're a different class of person. They don't get agitated afterwards. They just walk away and forget about it. Hubble was not the shooter. The way he had been dancing around in front of the reception counter disproved it. But I just shrugged and smiled.

'OK,' I said. 'You can let me go now, right?'

Finlay looked at me and shook his head.

'Wrong,' he said. 'I don't believe him. There were three guys involved here. You persuaded me of that yourself. So which one is Hubble claiming to be? I don't think he's the maniac. I can't see enough strength in him for that. I don't see him as the gofer. And he's definitely not the shooter, for God's sake. Guy like that couldn't shoot pool.'

I nodded. Like Finlay's partner. Worrying away at a problem.

'Got to throw his ass in the can for now,' he said. 'No option. He's confessed, couple of plausible details. But it definitely won't hold up.'

I nodded again. Sensed there was something more to come.

'Go on,' I said. With resignation.

Finlay looked at me. A level gaze.

'He wasn't even there at midnight,' he said. 'He was at some old couple's anniversary party. A family thing. Not far from where he lives. Got there around eight last night. He'd walked down with his wife. Didn't leave until after two o'clock in the morning. Two dozen people saw him arrive, two dozen people saw him leave. He got a ride home from his sister-in-law's brother-in-law. He got a ride because it was already pouring rain by then.'

'Go on, Finlay,' I said. 'Tell me.'

'His sister-in-law's brother-in-law?' he said. 'Drove him home, in the rain, two o'clock in the morning? Officer Stevenson.'

FIVE

Finlay leaned right back in his chair. His long arms were folded behind his head. He was a tall, elegant man. Educated in Boston. Civilized. Experienced. And he was sending me to jail for something I hadn't done. He levered himself upright. Spread his hands on the desk, palms up.

'I'm sorry, Reacher,' he said to me.

'You're sorry?' I said. 'You're sending two guys who couldn't have done it to jail and you're sorry?'

He shrugged. Looked unhappy about it.

'This is the way Chief Morrison wants it,' he said. 'He's calling it a done deal. Closing us down for the weekend. And he's the boss man, right?'

'You got to be joking,' I said. 'He's an asshole. He's calling Stevenson a liar. His own man.'

'Not exactly,' Finlay shrugged. 'He's saying it's maybe a conspiracy, you know, maybe Hubble wasn't literally there, but he recruited you to do it. A conspiracy, right? He reckons the confession is exaggerated because maybe Hubble's afraid of you and is scared to finger you right away. Morrison figures you were on your way down to Hubble's place to get paid when we hauled you in. He figures that's why you waited the eight hours. Figures that's why Hubble was at home today. Didn't go to work because he was waiting around to pay you off.'

I was silent. I was worried. Chief Morrison was dangerous. His theory was plausible. Until Finlay did the checking. If Finlay did the checking.

'So, Reacher, I'm sorry,' he said. 'You and Hubble stay in the bag until Monday. You'll get through it. Over in Warburton. Bad place, but the holding pens are OK. Worse if you go there for a stretch. Much worse. Meantime, I'll work on it before Monday. I'll ask Officer Roscoe to come in Saturday and Sunday. She's the pretty one outside. She's good, the best we got. If what you say is right, you'll be free and clear on Monday. OK?'

I stared at him. I was getting mad.

'No, Finlay, not OK,' I said. 'You know I didn't do a damn thing. You know it wasn't me. You're just shit scared of that useless fat bastard Morrison. So I'm going to jail because you're just a spineless damn coward.'

He took it pretty well. His dark face flushed darker. He sat quietly for a long time. I took a deep breath and glared at him. My glare subsided to a gaze as my temper cooled. Back under control. His turn to glare at me.

'Two things, Reacher,' he said. Precise articulation. 'First, if necessary I'll take care of Chief Morrison on Monday. Second, I am not a coward. You don't know me at all. Nothing about me.'

I gazed back at him. Six o'clock. Bus time.

'I know more than you think,' I said. 'I know you're a Harvard postgrad, you're divorced and you quit smoking in April.'

Finlay looked blank. Baker knocked and entered to say the prison bus had arrived. Finlay got up and walked around the desk. Told Baker he would bring me out himself. Baker went back to fetch Hubble.

'How do you know that stuff?' Finlay asked me. He was intrigued. He was losing the game.

'Easy,' I said. 'You're a smart guy, right? Educated in Boston, you told me. But when you were college age, Harvard wasn't taking too many black guys. You're smart, but you're no rocket scientist, so I figure Boston U for the first degree, right?'

'Right,' he conceded.

'And then Harvard for postgrad,' I said. 'You did well at Boston U, life moved on, you got into Harvard. You talk like a Harvard guy. I figured it straight away. PhD in criminology?'

'Right,' he said again. 'Criminology.'

'And then you got this job in April,' I said. 'You told me that. You've got a pension from Boston PD, because you did your twenty. So you've come down here with cash to spare. But you've come down here with no woman, because if you had, she'd have spent some of that spare cash on new clothes for you. She probably hated that wintry tweed thing you're wearing. She'd have junked it and put you in a Sunbelt outfit to start your new life on the right foot. But you're still wearing that terrible old suit, so the woman is gone. She either died or divorced you, so it was a fifty-fifty guess. Looks like I guessed right.'

He nodded blankly.

'And the smoking thing is easy,' I said. 'You were just stressed up and you were patting your pockets, looking for cigarettes. That means you quit fairly recently. Easy guess is you quit in April, you know, new life, new job, no more cigarettes. You figured quit now and you might beat the cancer thing.'

Finlay glared at me. A bit grudging.

'Very good, Reacher,' he said. 'Elementary deduction, right?'

I shrugged. Didn't say anything.

'So deduce who aced the guy up at the warehouse,' he said.

'I don't care who aced any guy anywhere,' I said. 'That's your problem, not mine. And it's the wrong question, Finlay. First you got to find out who the guy was, right?'

'So you got any way to do that, smart guy?' he asked me. 'No ID, no face left, nothing from the prints, Hubble won't say diddly?'

'Run the prints again,' I said. 'I'm serious, Finlay. Get Roscoe to do it.'

'Why?' he said.

'Something wrong there,' I said.

'What something?' he asked me.

'Run them again, OK?' I said. 'Will you do that?'

He just grunted. Didn't say yes or no. I opened the office door and stepped out. Roscoe had gone. Nobody was there except Baker and Hubble over at the cells. I could see the desk sergeant outside through the front doors. He was writing on a clipboard held by the prison bus driver. As a backdrop behind the two of them was the prison bus. It was stationary in the semicircular driveway. It filled the view through the big plate-glass entrance. It was a school bus painted light grey. On it was written: State of Georgia Department of Corrections. That inscription ran the full length of the bus, under the line of windows. Under the inscription was a crest. The windows had grilles welded over them.

Finlay came out of the office behind me. Touched my elbow and walked me over to Baker. Baker was holding three sets of handcuffs hooked over his thumb. They were painted bright orange. The paint was chipped. Dull steel showed through. Baker snapped a pair of handcuffs onto each of my wrists separately. He unlocked Hubble's cell and signalled the scared banker to come out. Hubble was blank and dazed, but he stepped out. Baker caught the dangling cuff on my left wrist and snapped it onto Hubble's right wrist. He put the third set of cuffs on Hubble's other wrist. Ready to go.

'Take his watch, Baker,' I said. 'He'll lose it in jail.'

He nodded. He knew what I meant. Guy like Hubble could lose a lot in jail. Baker unlatched the heavy Rolex from Hubble's wrist. The bracelet wouldn't slide over the handcuff, so Baker had to fiddle and fuss with taking the handcuff off and putting it back on again. The prison driver cracked the door and glared in. A man with a timetable. Baker dropped Hubble's watch on the nearest desk. Exactly where my friend Roscoe had put her coffee cup.

'OK, guys, let's hit the road,' Baker said.

He walked us to the doors. We went out into a dazzling hot bar of sunshine. Handcuffed together. Walking was awkward. Before crossing to the bus, Hubble stopped. He craned his neck and looked around carefully. He was being more vigilant than Baker or the prison driver. Maybe scared of a neighbour seeing him. But there was nobody around. We were three hundred yards north of the town. I could see the church steeple in the distance. We walked over to the bus through the evening warmth. My right cheek tingled in the low sun.

The driver pushed the bus door inward. Hubble shuffled sideways onto the step. I followed him. Made a clumsy turn into the aisle. The bus was empty. The driver directed Hubble into a seat. He slid over the vinyl to the window. I was pulled alongside. The driver knelt on the seat in front and clicked our outer wrists to the chromium hoop which ran across the top. He rattled each of our three cuffs in turn. Wanted to know they were secure. I didn't blame him. I've done that job. Nothing worse than driving with prisoners loose behind you.

The driver walked forward to his seat. He started the engine with a loud diesel clatter. The bus filled with vibration. The air was hot. Stifling. There was no air-conditioning. None of the windows opened. I could smell fuel fumes. The gears clashed and ground and the bus moved off. I glanced out to my right. Nobody waving goodbye.

We drove north out of the police lot, turning our backs on the town, heading up towards the highway. We passed Eno's diner after a half-mile. His lot was empty. Nobody looking for an early dinner. We carried on north for a spell. Then we turned a tight left off the county road and struck out west down a road between fields. The bus settled to a noisy cruise. Endless rows of bushes flicked past. Endless drills of red earth between. Ahead of me the sun was on the way down. It was a giant red ball heading for the fields. The driver had the large sun visor down. On it were printed manufacturer's instructions about how to operate the bus.

Hubble rocked and bounced beside me. He said nothing. He had slumped down with his face parallel to the floor. His left arm was raised because

72

it was handcuffed to the chrome bar in front of us. His right arm rested inert between us. He still had his expensive sweater draped across his shoulders. Where the Rolex had been was a band of pale skin. The life force had just about drained out of him. He was in the grip of a paralyzing fear.

We rocked and bounced for the best part of another hour through the huge landscape. A small stand of trees flashed past on my right. Then way in the far distance I saw a structure. It sat alone in a thousand acres of flat farmland. Against the low red sun it looked like a protrusion from hell. Something forced up through the crust of the earth. It was a complex of buildings. Looked like a chemical factory or a nuclear place. Massive concrete bunkers and glittering metal walkways. Tubing running here and there with steam drifting. All surrounded with fencing punctuated by towers. As we drew closer I could see arc lights and razor wire. Searchlights and rifles in the towers. Layers of fences separated with ploughed red earth. Hubble didn't look up. I didn't nudge him. It wasn't the Magic Kingdom up ahead.

The bus slowed as we approached. The outer-most fence was about a hundred yards out forming a giant perimeter. It was a substantial fence. Possibly fifteen feet tall, studded along its entire length with pairs of sodium floodlights. One of each pair was trained inward across the hundred-yard breadth of ploughed earth. One was trained out over the surrounding farmland. All the flood-lights were lit. The whole complex blazed with yellow sodium light. Up close it was very bright. The yellow light turned the red earth to a ghastly tan.

The bus rattled to a halt. The idling engine set up a vibration. What little ventilation there had been ceased. It was stifling. Hubble finally looked up. He peered out through his gold rims. He looked around him and out the window. He groaned. It was a groan of hopeless dejection. He dropped his head.

The driver was waiting for a signal from the first gate guard. The guard was speaking into a radio. The driver blipped the engine and crunched into gear. The guard signalled to him, using his radio as a baton, waving us through. The bus ground forward into a cage. We passed a long low sign at the kerb: Warburton Correctional Facility, State of Georgia Department of Corrections. Behind us a gate swung closed. We were sealed in a wire cage. It was roofed with wire. At the far end a gate swung open. The bus ground through.

We drove the hundred yards to the next fence. There was another vehicle cage. The bus went in, waited, and drove on out. We drove right into the heart of the prison. We stopped opposite a concrete bunker. The reception area. The engine noise beat against the concrete surrounding us. Then it shut down and the vibration and clatter died away to silence. The driver swung out of his seat and walked up the aisle, stooping, pulling himself like a climber on the seatbacks. He pulled out his keys and unlocked the cuffs fixing us to the seat in front.

'OK, boys, let's go,' he grinned. 'Party time.'

We hauled ourselves out of our seat and shuffled down the bus. My left arm was pulled back by Hubble. The driver stopped us at the front. He removed all three sets of handcuffs and dropped them in a bin next to his cab. Hauled on a lever and sprang the door. We got out of the bus. A door opened opposite and a guard stepped out. Called us over. He was eating a doughnut and spoke with his mouth full. A sugar moustache frosted his lip. He was a pretty casual guy. We went through the door into a small concrete chamber. It was filthy. Deal chairs surrounded a painted table. Another guard sat on the table reading from a battered clipboard.

'Sit down, OK?' he said. We sat. He stood up. His partner with the doughnut locked the outer door and joined him.

'Here's the deal,' said the clipboard guy. 'You guys are Reacher and Hubble. In from Margrave. Not convicted of any crime. In custody pending investigation. No bail application for either of you. Hear what I say? Not convicted of any crime. That's the important thing. Excuses you from a lot of shit in here, OK? No uniform, no processing, no big deal, you understand? Nice accommodations on the top floor.'

'Right,' said the doughnut guy. 'Thing is, if you were convicts, we'd be poking and prodding and hitting on you, and you'd get the uniform, and we'd shove you on the convict floors with the other animals and we'd just set back and watch the fun, right?'

'Right,' his partner said. 'So what we're saying is this. We ain't here to give you a hard time, so don't you boys be giving us a hard time neither, you understand? This damn facility ain't got the manpower. Governor laid off about a half the staff, OK? Got to meet the budget, right? Got to cut the deficit, right? So we ain't got the men to do the job the way it ought to be done. Trying to do our job with half a crew on every shift, right? So what I'm saying is we shove you in there, and we don't want to see you again until we pull you out on

Monday. No hassle, right? We ain't got the manpower for hassle. We ain't got the manpower for hassle on the convict floors, let alone hassle on the holding floor, you understand? Yo, Hubble, you understand?'

Hubble looked up at him and nodded blankly. Didn't speak.

'Reacher?' the clipboard guy said. 'You understand?'

'Sure,' I said. I understood. This guy was understaffed. Having problems because of a budget. While his friends collected unemployment. Tell me about it.

'Good,' he said. 'So the deal is this. The two of us are off duty at seven o'clock. Which is in about one minute's time. We ain't staying late for you boys. We don't want to and the union wouldn't let us anyway. So you get a meal, then you're locked down in here until they got manpower to take you upstairs. No manpower until lights out, maybe ten o'clock, OK? But then no guards will move prisoners around after lights out anyway, right? Union won't let 'em. So Spivey will come get you himself. Assistant warden. Top boy tonight. About ten o'clock, OK? You don't like it, you don't tell me, you tell the governor, OK?'

The doughnut eater went out into the corridor and came back a long moment later with a tray. On it were covered plates, paper cups and a thermos. He put the tray on the table and the two of them swung out through the corridor. Locked the door from the outside. It went quiet as a tomb in there.

We ate. Fish and rice. Friday food. Coffee in the thermos. Hubble didn't speak. He left most of the coffee for me. Score one for Hubble. I put the debris on the tray and the tray on the floor. Another three hours to waste. I tipped my chair back and put my feet up on the table. Not comfortable, but as good as I was going to get. A warm evening. September in Georgia.

I looked over at Hubble without curiosity. He was still silent. I had never heard him speak except on Finlay's speakerphone. He looked back at me. His face was full of dejection and fear. He looked at me like I was a creature from another world. He stared at me like I worried him. Then he looked away.

Maybe I wouldn't head back to the Gulf. But it was too late in the year to head north. Too cold up there. Maybe skip right down to the islands. Jamaica, maybe. Good music there. A hut on the beach. Live out the winter in a hut on a Jamaica beach. Smoke a pound of grass a week. Do whatever Jamaica people do. Maybe two pounds of grass a week with someone to share the hut. Roscoe kept drifting into the picture. Her uniform shirt was fabulously crisp. A crisp tight blue shirt. I had never seen a shirt look better. On a Jamaica beach in the sun she wouldn't need a shirt. I didn't think that would prove to be any kind of a major problem.

It was her wink that did it to me. She took my coffee cup. She said I had nice eyes. And she winked. Got to mean something, right? The eyes thing, I've heard that before. An English girl I'd had good times with for a while, she liked my eyes. Said it all the time. They're blue. Equally people have said they look like icebergs in an Arctic sea. If I concentrate I can stop them blinking. Gives a stare an intimidating effect. Useful. But Roscoe's wink had been the best part of the day. The only

77

part of the day, really, except Eno's scrambled eggs, which weren't bad. Eggs you can get anywhere. But I'd miss Roscoe. I floated on through the empty evening.

Not long after ten the door from the corridor was unlocked. A uniformed man came in. He carried a clipboard. And a shotgun. I looked him over. A son of the South. A heavy, fleshy man. Reddened skin, a big hard belly and a wide neck. Small eyes. A tight greasy uniform straining to contain him. Probably born right there on the farm they commandeered to build the prison. Assistant Warden Spivey. This shift's top boy. Understaffed and harassed. Ushering the short-stay guests around by himself. With a shotgun in his big red farmer's hands.

He studied his clipboard.

'Which one of you is Hubble?' he asked.

He had a high-pitched voice. At odds with his bulk. Hubble raised his hand briefly, like a boy at grade school. Spivey's little eyes flicked over him. Up and down. Like a snake's eyes. He grunted and signalled with the clipboard. We formed up and moved out. Hubble was blank and acquiescent. Like an exhausted trooper.

'Turn left and follow the red line,' Spivey said.

He waved left with the shotgun. There was a red line painted on the wall at waist height. It was a fire lane guide. I guessed it must lead outside, but we were going in the wrong direction. Into the prison, not out of it. We followed the red line through corridors, up stairs and around corners. Hubble first, then me. Then Spivey with the shotgun. It was very dark. Just dim emergency lighting. Spivey called a halt on a landing. He overrode an electronic lock with his key. A lock which would spring the fire door when the alarm went.

'No talking,' he said. 'Rules here say absolute silence at all times after lights out. Cell at the end on the right.'

We stepped in through the out door. The foul odour of prison hit me. The night exhalation of countless dispirited men. It was nearly pitch black. A night-light glowed dimly. I sensed rather than saw rows of cells. I heard the babble of night sounds. Breathing and snoring. Muttering and whimpering. Spivey walked us to the end of the row. Pointed to an empty cell. We crowded in. Spivey swung the bars shut behind us. They locked automatically. He walked away.

The cell was very dark. I could just about see a bunk bed, a sink and a john. Not much floorspace. I took off my coat and lobbed it onto the top bunk. Reached up and remade the bed with the pillow away from the bars. I liked it better that way. Worn sheet and blanket, but they smelled clean enough.

Hubble sat quietly on the lower bed. I used the john and rinsed my face at the sink. Pulled myself up into bed. Took off my shoes. Left them on the foot of the bed. I wanted to know where they were. Shoes can get stolen, and these were good shoes. Bought many years ago in Oxford, England. A university town near the airbase where I was stationed. Big heavy shoes with hard soles and a thick welt.

The bed was too short for me, but most beds are. I lay there in the dark and listened to the restless prison. Then I closed my eyes and floated back to Jamaica with Roscoe. I must have fallen asleep there with her because the next thing I knew it was Saturday. I was still in prison. And an even worse day was beginning.

SIX

I was woken up by bright lights coming on. The prison had no windows. Day and night were created by electricity. At seven o'clock the building was suddenly flooded with light. No dawn or soft twilight. Just circuit-breakers thrown shut at seven.

The bright light did not make the cell look any better. The front wall was bars. Half would open outward on a hinge to form the door. The two stacked beds occupied just about half the width and most of the length. On the back wall were a steel sink and a steel toilet pan. The walls were masonry. Part poured concrete and part old bricks. All thickly covered with paint. The walls looked massively thick. Like a dungeon. Above my head was a low concrete ceiling. The cell didn't feel like a room bounded by walls, floor, ceiling. It felt like a solid block of masonry with a tiny living space grudgingly burrowed in.

Outside, the restless night mutter was replaced by the clatter of daytime. Everything was metal, brick, concrete. Noises were amplified and echoed around. It sounded like hell. Through the bars I could see nothing. Opposite our cell was a blank wall. Lying in bed I didn't have the angle to see down the row. I threw off the cover and found my shoes. Put them on and laced them up. Lay down again. Hubble was sitting on the bottom bunk. His tan boat shoes were planted on the concrete floor. I wondered if he'd sat like that all night or if he'd slept.

Next person I saw was a cleaner. He moved into view outside our bars. This was a very old guy with a broom. An old black man with a fringe of snow-white hair. Bent up with age. Fragile like a wizened old bird. His orange prison uniform was washed almost white. He must have been eighty. Must have been inside for sixty years. Maybe stole a chicken in the Depression. Still paying his debt to society.

He stabbed the broom randomly over the corridor. His spine forced his face parallel to the floor. He rolled his head like a swimmer to see from side to side. He caught sight of Hubble and me and stopped. Rested on his broom and shook his head. Gave a kind of reflective chuckle. Shook his head again. He was chuckling away. An appreciative, delighted chuckle. Like at long last, after all these years, he'd been granted the sight of a fabled thing. Like a unicorn or a mermaid. He kept trying to speak, raising his hand as if his point was going to require emphasis. But every time, he'd start up with the chuckling again and need to clutch the broom. I didn't hurry him. I could wait. I had all weekend. He had the rest of his life.

'Well, yes indeed,' he grinned. He had no teeth. 'Well, yes indeed.'

I looked over at him.

'Well, yes what, Granddad?' I grinned back.

He was cackling away. This was going to take a while.

'Yes indeed,' he said. Now he had the chuckling under control. 'I've been in this joint since God's dog was a puppy, yes sir. Since Adam was a young boy. But here's something I ain't never seen. No sir, not in all those years.'

'What ain't you never seen, old man?' I asked him.

'Well,' he said, 'I been here all these years, and I ain't never seen anybody in that cell wearing clothes like yours, man.'

'You don't like my clothes?' I said. Surprised.

'I didn't say that, no sir, I didn't say I don't like your clothes,' he said. 'I like your clothes just fine. A very fine set of clothes, yes sir, yes indeed, very fine.'

'So what's the story?' I asked.

The old guy was cackling away to himself.

'The quality of the clothes ain't the issue,' he said. 'No sir, that ain't the issue at all. It's the fact you're wearing them, man, like not wearing the orange uniform. I never saw that before, and like I say, man, I been here since the earth cooled, since the dinosaurs said enough is enough. Now I seen everything, I really have, yes sir.'

'But guys on the holding floor don't wear the uniform,' I said.

'Yes indeed, that sure is true,' the old man said. 'That's a fact, for sure.'

'The guards said so,' I confirmed.

'They would say so,' he agreed. 'Because that's the rules, and the guards, they know the rules, yes sir, they know them because they make them.'

'So what's the issue, old man?' I said.

'Well, like I say, you're not wearing the orange suit,' he said.

We were going around in circles here.

'But I don't have to wear it,' I said.

He was amazed. The sharp bird eyes locked in on me.

'You don't?' he said. 'Why's that, man? Tell me.'

'Because we don't wear it on the holding floor,' I said. 'You just agreed with that, right?'

There was a silence. He and I got the message simultaneously.

'You think this is the holding floor?' he asked me.

'Isn't this the holding floor?' I asked him at the same time.

The old guy paused a beat. Lifted his broom and crabbed back out of sight. Quickly as he could. Shouting incredulously as he went.

'This ain't the holding floor, man,' he whooped. 'Holding floor is the top floor. Floor six. This here is floor three. You're on floor three, man. This is lifers, man. This is categorized dangerous people, man. This ain't even general population. This is the worst, man. Yes, indeed, you boys are in the wrong place. You boys are in trouble, yes indeed. You gonna get visitors. They gonna check you boys out. Oh man, I'm out of here.'

Evaluate. Long experience had taught me to evaluate and assess. When the unexpected gets dumped on you, don't waste time. Don't figure out how or why it happened. Don't recriminate. Don't figure out whose fault it is. Don't work out how to avoid the same mistake next time. All of that you do later. If you survive. First of all you evaluate. Analyze the situation. Identify the downside. Assess the upside. Plan accordingly. Do all that and you give yourself a better chance of getting through to the other stuff later.

We were not in the holding pens on the sixth floor. Not where unconvicted prisoners should be. We were among dangerous lifers on the third. There was no upside. The downside was extensive. We were new boys on a convict floor. We would not survive without status. We had no status. We would be challenged. We would be made to embrace our position at the absolute bottom of the pecking order. We faced an unpleasant weekend. Potentially a lethal one.

I remembered an army guy, a deserter. Young guy, not a bad recruit, went AWOL because he got some nut religion. Got into trouble in Washington, demonstrating. Ended up thrown in jail, among bad guys like on this floor. Died on his first night. Anally raped. An estimated fifty times. And at the autopsy they found a pint of semen in his stomach. A new boy with no status. Right at the bottom of the pecking order. Available to all those above him.

Assess. I could call on some heavy training. And experience. Not intended for prison life, but it would help. I had gone through a lot of unpleasant education. Not just in the army. Stretching right back into childhood. Between grade school and high school military kids like me get to go to twenty, maybe thirty new schools. Some on bases, most in local neighbourhoods. In some tough places. Philippines, Korea, Iceland, Germany, Scotland, Japan, Vietnam. All over the world. The first day at each new school, I was a new boy. With no status. Lots of first days. I quickly learned how to get status. In sandy hot schoolyards, in cold wet schoolyards, my brother and I had slugged it out together, back to back. We had got status.

Then in the service itself, that brutality was refined. I was trained by experts. Guys who traced their own training back to World War Two, Korea, Vietnam. People who had survived things I had only read about in books. They taught me methods, details, skills. Most of all they taught me attitude. They taught me that inhibitions would kill me. Hit early, hit hard. Kill with the first blow. Get your retaliation in first. Cheat. The gentlemen who behaved decently weren't there to train anybody. They were already dead.

At seven-thirty there was a ragged clunk along the row of cells. The time switch had unlocked the cages. Our bars sagged open an inch. Hubble sat motionless. Still silent. I had no plan. Best option would be to find a guard. Explain and get transferred. But I didn't expect to find a guard. On floors like this they wouldn't patrol singly. They would move in pairs, possibly in groups of three or four. The prison was understaffed. That had been made clear last night. Unlikely to be enough manpower to provide groups of guards on each floor. Probability was I wouldn't see a guard all day. They would wait in a crew room. Operate as a crash squad responding to emergencies. And if I did see a guard, what would I say? I shouldn't be here? They must hear that all day long. They would ask, who put you here? I would say Spivey, the top boy. They would say, well that's OK then, right? So the only plan was no plan. Wait and see. React accordingly. Objective, survival until Monday.

I could hear the grinding as the other inmates swung back their gates and latched them open. I could hear movement and shouted conversation as they strolled out to start another pointless day. I waited.

Not long to wait. From my tight angle on the

bed, head away from the door, I saw our next-door neighbours stroll out. They merged with a small knot of men. They were all dressed the same. Orange prison uniform. Red bandannas tight over shaved heads. Huge black guys. Obviously body-builders. Several had torn the sleeves off their shirts. Suggesting that no available garment could contain their massive bulk. They may have been right. An impressive sight.

The nearest guy was wearing pale sunglasses. The sort which darken in the sun. Silver halide. The guy had probably last seen the sun in the seventies. May never see it again. So the shades were re-dundant, but they looked good. Like the muscles. Like the bandannas and the torn shirts. All image. I waited.

The guy with the sunglasses spotted us. His look of surprise quickly changed to excitement. He alerted the group's biggest guy by hitting his arm. The big man looked round. He looked blank. Then he grinned. I waited. The knot of men assembled outside our cell. They gazed in. The big guy pulled open our gate. The others passed it from hand to hand through its arc. They latched it open.

'Look what they sent us,' the big guy said. 'You know what they sent us?'

'What they sent us?' the sunglasses guy said.

'They sent us fresh meat,' the big guy answered.

'They sure did, man,' the sunglasses guy said. 'Fresh meat.'

'Fresh meat for everybody,' the big guy said.

He grinned. He looked around his gang and they all grinned back. Exchanged low fives. I waited. The big guy stepped half a pace into our cell. He was enormous. Maybe an inch or two shorter than me but probably twice as heavy. He filled the doorway. His dull eyes flicked over me, then Hubble.

'Yo, white boy, come here,' he said. To Hubble.

I could sense Hubble's panic. He didn't move.

'Come here, white boy,' the big guy repeated. Quietly.

Hubble stood up. Took half a pace toward the man at the door. The big guy was glaring with that rage glare that is supposed to chill you with its ferocity.

'This is Red Boy territory, man,' the big guy said. Explaining the bandannas. 'What's whitey doing in Red Boy territory?'

Hubble said nothing in reply.

'Residency tax, man,' the big guy said. 'Like they got in Florida hotels, man. You got to pay the tax. Give me your sweater, white boy.'

Hubble was rigid with fear.

'Give me your sweater, white boy,' he said again. Quietly.

Hubble unwrapped his expensive white sweater and held it out. The big man took it and threw it behind him without looking.

'Give me the eyeglasses, white boy,' he said.

Hubble flicked a despairing glance up at me. Took off his gold glasses. Held them out. The big man took them and dropped them to the floor. Crunched them under his shoe. Screwed his foot around. The glasses smashed and splintered. The big man scraped his foot back and flicked the wreckage backwards into the corridor. The other guys all took turns stamping on them.

'Good boy,' the big guy said. 'You paid the tax.'

Hubble was trembling.

'Now come here, white boy,' said his tormentor.

Hubble shuffled nearer.

'Closer, white boy,' the big man said.

Hubble shuffled nearer. Until he was a foot away. He was shaking.

'On your knees, white boy,' said the big guy.

Hubble knelt.

'Unzip me, whitey,' he said.

Hubble did nothing. Filled with panic.

'Unzip me, white boy,' the big guy said again. 'With your teeth.'

Hubble gave a gasp of fear and revulsion and jumped back. He scuttled backwards to the rear of the cell. Tried to hide behind the john. He was practically hugging the pan.

Time to intervene. Not for Hubble. I felt nothing for him. But I had to intervene for myself. Hubble's abject performance would taint me. We would be seen as a pair. Hubble's surrender would disqualify us both. In the status game.

'Come back, white boy, don't you like me?' the big guy called to Hubble.

I took a long silent breath. Swung my feet over the side of the bunk and landed lightly in front of the big man. He stared at me. I stared back, calmly.

'You're in my house, fat boy,' I said. 'But I'm going to give you a choice.'

'Choice of what?' said the big guy. Blankly. Surprised.

'A choice of exit strategies, fat boy,' I said.

'Say what?' he said.

'What I mean is this,' I said. 'You're going to leave. That's for sure. Your choice is about how you leave. Either you can walk out of here by yourself, or these other fat boys behind you are going to carry you out in a bucket.'

'Oh yeah?' he said.

'For sure,' I said. 'I'm going to count to three,

OK, so you better choose real quick, right?'

He glared at me.

'One,' I counted. No response.

'Two,' I counted. No response.

Then I cheated. Instead of counting three I headbutted him full in the face. Came off the back foot with a thrust up the legs and whipped my head forward and smashed it into his nose. It was beautifully done. The forehead is a perfect arch in all planes and very strong. The skull at the front is very thick. I have a ridge up there like concrete. The human head is very heavy. All kinds of neck muscles and back muscles balance it. It's like getting hit in the face with a bowling ball. It's always a surprise. People expect punching or kicking. A headbutt is always unexpected. It comes out of the blue.

It must have caved his whole face in. I guess I pulped his nose and smashed both his cheekbones. Jarred his little brain around real good. His legs crumpled and he hit the floor like a puppet with the strings cut. Like an ox in the slaughterhouse. His skull cracked on the concrete floor.

I stared around the knot of men. They were busy reassessing my status.

'Who's next?' I said. 'But this is like Vegas now, it's double or quits. This guy is going to the hospital, maybe six weeks in a metal mask. So the next guy gets twelve weeks in the hospital, you understand that? Couple of smashed elbows, right? So who's next?'

There was no reply. I pointed at the guy in sunglasses.

'Give me the sweater, fat boy,' I said.

He bent and picked up the sweater. Passed it to me. Leaned over and held it out. Didn't want to get too close. I took the sweater and tossed it onto Hubble's bunk.

'Give me the eyeglasses,' I said.

He bent and swept up the twisted gold wreckage. Handed it to me. I tossed it back at him.

'They're broken, fat boy,' I said. 'Give me yours.'

There was a long pause. He looked at me. I looked at him. Without blinking. He took off his sunglasses and handed them to me. I put them in my pocket.

'Now get this carcass out of here,' I said.

The bunch of men in their orange uniforms and their red bandannas straightened out the slack limbs and dragged the big man away. I crawled back up into my bunk. I was shaking with adrenalin rush. My stomach was churning and I was panting. My circulation had just about shut down. I felt terrible. But not as bad as I would have felt if I hadn't done it. They'd have finished with Hubble by then and started in on me.

I didn't eat any breakfast. No appetite. I just lay on the bunk until I felt better. Hubble sat on his bed. He was rocking back and forward. He still hadn't spoken. After a while I slid to the floor. Washed at the sink. People were strolling up to the doorway and gazing in. Strolling away. The word had gotten around fast. The new guy in the cell at the end had sent a Red Boy to the hospital. Check it out. I was a celebrity.

Hubble stopped his rocking and looked at me. Opened his mouth and closed it again. Opened it for a second time.

'I can't take this,' he said.

They were the first words I had heard him say since his assured banter on Finlay's speakerphone.

His voice was low, but his statement was definite. Not a whine or a complaint, but a statement of fact. He couldn't take this. I looked over at him. Considered his statement for a long moment.

'So why are you here?' I asked him. 'What are you doing?'

'I'm not doing anything,' he said. Blankly.

'You confessed to something you didn't do,' I said. 'You asked for this.'

'No,' said Hubble. 'I did what I said. I did it and I told the detective.'

'Bullshit, Hubble,' I said. 'You weren't even there. You were at a party. The guy who drove you home is a policeman, for God's sake. You didn't do it, you know that, everybody knows that. Don't give me that shit.'

Hubble looked down at the floor. Thought for a moment.

'I can't explain it,' he said. 'I can't say anything about it. I just need to know what happens next.'

I looked at him again.

'What happens next?' I said. 'You stay here until Monday morning, and then you go back to Margrave. Then I guess they'll let you go.'

'Will they?' he said. Like he was debating with himself.

'You weren't even there,' I said again. 'They know that. They might want to know why you confessed, when you didn't do anything. And they'll want to know why the guy had your phone number.'

'What if I can't tell them?' he said.

'Can't or won't?' I asked him.

'I can't tell them,' he said. 'I can't tell anybody anything.'

He looked away and shuddered. Very frightened.

'But I can't stay in here,' he said. 'I can't stand it.'

Hubble was a financial guy. They give out their phone numbers like confetti. Talking to anybody they meet about hedge funds or tax havens. Anything to transfer some guy's hard-earned dollars their way. But this phone number was printed on a scrap of torn computer paper. Not engraved on a business card. And hidden in a shoe, not stuffed in a wallet. And playing in the background like a rhythm section was the fear coming out of the guy.

'Why can't you tell anybody?' I asked him.

'Because I can't,' he said. Wouldn't say anything more.

I was suddenly weary. Twenty-four hours ago I had jumped off a Greyhound at a cloverleaf and walked down a new road. Striding out happily through the warm morning rain. Avoiding people, avoiding involvement. No baggage, no hassle. Freedom. I didn't want it interrupted by Hubble, or by Finlay, or by some tall guy who got himself shot in his shaved head. I didn't want any part of it. I just wanted some peace and quiet and to go looking for Blind Blake. I wanted to find some eighty-year-old who might remember him from some bar. I should be talking to that old guy who swept up around the prison, not Hubble. Yuppie asshole.

He was thinking hard. I could see what Finlay had meant. I had never seen anybody think so visibly. His mouth was working soundlessly and he was fiddling with his fingers. Like he was checking off positives and negatives. Weighing things up. I watched him. I saw him make his decision. He turned and looked over at me.

'I need some advice,' he said. 'I've got a problem.'

I laughed at him.

'Well, what a surprise,' I said. 'I'd never have guessed. I thought you were here because you were bored with playing golf on the weekend.'

'I need help,' he said.

'You've had all the help you're going to get,' I said. 'Without me, you'd be bent forward over your bed right now, with a line of big horny guys forming at the door. And so far you haven't exactly overwhelmed me with gratitude for that.'

He looked down for a moment. Nodded.

'I'm sorry,' he said. 'I'm very grateful. Believe me, I am. You saved my life. You took care of it. That's why you've got to tell me what to do. I'm being threatened.'

I let the revelation hang in the air for a moment.

'I know that,' I said. 'That's pretty obvious.'

'Well, not just me,' he said. 'My family as well.'

He was getting me involved. I looked at him. He started thinking again. His mouth was working. He was pulling on his fingers. Eyes flicking left and right. Like over here was a big pile of reasons, and over there was another big pile of reasons. Which pile was bigger?

'Have you got family?' he asked me.

'No,' I said. What else could I say? My parents were both dead. I had a brother somewhere who I never saw. So I had no family. No idea whether I wanted one, either. Maybe, maybe not.

'I've been married ten years,' Hubble said. 'Ten years last month. Had a big party. I've got two children. Boy, age nine, girl, age seven. Great wife, great kids. I love them like crazy.'

He meant it. I could see that. He lapsed into

silence. Misting over as he thought about his family. Wondering how the hell he came to be in here without them. He wasn't the first guy to sit in this cell wondering that. And he wouldn't be the last.

'We've got a nice place,' he said. 'Out on Beckman Drive. Bought there five years ago. A lot of money, but it was worth it. You know Beckman?'

'No,' I said again. He was afraid to get to the point. Pretty soon he'd be telling me about the wallpaper in the downstairs half bath. And how he planned to pay for his daughter's orthodonture. I let him talk. Prison conversation.

'Anyway,' he said eventually. 'It's all falling apart now.'

He sat there in his chinos and his polo shirt. He had picked up his white sweater and wrapped it around his shoulders again. Without his glasses he looked older, more vacant. People who wear glasses, without them they always look unfocused, vulnerable. Out in the open. A layer removed. He looked like a tired old man. One leg was thrust forward. I could see the patterned sole of his shoe.

What did he call a threat? Some kind of exposure or embarrassment? Something that might blow away the perfect life he'd described on Beckman Drive? Maybe it was his wife who was involved in something. Maybe he was covering for her. Maybe she'd been having an affair with the tall dead guy. Maybe lots of things. Maybe anything. Maybe his family was threatened by disgrace, bankruptcy, stigma, cancellation of country club membership. I went around in circles. I didn't live in Hubble's world. I didn't share his frame of reference. I had seen him trembling and shaking with fear. But I had no idea how much it took to make a guy like that afraid. Or how little. When I first saw him at the station house yesterday he had looked upset and agitated. Since then he had been from time to time trembling, paralyzed, staring with fear. Sometimes resigned and apathetic. Clearly very afraid of something. I leaned on the cell wall and waited for him to tell me what.

'They're threatening us,' he said again. 'If I ever tell anybody what's going on, they said they'll break into our house. Round us all up. In my bedroom. They said they'll nail me to the wall and cut my balls off. Then they'll make my wife eat them. Then they'll cut our throats. They said they'll make our children watch and then they'll do things to them after we're dead that we'll never know about.'

SEVEN

'So what should I do?' Hubble asked me. 'What would you do?'

He was staring over at me. Waiting for a reply. What would I do? If somebody threatened me like that, they would die. I'd rip them apart. Either as they spoke, or days or months or years later. I would hunt them down and rip them apart. But Hubble couldn't do that. He had a family. Three hostages waiting to be taken. Three hostages already taken. Taken as soon as the threat was made.

'What should I do?' he asked me again.

I felt pressure. I had to say something. And my forehead hurt. It was bruising up after the massive impact with the Red Boy's face. I stepped to the bars and glanced down the row of cells. Leaned against the end of the bunk. Thought for a moment. Came up with the only possible answer. But not the answer Hubble wanted to hear.

'Nothing you can do,' I said. 'You've been told to keep your mouth shut, so you keep it shut. Don't tell anybody what's going on. Ever.'

He looked down at his feet. Dropped his head into his hands. Gave a moan of abject misery. Like he was crushed with disappointment.

'I've got to talk to somebody,' he said. 'I've got to get out of this. I mean it, I've got to get out. I've got to talk to somebody.'

I shook my head at him.

'You can't do that,' I said. 'They've told you to say nothing, so you say nothing. That way you stay alive. You and your family.'

He looked up. Shuddered.

'Something very big is going on,' he said. 'I've got to stop it if I can.'

I shook my head again. If something very big was going on around people who used threats like that, then he was never going to stop it. He was on board, and he was going to stay on board. I smiled a bleak smile at him and shook my head for the third time. He nodded like he understood. Like he finally accepted the situation. He went back to rocking and staring at the wall. His eyes were open. Red and naked without the gold rims. He sat silently for a long time.

I couldn't understand the confession. He should have kept his mouth shut. He should have denied any involvement with the dead guy. Should have said he had no idea why his phone number was written down in the guy's shoe. Should have said he had no idea what Pluribus was. Then he could have just gone home.

'Hubble?' I said. 'Why did you confess?'

He looked up. Waited a long moment before replying.

'I can't answer that,' he said. 'I'd be telling you more than I should.'

'I already know more than I should,' I said. 'Finlay asked about the dead guy and Pluribus and you flipped. So I know there's a link between you and the dead guy and whatever Pluribus is.'

He gazed at me. Looking vague.

'Is Finlay that black detective?' he said.

'Yes,' I said. 'Finlay. Chief of detectives.'

'He's new,' Hubble said. 'Never seen him before. It was always Gray. He was there years, since I was a kid. There's only one detective, you know, don't know why they say chief of detectives when there's only one. There's only eight people in the whole police department. Chief Morrison, he's been there years, then the desk man, four uniformed men, a woman, and the detective, Gray. Only now it's Finlay. The new man. Black guy, the first we've ever had. Gray killed himself, you know. Hung himself from a rafter in his garage. February, I think.'

I let him ramble on. Prison conversation. It passes the time. That's what it's for. Hubble was good at it. But I still wanted him to answer my question. My forehead hurt and I wanted to bathe it with cold water. I wanted to walk around for a while. I wanted to eat. I wanted coffee. I waited without listening as Hubble rambled through the municipal history of Margrave. Suddenly he stopped.

'What were you asking me?' he said.

'Why did you confess to killing the guy?' I repeated.

He looked around. Then he looked straight at me.

'There's a link,' he said. 'That's all it's safe to say right now. The detective mentioned the guy, and used the word "Pluribus", which made me jump. I was startled. I couldn't believe he knew the connection. Then I realized he hadn't known there was a connection, but I'd just told him by being startled. You see? I'd given it away. I felt I'd blown it. Given away the secret. And I mustn't do that, because of the threat.'

He tailed off and went quiet. An echo of the fright and panic he had felt in Finlay's office was back. He looked up again. Took a deep breath.

'I was terrified,' he said. 'But then the detective told me the guy was dead. He'd been shot. I got scared because if they had killed him, they might kill me, too. I can't really tell you why. But there's a link, like you worked out. If they got that particular guy, does that mean they are going to get me too? Or doesn't it? I had to think it out. I didn't even know for sure who had killed the guy. But then the detective told me about the violence. Did he tell you about that?'

I nodded.

'The injuries?' I said. 'Sounded pretty unpleasant.'

'Right,' Hubble said. 'And it proves it was who I thought it was. So I was really scared. I was thinking, are they looking for me too? Or aren't they? I just didn't know. I was terrified. I thought for ages. It was going around and around in my head. The detective was going crazy. I didn't say anything because I was thinking. Seemed like hours. I was terrified, you know?'

He fell back into silence. He was running it through his head again. Probably for the thousandth time. Trying to figure out if his decision had been the right one.

'I suddenly figured out what to do,' he said. 'I had three problems. If they were after me too, I had to avoid them. Hide, you know? To protect myself. But if they weren't after me, then I had to stay silent, right? To protect my wife and kids. And from their point of view that particular guy needed shooting. Three problems. So I confessed.'

I didn't follow his reasoning. Didn't make much sense, the way he was explaining it to me. I looked blankly at him.

'Three separate problems, right?' he said. 'I decided to get arrested. Then I was safe if they were after me. Because they can't get at me in here, right? They're out there and I'm in here. That's problem number one solved. But I also figured, this is the complicated bit, if they actually were not after me at all, then why don't I get arrested but don't say anything about them? They would think I had got arrested by mistake or whatever, and they see that I'm not talking. They see, OK? It proves I'm safe. It's like a demonstration that I'm dependable. A sort of proof. Trial by ordeal sort of a thing. That's problem number two solved. And by saying it was me actually killed the guy, it sort of definitely puts me on their side. It's like a statement of loyalty, right? And I thought they might be grateful I'd pointed the heat in the wrong direction for a while. So that was problem number three solved.'

I stared at him. No wonder he had clammed up and thought like crazy for forty minutes when he was in with Finlay. Three birds with one stone. That's what he had been aiming for.

The part about proving he could be trusted not to spill his guts was OK. Whoever they were, they would notice that. A spell in jail without talking was a rite of passage. A badge of honour. Counted for a lot. Good thinking, Hubble.

Unfortunately the other part was pretty shaky.

100

They couldn't get to him in here? He had to be joking. No better place in the world to ace a guy than prison. You know where he is, you've got all the time you need. Lots of people who'll do it for you. Lots of opportunity. Cheap, too. On the street, a hit would cost you what? A grand, two grand? Plus a risk. Inside, it costs you a carton of cigarettes. Plus no risk. Because nobody would notice. No, prison was not a safe hiding place. Bad thinking, Hubble. And there was another flaw, too.

'What are you going to do on Monday?' I asked him. 'You'll be back home, doing whatever you do. You'll be walking around Margrave or Atlanta or wherever it is you walk around. If they're after you, won't they get you then?'

He started up with the thinking again. Going at it like crazy. He hadn't thought very far ahead before. Yesterday afternoon it had been blind panic. Deal with the present. Not a bad principle. Except pretty soon the future rolls in and that needs dealing with, too.

'I'm just hoping for the best,' Hubble said. 'I sort of felt if they wanted to get me, they might cool off after a while. I'm very useful to them. I hope they'll think about that. Right now it's a very tense situation. But it's all going to calm back down very soon. I might just make it through. If they get me, they get me. I don't care any more. It's my family I'm worried about.'

He stopped and shrugged. Blew a sigh. Not a bad guy. He hadn't set out to be some big criminal. It had crept up on the blind side. Sucked him in so gently he hadn't noticed. Until he wanted out. If he was very lucky they wouldn't break all his bones until after he was dead.

'How much does your wife know?' I asked him.

He glanced over. An expression of horror on his face.

'Nothing,' he said. 'Nothing at all. I haven't told her anything. Not a thing. I couldn't. It's all my secret. Nobody else knows a thing.'

'You'll have to tell her something,' I said. 'She's sure to have noticed you're not at home, vacuuming the pool or whatever you do on the weekend.'

I was just trying to lighten it up, but it didn't work out. Hubble went quiet. Misting over again at the thought of his backyard in the early fall sunlight. His wife maybe fussing over rose bushes or whatever. His kids darting about shrieking. Maybe they had a dog. And a three-car garage with European sedans waiting to be hosed off. A basketball hoop over the middle door waiting for the nine-year-old to grow strong enough to dunk the heavy ball. A flag over the porch. Early leaves waiting to be swept. Family life on a Saturday. But not this Saturday. Not for this guy.

'Maybe she'll think it's all a mistake,' he said. 'Maybe they've told her, I don't know. We know one of the policemen, Dwight Stevenson. My brother married his wife's sister. I don't know what he'll have said to her. I guess I'll deal with that on Monday. I'll say it was some kind of terrible mistake. She'll believe it. Everybody knows mistakes are made.'

He was thinking out loud.

'Hubble?' I said. 'What did the tall guy do to them that was liable to get himself shot in the head?'

He stood up and leaned on the wall. Rested his foot on the edge of the steel toilet pan. Looked at me. Wouldn't answer. Now for the big question.

'What about you?' I asked him. 'What have you

done to them liable to get yourself shot in the head?'

He wouldn't answer. The silence in our cell was terrible. I let it crash around for a while. Couldn't think of anything more to say. Hubble clunked his shoe against the metal toilet pan. A rattly little rhythm. Sounded like a Bo Diddley riff.

'You ever heard of Blind Blake?' I asked him.

He stopped clunking and looked up.

'Who?' he said blankly.

'Doesn't matter,' I said. 'I'm going to find a bathroom. I need to put a wet towel on my head. It hurts.'

'I'm not surprised,' he said. 'I'll come with you.'

He was anxious not to be left alone. Understandable. I was going to be his minder for the weekend. Not that I had any other plans.

We walked down the cell row to a kind of open area at the end. I saw the fire door Spivey had used the night before. Beyond it was a tiled opening. Over the opening was a clock. Nearly twelve noon. Clocks in prisons are bizarre. Why measure hours and minutes when people think in years and decades?

The tiled entrance was clogged with men. I pushed through and Hubble followed. It was a large tiled room, square. A strong disinfectant stink. One wall had the doorway. On the left was a row of shower stalls. Open. The back wall was a row of toilet cubicles. Open at the front, divided by waist-high partitions. The right wall was a row of washbasins. Very communal. Not a big deal if you'd been in the army all your life, but Hubble wasn't happy. Not what he was used to at all.

All the fittings were steel. Everything that would

103

normally be porcelain was stainless steel. For safety. A smashed-up porcelain washbasin yields some pretty good shards. A decent-sized sharp piece would make a good weapon. For the same reason the mirrors over the basins were sheets of polished steel. A bit dull, but fit for the purpose. You could see yourself in them, but you couldn't smash them up and stab somebody with a fragment.

I stepped over to a basin and ran cold water. Took a wad of paper towels from the dispenser and soaked them. Held them to my bruised forehead. Hubble stood around doing nothing. I kept the cold towels on for a while and then took some more. Water ran down my face. Felt good. There was no real injury. No flesh there, just skin over solid bone. Not much to injure, and impossible to break. A perfect arch, nature's strongest structure. That's why I avoid hitting anything with my hands. Hands are pretty fragile. All kinds of small bones and tendons in there. A punch big enough to deck that Red Boy would have smashed my hand up pretty good. I'd have joined him in the hospital. Not much point in that.

I patted my face dry and leaned up close to the steel mirror to check out the damage. Not bad. I combed my hair with my fingers. As I leaned against the sink I could feel the sunglasses in my pocket. The Red Boy's shades. The spoils of victory. I took them out and put them on. Gazed at my dull reflection.

As I messed about in front of the steel mirror I saw the start of some kind of a commotion happening behind me. I heard a brief warning from Hubble and I turned around. The sunglasses dimmed the bright light. Five white guys were trawling across the room. Biker types. Orange suits, of course, more torn-off sleeves, but with black leather additions. Caps, belts, fingerless gloves. Big beards. All five were big, heavy men, with that hard, slabby fat which is almost muscle but not quite. All five had crude tattoos on their arms and their faces. Swastikas. On their cheeks under their eyes and on their foreheads. The Aryan Brotherhood. White trash prison gang.

As the five swept the room, the other occupants melted away. Any who didn't get the message were seized and hustled to the door. Thrown out into the corridor. Even the soapy naked guys from the shower stalls. Within seconds the big bathroom was empty. Except for the five bikers and Hubble and me. The five big men fanned out in a loose arc around us. These were big ugly guys. The swastika tattoos on their faces were scratched in. Roughly inked.

My assumption was they'd come to recruit me. Somehow hijack the fact that I'd knocked over a Red Boy. Claim my bizarre celebrity for their cause. Turn it into a race triumph for the Brotherhood. But I was wrong. My assumption was way out. So I was left unprepared. The guy in the middle of the five was looking back and forth between Hubble and me. His eyes flicked across. They stopped on me.

'OK, he's the one,' he said. Looking straight at me.

Two things happened. The end two bikers grabbed Hubble and ran him to the door. And the boss man swung a big fist at my face. I saw it late. Dodged left and it caught me on the shoulder. I was spun around by the blow. Grabbed from behind by the neck. Two huge hands at my throat.

Strangling me. The boss man lined up for another shot at my gut. If it landed, I was a dead man. I knew that much. So I leaned back and kicked out. Smashed the boss man's balls like I was trying to punt a football right out of the stadium. The big Oxford shoe crunched him real good. The welt hit him like a blunt axe.

My shoulders were hunched and I was pumping up my neck to resist the strangler. He was wrenching hard. I was losing it. I reached up and broke his little fingers. I heard the knuckles splinter over the roaring in my ears. Then I broke his ring fingers. More splintering. Like pulling a chicken apart. He let go.

The third guy waded in. He was a solid mountain of lard. Sheathed with heavy slabs of meat. Like armour. Nowhere to hit him. He was pounding me with short jabs to the arm and chest. I was jammed back between two sinks. The mountain of lard pressing up. Nowhere to hit him. Except his eyes. I jammed my thumb into his eye. Hooked the tips of my fingers in his ear and squeezed. My thumbnail popped his eyeball sideways. I pushed my thumb in. His eyeball was nearly out. He was screaming and pulling on my wrist. I held on.

The boss man was up on one knee. I kicked hard at his face. Missed. Caught him in the throat instead. Smashed his voicebox. He went back down. I went for the big guy's other eye. Missed. I held on with my thumb. Like pushing it through a bloody steak. He went down. I spun away from the wall. The guy with the broken fingers ran for the door. The guy with the eye out was flopping about on the floor. Screaming. The boss man was choking on his smashed voicebox.

I was grabbed from behind again. I twisted away.

A Red Boy. Two of them. I was dizzy. I was going to lose it now. But they just grabbed me and ran me to the door. Sirens were going off.

'Get out of here, man,' screamed the Red Boys over the sirens. 'This is ours. We did this. Understand? Red Boys did this. We'll take the fall, man.'

They hurled me into the crowd outside. I understood. They were going to say they did it. Not because they wanted to protect me from the blame. Because they wanted to claim the credit. A race victory.

I saw Hubble bouncing around in the crowd. I saw guards. I saw hundreds of men. I saw Spivey. I grabbed Hubble and we hustled back to the cell. Sirens were blasting. Guards were tumbling out of a door. I could see shotguns and clubs. Boots clattered. Shouting and screaming. Sirens. We raced to the cell. Fell inside. I was dizzy and panting. I had taken a battering. The sirens were deafening. Couldn't talk. I splashed water on my face. The sunglasses were gone. Must have fallen off.

I heard screaming at the door. I turned and saw Spivey. He was screaming at us to get out. He rushed into the cell. I grabbed my coat from the bunk. Spivey seized Hubble by the elbow. Then he grabbed me and straight-armed both of us out of there. He was screaming at us to run. Sirens were blasting. He ran us to the emergency door where the guards had rushed out. Shoved us through and ran us up stairs. Up and up. My lungs were giving out. There was a door at the top of the last flight painted with a big figure six. We crashed through. He hustled us down a row of cells. Shoved us into an empty cell and flung the iron gate shut. It crashed and locked. He ran off. I collapsed on the bed, eyes tight shut.

When I opened them again Hubble was sitting on a bed looking over at me. We were in a big cell. Probably twice as wide as the last one. Two separate beds, one on each side. A sink, a john. A wall of bars. Everything was brighter and cleaner. It was very quiet. The air smelled better. This was the holding floor. This was floor six. This was where we should have been all the time.

'What the hell happened to you in there?' Hubble asked.

I just shrugged at him. A meal cart appeared outside our cell. It was dragged by an old white guy. Not a guard, some kind of an orderly. Looked more like an old steward on an ocean liner. He passed a tray through an oblong slot in the bars. Covered plates, paper cups, thermos. We ate the food sitting on our beds. I drank all the coffee. Then I paced the cell. Shook the gate. It was locked. The sixth floor was calm and quiet. A big clean cell. Separate beds. A mirror. Towels. I felt much better up here.

Hubble piled the meal debris on the tray and shoved it out under the gate into the corridor. He lay down on his bed. Put his hands behind his head. Stared at the ceiling. Doing time. I did the same. But I was thinking hard. Because they had definitely gone through a selection process. They had looked us both over very carefully and chosen me. Quite definitely chosen me. Then they had tried to strangle me.

They would have killed me. Except for one thing. The guy with his hands around my throat had made a mistake. He had me from behind, which was in his favour, and he was big enough and strong enough. But he hadn't balled up his fingers. The best way is to use the thumbs on the back of the neck but fold up the fingers. Do it with knuckle pressure, not finger pressure. The guy had left his fingers out straight. So I had been able to reach up and snap them off. His mistake had saved my life. No doubt about that. Soon as he was neutralized, it was two against one. And I'd never had a problem with those kind of odds.

But it was still a straightforward attempt to kill me. They came in, chose me, tried to kill me. And Spivey had just happened to be outside the bathroom. He had set it up. He had employed the Aryan Brotherhood to kill me. He had ordered the attack and waited ready to burst in and find me dead.

And he had planned it yesterday before ten in the evening. That was clear. That's why he had left us on the wrong floor. On the third, not the sixth. On a convict floor, not the holding floor. Everybody had known we should have been on the holding floor. The two guards last night in the reception bunker, they had been totally clear about it. It had said so on their battered clipboard. But at ten o'clock, Spivey had left us on the third floor where he knew he could have me killed. He'd told the Aryans to attack me at twelve o'clock the next day. He had been waiting outside that bathroom at twelve o'clock ready to burst in. Ready to see my body lying on the tiles.

But then his plan had fouled up. I wasn't killed. The Aryans were beaten off. The Red Boys had piled in to seize the moment. Mayhem had broken out. A riot was starting. Spivey was panicking. He hit the alarms and called the crash squads. Rushed us off the floor, up to the sixth, and left us up here.

According to all the paperwork, the sixth floor is where we'd been all the time.

A neat fallback. It made me fireproof as far as investigation went. Spivey had chosen the fallback option which said we were never there. He had a couple of serious injuries on his hands, probably even a dead guy. I figured the boss man must have choked to death. Spivey must know I had done it. But he could never say so now. Because according to him, I was never there.

I lay on the bed and stared at the concrete ceiling. I exhaled gently. The plan was clear. No doubt about Spivey's plan at all. The fallback was coherent. An aborted plan with a neat fallback position. But why? I didn't understand it. Let's say the strangler had balled up his fingers. They would have got me then. I would have been dead. Dumped on the bathroom floor with my big swollen tongue sticking out. Spivey would have rushed in and found me. Why? What was Spivey's angle? What did he have against me? I'd never seen him before. Never been anywhere near him or his damn prison. Why the hell should he operate an elaborate plan to get me dead? I couldn't begin to figure it out.

EIGHT

Hubble slept for a while on the cot across from mine. Then he stirred and woke up. Writhed around. Looked disoriented for a moment, until he remembered where he was. Tried to check the time on his watch but saw only a band of pale skin where the heavy Rolex had been. Pushed against the bridge of his nose and remembered he'd lost his eyeglasses. Sighed and flopped his head back onto the striped prison pillow. One very miserable guy.

I could understand his fear. But he also looked defeated. Like he'd just rolled the dice and lost. Like he'd been counting on something to happen, and it hadn't happened, so now he was back in despair.

Then I began to understand that, too.

'The dead guy was trying to help you, wasn't he?' I said.

The question scared him.

'I can't tell you that, can I?' he answered.

'I need to know,' I said. 'Maybe you approached

111

the guy for help. Maybe you talked to him. Maybe that's why he got killed. Maybe it looks like now you'll start talking to me. Which could get me killed, too.'

Hubble nodded and rocked back and forth on his bed. Took a deep breath. Looked straight at me.

'He was an investigator,' he said. 'I brought him down here because I want this whole thing stopped. I don't want to be involved any more. I'm not a criminal. I'm scared to death and I want out. He was going to get me out and take down the scam. But he slipped up somehow and now he's dead and I'm never going to get out. And if they find out it was me brought him down here, they'll kill me. And if they don't kill me, I'll probably go to jail for a thousand years anyway, because right now the whole damn thing is very exposed and very dangerous.'

'Who was the guy?' I asked him.

'He didn't have a name,' Hubble said. 'Just a contact code. He said it was safer that way. I can't believe they got him. He seemed like a capable guy to me. Tell the truth, you remind me of him. You seem like a capable guy to me, too.'

'What was he doing up there at the warehouse?' I asked him.

He shrugged and shook his head.

'I don't understand that situation,' he said. 'I put him together with another guy, and he was meeting with him up there, but wouldn't they have shot the other guy as well? I don't understand why they only got one of them.'

'Who was the other guy he was meeting with?' I said.

He stopped and shook his head.

'I've told you way too much already,' he said. 'I must be crazy. They'll kill me.'

'Who's on the inside of this thing?' I asked him.

'Don't you listen?' he said. 'I'm not saying another word.'

'I don't want names,' I said. 'Is it a big deal?'

'It's huge,' he said. 'Biggest thing you ever heard of.'

'How many people?' I said.

He shrugged and thought about it. Counted up in his head.

'Ten people,' he said. 'Not counting me.'

I looked at him and shrugged.

'Ten people doesn't sound like a big deal,' I said.

'Well, there's hired help,' he said. 'They're around when they're needed. I mean a core of ten people around here. Ten people in the know, not counting me. It's a very tight situation, but believe me, it's a big deal.'

'What about the guy you sent to meet with the investigator?' I said. 'Is he one of the ten people?'

Hubble shook his head.

'I'm not counting him either,' he said.

'So there's you and him and ten others?' I said. 'Some kind of a big deal?'

He nodded glumly.

'Biggest thing you ever heard of,' he said again.

'And right now it's very exposed?' I asked him. 'Why? Because of this investigator poking about?'

Hubble shook his head again. He was writhing around like my questions were tearing him up.

'No,' he said. 'For another reason altogether. It's like a window of vulnerability is wide open right now. An exposure. It's been very risky, getting worse all the time. But now it could go either way.

If we get through it, nobody will ever know anything. But if we don't get through it, it'll be the biggest sensation you ever heard of, believe me. Either way, it's going to be a close call.'

I looked at him. He didn't look to me much like the sort of a guy who could cause the biggest sensation I ever heard of.

'So how long is this exposure going to last?' I asked him.

'It's nearly over,' he said. 'Maybe a week. A week tomorrow is my guess. Next Sunday. Maybe I'll live to see it.'

'So after next Sunday you're not vulnerable any more?' I said. 'Why not? What's going to happen next Sunday?'

He shook his head and turned his face away. It was like if he couldn't see me, I wasn't there, asking him questions.

'What does Pluribus mean?' I asked him.

He wouldn't answer. Just kept on shaking his head. His eyes were screwed shut with terror.

'Is it a code for something?' I said.

He wasn't hearing me. The conversation was over. I gave it up and we lapsed back into silence. That suited me well enough. I didn't want to know anything more. I didn't want to know anything at all. Being an outsider and knowing Hubble's business didn't seem to be a very smart combination. It hadn't done the tall guy with the shaved head a whole lot of good. I wasn't interested in sharing the same fate as him, dead at a warehouse gate, partially hidden under some old cardboard, two holes in my head, all my bones smashed. I just wanted to pass the time until Monday, and then get the hell out. By next Sunday, I planned to be a very long way away indeed.

'OK, Hubble,' I said. 'No more questions.'

He shrugged and nodded. Sat silent for a long time. Then he spoke, quietly, with a lot of resignation in his voice.

'Thanks,' he said. 'It's better that way.'

I was rolled over on the narrow cot trying to float away into some kind of limbo. But Hubble was restless. He was tossing and turning and blowing tight sighs. He was coming close to irritating me again. I turned to face him.

'I'm sorry,' he said. 'I'm very uptight. It was doing me good just to talk to somebody. I'd go crazy in here on my own. Can't we talk about something else? What about you? Tell me about yourself. Who are you, Reacher?'

I shrugged at him.

'I'm nobody,' I said. 'Just a guy passing through. I'll be gone on Monday.'

'Nobody's nobody,' he said. 'We've all got a story. Tell me.'

So I talked for a while, lying on my bed, running through the last six months. He lay on his bed, looking at the concrete ceiling, listening, keeping his mind off his problems. I told him about leaving from the Pentagon. Washington, Baltimore, Philadelphia, New York, Boston, Pittsburgh, Detroit, Chicago. Museums, music, cheap hotels, bars, buses and trains. Solitude. Travelling through the land of my citizenship like a cheap tourist. Seeing most things for the first time. Looking at the history I'd learned in dusty schoolrooms half a world away. Looking at the big things that had shaped the nation. Battlefields, factories, declarations, revolutions. Looking for the small things. Birthplaces, clubs, roads, legends. The big things and the small things which were supposed to represent home. I'd found some of them.

I told Hubble about the long hop through the endless plains and deltas all the way down from Chicago to New Orleans. Sliding around the Gulf Coast as far as Tampa. Then the Greyhound blasting north toward Atlanta. The crazy decision to bail out near Margrave. The long walk in the rain yesterday morning. Following a whim. Following some half-remembered note from my brother saying he'd been through some little place where Blind Blake might have died over sixty years ago. As I told him about it, I felt pretty stupid. Hubble was scuffling with a nightmare and I was following a meaningless pilgrimage. But he understood the urge.

'I did that once,' he said. 'On our honeymoon. We went to Europe. We stopped off in New York and I spent half a day looking for the Dakota building, you know, where John Lennon was shot. Then we spent three days in England walking around Liverpool, looking for the Cavern Club. Where the Beatles started out. Couldn't find it, I guess they knocked it down.'

He talked on for a while. Mostly about travelling. He'd taken plenty of trips with his wife. They'd enjoyed it. Been all over, Europe, Mexico, the Caribbean. All over the States and Canada. Had a great time together.

'Don't you get lonely?' he asked me. 'Travelling on your own all the time?'

I told him no, I enjoyed it. I told him I appreciated the solitude, the anonymity. Like I was invisible.

'How do you mean, invisible?' he said. He seemed interested.

'I travel by road,' I said. 'Always by road. Walk a bit, and ride the buses. Sometimes trains. Always pay cash. That way there's never a paper trail. No credit card transactions, no passenger manifests, nothing. Nobody could trace me. I never tell anybody my name. If I stay in a hotel, I pay cash and give them a made-up name.'

'Why?' he said. 'Who the hell's after you?'

'Nobody,' I said. 'It's just a bit of fun. I like anonymity. I feel like I'm beating the system. And right now, I'm truly pissed at the system.'

I saw him fall back to thinking. He thought a long time. I could see him deflate as he struggled with the problems that wouldn't go away. I could see his panic come and go like a tide.

'So give me your advice about Finlay,' he said. 'When he asks me about the confession, I'll say I was stressed out because of some business situation. I'll say there was some kind of rivalry, threats against my family. I'll say I don't know anything about the dead guy or anything about the phone number. I'll deny everything. Then I'll just try to settle everything down. What do you think?'

I thought it sounded like a pretty thin plan.

'Tell me one thing,' I said. 'Without giving me any more details, do you perform a useful function for them? Or are you just some kind of onlooker?'

He pulled on his fingers and thought for a moment.

'Yes, I perform a useful function for them,' he said. 'Crucial, even.'

'And if you weren't there to do it?' I asked him. 'Would they have to recruit someone else?'

'Yes, they would,' he said. 'And it would be

117

moderately difficult to do that, given the parameters of the function.'

He was rating his chances of staying alive like he would rate a credit application up at his office.

'OK,' I said. 'Your plan is as good as you're going to get. Go for it.'

I didn't see what else he could do. He was a small cog in some kind of a big operation. But a crucial cog. And nobody wrecks a big operation for no reason. So his future was actually clear-cut. If they ever figured it was him who had brought in the outside investigator, then he was definitely dead. But if they never found that out, then he was definitely safe. Simple as that. I figured he had a good enough chance, because of one very persuasive fact.

He had confessed because he had thought prison was some kind of a safe sanctuary where they couldn't get him. That had been part of his thinking behind it. It was bad thinking. He'd been wrong. He wasn't safe from attack, quite the reverse. They could have got him if they had wanted to. But the other side of that particular coin was that he hadn't been attacked. As it happened, I had been. Not Hubble. So I figured there was some kind of a proof there that he was OK. They weren't out to get him, because if they had wanted to kill him, they could have killed him by now, and they would have killed him by now. But they hadn't. Even though they were apparently very uptight right now because of some kind of a temporary risk. So it seemed like proof. I began to think he would be OK.

'Yes, Hubble,' I said again. 'Go for it, it's the best you can do.'

The cell stayed locked all day. The floor was

silent. We lay on our beds and drifted through the rest of the afternoon. No more talking. We were all talked out. I was bored and wished I had brought that newspaper with me from the Margrave station house. I could have read it all over again. All about the President cutting crime prevention so he could get re-elected. Saving a buck on the Coast Guard today so he could spend ten bucks on prisons like this one tomorrow.

At about seven the old orderly came by with dinner. We ate. He came back and picked up the tray. We drifted through the empty evening. At ten the power banged off and we were in darkness. Nightfall. I kept my shoes on and slept lightly. Just in case Spivey had any more plans for me.

At seven in the morning the lights came back on. Sunday. I woke up tired, but I forced myself to get up. Forced myself to do a bit of stretching to ease off my sore body. Hubble was awake, but silent. He was vaguely watching me exercise. Still drifting. Breakfast arrived before eight. The same old guy dragging the meal cart. I ate the breakfast and drank the coffee. As I finished up the flask, the gate lock clunked and sprang the door. I pushed it open and stepped out and bumped into a guard aiming to come in.

'It's your lucky day,' the guard said. 'You're getting out.'

'I am?' I said.

'You both are,' he said. 'Reacher and Hubble, released by order of the Margrave PD. Be ready in five minutes, OK?'

I stepped back into the cell. Hubble had hauled himself up onto his elbows. He hadn't eaten his breakfast. He looked more worried than ever.

'I'm scared,' he said.

'You'll be OK,' I said.

'Will I?' he said. 'Once I'm out of here, they can get to me.'

I shook my head.

'It would have been easier for them to get you in here,' I said. 'Believe me, if they were looking to kill you, you'd be dead by now. You're in the clear, Hubble.'

He nodded to himself and sat up. I picked up my coat and we stood together outside the cell, waiting. The guard was back within five minutes. He walked us along a corridor and through two sets of locked gates. Put us in a back elevator. Stepped in and used his key to send it down. Stepped out again as the doors began to close.

'So long,' he said. 'Don't come back.'

The elevator took us down to a lobby and then we stepped outside into a hot concrete yard. The prison door sucked shut and clicked behind us. I stood face up to the sun and breathed in the outside air. I must have looked like some guy in a corny old movie who gets released from a year in solitary.

There were two cars parked in the yard. One was a big dark sedan, an English Bentley, maybe twenty years old, but it looked brand-new. There was a blonde woman in it, who I guessed was Hubble's wife, because he was on his way over to her like she was the sweetest sight he ever saw. The other car had Officer Roscoe in it.

She got out and walked straight over to me. Looked wonderful. Out of uniform. Dressed in jeans and a soft cotton shirt. Leather jacket. Calm intelligent face. Soft dark hair. Huge eyes. I'd thought she was nice on Friday. I'd been right.

'Hello, Roscoe,' I said.

'Hello, Reacher,' she said, and smiled.

Her voice was wonderful. Her smile was great. I watched it for as long as it lasted, which was a good long time. Ahead of us, the Hubbles drove off in the Bentley, waving. I waved back and wondered how things would turn out for them. Probably I would never know, unless they got unlucky and I happened to read about it in a newspaper somewhere.

Roscoe and I got into her car. Not really hers, she explained, just a department unmarked she was using. A brand-new Chevrolet something, big, smooth and quiet. She'd kept the motor running and the air on and inside it was cool. We wafted out of the concrete yard and shunted through the wire vehicle cages. Outside the last cage Roscoe spun the wheel and we blasted away down the road. The nose of the car rose up and the back end squatted down on the soft suspension. I didn't look back. I just sat there, feeling good. Getting out of prison is one of life's good feelings. So is not knowing what tomorrow holds. So is cruising silently down a sunny road with a pretty woman at the wheel.

'So what happened?' I said after a mile. 'Tell me.'

She told me a pretty straightforward story. They'd started work on my alibi late Friday evening. She and Finlay. A dark squad room. A couple of desk lights on. Pads of paper. Cups of coffee. Telephone books. The two of them cradling phones and chewing pencils. Low voices. Patient enquiries. A scene I'd been in myself a thousand times.

They'd called Tampa and Atlanta and by

121

midnight they'd gotten hold of a passenger from my bus and the ticket clerk at the Tampa depot. Both of them remembered me. Then they got the bus driver as well. He confirmed he'd stopped at the Margrave cloverleaf to let me out, eight o'clock Friday morning. By midnight my alibi was looking rock-solid, just like I'd said it would be.

Saturday morning, a long fax was in from the Pentagon about my service record. Thirteen years of my life, reduced to a few curling fax pages. It felt like somebody else's life now, but it backed my story. Finlay had been impressed by it. Then my prints came back from the FBI database. They'd been matched by the tireless computer at two-thirty in the morning. US Army, printed on induction, thirteen years ago. My alibi was solid, and my background checked out.

'Finlay was satisfied,' Roscoe told me. 'You are who you say you are, and midnight Thursday you were over four hundred miles away. That was nailed down. He called the medical examiner again just in case he had a new opinion on the time of death, but no, midnight was still about right.'

I shook my head. Finlay was one very cautious guy.

'What about the dead guy?' I said. 'Did you run his prints again?'

She concentrated on passing a farm truck. The first vehicle we'd seen in a quarter-hour. Then she looked across and nodded.

'Finlay told me you wanted me to,' she said. 'But why?'

'They came back too quickly for a negative result,' I said.

'Too quickly?' she said.

'You told me there was a pyramid system, right?'

I said. 'The top ten, then the top hundred, then the top thousand, all the way down, right?'

She nodded again.

'So take me as an example,' I said. 'I'm in the database, but I'm pretty low down the pyramid. You just said it took fourteen hours to get down to me, right?'

'Right,' she said. 'I sent your prints in about twelve-thirty at lunchtime and they were matched at two-thirty in the morning.'

'OK,' I said. 'Fourteen hours. So if it takes fourteen hours to reach nearly to the bottom of the pyramid, it's got to take more than fourteen hours to get all the way down to the bottom. That's logical, right?'

'Right,' she said.

'But what happened with this dead guy?' I said. 'The body was found at eight o'clock, so the prints went in when? Eight-thirty, earliest. But Baker was already telling me there was no match on file when they were talking to me at two-thirty. I remember the time, because I was looking at the clock. That's only six hours. If it took fourteen hours to find out that I'm in there, how could it take just six hours to say the dead guy's not in there?'

'God,' she said. 'You're right. Baker must have screwed up. Finlay took the prints and Baker sent them. He must have screwed up the scan. You got to be careful, or it doesn't transmit clearly. If the scan's not clear, the database tries to decipher it, then it comes back as unreadable. Baker must have thought that meant a null result. The codes are similar. Anyway, I sent them again, first thing. We'll know soon enough.'

We drove on east and Roscoe told me she'd pushed Finlay to get me out of Warburton right away yesterday afternoon. Finlay had grunted and agreed, but there was a problem. They'd had to wait until today, because yesterday afternoon Warburton had been just about shut down. They had told Finlay there had been some trouble in a bathroom. One convict was dead, one had lost an eye, and a full-scale riot had started, black and white gangs at war.

I just sat there next to Roscoe and watched the horizon reeling in. I'd killed one guy and blinded another. Now I'd have to confront my feelings. But I didn't feel much at all. Nothing, in fact. No guilt, no remorse. None at all. I felt like I'd chased two roaches around that bathroom and stomped on them. But at least a roach is a rational, reasonable, evolved sort of a creature. Those Aryans in that bathroom had been worse than vermin. I'd kicked one of them in the throat and he had suffocated on his smashed larynx. Well, tough shit. He started it, right? Attacking me was like pushing open a forbidden door. What waited on the other side was his problem. His risk. If he didn't like it, he shouldn't have pushed open the damn door. I shrugged and forgot about it. Looked over at Roscoe.

'Thank you,' I said. 'I mean it. You worked hard to help me out.'

She waved away my thanks with a blush and a small gesture and just drove on. I was starting to like her a lot. But probably not enough to stop me getting the hell out of Georgia as soon as I could. Maybe I might just stay an hour or two and then get her to drive me to a bus depot somewhere.

'I want to take you to lunch,' I said. 'Kind of a thank-you thing.'

She thought about it for a quarter-mile and then smiled across at me.

'OK,' she said.

She jinked the right turn onto the county road and accelerated south towards Margrave. Drove past Eno's shiny new place and headed down to town.

NINE

I got her to duck in at the station house and bring me out the property bag with my money in it. Then we drove on and she dropped me in the centre of Margrave and I arranged to meet her up at the station house in a couple of hours. I stood on the sidewalk in the fierce Sunday morning heat and waved her off. I felt a whole lot better. I was back in motion. I was going to check out the Blind Blake story, then take Roscoe to lunch, then get the hell out of Georgia and never come back.

So I spent a while wandering around looking at the town, doing the things I should have been doing on Friday afternoon. There wasn't really much to the place. The old county road ran straight through, north to south, and for about four blocks it was labelled Main Street. Those four blocks had small stores and offices facing each other across the width of the road, separated by little service alleys which ran round to the back of the buildings. I saw a small grocery, a barbershop, an outfitters, a doctor's office, a lawyer's office and a dentist's office. In back of the commercial buildings was parkland with white picket fences and ornamental trees. On the street, the stores and offices had awnings over wide sidewalks. There were benches set on the sidewalks, but they were empty. The whole place was deserted. Sunday morning, miles from anywhere.

Main Street ran north, straight as a die, past a few hundred yards of more parkland up to the station house and the fire house, and a half-mile farther on than that was Eno's diner. A few miles beyond Eno's was the turn west out to Warburton where the prison was. North of that junction there was nothing on the county road until you reached the warehouses and the highway cloverleaf, fourteen empty miles from where I stood.

On the south edge of town I could see a little village green with a bronze statue and a residential street running away to the west. I strolled down there and saw a discreet green sign which read: Beckman Drive. Hubble's street. I couldn't see any real distance down it because pretty much straight away it looped left and right around a wide grass square with a big white wooden church set on it. The church was ringed by cherry trees and the lawn was circled by cars with clean quiet paint parked in neat lines. I could just about make out the growl of the organ and the sound of the people singing.

The statue on the village green was of a guy called Caspar Teale who'd done something or other about a hundred years ago. More or less opposite Beckman Drive on the other side of the green was another residential street, running east, with a convenience store standing alone on the corner. And that was it. Not much of a town. Not much going on. Took me less than thirty minutes to look over everything the place had to offer.

But it was the most immaculate town I had ever seen. It was amazing. Every single building was either brand-new or recently refurbished. The roads were smooth as glass, and the sidewalks were flat and clean. No potholes, no cracks, no heave. The little offices and stores looked like they got repainted every week. The lawns and the plantings and the trees were clipped to perfection. The bronze statue of old Caspar Teale looked like somebody licked it clean every morning. The paint on the church was so bright it hurt my eyes. Flags flew everywhere, sparkling white and glowing red and blue in the sun. The whole place was so tidy it could make you nervous to walk around in case you left a dirty footprint somewhere.

The convenience store on the southeastern corner was selling the sort of stuff which gave it a good enough excuse to be open on a Sunday morning. Open, but not busy. There was nobody in there except the guy behind the register. But he had coffee. I sat up at the little counter and ordered a big mug and bought a Sunday newspaper.

The President was still on the front page. Now he was in California. He was explaining to defence contractors why their gravy train was grinding to a halt after fifty glorious years. The aftershock from his Pensacola announcement about the Coast Guard was still rumbling on. Their boats were returning to their harbours on Saturday night. They wouldn't go out again without new funding. The paper's editorial guys were all stirred up about it.

I stopped reading and glanced up when I heard the door open. A woman came in. She took a stool at the opposite end of the counter. She was older than me, maybe forty. Dark hair, very slender, expensively dressed in black. She had very pale skin. So pale, it was almost luminous. She moved with a kind of nervous tension. I could see tendons like slim ropes in her wrists. I could see some kind of an appalling strain in her face. The counter guy slid over to her and she ordered coffee in a voice so quiet I could barely hear it, even though she was pretty close by and it was a silent room.

She didn't stay long. She got through half her coffee, watching the window all the time. Then a big black pickup truck pulled up outside and she shivered. It was a brand-new truck and obviously it had never hauled anything worth hauling. I caught a glimpse of the driver as he leaned over inside to spring the door. He was a tough-looking guy. Pretty tall. Broad shoulders and a thick neck. Black hair. Black hair all over long knotted arms. Maybe thirty years old. The pale woman slid off her stool like a ghost and stood up. Swallowed once. As she opened the shop door I heard the burble of a big motor idling. The woman got into the truck, but it didn't move away. Just sat there at the kerb. I swivelled on my stool to face the counter guy.

'Who is that?' I asked him.

The guy looked at me like I was from another planet.

'That's Mrs Kliner,' he said. 'You don't know the Kliners?'

'I heard about them,' I said. 'I'm a stranger in town. Kliner owns the warehouses up near the highway, right?'

'Right,' he said. 'And a whole lot more besides. Big deal round here, Mr Kliner.'

'He is?' I said.

'Sure,' the guy said. 'You heard about the Foundation?'

I shook my head. Finished my coffee and pushed the mug over for a refill.

'Kliner set up the Kliner Foundation,' the guy said. 'Benefits the town in a lot of ways. Came here five years ago, been like Christmas ever since.'

I nodded.

'Is Mrs Kliner OK?' I asked him.

He shook his head as he filled my mug.

'She's a sick woman,' he said. 'Very sick. Very pale, right? Sort of wan? A very sick woman. Could be tuberculosis. I seen tuberculosis do that to folks. She used to be a fine-looking woman, but now she looks like something grown in a closet, right? A very sick woman, that's for damn sure.'

'Who's the guy in the truck?' I said.

'Stepson,' he said. 'Kliner's kid by his first wife. Mrs Kliner's his second. I've heard she don't get along so good with the kid.'

He gave me the sort of nod that terminates casual conversations. Moved away to wipe off some kind of a chromium machine behind the other end of the counter. The black pickup was still waiting outside. I agreed with the guy that the woman looked like something grown in a closet. She looked like some kind of a rare orchid starved of light and sustenance. But I didn't agree with him that she looked sick. I didn't think she had tuberculosis. I thought she was suffering from something else. Something I'd seen once or twice before. I thought she was suffering from sheer terror. Terror of what, I didn't know. Terror of what, I didn't want to know. Not my problem. I stood up and dropped a five on the counter. The guy made change all in coins. He had no dollar bills. The pickup was still there, stationary at the kerb. The driver was leaning up, chest against the wheel, looking sideways across his stepmother, staring in straight at me.

There was a mirror opposite me behind the counter. I looked exactly like a guy who'd been on an all-night bus and then spent two days in jail. I figured I needed to get cleaned up before I took Roscoe to lunch. The counter guy saw me figuring.

'Try the barbershop,' he said.

'On a Sunday?' I said.

The guy shrugged.

'They're always in there,' he said. 'Never exactly closed. Never exactly open, either.'

I nodded and pushed out through the door. I saw a small crowd of people coming out of the church and chatting on the lawns and getting into their cars. The rest of the town was still deserted. But the black pickup was still at the kerb, right outside the convenience store. The driver was still staring at me.

I walked north in the sun and the pickup moved slowly alongside, keeping pace. The guy was still hunched forward, staring sideways. I stretched out a couple of steps and the truck sped up to keep station. Then I stopped dead and he overshot. I stood there. The guy evidently decided backing up wasn't on his agenda. He floored it and took off with a roar. I shrugged and carried on. Reached the barbershop. Ducked under the striped awning and tried the door. Unlocked. I went in.

Like everything else in Margrave, the barbershop looked wonderful. It gleamed with ancient chairs and fittings lovingly polished and maintained. It had the kind of barbershop gear everybody tore out thirty years ago. Now everybody wants it back.

They pay a fortune for it because it recreates the way people want America to look. The way they think it used to look. It's certainly the way I thought it used to look. I would sit in some schoolyard in Manila or Munich and imagine green lawns and trees and flags and a gleaming chrome barbershop like this one.

It was run by two old black guys. They were just hanging out there. Not really open for business, not really closed. But they indicated they would serve me. Like they were there, and I was there, so why not? And I guess I looked like an urgent case. I asked them for the works. A shave, a haircut, a hot towel and a shoeshine. There were framed newspaper front pages here and there on the walls. Big headlines. Roosevelt dies, VJ Day, JFK assassinated, Martin Luther King murdered. There was an old mahogany table radio thumping warmly away. The new Sunday paper was crisply folded on a bench in the window.

The old guys mixed up soapy lather in a bowl, stropped a straight razor, rinsed a shaving brush. They shrouded me with towels and got to work. One guy shaved me with the old straight razor. The other guy stood around doing not much of anything. I figured maybe he came into play later. The busy guy started chatting away, like barbers do. Told me the history of his business. The two of them had been buddies since childhood. Always lived here in Margrave since way back. Started out as barbers way before World War Two. Apprenticed in Atlanta. Opened a shop together as young men. Moved it to this location when the old neighbourhood was razed. He told me the history of the county from a barber's perspective. Listed the personalities who'd been in and out of these old chairs. Told me about all kinds of people.

'So tell me about the Kliners,' I said.

He was a chatty guy, but that question shut him up. He stopped work and thought about it.

'Can't help you with that enquiry, that's for sure,' he said. 'That's a subject we prefer not to discuss in here. Best if you ask me about somebody else altogether.'

I shrugged under the shroud of towels.

'OK,' I said. 'You ever heard of Blind Blake?'

'Him I heard of, that's for sure,' the old man said. 'That's a guy we can discuss, no problem at all.'

'Great,' I said. 'So what can you tell me?'

'He was here, time to time, way back,' he said. 'Born in Jacksonville, Florida, they say, just over the state line. Used to kind of trek on up from there, you know, through here, through Atlanta, all the way up north to Chicago, and then trek all the way back down again. Back through Atlanta, back through here, back home. Very different then, you know. No highway, no automobiles, at least not for a poor black man and his friends. All walking or riding on the freight cars.'

'You ever hear him play?' I asked him.

He stopped work again and looked at me.

'Man, I'm seventy-four years old,' he said. 'This was back when I was just a little boy. We're talking about Blind Blake here. Guys like that played in bars. Never was in no bars when I was a little boy, you understand. I would have got my behind whupped real good if I had been. You should talk to my partner here. He's a whole lot older than I am. He may have heard him play, only he may not remember it because he don't remember much. Not even what he ate for breakfast. Am I right?

133

Hey, my old friend, what you eat for breakfast?'

The other old guy creaked over and leaned up on the next sink to mine. He was a gnarled old fellow the colour of the mahogany radio.

'I don't know what I ate for breakfast,' he said. 'Don't even know if I ate any breakfast at all. But listen up. I may be an old guy, but the truth is old guys remember stuff real well. Not recent things, you understand, but old things. You got to imagine your memory is like an old bucket, you know? Once it's filled up with old stuff there ain't no way to get new stuff in. No way at all, you understand? So I don't remember any new stuff because my old bucket is all filled up with old stuff that happened way back. You understand what I'm saying here?'

'Sure I understand,' I said. 'So way back, did you ever hear him play?'

'Who?' he said.

I looked at both of them in turn. I wasn't sure whether this was some kind of a rehearsed routine.

'Blind Blake,' I said. 'Did you ever hear him play?'

'No, I never heard him play,' the old guy said. 'But my sister did. Got me a sister more than about ninety years old or thereabouts, may she be spared. Still alive. She did a little singing way back and she sang with old Blind Blake many a time.'

'She did?' I said. 'She sang with him?'

'She sure did,' said the gnarled old guy. 'She sang with just about anybody passing through. You got to remember this old town lay right on the big road to Atlanta. That old county road out there used to come on down through here straight on south into Florida. It was the only route through Georgia north to south. Of course now you got the highway runs right by without stopping off, and you got airplanes and all. No importance to Margrave now, nobody coming on through any more.'

'So Blind Blake stopped off here?' I prompted him. 'And your sister sang with him?'

'Everybody used to stop off here,' he said. 'North side of town was just pretty much a mess of bars and rooming houses to cater to the folks passing through. All these fancy gardens between here and the fire house is where the bars and rooming houses used to be. All tore down now, or else all fell down. Been no passing trade at all for a real long time. But back then, it was a different kind of a town altogether. Streams of people in and out, the whole time. Workers, crop pickers, drummers, fighters, hoboes, truckers, musicians. All kinds of those guys used to stop off and play and my old sister would be right in there singing with them all.'

'And she remembers Blind Blake?' I asked him.

'She sure does,' the old man said. 'Used to think he was the greatest thing alive. Says he used to play real sporty. Real sporty indeed.'

'What happened to him?' I said. 'Do you know?'

The old guy thought hard. Trawled back through his fading memories. He shook his grizzled head a couple of times. Then he took a wet towel from a hot box and put it over my face. Started cutting my hair. Ended up shaking his head with some kind of finality.

'Can't rightly say,' he said. 'He came back and forth on the road, time to time. I remember that pretty well. Three, four years later he was gone. I was up in Atlanta for a spell, wasn't here to know. Heard tell somebody killed him, maybe right here in Margrave, maybe not. Some kind of big trouble, got him killed stone dead.'

I sat listening to their old radio for a while. Then

I gave them a twenty off my roll of bills and hurried out onto Main Street. Strode out north. It was nearly noon and the sun was baking. Hot for September. Nobody else was out walking. The black road blasted heat at me. Blind Blake had walked this road, maybe in the noon heat. Back when those old barbers had been boys this had been the artery reaching north to Atlanta, Chicago, jobs, hope, money. Noon heat wouldn't have stopped anybody getting where they were going. But now the road was just a smooth blacktop byway going nowhere at all.

It took me a few minutes in the heat to get up to the station house. I walked across its springy lawn past another bronze statue and pulled open the heavy glass entrance door. Stepped into the chill inside. Roscoe was waiting for me, leaning on the reception counter. Behind her in the squad room, I could see Stevenson talking urgently into a telephone. Roscoe was pale and looking very worried.

'We found another body,' she said.

'Where?' I asked her.

'Up at the warehouse again,' she said. 'The other side of the road this time, underneath the cloverleaf, where it's raised up.'

'Who found it?' I said.

'Finlay,' she said. 'He was up there this morning, poking around, looking for something to help us with the first one. Some help, right? All he finds is another one.'

'Do you know who this one is?' I asked her.

She shook her head.

'Unidentified,' she said. 'Same as the first one.'

'Where's Finlay now?' I asked her.

'Gone to get Hubble,' she said. 'He thinks Hubble may know something about it.'

I nodded.

'How long was this one up there?' I said.

'Two or three days, maybe,' she said. 'Finlay says it could have been a double homicide on Thursday night.'

I nodded again. Hubble did know something about it. This was the guy he had sent to meet with the tall investigator with the shaved head. He couldn't figure out how the guy had gotten away with it. But the guy hadn't gotten away with it.

I heard a car in the lot outside and then the big glass door sucked open. Finlay stuck his head in.

'Morgue, Roscoe,' he said. 'You too, Reacher.'

We followed him back outside into the heat. We all got into Roscoe's unmarked sedan. Left Finlay's car where he'd parked it. Roscoe drove. I sat in the back. Finlay sat in the front passenger seat, twisted around so he could talk to the both of us at once. Roscoe nosed out of the police lot and headed south.

'I can't find Hubble,' Finlay said. Looking at me. 'There's nobody up at his place. Did he say anything to you about going anywhere?'

'No,' I said. 'Not a word. We hardly spoke all weekend.'

Finlay grunted at me.

'I need to find out what he knows about all this,' he said. 'This is serious shit and he knows something about it, that's for damn sure. What did he tell you about it, Reacher?'

I didn't answer. I wasn't entirely sure whose side I was on yet. Finlay's, probably, but if Finlay started blundering around in whatever Hubble was mixed up in, Hubble and his family were going to end up dead. No doubt about that. So I figured I should just stay impartial and then get the hell out of there as fast as possible. I didn't want to get involved.

'You try his mobile number?' I asked him.

Finlay grunted and shook his head.

'Switched off,' he said. 'Some automatic voice came on and told me.'

'Did he come by and pick up his watch?' I asked him.

'His what?' he said.

'His watch,' I said. 'He left a ten-thousand-dollar Rolex with Baker on Friday. When Baker was cuffing us for the ride out to Warburton. Did he come pick it up?'

'No,' Finlay said. 'Nobody said so.'

'OK,' I said. 'So he's got some urgent business somewhere. Not even an asshole like Hubble's going to forget about a ten-thousand-dollar watch, right?'

'What urgent business?' Finlay said. 'What did he tell you about it?'

'He didn't tell me diddly,' I said. 'Like I told you, we hardly spoke.'

Finlay glared at me from the front seat.

'Don't mess with me, Reacher,' he said. 'Until I get hold of Hubble, I'm going to keep hold of you and sweat your ass for what he told you. And don't make out he kept his mouth shut all weekend, because guys like that never do. I know that and you know that, so don't mess with me, OK?'

I just shrugged at him. He wasn't about to arrest me again. Maybe I could get a bus from wherever the morgue was. I'd have to pass on lunch with Roscoe. Pity.

'So what's the story on this one?' I asked him.

'Pretty much the same as the last one,' Finlay

said. 'Looks like it happened at the same time. Shot to death, probably the same weapon. This one didn't get kicked around afterwards, but it was probably part of the same incident.'

'You don't know who it is?' I said.

'His name is Sherman,' he said. 'Apart from that, no idea.'

'Tell me about it,' I said. I was asking out of habit. Finlay thought for a moment. I saw him decide to answer. Like we were partners.

'Unidentified white male,' he said. 'Same deal as the first one, no ID, no wallet, no distinguishing marks. But this one had a gold wristwatch, engraved on the back: to Sherman, love Judy. He was maybe thirty or thirty-five. Hard to tell, because he'd been lying there for three nights and he was well gnawed by the small animals, you know? His lips are gone, and his eyes, but his right hand was OK because it was folded up under his body, so I got some decent prints. We ran them an hour ago and something may come of that, if we're lucky.'

'Gunshot wounds?' I asked him.

Finlay nodded.

'Looks like the same gun,' he said. 'Small-calibre, soft-nose shells. Looks like maybe the first shot only wounded him and he was able to run. He got hit a couple more times but made it to cover under the highway. He fell down and bled to death. He didn't get kicked around because they couldn't find him. That's how it looks to me.'

I thought about it. I'd walked right by there at eight o'clock on Friday morning. Right between the two bodies.

'And you figure he was called Sherman?' I said.

'His name was on his watch,' Finlay said.

'Might not have been his watch,' I said. 'The guy could have stolen it. Could have inherited it, bought it from a pawnshop, found it in the street.'

Finlay just grunted again. We must have been more than ten miles south of Margrave. Roscoe was keeping up a fast pace down the old county road. Then she slowed and slid down a left fork which led straight to the distant horizon.

'Where the hell are we going?' I said.

'County hospital,' Finlay said. 'Down in Yellow Springs. Next-but-one town to the south. Not long now.'

We drove on. Yellow Springs became a smudge in the heat haze on the horizon. Just inside the town limit was the county hospital, standing more or less on its own. Put there back when diseases were infectious and sick people were isolated. It was a big hospital, a warren of wide low buildings sprawled over a couple of acres. Roscoe slowed and swung into the entrance lane. We wallowed over speed bumps and threaded our way around to a spread of buildings clustered on their own in back. The mortuary was a long shed with a big roll-up door standing open. We stopped well clear of the door and left the car in the yard. We looked at each other and went in.

A medical guy met us and led us into an office. He sat behind a metal desk and waved Finlay and Roscoe to some stools. I leaned on a counter, between a computer terminal and a fax machine. This was not a big-budget facility. It had been cheaply equipped some years ago. Everything was worn and chipped and untidy. Very different from the station house up at Margrave. The guy at the desk looked tired. Not old, not young, maybe

Finlay's sort of age. White coat. He looked like the type of guy whose judgement you wouldn't worry about too much. He didn't introduce himself. Just took it for granted we all knew who he was and what he was for.

'What can I tell you folks?' he said.

He looked at all three of us in turn. Waited. We looked back.

'Was it the same incident?' Finlay asked. His deep Harvard tones sounded out of place in the shabby office. The medical guy shrugged at him.

'I've only had the second corpse for an hour,' he said. 'But, yes, I would say it's the same incident. It's almost certainly the same weapon. Looks like small-calibre soft-nose bullets in both cases. The bullets were slow, looks like the gun had a silencer.'

'Small calibre?' I said. 'How small?'

The doctor swivelled his tired gaze my way.

'I'm not a firearms expert,' he said. 'But I'd vote for a twenty-two. Looks that small to me. I'd say we're looking at soft-nose twenty-two-gauge shells. Take the first guy's head, for example. Two small splintery entry wounds and two big messy exit wounds, characteristic of a small soft-nose bullet.'

I nodded. That's what a soft-nose bullet does. It goes in and flattens out as it does so. Becomes a blob of lead about the size of a quarter tumbling through whatever tissue it meets. Rips a great big exit hole for itself. And a nice slow soft-nose .22 makes sense with a silencer. No point using a silencer except with a subsonic muzzle velocity. Otherwise the bullet is making its own sonic boom all the way to the target, like a tiny fighter plane.

'OK,' I said. 'Were they killed up there where they were found?'

'No doubt about it,' the guy said. 'Hypostasis is clear in both corpses.'

He looked at me. Wanted me to ask him what hypostasis was. I knew what it was, but I felt polite. So I looked puzzled for him.

'Postmortem hypostasis,' he said. 'Lividity. When you die, your circulation stops, right? Heart isn't beating any more. Your blood obeys the law of gravity. It settles to the bottom of your body, into the lowest available vessels, usually into the tiny capillaries in the skin next to the floor or whatever you've fallen down onto. The red cells settle first. They stain the skin red. Then they clot, so the stain is fixed, like a photograph. After a few hours, the stains are permanent. The stains on the first guy are entirely consistent with his position on the warehouse forecourt. He was shot, he fell down dead, he was kicked around in some sort of mad frenzy for a few minutes, then he lay there for around eight hours. No doubt about it.'

'What do you make of the kicking?' Finlay asked him.

The doctor shook his head and shrugged.

'Never seen anything like it,' he said. 'I've read about it in the journals, time to time. Some kind of a psychopathic thing, obviously. No way to explain it. It didn't make any difference to the dead guy. Didn't hurt him, because he was dead. So it must have gratified the kicker somehow. Unbelievable fury, tremendous strength. The injuries are grievous.'

'What about the second guy?' Finlay asked.

'He ran for it,' the doctor said. 'He was hit close up in the back with the first shot, but it didn't drop him, and he ran. He took two more on the way. One in the neck, and the fatal shot in the thigh.

142

Blew away his femoral artery. He made it as far as the raised-up section of highway, then lay down and bled to death. No doubt about that. If it hadn't rained all night Thursday, I'm sure you'd have seen the trail of blood on the road. There must have been about a gallon and a half lying about somewhere, because it sure as hell isn't inside the guy any more.'

We all fell quiet. I was thinking about the second guy's desperate sprint across the road. Trying to reach cover while the bullets smashed into his flesh. Hurling himself under the highway ramp and dying amid the quiet scuffling of the small night animals.

'OK,' Finlay said. 'So we're safe to assume the two victims were together. The shooter is in a group of three, he surprises them, shoots the first guy in the head twice, meanwhile the second guy takes off and gets hit by three shots as he runs, right?'

'You're assuming there were three assailants?' the doctor said.

Finlay nodded across to me. It was my theory, so I got to explain it.

'Three separate personality characteristics,' I said. 'A competent shooter, a frenzied maniac, and an incompetent concealer.'

The doctor nodded slowly.

'I'll buy that,' he said. 'The first guy was hit at point-blank range, so maybe we should assume he knew the assailants and allowed them to get next to him?'

Finlay nodded.

'Had to be that way,' he said. 'Five guys meeting together. Three of them attack the other two. This is some kind of a big deal, right?'

'Do we know who the assailants were?' the doctor asked.

'We don't even know who the victims were,' Roscoe said.

'Got any theories on the victims?' Finlay asked the doctor.

'Not on the second guy, apart from the name on his watch,' the doctor said. 'I only just got him on the table an hour ago.'

'So you got theories on the first guy?' Finlay said.

The doctor started shuffling some notes on his desk, but his telephone rang. He answered it and then held it out to Finlay.

'For you,' he said. Finlay crouched forward on his stool and took the call. Listened for a moment.

'OK,' he said into the phone. 'Just print it out and fax it to us here, will you?'

Then he passed the phone back to the doctor and rocked back on his stool. He had the beginnings of a smile on his face.

'That was Stevenson, up at the station house,' he said. 'We finally got a match on the first guy's prints. Seems like we did the right thing to run them again. Stevenson's faxing it through to us here in a minute, so tell us what you got, doc, and we'll put it all together.'

The tired guy in the white coat shrugged and picked up a sheet of paper.

'The first guy?' he said. 'I haven't got much at all. The body was in a hell of a mess. He was tall, he was fit, he had a shaved head. The main thing is the dental work. Looks like the guy got his teeth fixed all over the place. Some of it is American, some of it looks American, some of it is foreign.'

Next to my hip, the fax machine started beeping and whirring. A sheet of thin paper fed itself in.

'So what do we make of that?' Finlay said. 'The

guy was foreign? Or an American who lived abroad or what?'

The thin sheet of paper fed itself out, covered in writing. Then the machine stopped and went quiet. I picked up the paper and glanced at it. Then I read it through twice. I went cold. I was gripped by an icy paralysis and I couldn't move. I just couldn't believe what I was seeing on that piece of fax paper. The sky crashed in on me. I stared at the doctor and spoke.

'He grew up abroad,' I said. 'He had his teeth fixed wherever he was living. He broke his right arm when he was eight and had it set in Germany. He had his tonsils out in the hospital in Seoul.'

The doctor looked up at me.

'They can tell all that from his fingerprints?' he said.

I shook my head.

'The guy was my brother,' I said.

TEN

Once I saw a navy film about expeditions in the frozen Arctic. You could be walking over a solid glacier. Suddenly the ice would heave and shatter. Some kind of unimaginable stresses in the floes. A whole new geography would be forced up. Massive escarpments where it had been flat. Huge ravines behind you. A new lake in front of you. The world all changed in a second. That's how I felt. I sat there rigid with shock on the counter between the fax machine and the computer terminal and felt like an Arctic guy whose whole world changes in a single step.

They walked me through to the cold store in back to make a formal identification of his body. His face had been blown away by the gunshots and all his bones were broken but I recognized the star-shaped scar on his neck. He'd got it when we were messing with a broken bottle, twenty-nine years ago. Then they took me back up to the station house in Margrave. Finlay drove. Roscoe sat with me in the back of the car and held my hand all the way. It was only a twenty-minute ride, but in that time I lived through two whole lifetimes. His and mine.

My brother Joe. Two years older than me. He was born on a base in the Far East right at the end of the Eisenhower era. Then I had been born on a base in Europe, right at the start of the Kennedy era. Then we'd grown up together all over the world inside that tight isolated transience that service families create for themselves. Life was all about moving on at random and unpredictable intervals. It got so that it felt weird to do more than a semester and a half in any one place. Several times we went years without seeing a winter. We'd get moved out of Europe at the start of the fall and go down to the Pacific somewhere and summer would begin all over again.

Our friends kept just disappearing. Some unit would get shipped out somewhere and a bunch of kids would be gone. Sometimes we saw them again months later in a different place. Plenty of them we never saw again. Nobody ever said hello or good-bye. You were just either there or not there.

Then as Joe and I got older, we got moved around more. The Vietnam thing meant the military started shuffling people around the world faster and faster. Life became just a blur of bases. We never owned anything. We were only allowed one bag each on the transport planes.

We were together in that blur for sixteen years. Joe was the only constant thing in my life. And I loved him like a brother. But that phrase has a very precise meaning. A lot of those stock sayings do. Like when people say they slept like a baby. Do they mean they slept well? Or do they mean they woke up every ten minutes, screaming? I loved Joe

147

like a brother, which meant a lot of things in our family.

The truth was I never knew for sure if I loved him or not. And he never knew for sure if he loved me or not, either. We were only two years apart, but he was born in the fifties and I was born in the sixties. That seemed to make a lot more than two years' worth of a difference to us. And like any pair of brothers two years apart, we irritated the hell out of each other. We fought and bickered and sullenly waited to grow up and get out from under. Most of those sixteen years, we didn't know if we loved each other or hated each other.

But we had the thing that army families have. Your family was your unit. The men on the bases were taught total loyalty to their units. It was the most fundamental thing in their lives. The boys copied them. They translated that same intense loyalty onto their families. So time to time you might hate your brother, but you didn't let anybody mess with him. That was what we had, Joe and I. We had that unconditional loyalty. We stood back to back in every new schoolyard and punched our way out of trouble together. I watched out for him, and he watched out for me, like brothers did. For sixteen years. Not much of a normal childhood, but it was the only childhood I was ever going to get. And Joe was just about the beginning and end of it. And now somebody had killed him. I sat there in the back of the police Chevrolet listening to a tiny voice in my head asking me what the hell I was going to do about that.

Finlay drove straight through Margrave and parked up outside the station house. Right at the kerb opposite the big plate-glass entrance doors. He and Roscoe got out of the car and stood there waiting for me, just like Baker and Stevenson had forty-eight hours before. I got out and joined them in the noontime heat. We stood there for a moment and then Finlay pulled open the heavy door and we went inside. Walked back through the empty squad room to the big rosewood office.

Finlay sat at the desk. I sat in the same chair I'd used on Friday. Roscoe pulled a chair up and put it next to mine. Finlay rattled open the desk drawer. Took out the tape recorder. Went through his routine of testing the microphone with his fingernail. Then he sat still and looked at me.

'I'm very sorry about your brother,' he said.

I nodded. Didn't say anything.

'I'm going to have to ask you a lot of questions, I'm afraid,' he said.

I just nodded again. I understood his position. I'd been in his position plenty of times myself.

'Who would be his next of kin?' he asked.

'I am,' I said. 'Unless he got married without telling me.'

'Do you think he might have done that?' Finlay asked me.

'We weren't close,' I said. 'But I doubt it.'

'Your parents dead?'

I nodded. Finlay nodded. Wrote me down as next of kin.

'What was his full name?'

'Joe Reacher,' I said. 'No middle name.'

'Is that short for Joseph?'

'No,' I said. 'It was just Joe. Like my name is just Jack. We had a father who liked simple names.'

'OK,' Finlay said. 'Older or younger?'

'Older,' I said. I gave him Joe's date of birth.

'Two years older than me.'

'So he was thirty-eight?'

I nodded. Baker had said the victim had been maybe forty. Maybe Joe hadn't worn well.

'Do you have a current address for him?'

I shook my head.

'No,' I said. 'Washington DC, somewhere. Like I said, we weren't close.'

'OK,' he said again. 'When did you last see him?'

'About twenty minutes ago,' I said. 'In the morgue.'

Finlay nodded gently. 'Before that?'

'Seven years ago,' I said. 'Our mother's funeral.'

'Have you got a photograph of him?'

'You saw the stuff in the property bag,' I said. 'I haven't got a photograph of anything.'

He nodded again. Went quiet. He was finding this difficult.

'Can you give me a description of him?'

'Before he got his face shot off?'

'It might help, you know,' Finlay said. 'We need to find out who saw him around, when and where.'

I nodded.

'He looked like me, I guess,' I said. 'Maybe an inch taller, maybe ten pounds lighter.'

'That would make him what, about six-six?' he asked.

'Right,' I said. 'About two hundred pounds, maybe.'

Finlay wrote it all down.

'And he shaved his head?' he said.

'Not the last time I saw him,' I said. 'He had hair like anybody else.'

'Seven years ago, right?' Finlay said.

I shrugged.

'Maybe he started going bald,' I said. 'Maybe he was vain about it.'

Finlay nodded.

'What was his job?' he asked.

'Last I heard, he worked for the Treasury Department,' I said. 'Doing what, I'm not sure.'

'What was his background?' he asked. 'Was he in the service too?'

I nodded.

'Military Intelligence,' I said. 'Quit after a while, then he worked for the government.'

'He wrote you that he had been here, right?' he asked.

'He mentioned the Blind Blake thing,' I said. 'Didn't say what brought him down here. But it shouldn't be difficult to find out.'

Finlay nodded.

'We'll make some calls first thing in the morning,' he said. 'Until then, you're sure you got no idea why he should be down here?'

I shook my head. I had no idea at all why he had come down here. But I knew Hubble did. Joe had been the tall investigator with the shaved head and the code name. Hubble had brought him down here and Hubble knew exactly why. First thing to do was to find Hubble and ask him about it.

'Did you say you couldn't find Hubble?' I asked Finlay.

'Can't find him anywhere,' he said. 'He's not up at his place on Beckman Drive and nobody's seen him around town. Hubble knows all about this, right?'

I just shrugged. I felt like I wanted to keep some of the cards pretty close to my chest. If I was going to have to squeeze Hubble for something he wasn't very happy to talk about, then I wanted to do it in private. I didn't particularly want Finlay watching over my shoulder while I was doing it. He might think I was squeezing too hard. And I definitely didn't want to have to watch anything over Finlay's shoulder. I didn't want to leave the squeezing to him. I might think he wasn't squeezing hard enough. And anyway, Hubble would talk to me faster than he would talk to a policeman. He was already halfway there with me. So exactly how much Hubble knew was going to stay my secret. Just for now.

'No idea what Hubble knows,' I said. 'You're the one claims he fell apart.'

Finlay just grunted again and looked across the desk at me. I could see him settling into a new train of thought. I was pretty sure what it was. I'd been waiting for it to surface. There's a rule of thumb about homicide. It comes from a lot of statistics and a lot of experience. The rule of thumb says: when you get a dead guy, first you take a good look at his family. Because a hell of a lot of homicide gets done by relatives. Husbands, wives, sons. And brothers. That was the theory. Finlay would have seen it in action a hundred times in his twenty years up in Boston. Now I could see him trying it out in his head down in Margrave. I needed to run interference on it. I didn't want him thinking about it. I didn't want to waste any more of my time in a cell. I figured I might need that time for something else.

'You're happy with my alibi, right?' I said.

He saw where I was going. Like we were colleagues on a knotty case. He flashed me a brief grin.

'It held up,' he said. 'You were in Tampa when this was going down.'

'OK,' I said. 'And is Chief Morrison comfortable with that?'

'He doesn't know about it,' Finlay said. 'He's not answering his phone.'

'I don't want any more convenient mistakes,' I said. 'The fat moron said he saw me up there. I want him to know that won't fly any more.'

Finlay nodded. Picked up the phone on the desk and dialled a number. I heard the faint purr of the ring tone from the earpiece. It rang for a long time and cut off when Finlay put the phone back down.

'Not at home,' he said. 'Sunday, right?'

Then he pulled the phone book out of a drawer. Opened it to H. Looked up Hubble's number on Beckman Drive. Dialled it and got the same result. A lot of ring tone and nobody home. Then he tried the mobile number. An electronic voice started to tell him the phone was switched off. He hung up before it finished.

'I'm going to bring Hubble in, when I find him,' Finlay said. 'He knows stuff he should be telling us. Until then, not a lot I can do, right?'

I shrugged. He was right. It was a pretty cold trail. The only spark that Finlay knew about was the panic Hubble had shown on Friday.

'What are you going to do, Reacher?' he asked me.

'I'm going to think about that,' I said.

Finlay looked straight at me. Not unfriendly, but very serious, like he was trying to communicate an order and an appeal with a single stern eye-to-eye gaze.

'Let me deal with this, OK?' he said. 'You're going to feel pretty bad, and you're going to want to see justice done, but I don't want any independent action going on here, OK? This is police business. You're a civilian. Let me deal with it, OK?'

I shrugged and nodded. Stood up and looked at them both.

'I'm going for a walk,' I said.

I left the two of them there and strolled through the squad room. Pushed out through the glass doors into the hot afternoon. Wandered through the parking lot and crossed the wide lawn in front, over as far as the bronze statue. It was another tribute to Caspar Teale, whoever the hell he had been. Same guy as on the village green on the southern edge of town. I leaned up against his warm metal flank and thought.

The United States is a giant country. Millions of square miles. Best part of three hundred million people. I hadn't seen Joe for seven years, and he hadn't seen me, but we'd ended up in exactly the same tiny spot, eight hours apart. I'd walked within fifty yards of where his body had been lying. That was one hell of a big coincidence. It was almost unbelievable. So Finlay was doing me a big favour by treating it like a coincidence. He should be trying to tear my alibi apart. Maybe he already was. Maybe he was already on the phone to Tampa, checking again.

But he wouldn't find anything, because it was a coincidence. No point going over and over it. I was only in Margrave because of a crazy last-minute whim. If I'd taken a minute longer looking at the guy's map, the bus would have been past the cloverleaf and I'd have forgotten all about Margrave. I'd have gone on up to Atlanta and never known anything about Joe. It might have taken another seven years before the news caught up with me. So there was no point getting all stirred up about the coincidence. The only thing I had to do was to decide what the hell I was going to do about it.

I was about four years old before I caught on to the loyalty thing. I suddenly figured I was supposed to watch out for Joe the way he was watching out for me. After a while, it became second nature, like an automatic thing. It was always in my head to scout around and check he was OK. Plenty of times I would run out into some new schoolyard and see a bunch of kids trying it on with the tall skinny newcomer. I'd trot over there and haul them off and bust a few heads. Then I'd go back to my own buddies and play ball or whatever we were doing. Duty done, like a routine. It was a routine which lasted twelve years, from when I was four right up to the time Joe finally left home. Twelve years of that routine must have left faint tracks in my mind, because for ever afterwards I always carried a faint echo of the question: where's Joe? Once he was grown up and away, it didn't much matter where he was. But I was always aware of the faint echo of that old routine. Deep down, I was always aware I was supposed to stand up for him, if I was needed.

But now he was dead. He wasn't anywhere. I leaned up against the statue in front of the station house and listened to the tiny voice inside my head saying: you're supposed to do something about that.

The station house door sucked open. I squinted through the heat and saw Roscoe step out. The sun was behind her and it lit her hair like a halo. She scanned around and saw me leaning on the statue in the middle of the lawn. Started over toward me. I pushed off the warm bronze.

'You OK?' she asked me.

'I'm fine,' I said.

'You sure?' she said.

'I'm not falling apart,' I said. 'Maybe I should be, but I'm not. I just feel numb, to be honest.'

It was true. I wasn't feeling much of anything. Maybe it was some kind of a weird reaction, but that was how I felt. No point in denying it.

'OK,' Roscoe said. 'Can I give you a ride somewhere?'

Maybe Finlay had sent her out to keep track of me, but I wasn't about to put up a whole lot of objections to that. She was standing there in the sun looking great. I realized I liked her more every time I looked at her.

'Want to show me where Hubble lives?' I asked her.

I could see her thinking about it.

'Shouldn't we leave that to Finlay?' she said.

'I just want to see if he's back home yet,' I said. 'I'm not going to eat him. If he's there, we'll call Finlay right away, OK?'

'OK,' she said. She shrugged and smiled. 'Let's go.'

We walked together back over the lawn and got into her police Chevy. She started it up and pulled out of the lot. Turned left and rolled south through the perfect little town. It was a gorgeous September day. The bright sun turned it into a fantasy. The brick sidewalks were glowing and the white paint was blinding. The whole place was quiet and basking in the Sunday heat. Deserted.

Roscoe hung a right at the little village green and made the turn into Beckman Drive. Skirted around the square with the church on it. The cars were gone and the place was quiet. Worship was over. Beckman opened out into a wide tree-lined residential street, set on a slight rise. It had a rich feel. Cool and shady and prosperous. It was what real-estate people mean when they talk about location. I couldn't see the houses. They were set far back behind wide grassy shoulders, big trees, high hedges. Their driveways wound out of sight. Occasionally I glimpsed a white portico or a red roof. The further out we got, the bigger the lots became. Hundreds of yards between mailboxes. Enormous mature trees. A solid sort of a place. But a place with stories hiding behind the leafy facades. In Hubble's case, some sort of a desperate story which had caused him to reach out to my brother. Some sort of a story which had got my brother killed.

Roscoe slowed at a white mailbox and turned left into the drive of number twenty-five. About a mile from town, on the left, its back to the afternoon sun. It was the last house on the road. Up ahead, peach groves stretched into the haze. We nosed slowly up a winding driveway around massed banks of garden. The house was not what I had imagined. I had pictured a big white place, like a normal house, but bigger. This was more splendid. A palace. It was huge. Every detail was expensive. Expanses of gravel drive, expanses of velvet lawn, huge exquisite trees, everything shining and dappled in the blazing sun. But there was no sign of the dark Bentley I'd seen up at the prison. It looked like there was nobody home.

Roscoe pulled up near the front door and we got out. It was silent. I could hear nothing except the heavy buzz of afternoon heat. We rang on the bell and knocked on the door. No response from inside. We shrugged at each other and walked across a lawn around the side of the house. There were acres of grass and a blaze of some kind of flowers surrounding a garden room. Then a wide patio and a long lawn sloping down to a giant swimming pool. The water was bright blue in the sun. I could smell the chlorine hanging in the hot air.

'Some place,' Roscoe said.

I nodded. I was wondering if my brother had been there.

'I hear a car,' she said.

We got back to the front of the house in time to see the big Bentley easing to a stop. The blonde woman I'd seen driving away from the prison got out. She had two children with her. A boy and a girl. This was Hubble's family. He loved them like crazy. But he wasn't there with them.

The blonde woman seemed to know Roscoe. They greeted each other and Roscoe introduced me to her. She shook my hand and said her name was Charlene, but I could call her Charlie. She was an expensive-looking woman, tall, slim, good bones, carefully dressed, carefully looked after. But she had a seam of spirit running through her face like a flaw. Enough spirit there to make me like her. She held on to my hand and smiled, but it was a smile with a whole lot of strain behind it.

'This hasn't been the best weekend of my life, I'm afraid,' she said. 'But it seems that I owe you a great deal of thanks, Mr Reacher. My husband tells me you saved his life in prison.'

She said it with a lot of ice in her voice. Not aimed at me. Aimed at whatever circumstance it was forcing her to use the words 'husband' and 'prison' in the same sentence.

'No problem,' I said. 'Where is he?'

'Taking care of some business,' Charlie said. 'I expect him back later.'

I nodded. That had been Hubble's plan. He'd said he would spin her some kind of a yarn and then try to settle things down. I wondered if Charlie wanted to talk about it, but the children were standing silently next to her, and I could see she wouldn't talk in front of them. So I grinned at them. I hoped they would get all shy and run off somewhere, like children usually do with me, but they just grinned back.

'This is Ben,' Charlie said. 'And this is Lucy.'

They were nice-looking kids. The girl still had that little-girl chubbiness. No front teeth. Fine sandy hair in pigtails. The boy wasn't much bigger than his little sister. He had a slight frame and a serious face. Not a rowdy hooligan like some boys are. They were a nice pair of kids. Polite and quiet. They both shook hands with me and then stepped back to their mother's side. I looked at the three of them and I could just about see the terrible cloud hanging there over them. If Hubble didn't take care, he could get them all as dead as he'd gotten my brother.

'Will you come in for some iced tea?' Charlie asked us.

She stood there, her head cocked like she was waiting for an answer. She was maybe thirty, similar age to Roscoe. But she had a rich woman's ways. A hundred and fifty years ago, she'd have been the mistress of a big plantation.

'OK,' I said. 'Thanks.'

The kids ran off to play somewhere and Charlie ushered us in through the front door. I didn't really want to drink any iced tea, but I did want to stick around in case Hubble got back. I wanted to catch him on my own for five minutes. I wanted to ask him some pretty urgent questions before Finlay started in with the Miranda warnings.

It was a fabulous house. Huge. Beautifully furnished. Light and fresh. Cool creams and sunny yellows. Flowers. Charlie led us through to the garden room we'd seen from the outside. It was like something from a magazine. Roscoe went off with her to help fix the tea. Left me alone in the room. It made me uneasy. I wasn't accustomed to houses. Thirty-six years old and I'd never lived in a house. Lots of service accommodations and a terrible bare dormitory on the Hudson when I was up at the Point. That's where I'd lived. I sat down like an ugly alien on a flowered cushion on a cane sofa and waited. Uneasy, numb, in that dead zone between action and reaction.

The two women came back with the tea. Charlie was carrying a silver tray. She was a handsome woman, but she was nothing next to Roscoe. Roscoe had a spark in her eyes so electric it made Charlie just about invisible.

Then something happened. Roscoe sat down next to me on the cane sofa. As she sat, she pushed my leg to one side. It was a casual thing but it was very intimate and familiar. A numbed nerve end suddenly clicked in and screamed at me: she likes you too. She likes you too. It was the way she touched my leg.

I went back and looked at things in that new light. Her manner as she took the fingerprints and the photographs. Bringing me the coffee. Her smile and her wink. Her laugh. Working Friday night and Saturday so she could get me out of Warburton.

Driving all the way over there to pick me up. Holding my hand after I'd seen my brother's broken body. Giving me a ride over here. She liked me too.

All of a sudden I was glad I had jumped off that damn bus. Glad I made that crazy last-minute decision. I suddenly relaxed. Felt better. The tiny voice in my head quieted down. Right then there was nothing for me to do. I'd speak to Hubble when I saw him. Until then I would sit on a sofa with a good-looking friendly dark-haired woman in a soft cotton shirt. The trouble would start soon enough. It always does.

Charlie Hubble sat down opposite us and started pouring the iced tea from the pitcher. The smell of lemon and spices drifted over. She caught my eye and smiled the same strained smile she'd used before.

'Normally, at this point, I'd ask you how you were enjoying your visit with us here in Margrave,' she said, looking at me, strained, smiling.

I couldn't think of a reply to that. I just shrugged. It was clear Charlie didn't know anything. She thought her husband had been arrested because of some kind of a mistake. Not because he was grabbed up in some kind of trouble which had just got two people murdered. One of which was the brother of the stranger she was busy smiling at. Roscoe rescued the conversation and the two of them started passing the time of day. I just sat there and drank the tea and waited for Hubble. He didn't show up. Then the conversation died and we had to get out of there. Charlie was fidgeting like she had things to do. Roscoe put her hand on my arm. Her touch burned me like electricity.

'Let's go,' she said. 'I'll give you a ride back to town.'

I felt bad I wasn't staying to wait for Hubble. It made me feel disloyal to Joe. But I just wanted to be on my own with Roscoe. I was burning up with it. Maybe some kind of repressed grief was intensifying it. I wanted to leave Joe's problems until tomorrow. I told myself I had no choice anyway. Hubble hadn't shown up. Nothing else I could do. So we got back in the Chevy together and nosed down the winding driveway. Cruised down Beckman. The buildings thickened up at the bottom of the mile. We jinked around the church. The little village green with the statue of old Caspar Teale was ahead.

'Reacher?' Roscoe said. 'You'll be around for a while, right? Until we get this thing about your brother straightened out?'

'I guess I will,' I said.

'Where are you going to stay?' she asked.

'I don't know,' I said.

She pulled over to the kerb near the lawn. Nudged the selector into Park. She had a tender look on her face.

'I want you to come home with me,' she said.

I felt like I was out of my mind, but I was burning up with it so I pulled her to me and we kissed. That fabulous first kiss. The new and unfamiliar mouth and hair and taste and smell. She kissed hard and long and held on tight. We came up for air a couple of times before she took off again for her place.

She blasted a quarter-mile down the street which opened up opposite Beckman Drive. I saw a blur of greenery in the sun as she swooped into her driveway. The tyres chirped as she stopped. We more or less tumbled out and ran to the door. She used her key and we went in. The door swung shut and before it clicked she was back in my arms. We kissed and stumbled through to her living room. She was a foot shorter than me and her feet were off the ground.

We tore each other's clothes off like they were on fire. She was gorgeous. Firm and strong and a shape like a dream. Skin like silk. She pulled me to the floor through bars of hot sunlight from the window. It was frantic. We were rolling and nothing could have stopped us. It was like the end of the world. We shuddered to a stop and lay gasping. We were bathed in sweat. Totally spent.

We lay there clasped and caressing. Then she got off me and pulled me up. We kissed again as we staggered through to her bedroom. She pulled back the covers on the bed and we collapsed in. Held each other and fell into a deep afterglow stupor. I was wrecked. I felt like all my bones and sinews were rubber. I lay in the unfamiliar bed and drifted away to a place far beyond relaxation. I was floating. Roscoe's warm heft was snuggled beside me. I was breathing through her hair. Our hands were lazily caressing unfamiliar contours.

She asked me if I wanted to go find a motel. Or to stay there with her. I laughed and told her the only way to get rid of me now would be to go fetch a shotgun from the station house and chase me away. I told her even that might not work. She giggled and pressed even closer.

'I wouldn't fetch a shotgun,' she whispered. 'I'd fetch some handcuffs. I'd chain you to the bed and keep you here for ever.'

We dozed through the afternoon. I called the Hubble place at seven in the evening. He still wasn't back. I left Roscoe's number with Charlie and told her to have Hubble call me as soon as he got in. Then we drifted on through the rest of the evening. Fell fast asleep at midnight. Hubble never called.

Monday morning I was vaguely aware of Roscoe getting up for work. I heard the shower and I knew she kissed me tenderly and then the house was hot and quiet and still. I slept on until after nine. The phone didn't ring. That was OK. I needed some quiet thinking time. I had decisions to make. I stretched out in Roscoe's warm bed and started answering the question the tiny voice in my head was asking me again.

What was I going to do about Joe? My answer came very easily. I knew it would. I knew it had been waiting there since I first stood next to Joe's broken body in the morgue. It was a very simple answer. I was going to stand up for him. I was going to finish his business. Whatever it was. Whatever it took.

I didn't foresee any major difficulties. Hubble was the only link I had, but Hubble was the only link I needed. He would co-operate. He'd depended on Joe to help him out. Now he'd depend on me. He'd give me what I needed. His masters were vulnerable for a week. What had he said? A window of exposure wide open until Sunday? I'd use it to tear them apart. My mind was made up. I couldn't do it any other way. I couldn't leave it to Finlay. Finlay wouldn't understand all those years of history. Finlay wouldn't sanction the sort of punishments that were going to be necessary. Finlay couldn't understand the simple truth I'd learned at the age of four: you don't mess with my brother. So this was my business. It was between me and Joe. It was duty.

I lay there in Roscoe's warm bed and scoped it out. It was going to be a simple process. About as simple as you could get. Getting hold of Hubble wasn't going to be difficult. I knew where he lived. I knew his phone number. I stretched and smiled and filled with restless energy. Got out of bed and found coffee. There was a note propped against the pot. The note said: *Early lunch at Eno's? Eleven o'clock? Leave Hubble to Finlay, OK?* The note was signed with lots of kisses and a little drawing of a pair of handcuffs. I read it and smiled at the drawing, but I wasn't going to leave Hubble to Finlay. No way. Hubble was my business. So I looked up the number again and called Beckman Drive. There was nobody home.

I poured a big mug of coffee and wandered through to the living room. The sun was blinding outside. It was another hot day. I walked through the house. It was a small place. A living room, an eat-in kitchen, two bedrooms, one and a half baths. Very new, very clean. Decorated in a cool, simple way. What I would expect from Roscoe. A cool simple style. Some nice Navajo art, some bold rugs, white walls. She must have been to New Mexico and liked it.

It was still and quiet. She had a stereo, a few records and tapes, more sweet and melodic than the howl and buzz that I call music. I got more coffee from her kitchen. Went out back. There was a small yard out there, a neat coarse lawn and some recent evergreen planting. Shredded bark to smother weeds and rough timber edging against the planted areas. I stood in the sun and sipped the coffee.

Then I ducked back inside and tried Hubble's number again. No reply. I showered and dressed. Roscoe had a small shower stall, the head set low, feminine soaps in the dish. I found a towel in a closet and a comb on a vanity. No razor. I put my clothes on and rinsed out the coffee mug. Tried Hubble's number again from the kitchen phone. I let it ring for a long time. Nobody home. I figured I'd get a ride up there from Roscoe after lunch. This thing wasn't going to wait for ever. I relocked the back door and went out the front.

It was about ten-thirty. A mile and a quarter up to Eno's place. A gentle half-hour stroll in the sun. It was already very hot. Well into the eighties. Glorious fall weather in the South. I walked the quarter-mile to Main Street up a gently winding rise. Everything was beautifully manicured. There were towering magnolia trees everywhere and late blossom in the shrubs.

I turned at the convenience store and strolled up Main Street. The sidewalks had been swept. I could see crews of gardeners in the little park areas. They were setting up sprinklers and barrowing stuff out of smart green trucks marked 'Kliner Foundation' in gold. A couple of guys were painting the picket fence. I waved in at the two old barbers in their shop. They were leaning up inside their doorway, like they were waiting for custom. They waved back and I strolled on.

Eno's came into sight. The polished aluminium siding gleamed in the sun. Roscoe's Chevrolet was in the lot. Standing next to it on the gravel was the black pickup I'd seen the day before outside the coffee shop. I reached the diner and pushed in through the door. I had been prodded out through it on Friday with Stevenson's shotgun pointed at my gut. I had been in handcuffs. I wondered if the diner people would remember me. I figured they probably would. Margrave was a very quiet place. Not a whole lot of strangers passing through.

Roscoe was in a booth, the same one I'd used on Friday. She was back in uniform and she looked like the sexiest thing on earth. I stepped over to her. She smiled a tender smile up at me and I bent to kiss her mouth. She slid over the vinyl to the window. There were two cups of coffee on the table. I passed hers across.

The driver from the black pickup was sitting at the lunch counter. The Kliner boy, the pale woman's stepson. He'd spun the stool and his back was against the counter. He was sitting legs apart, elbows back, head up, eyes blazing, staring at me again. I turned my back on him and kissed Roscoe again.

'Is this going to ruin your authority?' I asked her. 'To be seen kissing a vagrant who got arrested in here on Friday?'

'Probably,' she said. 'But who cares?'

So I kissed her again. The Kliner kid was watching. I could feel it on the back of my neck. I turned to look back at him. He held my gaze for a second, then he slid off his stool and left. Stopped in the doorway and glared at me one last time. Then he hustled over to his pickup and took off. I heard the roar of the motor and then the diner was quiet. It was more or less empty, just like on Friday. A couple of old guys and a couple of waitresses. They were the same women as on Friday. Both blonde, one taller and heavier than the other. Waitress uniforms. The shorter one wore eyeglasses. Not really alike, but similar. Like sisters or cousins. The same genes in there somewhere. Small town, miles from anywhere.

'I made a decision,' I said. 'I have to find out what happened with Joe. So I just want to apologize in advance in case that gets in the way, OK?'

Roscoe shrugged and smiled a tender smile. Looked concerned for me.

'It won't get in the way,' she said. 'No reason why it should.'

I sipped my coffee. It was good coffee. I remembered that from Friday.

'We got an ID on the second body,' she said. 'His prints matched with an arrest two years ago in Florida. His name was Sherman Stoller. That name mean anything at all to you?'

I shook my head.

'Never heard of him,' I said.

Then her beeper started going. It was a little black pager thing clipped to her belt. I hadn't seen it before. Maybe she was only required to use it during working hours. It was beeping away. She reached around and clicked it off.

'Damn,' she said. 'I've got to call in. Sorry. I'll use the phone in the car.'

I slid out of the booth and stepped back to let her by.

'Order me some food, OK?' she said. 'I'll have whatever you have.'

'OK,' I said. 'Which one is our waitress?'

'The one with the glasses,' she said.

She walked out of the diner. I was aware of her leaning into her car, using the phone. Then she was gesturing to me from the parking lot. Miming urgency. Miming that she had to get back. Miming that I should stay put. She jumped into the car and took off, south. I waved vaguely after her, not really looking, because I was staring at the waitresses instead. I had almost stopped breathing. I needed Hubble. And Roscoe had just told me Hubble was dead.

ELEVEN

I stared blankly over at the two blonde waitresses. One was perhaps three inches taller than the other. Perhaps fifteen pounds heavier. A couple of years older. The smaller woman looked petite in comparison. Better looking. She had longer, lighter hair. Nicer eyes behind the glasses. As a pair, the waitresses were similar in a superficial kind of a way. But not alike. There were a million differences between them. No way were they hard to distinguish one from the other.

I'd asked Roscoe which was our waitress. And how had she answered? She hadn't said the smaller one, or the one with the long hair, or the blonder one, or the slimmer one, or the prettier one or the younger one. She'd said the one with glasses. One was wearing glasses, the other wasn't. Ours was the one with glasses. Wearing glasses was the major difference between them. It overrode all the other differences. The other differences were matters of degree. Taller, heavier, longer, shorter, smaller, prettier, darker, younger. The glasses were not a matter of degree. One woman wore them, the other didn't. An absolute difference. No confusion. Our waitress was the one with glasses.

That's what Spivey had seen on Friday night. Spivey had come into the reception bunker a little after ten o'clock. With a shotgun and a clipboard in his big red farmer's hands. He had asked which one of us was Hubble. I remembered his high voice in the stillness of the bunker. There was no reason for his question. Why the hell should Spivey care which one of us was which? He didn't need to know. But he'd asked. Hubble had raised his hand. Spivey had looked him over with his little snake eyes. He had seen that Hubble was smaller, shorter, lighter, sandier, balder, younger than me. But what was the major difference he had hung on to? Hubble wore glasses. I didn't. The little gold rims. An absolute difference. Spivey had said to himself that night: Hubble's the one with glasses.

But by the next morning I was the one with glasses, not Hubble. Because Hubble's gold rims had been smashed up by the Red Boys outside our cell. First thing in the morning. The little gold rims were gone. I had taken some shades from one of them as a trophy. Taken them and forgotten about them. I'd leaned up against the sink in that bathroom inspecting my tender forehead in the steel mirror. I'd felt those shades in my pocket. I'd pulled them out and put them on. They weren't dark because they were supposed to react to sunlight. They looked like ordinary glasses. I'd been standing there with them on when the Aryans came trawling into the bathroom. Spivey had just told them: find the new boys and kill the one with

171

glasses. They'd tried hard. They'd tried very hard to kill Paul Hubble.

They had attacked me because the description they'd been given was suddenly the wrong description. Spivey had reported that back long ago. Whoever had set him on Hubble hadn't given up. They'd made a second attempt. And the second attempt had succeeded. The whole police department had been summoned up to Beckman Drive. Up to number twenty-five. Because somebody had discovered an appalling scene there. Carnage. He was dead. All four of them were dead. Tortured and butchered. My fault. I hadn't thought hard enough.

I ran over to the counter. Spoke to our waitress. The one with glasses.

'Can you call me a taxi?' I asked her.

The cook was watching from the kitchen hatch. Maybe he was Eno himself. Short, stocky, dark, balding. Older than me.

'No, we can't,' he called through. 'What do you think this place is? A hotel? This ain't the Waldorf-Astoria, pal. You want a taxi, you find it yourself. You ain't particularly welcome here, pal. You're trouble.'

I gazed back at him bleakly. Too drained for any reaction. But the waitress just laughed at him. Put her hand on my arm.

'Don't pay no mind to Eno,' she said. 'He's just a grumpy old thing. I'll call you the taxi. Just wait out in the parking lot, OK?'

I waited out on the road. Five minutes. The taxi drove up. Brand-new and immaculate, like everything else in Margrave.

'Where to, sir?' the driver asked.

I gave him Hubble's address and he made a wide, slow turn, shoulder to shoulder across the county road. Headed back to town. We passed the fire house and the police headquarters. The lot was empty. Roscoe's Chevy wasn't there. No cruisers. They were all out. Up at Hubble's. We made the right at the village green and swung past the silent church. Headed up Beckman. In a mile I would see a cluster of vehicles outside number twenty-five. The cruisers with their light bars flashing and popping. Unmarked cars for Finlay and Roscoe. An ambulance or two. The coroner would be there, up from his shabby office in Yellow Springs.

But the street was empty. I walked into Hubble's driveway. The taxi turned and drove back to town. Then it was silent. That heavy silence you get in a quiet street on a hot, quiet day. I rounded the big banks of garden. There was nobody there. No police cars, no ambulances, no shouting. No clattering gurneys, no gasps of horror. No police photographers, no tape sealing off the access.

The big dark Bentley was parked up on the gravel. I walked past it on my way to the house. The front door crashed open. Charlie Hubble ran out. She was screaming. She was hysterical. But she was alive.

'Hub's disappeared,' she screamed.

She ran over the gravel. Stood right in front of me.

'Hub's gone,' she screamed. 'He's disappeared. I can't find him.'

It was just Hubble on his own. They'd taken him and dumped him somewhere. Someone had found the body and called the police. A screaming, gagging phone call. The cluster of cars and ambulances was there. Not here on Beckman. Somewhere else. But it was just Hubble on his own.

'Something's wrong,' Charlie wailed. 'This prison thing. Something's gone wrong at the bank. It must be that. Hub's been so uptight. Now he's gone. He's disappeared. Something's happened, I know it.'

She screwed her eyes tight shut. Started screaming. She was losing it. Getting more and more hysterical. I didn't know how to handle her.

'He got back late last night,' she screamed. 'He was still here this morning. I took Ben and Lucy to school. Now he's gone. He hasn't gone to work. He got a call from his office telling him to stay home, and his briefcase is still here, his phone is still here, his jacket is still here, his wallet is still here, his credit cards are in it, his driver's licence is in it, his keys are in the kitchen. The front door was standing wide open. He hasn't gone to work. He's just disappeared.'

I stood still. Paralyzed. He'd been dragged out of there by force and killed. Charlie sagged in front of me. Then she started whispering to me. The whispering was worse than the screaming.

'His car is still here,' she whispered. 'He can't have walked anywhere. He never walks anywhere. He always takes his Bentley.'

She waved vaguely toward the back of the house.

'Hub's Bentley is green,' she said. 'It's still in the garage. I checked. You've got to help us. You've got to find him. Mr Reacher, please. I'm asking you to help us. Hub's in trouble, I know it. He's vanished. He said you might help. You saved his life. He said you knew how to do things.'

She was hysterical. She was pleading. But I

174

couldn't help her. She would know that soon enough. Baker or Finlay would come up to the house very soon. They would tell her the shattering news. Probably Finlay would handle it. Probably he was very good at it. Probably he had done it a thousand times in Boston. He had dignity and gravity. He would break the news, gloss over the details, drive her down to the morgue to identify the body. The morgue people would shroud the corpse with heavy gauze to hide the appalling wounds.

'Will you help us?' Charlie asked me.

I decided not to wait with her. I decided to go down to the station house. Find out details like where and when and how. But I'd come back with Finlay. This was my fault, so I should come back.

'You stay here,' I said. 'You'll have to lend me your car, OK?'

She rooted in her bag and pulled out a big bunch of keys. Handed them to me. The car key had a big letter 'B' embossed on it. She nodded vaguely and stayed where she was. I stepped over to the Bentley and slid into the driver's seat. Backed it up and swung it down the curving driveway. Glided down Beckman in silence. Made the left onto Main Street up toward the station house.

There were cruisers and unmarked units sprawled right across the police parking lot. I left Charlie's Bentley at the kerb and stepped inside. They were all milling around the open area. I saw Baker, Stevenson, Finlay. I saw Roscoe. I recognized the backup team from Friday. Morrison wasn't there. Nor was the desk guy. The long counter was unattended. Everybody was stunned. They were all vague and staring. Horrified. Distracted. Nobody

175

would talk to me. They looked over bleakly. Didn't really look away, it was like they didn't see me at all. There was total silence. Finally Roscoe came over. She'd been crying. She walked up to me. Pressed her face against my chest. She was burning up. She put her arms around me and held on.

'It was horrible,' she said. Wouldn't say any more.

I walked her around to her desk and sat her down. Squeezed her shoulder and stepped over towards Finlay. He was sitting on a desk, looking blank. I nodded him over to the big office in back. I needed to know, and Finlay was the guy who would tell me. He followed me into the office. Sat down in the chair in front of the desk. Where I had sat in handcuffs on Friday. I sat behind the desk. Roles reversed.

I watched him for a while. He was really shaken up. I went cold inside all over again. Hubble must have been left in a hell of a mess to be getting a reaction like that from Finlay. He was a twenty-year man from a big city. He must have seen all there is to see. But now he was really shaken up. I sat there and burned with shame. Sure, Hubble, I'd said, you look safe enough to me.

'So what's the story?' I said.

He lifted his head up with an effort and looked at me.

'Why should you care?' he said. 'What was he to you?'

A good question. One I couldn't answer. Finlay didn't know what I knew about Hubble. I'd kept quiet about it. So Finlay didn't see why Hubble was so important to me.

'Just tell me what happened,' I said.

'It was pretty bad,' he said. Wouldn't go on.

176

He was worrying me. My brother had been shot in the head. Two big messy exit wounds had removed his face. Then somebody had turned his corpse into a bag of pulp. But Finlay hadn't fallen apart over that. The other guy had been all gnawed up by rats. There wasn't a drop of blood left in him. But Finlay hadn't fallen apart over that, either. Hubble was a local guy, which made it a bit worse, I could see that. But on Friday, Finlay hadn't even known who Hubble was. And now Finlay was acting like he'd seen a ghost. So it must have been some pretty spectacular work.

Which meant that there was some kind of a big deal going down in Margrave. Because there's no point in spectacular work unless it serves a purpose. The threat of it beforehand works on the guy himself. It had certainly worked on Hubble. He had taken a lot of notice of it. That's the point of a threat. But to actually carry out something like that has a different point. A different purpose. Carrying it out is not about the guy himself. It's about backing up the threat against the next guy in line. It says, see what we did to that other guy? That's what we could do to you. So by doing some spectacular work on Hubble, somebody had just revealed there was a high-stakes game going down, with other guys waiting next in line, right there in the locality.

'Tell me what happened, Finlay,' I said again.

He leaned forward. Cupped his mouth and nose with his hands and sighed heavily into them.

'OK,' he said. 'It was pretty horrible. One of the worst I've ever seen. And I've seen a few, let me tell you. I've seen some pretty bad ones, but this was something else. He was naked. They nailed him to the wall. Six or seven big carpentry nails through his hands and up his arms. Through the fleshy parts. They nailed his feet to the floor. Then they sliced his balls off. Just hacked them off. Blood everywhere. Pretty bad, let me tell you. Then they slit his throat. Ear to ear. Bad people, Reacher. These are bad people. As bad as they come.'

I was numb. Finlay was waiting for a comment. I couldn't think of anything. I was thinking about Charlie. She would ask if I'd found anything out. Finlay should go up there. He should go up there right now and break the news. It was his job, not mine. I could see why he was reluctant. Difficult news to break. Difficult details to gloss over. But it was his job. I'd go with him. Because it was my fault. No point running away from that.

'Yes,' I said to him. 'It sounds pretty bad.'

He leaned his head back and looked around. Blew another sigh up at the ceiling. A sombre man.

'That's not the worst of it,' he said. 'You should have seen what they did to his wife.'

'His wife?' I said. 'What the hell do you mean?'

'I mean his wife,' he said. 'It was like a butcher's shop.'

For a moment I couldn't speak. The world was spinning backwards.

'But I just saw her,' I said. 'Twenty minutes ago. She's OK. Nothing happened to her.'

'You saw who?' Finlay said.

'Charlie,' I said.

'Who the hell is Charlie?' he asked.

'Charlie,' I said blankly. 'Charlie Hubble. His wife. She's OK. They didn't get her.'

'What's Hubble got to do with this?' he said.

I just stared at him.

'Who are we talking about?' I said. 'Who got killed?'

Finlay looked at me like I was crazy.

'I thought you knew,' he said. 'Chief Morrison. The chief of police. Morrison. And his wife.'

TWELVE

I was watching Finlay very carefully, trying to decide how far I should trust him. It was going to be a life or death decision. In the end I figured his answer to one simple question would make up my mind for me.

'Are they going to make you chief now?' I asked him.

He shook his head.

'No,' he said. 'They're not going to make me chief.'

'You sure about that?' I said.

'I'm sure,' he said.

'Whose decision is it?' I asked him.

'The mayor's,' Finlay said. 'Town mayor appoints the chief of police. He's coming over. Guy named Teale. Some kind of an old Georgia family. Some ancestor was a railroad baron who owned everything in sight around here.'

'Is that the guy you've got statues of?' I said.

Finlay nodded.

'Caspar Teale,' he said. 'He was the first.

They've had Teales here ever since. This mayor must be the great-grandson or something.'

I was in a minefield. I needed to find a clear lane through.

'What's the story with this guy Teale?' I asked him.

Finlay shrugged. Tried to find a way to explain it.

'He's just a southern asshole,' he said. 'Old Georgia family, probably a long line of southern assholes. They've been the mayors around here since the beginning. I dare say this one's no worse than the others.'

'Was he upset?' I said. 'When you called him about Morrison?'

'Worried, I think,' Finlay said. 'He hates mess.'

'Why won't he make you chief?' I said. 'You're the senior guy, right?'

'He just won't,' Finlay said. 'Why not is my business.'

I watched him for a moment longer. Life or death.

'Somewhere we can go to talk?' I said.

He looked over the desk at me.

'You thought it was Hubble got killed, right?' he said. 'Why?'

'Hubble did get killed,' I said. 'Fact that Morrison got killed as well doesn't change it.'

We walked down to the convenience store. Sat side by side at the empty counter, near the window. I sat at the same place the pale Mrs Kliner had used when I was in there the day before. That seemed like a long time ago. The world had changed since then. We got tall mugs of coffee and a big plate of doughnuts. Didn't look at each other directly. We looked at each other in the mirror behind the counter.

'Why won't you get the promotion?' I asked him.

His reflection shrugged in the mirror. He was looking puzzled. He couldn't see the connection. But he'd see it soon enough.

'I should get it,' he said. 'I'm better qualified than all the others put together. I've done twenty years in a big city. A real police department. What the hell have they done? Look at Baker, for instance. He figures himself for a smart boy. But what has he done? Fifteen years in the sticks? In this backwater? What the hell does he know?'

'So why won't you get it?' I said.

'It's a personal matter,' he said.

'You think I'm going to sell it to the newspaper?' I asked him.

'It's a long story,' he said.

'So tell it to me,' I said. 'I need to know.'

He looked at me in the mirror. Took a deep breath.

'I finished in Boston in March,' he said. 'Done my twenty years. Unblemished record. Eight commendations. I was one hell of a detective, Reacher. I had retirement on full pension to look forward to. But my wife was going crazy. Since last fall, she was getting agitated. It was so ironic. We were married all through those twenty years. I was working my ass off. Boston PD was a madhouse. We were working seven days a week. All day and all night. All around me guys were seeing their marriages fall apart. They were all getting divorced. One after the other.'

He stopped for a long pull on his coffee. Took a bite of doughnut.

'But not me,' he said. 'My wife could take it. Never

complained, never once. She was a miracle. Never gave me a hard time.'

He lapsed back into silence. I thought about twenty years in Boston. Working around the clock in that busy old city. Grimy nineteenth-century precincts. Overloaded facilities. Constant pressure. An endless parade of freaks, villains, politicians, problems. Finlay had done well to survive.

'It started last fall,' he said again. 'We were within six months of the end. It was all going to be over. We were thinking of a cabin somewhere, maybe. Vacations. Plenty of time together. But she started panicking. She didn't want plenty of time together. She didn't want me to retire. She didn't want me at home. She said she woke up to the fact that she didn't like me. Didn't love me. Didn't want me around. She'd loved the twenty years. Didn't want it to change. I couldn't believe it. It had been my dream. Twenty years and then retire at forty-five. Then maybe another twenty years enjoying ourselves together before we got too old, you know? It was my dream and I'd worked towards it for twenty years. But she didn't want it. She ended up saying the thought of twenty more years with me in a cabin in the woods was making her flesh crawl. It got really bitter. We fell apart. I was a total basket case.'

He tailed off again. We got more coffee. It was a sad story. Stories about wrecked dreams always are.

'So obviously, we got divorced,' he said. 'Nothing else to do. She demanded it. It was terrible. I was totally out of it. Then in my last month in the department I started reading the union vacancy lists again. Saw this job down here. I called an old buddy in Atlanta FBI and asked him about it. He warned me off. He said forget it. He said it was a Mickey Mouse department in a town that wasn't even on the map. The job was called the chief of detectives, but there was only one detective. The previous guy was a weirdo who hung himself. The department was run by a fat moron. The town was run by some old Georgia type who couldn't remember slavery had been abolished. My friend up in Atlanta said forget it. But I was so screwed up I wanted it. I thought I could bury myself down here as a punishment, you know? A kind of penance. Also, I needed the money. They were offering top dollar and I was looking at alimony and lawyer bills, you know? So I applied for it and came down. It was Mayor Teale and Morrison who saw me. I was a basket case, Reacher. I was a wreck. I couldn't string two words together. It had to be the worst job application in the history of the world. I must have come across as an idiot. But they gave me the job. I guess they needed a black guy to look good. I'm the first black cop in Margrave's history.'

I turned on the stool and looked straight at him.

'So you figure you're just a token?' I said. 'That's why Teale won't make you chief?'

'It's obvious, I guess,' he said. 'He's got me marked down as a token and an idiot. Not to be promoted further. Makes sense in a way. Can't believe they gave me the job in the first place, token or not.'

I waved to the counter guy for the check. I was happy with Finlay's story. He wasn't going to be chief. So I trusted him. And I trusted Roscoe. It was going to be the three of us, against whoever. I shook my head at him in the mirror.

'You're wrong,' I said. 'That's not the real

184

reason. You're not going to be chief because you're not a criminal.'

I paid the check with a ten and got all quarters for change. The guy still had no dollar bills. Then I told Finlay I needed to see the Morrison place. Told him I needed all the details. He just shrugged and led me outside. We turned and walked south. Passed by the village green and put the town behind us.

'I was the first one there,' he said. 'About ten this morning. I hadn't seen Morrison since Friday and I needed to update the guy, but I couldn't get him on the phone. It was middle of the morning on a Monday and we hadn't done anything worth a damn about a double homicide from last Thursday night. We needed to get our asses in gear. So I went up to his house to start looking for him.'

He went quiet and walked on. Revisiting in his mind the scene he'd found.

'Front door was standing open,' he said. 'Maybe a half-inch. It had a bad feel. I went in, found them upstairs in the master bedroom. It was like a butcher's shop. Blood everywhere. He was nailed to the wall, sort of hanging off. Both of them sliced up, him and his wife. It was terrible. About twenty-four hours of decomposition. Warm weather. Very unpleasant. So I called in the whole crew and we went over every inch and pieced it all together. Literally, I'm afraid.'

He tailed off again. Just went quiet.

'So it happened Sunday morning?' I said.

He nodded.

'Sunday papers on the kitchen table,' he said. 'Couple of sections opened out and the rest untouched. Breakfast things on the table. Medical

185

examiner says about ten o'clock Sunday morning.'

'Any physical evidence left behind?' I asked him.

He nodded again. Grimly.

'Footprints in the blood,' he said. 'The place was a lake of blood. Gallons of it. Partly dried up now, of course. They left footprints all over. But they were wearing rubber overshoes, you know? Like you get for the winter up north? No chance of tracing them. They must sell millions every year.'

They had come prepared. They'd known there was going to be a lot of blood. They'd brought overshoes. They must have brought overalls. Like the nylon bodysuits they wear in the slaughter-house. On the killing floor. Big white nylon suits, hooded, the white nylon splashed and smeared with bright red blood.

'They wore gloves, too,' he said. 'There are rubbery smears in the blood on the walls.'

'How many people?' I asked him. I was trying to build up a picture.

'Four,' he said. 'The footprints are confused, but I think I can see four.'

I nodded. Four sounded right. About the minimum, I reckoned. Morrison and his wife would have been fighting for their lives. It would take four of them, at least. Four out of the ten Hubble had mentioned.

'Transport?' I said.

'Can't really tell,' Finlay said. 'Gravel driveway, washed into ruts here and there. I saw some wide ruts which look new, maybe. Could have been wide tyres. Maybe a big four-wheel-drive or a small truck.'

We were a couple of hundred yards south of where Main Street had petered out. We turned west up a gravel driveway which must have been just about parallel with Beckman Drive. At the end of the driveway was Morrison's house. It was a big formal place, white columns at the front, symmetrical evergreen trees dotted about. There was a new Lincoln parked near the door and a lot of police tape strung at waist height between the columns.

'We going in?' Finlay asked.

'May as well,' I said.

We ducked under the tape and pushed in through Morrison's front door. The house was a wreck. Grey metallic fingerprint powder everywhere. Everything tossed and searched and photographed.

'You won't find anything,' Finlay said. 'We went over the whole place.'

I nodded and headed for the staircase. Went up and found the master bedroom. Stopped at the door and peered in. There was nothing to see except the ragged outline of the nail holes in the wall and the massive bloodstains. The blood was turning black. It looked like somebody had flung buckets of tar around. The carpet was crusty with it. On the parquet in the doorway I could see the footprints from the overshoes. I could make out the intricate pattern of the treads. I headed back downstairs and found Finlay leaning on a porch column out front.

'OK?' he asked me.

'Terrific,' I said. 'You search the car?'

He shook his head.

'That's Morrison's,' he said. 'We just looked for stuff the intruders might have left behind.'

I stepped over to the Lincoln and tried the door. Unlocked. Inside, there was a strong new-car smell and not much else. This was a chief's car. It wasn't going to be full of cheeseburger wrappings and soda cans like a patrolman's would be. But I checked it out. Poked around in the door pockets and under the seats. Found nothing at all. Then I opened the glovebox and found something. There was a switchblade in there. It was a handsome thing. Ebony handle with Morrison's name in gold-filled engraving. I popped the blade. Double edged, seven inches, Japanese surgical steel. Looked good. Brand new, never been used. I closed it up and slipped it into my pocket. I was unarmed and facing big trouble. Morrison's switchblade might make a difference. I slid out of the Lincoln and rejoined Finlay on the gravel.

'Find anything?' he asked.

'No,' I said. 'Let's go.'

We crunched back down the driveway together and turned north on the county road. Headed back to town. I could see the church steeple and the bronze statue in the distance, waiting for us.

THIRTEEN

'Something I need to check with you,' I said.

Finlay's patience was running thin. He looked at his watch.

'You better not be wasting my time, Reacher,' he said.

We walked on north. The sun was dropping away from overhead, but the heat was still fierce. I didn't know how Finlay could wear a tweed jacket. And a moleskin vest. I led him over to the village green. We crossed the grass and leaned up on the statue of old Caspar Teale, side by side.

'They cut his balls off, right?' I said.

He nodded. Looked at me, waiting.

'OK,' I said. 'So the question is this: did you find his balls?'

He shook his head.

'No,' he said. 'We went over the whole place. Ourselves and the medical examiner. They weren't there. His testicles are missing.'

He smiled as he said it. He was recovering his cop's sense of humour.

'OK,' I said. 'That's what I needed to know.'

His smile widened. Reached his eyes.

'Why?' he said. 'Do you know where they are?'

'When's the autopsy?' I asked him.

He was still smiling.

'His autopsy won't help,' he said. 'They were cut off. They're not connected to him any more. They weren't there. They're missing. So how can they find them at his autopsy?'

'Not his autopsy,' I said. 'Her autopsy. His wife's. When they check what she ate.'

Finlay stopped smiling. Went quiet. Just looked at me.

'Talk, Reacher,' he said.

'OK,' I said. 'That's why we came out here, remember? So answer another question for me. How many homicides have they had in Margrave?'

He thought about it. Shrugged.

'None,' he said. 'At least, not for maybe thirty years or so. Not since voter registration days, I guess.'

'And now you've had four in four days,' I said. 'And pretty soon you'll find the fifth.'

'Fifth?' he said. 'Who's the fifth?'

'Hubble,' I said. 'My brother, this Sherman Stoller guy, the two Morrisons and Hubble makes five. No homicides in thirty years and now you've got five all at once. That can't be any kind of a co-incidence, right?'

'No way,' he said. 'Of course not. They're linked.'

'Right,' I said. 'Now I'll tell you some more links. But first of all, you got to understand something, right? I was just passing through here. On Friday and Saturday and Sunday right up to the time those prints came through on my brother, I wasn't paying

190

the slightest bit of attention to anything at all. I was just figuring I'd wait around and get the hell out of here as soon as possible.'

'So?' he said.

'So I was told stuff,' I said. 'Hubble told me things in Warburton, but I didn't pay a lot of attention. I wasn't interested in him, OK? He told me things, and I didn't follow them up with him and I probably don't recall some of them.'

'Like what things?' Finlay said.

So I told him the things I remembered. I started the same way Hubble had started. Trapped inside some kind of a racket, terrorized by a threat against himself and his wife. A threat consisting of the same things, word for word, that Finlay had just seen for himself that morning.

'You sure about that?' he said. 'Exactly the same?'

'Word for word,' I said. 'Totally identical. Nailed to the wall, balls cut off, the wife forced to eat the balls, then they get their throats cut. Word-for-word identical, Finlay. So unless we got two threateners at the same time in the same place making the exact same threat, that's another link.'

'So Morrison was inside the same scam as Hubble?' he said.

'Owned and operated by the same people,' I said.

Then I told him Hubble had been talking to an investigator. And I told him the investigator had been talking to Sherman Stoller, whoever he had been.

'Who was the investigator?' he asked. 'And where does Joe fit in?'

'Joe was the investigator,' I said. 'Hubble told me the tall guy with the shaved head was an investigator, trying to get him free.'

'What sort of an investigator was your brother?' Finlay said. 'Who the hell was he working for?'

'Don't know,' I said. 'Last I heard he was working for the Treasury Department.'

Finlay pushed off the statue and started walking back north.

'I got to make some calls,' he said. 'Time to go to work on this thing.'

'Walk slow,' I said. 'I haven't finished yet.'

Finlay was on the sidewalk. I was in the road, staying clear of the low awnings in front of every store. There was no traffic on the street to worry about. Monday, two o'clock in the afternoon, and the town was deserted.

'How do you know Hubble's dead?' Finlay asked me.

So I told him how I knew. He thought about it. He agreed with me.

'Because he was talking to an investigator?' he said.

I shook my head. Stopped outside the barbershop.

'No,' I said. 'They didn't know about that. If they had, they'd have got to him much earlier. Thursday at the latest. I figure they took the decision to waste him Friday, about five o'clock. Because you pulled him in with the phone number in Joe's shoe. They figured he couldn't be allowed to talk to cops or prison guards. So they set it up with Spivey. But Spivey's boys blew it, so they tried over again. His wife said he got a call to wait at home today. They were setting him up for a second attempt. Looks like it worked.'

Finlay nodded slowly.

'Shit,' he said. 'He was the only link we had to

exactly what the hell is going on here. You should have hit on him while you had the chance, Reacher.'

'Thanks, Finlay,' I said. 'If I'd known the dead guy was Joe, I'd have hit on him so hard, you'd have heard him yelling all the way over here.'

He just grunted. We moved over and sat together on the bench under the barbershop window.

'I asked him what Pluribus was,' I said. 'He wouldn't answer. He said there were ten local people involved in the scam, plus hired help in from the outside when necessary. And he said the scam is vulnerable until something happens on Sunday. Exposed, somehow.'

'What happens on Sunday?' Finlay asked.

'He didn't tell me,' I said.

'And you didn't press him?' he asked.

'I wasn't very interested,' I said. 'I told you that.'

'And he gave you no idea what the scam is all about?' he asked.

'No idea,' I said.

'Did he say who these ten people are?' he asked.

'No,' I said.

'Christ, Reacher, you're a big help, you know that?' he said.

'I'm sorry, Finlay,' I said. 'I thought Hubble was just some asshole. If I could go back and do it again, I'd do it a lot different, believe me.'

'Ten people?' he said again.

'Not counting himself,' I said. 'Not counting Sherman Stoller, either. But I assume he was counting Chief Morrison.'

'Great,' Finlay said. 'That only leaves me another nine to find.'

'You'll find one of them today,' I said.

* * *

193

The black pickup I'd last seen leaving Eno's parking lot pulled up short at the opposite kerb. It waited there, motor running. The Kliner kid leaned his head on his forearm and stared out of the window at me from across the street. Finlay didn't see him. He was looking down at the sidewalk.

'You should be thinking about Morrison,' I said to him.

'What about him?' he said. 'He's dead, right?'

'But dead how?' I said. 'What should that be saying to you?'

He shrugged.

'Somebody making an example of him?' he said. 'A message?'

'Correct, Finlay,' I said. 'But what had he done wrong?'

'Screwed something up, I guess,' he said.

'Correct, Finlay,' I said again. 'He was told to cover up what went down at the warehouse Thursday night. That was his task for the day. He was up there at midnight, you know.'

'He was?' Finlay said. 'You said that was a bullshit story.'

'No,' I said. 'He didn't see me up there. That part was the bullshit story. But he was up there himself. He saw Joe.'

'He did?' Finlay said. 'How do you know that?'

'First time he saw me was Friday, right?' I said. 'In the office? He was staring at me like he'd seen me before, but he couldn't place where. That was because he'd seen Joe. He noticed a resemblance. Hubble said the same thing. He said I reminded him of his investigator.'

'So Morrison was there?' Finlay said. 'Was he the shooter?'

'Can't figure it that way,' I said. 'Joe was a

194

reasonably smart guy. He wouldn't let a fat idiot like Morrison shoot him. The shooter must have been somebody else. I can't figure Morrison for the maniac, either. That much physical exertion would have dropped him with a heart attack. I think he was the third guy. The clean-up guy. But he didn't search Joe's shoes. And because of that, Hubble got hauled in. That got somebody mad. It meant they had to waste Hubble, so Morrison was wasted as a punishment.'

'Some punishment,' Finlay said.

'Also a message,' I said. 'So think about it.'

'Think about what?' he said. 'Wasn't a message for me.'

'So who was it a message for?' I said.

'Who is any such message for?' he said. 'The next guy in line, right?'

I nodded.

'See why I was worried who was going to be the next chief?' I said.

Finlay dropped his head again and stared at the sidewalk.

'Christ,' he said. 'You think the next chief will be in the scam?'

'Got to be,' I said. 'Why would they have Morrison inside? Not for his wonderful personality, right? They had him inside because they need the chief on board. Because that's useful to them in some particular way. So they wouldn't waste Morrison unless they had a replacement ready. And whoever it is, we're looking at a very dangerous guy. He'll be going in there with Morrison's example staring him in the face. Somebody will have just whispered to him: see what we did to Morrison? That's what we'll do to you if you screw up the way he did.'

'So who is it?' Finlay said. 'Who's going to be the new chief?'

'That's what I was asking you,' I said.

We sat quiet on the bench outside the barbershop for a moment. Enjoyed the sun creeping in under the edge of the striped awning.

'It's you, me and Roscoe,' I said. 'Right now, the only safe thing is to assume everybody else is involved.'

'Why Roscoe?' he said.

'Lots of reasons,' I said. 'But mainly because she worked hard to get me out of Warburton. Morrison wanted me in there as a fall guy for Thursday night, right? So if Roscoe was inside the scam, she'd have left me in there. But she got me out. She pulled in the exact opposite direction from Morrison. So if he was bent, she isn't.'

He looked at me. Grunted.

'Only three of us?' he said. 'You're a cautious guy, Reacher.'

'You bet your ass I'm a cautious guy, Finlay,' I said. 'People are getting killed here. One of them was my only brother.'

We stood up from the bench on the sidewalk. Across the street, the Kliner kid killed his motor and got out of the pickup. Started walking slowly over. Finlay rubbed his face with his hands, like he was washing without water.

'So what now?' he said.

'You got things to do,' I said. 'You need to get Roscoe on one side and fill her in with the details, OK? Tell her to take a lot of care. Then you need to make some calls and find out from Washington what Joe was doing down here.'

'OK,' Finlay said. 'What about you?'

I nodded across at the Kliner kid.

'I'm going to have a talk with this guy,' I said. 'He keeps looking at me.'

Two things happened as the Kliner kid came near. First, Finlay left in a hurry. He just strode off north without another word. Second, I heard the barbershop blinds coming down in the window behind me. I glanced around. There could have been nobody else on the planet except for me and the Kliner kid.

Up close, the kid was an interesting study. He was no lightweight. Probably six-two, maybe one ninety, shot through with some kind of a restless energy. There was a lot of intelligence in his eyes, but there was also some kind of an eerie light burning in there. His eyes told me this probably wasn't the most rational character I was ever going to meet in my whole life. He came close and stood in front of me. Just stared at me.

'You're trespassing,' he said.

'This is your sidewalk?' I said.

'It sure is,' the kid said. 'My daddy's Foundation paid for every inch of it. Every brick. But I'm not talking about the sidewalk. I'm talking about Miss Roscoe. She's mine. She's mine, right from when I first saw her. She's waiting for me. Five years, she's been waiting for me, until the time is right.'

I gazed back at him.

'You understand English?' I said.

The kid tensed up. He was just about hopping from foot to foot.

'I'm a reasonable guy,' I said. 'First time Miss Roscoe tells me she wants you instead of me, I'm out of here. Until then, you back off. Understand that?'

The kid was boiling. But then he changed. It was

like he was operated by a remote control and somebody had just hit a button and switched the channel. He relaxed and shrugged and smiled a wide, boyish smile.

'OK,' he said. 'No hard feelings, right?'

He stuck out his hand to shake on it and he nearly fooled me. Right at the last split second I pulled my own hand back a fraction and closed around his knuckles, not his palm. It's an old army trick. They go to shake your hand, but they're aiming to crush it. Some big macho ritual. The way out is to be ready. You pull back a fraction and you squeeze back. You're squeezing their knuckles, not the meat of their palm. Their grip is neutralized. If you catch it right, you can't lose.

He started crushing, but he never stood a chance. He was going for the steady squeeze, so he could stare into my eyes while I sweated it out. But he never got near. I crunched his knuckles once, then twice, a little harder, and then I dropped his hand and turned away. I was a good sixty yards north before I heard the truck start up. It rumbled south and its noise was lost in the buzz of the heat.

FOURTEEN

Back at the station house there was a big white Cadillac parked right across the entrance. Brand-new, fully loaded. Full of puffy black leather and fake wood. It looked like a Vegas whorehouse after the stern walnut and old hide in Charlie Hubble's Bentley. Took me five strides to get around its hood to the door.

Inside in the chill everybody was milling around a tall old guy with silver hair. He was in an old-fashioned suit. Bootlace tie with a silver clasp. Looked like a real asshole. Some kind of a politician. The Cadillac driver. He must have been about seventy-five years old and he was limping around, leaning on a thick cane with a huge silver knob at the top. I guessed this was Mayor Teale.

Roscoe was coming out of the big office in back. She had been pretty shaken up after being at the Morrison place. Wasn't looking too good now, but she waved and tried a smile. Gestured me over. Wanted me to go into the office with her. I took another quick glance at Mayor Teale and walked over to her.

'You OK?' I said.

'I've had better days,' she said.

'You up to speed?' I asked her. 'Finlay give you the spread?'

She nodded.

'Finlay told me everything,' she said.

We ducked into the big rosewood office. Finlay was sitting at the desk under the old clock. It showed a quarter of four. Roscoe closed the door and I looked back and forth between the two of them.

'So who's getting it?' I said. 'Who's the new chief?'

Finlay looked up at me from where he was sitting. Shook his head.

'Nobody,' he said. 'Mayor Teale is going to run the department himself.'

I went back to the door and cracked it open an inch. Peered out and looked at Teale across the squad room. He had Baker pinned up against the wall. Looked like he was giving him a hard time about something. I watched him for a moment.

'So what do you make of that?' I asked them.

'Everybody else in the department is clean,' Roscoe said.

'Looks that way, I guess,' I said. 'But it proves Teale himself is on board. Teale's their replacement, so Teale's their boy.'

'How do we know he's just their boy?' she said. 'Maybe he's the big boss. Maybe he's running the whole thing.'

'No,' I said. 'The big boss had Morrison carved up as a message. If Teale was the big boss, why would he send a message to himself? He belongs to somebody. He's been put in here to run interference.'

'That's for sure,' Finlay said. 'Started already. Told us Joe and Stoller are going on the back burner. We're throwing everything at the Morrison thing. Doing it ourselves, no outside help, no FBI, no nothing. He says the pride of the department is at stake. And he's already driving us up a blind alley. Says it's obvious Morrison was killed by somebody just out of prison. Somebody Morrison himself put away a long time ago, out for revenge.'

'And it's a hell of a blind alley,' Roscoe said. 'We've got to trawl through twenty years of old files and cross-check every name in every file against parole records from across the entire country. It could take us months. He's pulled Stevenson in off the road for it. Until this is over, he drives a desk. So do I.'

'It's worse than a blind alley,' Finlay said. 'It's a coded warning. Nobody in our files looks good for violent revenge. Never had that sort of crime here. We know that. And Teale knows we know that. But we can't call his bluff, right?'

'Can't you just ignore him?' I said. 'Just do what needs doing?'

He leaned back in his chair. Blew a sigh at the ceiling and shook his head.

'No,' he said. 'We're working right under the enemy's nose. Right now, Teale's got no reason to think we know anything about any of this. And we've got to keep it that way. We've got to play dumb and act innocent, right? That's going to limit our scope. But the big problem is authorization. If I need a warrant or something, I'm going to need his signature. And I'm not going to get it, am I?'

I shrugged at him.

'I'm not planning on using warrants,' I said. 'Did you call Washington?'

'They're getting back to me,' he said. 'Just hope Teale doesn't grab the phone before I can.'

I nodded.

'What you need is somewhere else to work,' I said. 'What about that buddy of yours up in Atlanta FBI? The one you told me about? Could you use his office as a kind of private facility?'

Finlay thought about it. Nodded.

'Not a bad idea,' he said. 'I'll have to go off the record. I can't ask Teale to make a formal request, right? I'll call from home, tonight. Guy called Picard. Nice guy, you'll like him. He's from the Quarter, down in New Orleans. He did a spell in Boston about a million years ago. Great big guy, very smart, very tough.'

'Tell him we need it kept very quiet,' I said. 'We don't want his agents down here until we're ready.'

'What are you going to do about Teale?' Roscoe asked me. 'He works for the guys who killed your brother.'

I shrugged again.

'Depends how involved he was,' I said. 'He wasn't the shooter.'

'He wasn't?' Roscoe said. 'How do you know that?'

'Not fast enough,' I said. 'Limps around with a cane in his hand. Too slow to pull a gun. Too slow to get Joe, anyway. He wasn't the kicker, either. Too old, not vigorous enough. And he wasn't the gofer. That was Morrison. But if he starts messing with me, then he's in deep shit. Otherwise, to hell with him.'

'So what now?' she said.

I shrugged at her. Didn't reply.

'I think Sunday is the thing,' Finlay said. 'Sunday is going to solve some kind of a problem for them. Teale being put in here feels so temporary, you know? The guy's seventy-five years old. He's got no police experience. It's a temporary fix, to get them through until Sunday.'

The buzzer on the desk went off. Stevenson's voice came over the intercom asking for Roscoe. They had files to check. I opened the door for her. But she stopped. She'd just thought of something.

'What about Spivey?' she said. 'Over at Warburton? He was ordered to arrange the attack on Hubble, right? So he must know who gave him the order. You should go ask him. Might lead somewhere.'

'Maybe,' I said. Closed the door behind her.

'Waste of time,' Finlay said to me. 'You think Spivey's just going to tell you a thing like that?'

I smiled at him.

'If he knows, he'll tell me,' I said to him. 'A question like that, it's how you ask it, right?'

'Take care, Reacher,' he said. 'They see you getting close to what Hubble knew, they'll waste you like they wasted him.'

Charlie and her kids flashed into my mind and I shivered. They would figure Charlie was close to what Hubble had known. That was inevitable. Maybe even his kids as well. A cautious person would assume kids could have overheard something. It was four o'clock. The kids would be out of school. There were people out there who had loaded up with rubber overshoes, nylon bodysuits and surgical gloves. And sharp knives. And a bag of nails. And a hammer.

'Finlay, call your buddy Picard right now,' I said. 'We need his help. We've got to put Charlie

Hubble somewhere safe. And her kids. Right now.'

Finlay nodded gravely. He saw it. He understood.

'For sure,' he said. 'Get your ass up to Beckman. Right now. Stay there. I'll organize Picard. You don't leave until he shows up, OK?'

He picked up the phone. Dialled an Atlanta number from memory.

Roscoe was back at her desk. Mayor Teale was handing her a thick wad of file folders. I stepped over to her and pulled up a spare chair. Sat down next to her.

'What time do you finish?' I said.

'About six, I guess,' she said.

'Bring some handcuffs home, OK?' I said.

'You're a fool, Jack Reacher,' she said.

Teale was watching so I got up and kissed her hair. Went out into the afternoon and headed for the Bentley. The sun was dropping away and the heat was gone. Shadows were lengthening up. Felt like the fall was on its way. Behind me I heard a shout. Mayor Teale had followed me out of the building. He called me back. I stayed where I was. Made him come to me. He limped over, tapping his cane, smiling. Stuck out his hand and introduced himself. Said his name was Grover Teale. He had that politician's knack of fixing you with a look and a smile like a searchlight. Like he was thrilled to bits just to be talking to me.

'Glad I caught you,' he said. 'Sergeant Baker has brought me up to date on the warehouse homicides. It all seems pretty clear to me. We made a clumsy mistake in apprehending you, and we're all very sorry indeed about your brother, and we'll certainly let you know just as soon as we get to any conclusions. So before you get on your way, I'd be grateful if you'd kindly accept my apology on behalf of this department. I wouldn't want you to take away a bad impression of us. May we just call it a mistake?'

'OK, Teale,' I said. 'But why do you assume I'm leaving?'

He came back smoothly. Not more than a tiny hesitation.

'I understood you were just passing through,' he said. 'We have no hotel here in Margrave and I imagined you would find no opportunity to stay.'

'I'm staying,' I said. 'I received a generous offer of hospitality. I understand that's what the South is famous for, right? Hospitality?'

He beamed at me and grasped his embroidered lapel.

'Oh, undoubtedly that's true, sir,' he said. 'The South as a whole, and Georgia in particular, is indeed famous for the warmth of its welcome. However, as you know, just at the present time, we find ourselves in a most awkward predicament. In the circumstances, a motel in Atlanta or Macon would really suit you much better. Naturally, we would keep in close touch, and we would extend you every assistance in arranging your brother's funeral, when that sad time comes. Here in Margrave, I'm afraid, we're all going to be very busy. It'll be boring for you. Officer Roscoe's going to have a lot of work to do. She shouldn't be distracted just at the moment, don't you think?'

'I won't distract her,' I said evenly. 'I know she's doing vital work.'

He looked at me. An expressionless gaze. Eye to eye, but he wasn't really tall enough. He'd get a crick in his scrawny old neck. And if he kept on staring at me like that, he'd get his scrawny old neck broken. I gave him a wintry smile and stepped away to the Bentley. Unlocked it and got in. Gunned the big motor and whirred the window down.

'See you later, Teale,' I called as I drove away.

The end of the school day was the busiest I'd ever seen the town. I passed two people on Main Street and saw another four in a knot near the church. Some kind of an afternoon club, maybe. Reading the Bible or bottling peaches for the winter. I drove past them and hustled the big car up the sumptuous mile of Beckman Drive. Turned in at the Hubbles' white mailbox and spun the old Bakelite steering wheel through the driveway curves.

The problem with trying to warn Charlie was I didn't know how much I wanted to tell her. Certainly I wasn't about to give her the details. Didn't even feel right to tell her Hubble was dead at all. We were stuck in some kind of a limbo. But I couldn't keep her in the dark for ever. She needed to know some context. Or else she wouldn't listen to the warning.

I parked her car at her door and rang her bell. The children dashed around from somewhere as Charlie opened up and let me in. She was looking pretty tired and strained. The children looked happy enough. They hadn't picked up on their mother's worries. She chased them off and I followed her back to the kitchen. It was a big, modern room. I got her to make me some coffee. I could see she was anxious to talk, but she was having trouble getting started. I watched her fiddling with the filter machine.

'Don't you have a maid?' I asked her.

She shook her head.

'I don't want one,' she said. 'I like to do things myself.'

'It's a big house,' I said.

'I like to keep busy, I guess,' she said.

Then we were silent. Charlie switched on the coffee machine and it started with a faint hiss. I sat at a table in a window nook. It overlooked an acre of velvet lawn. She came and sat opposite me. Folded her hands in front of her.

'I heard about the Morrisons,' she said at last. 'Is my husband involved in all of this?'

I tried to think exactly what I could say to her. She waited for an answer. The coffee machine burbled away in the big silent kitchen.

'Yes, Charlie,' I said. 'I'm afraid he was. But he didn't want to be involved, OK? Some kind of blackmail was going on.'

She took it well. She must have figured it out for herself, anyway. Must have run every possible speculation through her head. This explanation was the one which fit. That was why she didn't look surprised or outraged. She just nodded. Then she relaxed. She looked like it had done her good to hear someone else say it. Now it was out in the open. It was acknowledged. It could be dealt with.

'I'm afraid that makes sense,' she said.

She got up to pour the coffee. Kept talking as she went.

'That's the only way I can explain his behaviour,' she said. 'Is he in danger?'

'Charlie, I'm afraid I have no idea where he is,' I said.

She handed me a mug of coffee. Sat down again on the kitchen counter.

'Is he in danger?' she asked again.

I couldn't answer. Couldn't get any words out. She moved off the counter and came to sit opposite me again at the table in the window. She cradled her cup in front of her. She was a fine-looking woman. Blonde and pretty. Perfect teeth, good bones, slim, athletic. A lot of spirit. I had seen her as a plantation type. What they call a belle. I had said to myself that a hundred and fifty years ago she would have been a slaveowner. I began to change that opinion. I felt a crackle of toughness coming from her. She enjoyed being rich and idle, sure. Beauty parlours and lunch with the girls in Atlanta. The Bentley and the gold cards. The big kitchen which cost more than I ever made in a year. But if it came to it, here was a woman who might get down in the dirt and fight. Maybe a hundred and fifty years ago she would have been on a wagon train heading west. She had enough spirit. She looked hard at me across the table.

'I panicked this morning,' she said. 'That's not really like me at all. I must have given you a very bad impression, I'm afraid. After you left, I calmed down and thought things out. I came to the same conclusion you've just described. Hub's blundered into something and he's got all tangled up in it. So what am I going to do about it? Well, I'm going to stop panicking and start thinking. I've been a mess since Friday and I'm ashamed of it. That's not the real me at all. So I did something, and I hope you'll forgive me for it?'

'Go on,' I said.

'I called Dwight Stevenson,' she said. 'He had mentioned he had seen a fax from the Pentagon about your service as a military policeman. I asked him to find it and read it to me. I thought it was an excellent record.'

She smiled at me. Hitched her chair in closer.

'So what I want to do is to hire you,' she said. 'I want to hire you in a private capacity to solve my husband's problem. Would you consider doing that for me?'

'No,' I said. 'I can't do that, Charlie.'

'Can't or won't?' she said.

'There would be a sort of a conflict of interest,' I said. 'It might mean I couldn't do a proper job for you.'

'A conflict?' she said. 'In what way?'

I paused for a long moment. Tried to figure out how to explain it.

'Your husband felt bad, OK?' I said. 'He got hold of some kind of an investigator, a government guy, and they were trying to fix the situation. But the government guy got killed. And I'm afraid my interest is in the government guy, more than your husband.'

She followed what I was saying and nodded.

'But why?' she asked. 'You don't work for the government.'

'The government guy was my brother,' I told her. 'Just a crazy coincidence, I know, but I'm stuck with it.'

She went quiet. She saw where the conflict could lie.

'I'm very sorry,' she said. 'You're not saying Hub betrayed your brother?'

'No,' I said. 'That's the very last thing he would have done. He was depending on him to get him out from under. Something went wrong, is all.'

'May I ask you a question?' she said. 'Why do you refer to my husband in the past tense?'

I looked straight at her.

'Because he's dead,' I said. 'I'm very sorry.'

Charlie hung in there. She went pale and clenched her hands until her knuckles shone waxy white. But she didn't fall apart.

'I don't think he's dead,' she whispered. 'I would know. I would be able to feel it. I think he's just hiding out somewhere. I want you to find him. I'll pay you whatever you want.'

I just slowly shook my head at her.

'Please,' she said.

'I won't do it, Charlie,' I said. 'I won't take your money for that. I would be exploiting you. I can't take your money because I know he's already dead. I'm very sorry, but there it is.'

There was a long silence in the kitchen. I sat there at the table, nursing the coffee she'd made for me.

'Would you do it if I didn't pay you?' she said. 'Maybe you could just look around for him while you find out about your brother?'

I thought about it. Couldn't see how I could say no to that.

'OK,' I said. 'I'll do that, Charlie. But like I say, don't expect miracles. I think we're looking at something very bad here.'

'I think he's alive,' she said. 'I would know if he wasn't.'

I started worrying about what would happen when his body was found. She was going to come face to face with reality the same way a runaway truck comes face to face with the side of a building.

'You'll need expense money,' Charlie said.

I wasn't sure about taking it, but she passed me a thick envelope.

'Will that do?' she asked.

I looked in the envelope. There was a thick wad of hundred dollar bills in there. I nodded. That would do.

'And please keep the car,' she said. 'Use it as long as you need it.'

I nodded again. Thought about what else I needed to say and forced myself to use the present tense.

'Where does he work?' I asked her.

'Sunrise International,' she said. 'It's a bank.'

She reeled off an Atlanta address.

'OK, Charlie,' I said. 'Now let me ask you something else. It's very important. Did your husband ever use the word "Pluribus"?'

She thought about it and shrugged.

'Pluribus?' she said. 'Isn't that something to do with politics? Like on the podium when the President gives a speech? I never heard Hub talking about it. He graduated in banking studies.'

'You never heard him use that word?' I asked her again. 'Not on the phone, not in his sleep or anything?'

'Never,' she said.

'What about next Sunday?' I asked her. 'Did he mention next Sunday? Anything about what's going to happen?'

'Next Sunday?' she repeated. 'I don't think he mentioned it. Why? What's going to happen next Sunday?'

'I don't know,' I said. 'That's what I'm trying to find out.'

She pondered it again for a long moment, but just shook her head and shrugged, palms upward, like it meant nothing to her.

'I'm sorry,' she said.

'Don't worry about it,' I said. 'Now you've got to do something.'

'What do I have to do?' she said.

'You've got to get out of here,' I said.

Her knuckles were still white, but she was staying in control.

'I've got to run and hide?' she said. 'But where to?'

'An FBI agent is coming here to pick you up,' I said.

She stared at me in panic.

'FBI?' she said. She went paler still. 'This is really serious, isn't it?'

'It's deadly serious,' I said. 'You need to get ready to leave right now.'

'OK,' she said, slowly. 'I can't believe this is happening.'

I walked out of her kitchen and into the garden room where we had drunk iced tea the day before. Stepped through the French doors and strolled a slow circuit outside the house. Down the driveway, through the banks of greenery, out onto Beckman Drive. Leaned up on the white mailbox on the shoulder. It was silent. I could hear nothing at all except the dry rustle of the grass cooling under my feet.

Then I could hear a car coming west out of town. It slowed just before the crest of the rise and I heard the automatic box slur a change down as the speed dropped. The car rose up over the crest into view. It was a brown Buick, very plain, two guys in it. They were small dark guys, Hispanic, loud shirts. They were slowing, drifting to the left of the road, looking for the Hubble mailbox. I was leaning on the Hubble mailbox, looking at them. Their eyes met mine. The car accelerated again and swerved away. Blasted on into the empty peach country. I stepped out and watched them go. I saw a dust plume rising as they drove off Margrave's immaculate blacktop onto the dusty rural roadway. Then I sprinted back up to the house. I wanted Charlie to hurry.

She was inside, flustered, chattering away like a kid going on vacation. Making lists out loud. Some kind of a mechanism to burn off the panic she was feeling. On Friday she'd been a rich idle woman married to a banker. Now on Monday a stranger who said the banker was dead was telling her to hurry up and run for her life.

'Take the mobile phone with you,' I called to her.

She didn't reply. I just heard a worried silence. Footsteps and closet doors banging. I sat in her kitchen with the rest of the coffee for most of an hour. Then I heard a car horn blow and the crunch of heavy steps on the gravel. A loud knock on the front door. I put my hand in my pocket and closed it around the ebony handle of Morrison's switch-blade. Walked out into the hallway and opened up.

There was a neat blue sedan next to the Bentley and a gigantic black guy standing back from the doorstep. He was as tall as me, maybe even taller, but he must have outweighed me by at least a hundred pounds. Must have been three-ten, three-twenty. Next to him, I was a featherweight. He stepped forward with the easy elastic grace of an athlete.

'Reacher?' the giant said. 'Pleased to meet you. I'm Picard, FBI.'

He shook hands with me. He was enormous. He had a casual competence about him which made me glad he was on my side. He looked like my type of a guy. Like he could be very useful in a tight corner. I suddenly felt a flood of encouragement.

I stood aside to let him into Charlie's house.

'OK,' Picard said to me. 'I got all the details from Finlay. Real sorry about your brother, my friend. Real sorry. Somewhere we can talk?'

I led him through to the kitchen. He loped beside me and covered the distance in a couple of strides. Glanced around and poured himself the dregs of the stewed coffee. Then he stepped over next to me and dropped his hand on my shoulder. Felt like somebody had hit me with a bag of cement.

'Ground rules,' he said. 'This whole thing is off the record, right?'

I nodded. His voice matched his bulk. It was a low rumble. It was what a brown bear would sound like if it learned to talk. I couldn't tell how old the guy was. He was one of those big fit men whose peak years stretch on for decades. He nodded and moved away. Rested his giant frame against the counter.

'This is a huge problem for me,' he said. 'Bureau can't act without a call from the responsible official in the local jurisdiction. That would be this guy Teale, right? And from what Finlay tells me, I assume old Teale's not going to be making that call. So I could end up with my big ass in a sling for this. But I'll bend the rules for Finlay. We go back quite a ways. But you got to remember, this is all unofficial, OK?'

I nodded again. I was happy with that. Very happy. Unofficial help suited me fine. It would get the job done without hanging me up on procedure. I had five clear days before Sunday. This morning, five days had seemed more than generous. But now, with Hubble gone, I felt like I was very short of time. Much too short of time to waste any of it on procedure.

'Where are you going to put them?' I asked him.

'Safe house up in Atlanta,' Picard said. 'Bureau place, we've had it for years. They'll be secure there, but I'm not going to say exactly where it is, and I'm going to have to ask you not to press Mrs Hubble about it afterwards, OK? I got to watch my back on this thing. I blow a safe house, I'm in really deep shit.'

'OK, Picard,' I said. 'I won't cause you a problem. And I appreciate it.'

He nodded, gravely, like he was way out on a limb. Then Charlie and the kids burst in. They were burdened down with badly packed bags. Picard introduced himself. I could see that Charlie's daughter was terrified by the size of the guy. The little boy's eyes grew round as he gazed at the FBI Special Agent's shield Picard was holding out. Then the five of us carried the bags outside and piled them in the blue sedan's trunk. I shook hands with Picard and Charlie. Then they all got in the car. Picard drove them away. I waved after them.

FIFTEEN

I headed over to Warburton a damn sight faster than the prison driver had and I was there in less than fifty minutes. It was a hell of a sight. There was a storm coming in quickly from the west and shafts of low afternoon sun were escaping the clouds and hitting the place. The glittering metal towers and turrets were catching the orange rays. I slowed up and pulled into the prison approach. Stopped outside the first vehicle cage. I wasn't going in there. I'd had enough of that. Spivey was going to have to come out to me. I got out of the Bentley and walked over to the guard. He seemed friendly enough.

'Spivey on duty?' I asked him.

'You want him?' the guard said.

'Tell him Mr Reacher's here,' I said.

The guy ducked under a Perspex hood and made a call. Ducked back out again and shouted over to me.

'He doesn't know any Mr Reacher,' he said.

'Tell him Chief Morrison sent me,' I said. 'Over from Margrave.'

216

The guy went under the Perspex thing again and started talking. After a minute he was back out.

'OK, drive on through,' he said. 'Spivey will meet you at reception.'

'Tell him he's got to come out here,' I said. 'Meet me on the road.'

I walked away and stood in the dust on the edge of the blacktop. It was a battle of nerves. I was betting Spivey would come on out. I'd know in five minutes. I waited. I could smell rain coming out of the west. In an hour, it was going to roll right over us. I stood and waited.

Spivey came out. I heard the grilles on the vehicle cage grinding across. I turned and saw a dirty Ford driving through. It came out and stopped next to the Bentley. Spivey heaved himself out. He walked over. Big guy, sweating, red face and hands. His uniform was dirty.

'Remember me?' I asked him.

His small snake eyes flicked around. He was adrift and worried.

'You're Reacher,' he said. 'So what?'

'Right,' I said. 'I'm Reacher. From Friday. What was the deal?'

He shifted from foot to foot. He was going to play hard to get. But he'd already showed his hand. He'd come out to meet me. He'd already lost the game. But he didn't speak.

'What was the deal on Friday?' I said again.

'Morrison is dead,' he said. Then he shrugged and clamped his thin lips. Wouldn't say any more.

I stepped casually to my left. Just a foot or so, to put Spivey's bulk between me and the gate guard. So the gate guard couldn't see. Morrison's switch-blade appeared in my hand. I held it up at Spivey's eye level for a second. Just long enough for him to

217

read the gold-filled engraving in the ebony. Then the blade popped out with a loud click. Spivey's small eyes were fixed on it.

'You think I used this on Morrison?' I said.

He was staring at the blade. It shone blue in the stormy sun.

'It wasn't you,' he said. 'But maybe you had good reason.'

I smiled at him. He knew it wasn't me who killed Morrison. Therefore he knew who had. Therefore he knew who Morrison's bosses were. Simple as that. Three little words, and I was getting somewhere. I moved the blade a fraction closer to his big red face.

'Want me to use this on you?' I said.

Spivey looked around wildly. Saw the gate guard thirty yards away.

'He's not going to help you,' I said. 'He hates your useless fat guts. He's just a guard. You sucked ass and got promotion. He wouldn't piss on you if you were on fire. Why should he?'

'So what do you want?' Spivey said.

'Friday,' I said. 'What was the deal?'

'And if I tell you?' he said.

I shrugged at him.

'Depends what you tell me,' I said. 'You tell me the truth, I'll let you go back inside. Want to tell me the truth?'

He didn't reply. We were just standing there by the road. A battle of nerves. His nerves were shot to hell. So he was losing. His little eyes were darting about. They always came back to the blade.

'OK, I'll tell you,' he said. 'Time to time, I helped Morrison out. He called me Friday. Said he was sending two guys over. Names meant nothing to me. Never heard of you or the other guy. I was supposed to get the Hubble guy killed. That's all. Nothing was supposed to happen to you, I swear it.'

'So what went wrong?' I asked him.

'My guys screwed up,' he said. 'That's all, I swear it. It was the other guy we were after. Nothing was supposed to happen to you. You got out of there, right? No damage done, right? So why give me a hard time?'

I flashed the blade up real quick and nicked his chin. He froze in shock. A moment later a fat worm of dark blood welled out of the cut.

'What was the reason?' I asked him.

'There's never a reason,' he said. 'I just do what I'm told.'

'You do what you're told?' I said.

'I do what I'm told,' he said again. 'I don't want to know any reasons.'

'So who told you what to do?' I said.

'Morrison,' he said. 'Morrison told me what to do.'

'And who told Morrison what to do?' I asked him.

I held the blade an inch from his cheek. He was just about whimpering with fear. I stared into his small snake eyes. He knew the answer. I could see that, far back in those eyes. He knew who told Morrison what to do.

'Who told him what to do?' I asked him again.

'I don't know,' he said. 'I swear it, grave of my mother.'

I stared at him for a long moment. Shook my head.

'Wrong, Spivey,' I said. 'You do know. You're going to tell me.'

Now Spivey shook his head. His big red face

jerked from side to side. The blood was running down his chin onto his slabby jowls.

'They'll kill me if I do,' he said.

I flicked the knife at his belly. Slit his greasy shirt.

'I'll kill you if you don't,' I said.

Guy like Spivey, he thinks short term. If he told me, he'd die tomorrow. If he didn't tell me, he'd die today. That's how he thought. Short term. So he set about telling me. His throat started working up and down, like it was too dry to speak. I stared into his eyes. He couldn't get any words out. He was like a guy in a movie who crawls up a desert dune and tries to call for water. But he was going to tell me.

Then he wasn't. Over his shoulder, I saw a dust plume far in the east. Then I heard the faint roar of a diesel engine. Then I made out the grey shape of the prison bus rolling in. Spivey snapped his head around to look at his salvation. The gate guard wandered out to meet the bus. Spivey snapped his head back to look at me. There was a mean gleam of triumph in his eyes. The bus was getting closer.

'Who was it, Spivey?' I said. 'Tell me now, or I'll come back for you.'

But he just backed off and turned and hustled over to his dirty Ford. The bus roared in and blew dust all over me. I closed up the switchblade and put it back in my pocket. Jogged over to the Bentley and took off.

The coming storm chased me all the way back east. I felt I had more than a storm after me. I was sick with frustration. This morning I had been just one conversation away from knowing everything. Now I knew nothing. The situation had suddenly turned sour.

I had no backup, no facilities, no help. I couldn't rely on Roscoe or Finlay. I couldn't expect either of them to agree with my agenda. And they had troubles of their own up at the station house. What had Finlay said? Working under the enemy's nose? And I couldn't expect too much from Picard. He was already way out on a limb. I couldn't count on anybody but myself.

On the other hand, I had no laws to worry about, no inhibitions, no distractions. I wouldn't have to think about Miranda, probable cause, constitutional rights. I wouldn't have to think about reasonable doubt or rules of evidence. No appeal to any higher authority for these guys. Was that fair? You bet your ass. These were bad people. They'd stepped over the line a long time ago. Bad people. What had Finlay said? As bad as they come. And they had killed Joe Reacher.

I rolled the Bentley down the slight hill to Roscoe's house. Parked on the road outside her place. She wasn't home. The Chevrolet wasn't there. The big chrome clock on the Bentley's dash showed ten of six. Ten minutes to wait. I got out of the front seat and got into the back. Stretched out on the big old car's leather bench.

I wanted to get away from Margrave for the evening. I wanted to get out of Georgia altogether. I found a map in a pocket on the back of the driver's seat. I peered at it and figured if we went west for an hour, hour and a half, back past Warburton again, we'd cross the state line into Alabama. That's what I wanted to do. Blast west with Roscoe into Alabama and pull into the first live music bar we came to. Put my troubles on hold until tomorrow. Eat some cheap food, drink some cold beer, hear some dirty music. With Roscoe. My idea of a hell of an evening. I settled back to wait for her. The dark was gathering in. I felt a faint chill in the evening air. About six o'clock huge drops started hammering on the roof of the Bentley. It felt like a big evening thunderstorm was moving in, but it never really arrived. It never really let loose. Just the big early drops spattering down like the sky was straining to unload but wouldn't let go. It went very dark and the heavy car rocked gently in the damp wind.

Roscoe was late. The storm had been threatening for about twenty minutes before I saw her Chevy winding down the rise. Her headlights swept and arced left and right. They washed over me as she swung into her driveway. They blazed against her garage door, then died as she cut the power. I got out of the Bentley and stepped over to her. We held each other and kissed. Then we went inside.

'You OK?' I asked her.

'I guess,' she said. 'Hell of a day.'

I nodded. It had been.

'Upset?' I asked her.

She was moving around switching lamps on. Pulling drapes.

'This morning was the worst thing I've ever seen,' she said. 'By far the worst thing. But I'm going to tell you something I would never tell anyone else. I wasn't upset. Not about Morrison. You can't get upset about a guy like that. But I'm upset about his wife. Bad enough living with a guy like Morrison without dying because of him too, right?'

'What about the rest of it?' I asked her. 'Teale?'

'I'm not surprised,' she said. 'That whole family has been scumbags for two hundred years. I know all about them. His family and my family go way

222

back together. Why should he be any different? But, God, I'm glad everybody else in the department turned out clean. I was dreading finding out one of those guys had been in it, too. I don't know if I could have faced that.'

She went into the kitchen and I followed. She went quiet. She wasn't falling apart, but she wasn't happy. She pulled open the refrigerator door. It was a gesture which said: the cupboard is bare. She smiled a tired smile at me.

'You want to buy me dinner?' she said.

'Sure,' I said. 'But not here. In Alabama.'

I told her what I wanted to do. She liked the plan. She brightened up and went to take a shower. I figured I could use a shower too, so I went with her. But we hit a delay because as soon as she started to unbutton her crisp uniform shirt, my priorities shifted. The lure of an Alabama bar receded. And the shower could wait, too. She was wearing black underwear beneath the uniform. Not very substantial items. We ended up in a frenzy on the bedroom floor. The thunderstorm was finally breaking outside. The rain was lashing the little house. Lightning was blazing and the thunder was crashing about.

We finally made it to the shower. By then, we really needed it. Afterwards I lay on the bed while Roscoe dressed. She put on faded denims and a silky shirt. We turned off the lamps again and locked up and took off in the Bentley. It was seven-thirty and the storm was drifting off to the east, heading for Charleston before boiling out over the Atlantic. Might hit Bermuda tomorrow. We headed west toward a pinker sky. I found the road back out to Warburton. Cruised down the farm roads between the endless dark fields and blasted past the prison. It squatted glowering in its ghastly yellow light.

A half-hour after Warburton we stopped to fill the old car's gigantic tank. Threaded through some tobacco country and crossed the Chattahoochee by an old river bridge in Franklin. Then a sprint down to the state line. We were in Alabama before nine o'clock. We agreed to take a chance and stop at the first bar.

We saw an old roadhouse maybe a mile later. Pulled into the parking lot and got out. Looked OK. Big enough place, wide and low, built from tarred boards. Plenty of neon, plenty of cars in the lot, and I could hear music. The sign at the door said The Pond, live music seven nights a week at nine-thirty. Roscoe and I held hands and walked in.

We were hit by bar noise and jukebox music and a blast of beery air. We pushed through to the back and found a wide ring of booths around a dance floor with a stage beyond. The stage was really just a low concrete platform. It might once have been some kind of a loading bay. The ceiling was low and the light was dim. We found an empty booth and slid in. Watched the band setting up while we waited for service. The waitresses were rushing around like basketball centres. One dived over and we ordered beers, cheeseburgers, fries, onion rings. Pretty much right away she ran back with a tin tray with our stuff on it. We ate and drank and ordered more.

'So what are you going to do about Joe?' Roscoe asked me.

I was going to finish his business. Whatever it was. Whatever it took. That was the decision I had taken in her warm bed that morning. But she was a police officer. She was sworn to uphold all kinds of laws. Laws that were designed to get in my way. I didn't know what to say. But she didn't wait for me to say anything.

'I think you should find out who it was killed him,' she said.

'And then what?' I asked her.

But that was as far as we got. The band started up. We couldn't talk any more. Roscoe gave an apologetic smile and shook her head. The band was loud. She shrugged, saying sorry for the fact that I couldn't hear her talking. She sketched me a tell-you-later gesture across the table and we turned to face the stage. I wished I could have heard her reply to my question.

The bar was called The Pond and the band was called Pond Life. They started pretty well. A classic trio. Guitar, bass, drums. Firmly into the Stevie Ray Vaughan thing. Since Stevie Ray died in his helicopter up near Chicago it seemed like you could count up all the white men under forty in the southern states, divide by three, and that was the number of Stevie Ray Vaughan tribute bands. Everybody was doing it. Because it didn't require much. Didn't matter what you looked like, didn't matter what gear you had. All you needed was to get your head down and play. The best of them could match Stevie Ray's on-a-dime changes from loose bar rock to the old Texas blues.

This lot was pretty good. Pond Life. They lived up to their ironic name. The bass and the drums were big messy guys, lots of hair all over, fat and dirty. The guitar player was a small dark guy, not unlike old Stevie Ray himself. The same gappy grin. He could play, too. He had a black Les Paul copy and a big Marshall stack. Good old-fashioned sound. The loose heavy strings and the big pickups overloading the ancient Marshall tubes, giving that glorious fat buzzy scream you couldn't get any other way.

We were having a good time. We drank a lot of beer, sat tight together in the booth. Then we danced for a while. Couldn't resist it. The band played on and on. The room got hot and crowded. The music got louder and faster. The waitresses sprinted back and forth with long-neck bottles.

Roscoe looked great. Her silky shirt was damp. She wasn't wearing anything underneath it. I could see that because of the way the damp silk stuck to her skin. I was in heaven. I was in a plain old bar with a stunning woman and a decent band. Joe was on hold until tomorrow. Margrave was a million miles away. I had no problems. I didn't want the evening to end.

The band played on until pretty late. Must have been way past midnight. We were juiced up and sloppy. Couldn't face the drive back. It was raining again, lightly. Didn't want to drive an hour and a half in the rain. Not so full of beer. Might end up in a ditch. Or in jail. There was a sign to a motel a mile further on. Roscoe said we should go there. She was giggly about it. Like we were eloping or something. Like I'd transported her across the state line for that exact purpose. I hadn't, specifically. But I wasn't about to put up a whole lot of objections.

So we stumbled out of the bar with ringing ears and got into the Bentley. We rolled the big old car cautiously and slowly down the streaming road for a mile. Saw the motel up ahead. A long, low old place, like something out of a movie. I pulled into the lot and went into the office. Roused the night guy at the desk. Gave him the money and arranged an early morning call. Got the key and went back out to the car. I pulled it around to our cabin and we went in. It was a decent, anonymous place. Could have been anywhere in America. But it felt warm and snug with the rain pattering on the roof. And it had a big bed.

I didn't want Roscoe to catch a chill. She ought to get out of that damp shirt. That's what I told her. She giggled at me. Said she hadn't realized I had medical qualifications. I told her we'd been taught enough for basic emergencies.

'Is this a basic emergency?' she giggled.

'It will be soon,' I laughed. 'If you don't take that shirt off.'

So she did take it off. Then I was all over her. She was so beautiful, so provocative. She was ready for anything.

Afterwards we lay in an exhausted tangle and talked. About who we were, about what we'd done. About who we wanted to be and what we wanted to do. She told me about her family. It was a bad luck story stretching back generations. They sounded like decent people, farmers, people who had nearly made it but never did. People who had struggled through the hard times before chemicals, before machinery, hostages to the power of nature. Some old ancestor had nearly made it big, but he lost his best land when Mayor Teale's great-grandfather built the railroad. Then some mortgages were called in and the grudge rolled on down the years so that now she loved Margrave but hated to see Teale walking around like he owned it, which he did, and which Teales always had.

I talked to her about Joe. I told her things I'd never told anybody else. All the stuff I'd kept to myself. All about my feelings for him and why I felt driven to do something about his death. And how I was happy to do it. We went through a lot of personal stuff. Talked for a long time and fell asleep in each other's arms.

Seemed like more or less straight away the guy was banging on the door with the early morning call. Tuesday. We got up and staggered around. The early sun was struggling against a damp dawn. Within five minutes we were back in the Bentley rolling east. The rising sun was blinding in the dewy screen.

Slowly we woke up. We crossed the state line back into Georgia. Crossed the river in Franklin. Settled into a fast cruise through the empty farming country. The fields were hidden under a floating quilt of morning mist. It hung over the red earth like steam. The sun climbed up and set about burning it off.

Neither of us spoke. We wanted to preserve the quiet intimate cocoon as long as possible. Arriving back in Margrave was going to burst the bubble soon enough. So I guided the big stately car down the country roads and hoped. Hoped there'd be plenty more nights like that one. And quiet mornings like this one. Roscoe was curled up on the big hide chair beside me. Lost in thought. She looked very content. I hoped she was.

We blasted past Warburton again. The prison floated like an alien city on the carpet of low mist. We passed the little copse I'd seen from the prison bus. Passed the rows of bushes invisible in the fields. Reached the junction and turned south onto the county road. Past Eno's diner and the station house and the fire house. Down onto Main Street.

We turned left at the statue of the man who took good land for the railroad. Down the slope to Roscoe's place. I parked at the kerb and we got out, yawning and stretching. We grinned briefly at each other. We'd had fun. We walked hand in hand down the driveway.

Her door was open. Not wide open, but an inch or two ajar. It was ajar because the lock was smashed. Someone had used a crowbar on it. The tangle of broken lock and splinters wouldn't allow the door to close all the way. Roscoe put her hand to her mouth and gave a silent gasp. Her eyes were wide. They slid from the door to me.

I grabbed her elbow and pulled her away. We stood flat against the garage door. Crouched down. Stuck close to the walls and circled right around the house. Listened hard at every window and risked ducking our heads up for a quick glance into every room. We arrived back at the smashed front door. We were wet from kneeling on the soaked ground and from brushing against the dripping evergreens. We stood up. Looked at each other and shrugged. Pushed the door open and went inside.

We checked everywhere. There was nobody in the house. No damage. No disturbance. Nothing was stolen. The stereo was still there, the TV was still there. Roscoe checked her closet. The police revolver was still on her belt. She checked her drawers and her bureau. Nothing had been touched. Nothing had been searched. Nothing was missing. We stood back in the hallway and looked at each other. Then I noticed something that had been left behind.

The low morning sun was coming in through the open door and playing a shallow beam over the floor. I could see a line of footprints on the parquet.

A lot of footprints. Several people had tracked through from the front door into the living room. The line of prints disappeared on the bold living room rug. Reappeared on the wood floor leading into the bedroom. Came back out, through the living room, back to the front door. They had been made by people coming in from the rainy night. A slight film of muddy rainwater had dried on the wood leaving faint prints. Faint, but perfect. I could see at least four people. In and out. I could see the tread patterns they had left behind. They had been wearing rubber overshoes. Like you get for the winter up north.

SIXTEEN

They had come for us in the night. They had come expecting a lot of blood. They had come with all their gear. Their rubber overshoes and their nylon bodysuits. Their knives, their hammer, their bag of nails. They had come to do a job on us, like they'd done on Morrison and his wife.

They had pushed open the forbidden door. They had made a second fatal mistake. Now they were dead men. I was going to hunt them down and smile at them as they died. Because to attack me was a second attack on Joe. He was no longer here to stand up for me. It was a second challenge. A second humiliation. This wasn't about self-defence. This was about honouring Joe's memory.

Roscoe was following the trail of footprints. Showing a classic reaction. Denial. Four men had come to butcher her in the night. She knew that, but she was ignoring it. Closing it out of her mind. Dealing with it by not dealing with it. Not a bad approach, but she'd fall off the high wire before long. Until then, she was making herself busy tracing the faint footprints on her floors.

They had searched the house for us. They had split up in the bedroom and looked around. Then they had regrouped in the bedroom and left. We looked for tracks outside on the road, but there was nothing. The smooth tarmac was wet and steaming. We went back inside. No evidence at all except the wrenched lock and the faint footprints throughout the house.

Neither of us spoke. I was burning with anger. Still watching Roscoe. Waiting for the dam to break. She'd seen the Morrison corpses. I hadn't. Finlay had sketched in the details for me. That was bad enough. He'd been there. He'd been shaken by the whole thing. Roscoe had been there too. She'd seen exactly what somebody wanted to do to the two of us.

'So who were they after?' she said at last. 'Me, you, both of us?'

'They were after both of us,' I said. 'They figure Hubble talked to me in prison. They figure I've told you all about it. So they think you and I know whatever it was Hubble knew.'

She nodded, vaguely. Then she moved away and leaned up near her back door. Looking out at her neat evergreen garden. I saw her go pale. She shuddered. The defences crashed down. She pressed herself into the corner by the door. Tried to flatten herself onto the wall. Stared into space like she was seeing all the nameless horrors. Started crying like her heart was broken. I stepped over and held her tight. Pressed her against me and held her as she cried out the fear and the tension. She cried for a long time. She felt hot and weak. My shirt was soaked with her tears.

'Thank God we weren't here last night,' she whispered.

I knew I had to sound confident. Fear wouldn't get her anywhere. Fear would just sap her energy. She had to face it down. And she had to face down the dark and the quiet again tonight, and every other night of her life.

'I wish we had been here,' I said. 'We could have gotten a few answers.'

She looked at me like I was crazy. Shook her head.

'What would you have done?' she said. 'Killed four men?'

'Only three,' I said. 'The fourth would have given us the answers.'

I said it with total certainty. Total conviction. Like absolutely no other possibility existed. She looked at me. I wanted her to see this huge guy. A soldier for thirteen long years. A bare-knuckle killer. Icy blue eyes. I was giving it everything I had. I was willing myself to project all the invincibility, all the implacability, all the protection I felt. I was doing the hard, no-blink stare that used to shrivel up drunken marines two at a time. I wanted Roscoe to feel safe. After what she was giving me, I wanted to give her that. I didn't want her to feel afraid.

'It's going to take more than four little country boys to get me,' I said. 'Who are they kidding? I've shit better opponents than that. They come in here again, they'll go out in a bucket. And I'll tell you what, Roscoe, someone even thinks about hurting you, they die before they finish thinking.'

It was working. I was convincing her. I needed her to be bright, tough, self-confident. I was

233

willing her to pick it up. It was working. Her amazing eyes were filling with spirit.

'I mean it, Roscoe,' I said. 'Stick with me and you'll be OK.'

She looked at me again. Pushed her hair back.

'Promise?' she said.

'You got it, babe,' I said. Held my breath.

She sighed a ragged sigh. Pushed off the wall and stepped over. Tried a brave smile. The crisis was gone. She was up and running.

'Now we get the hell out of here,' I said. 'We can't stay around like sitting targets. So throw what you need into a bag.'

'OK,' she said. 'Are we going to fix my door first?'

I thought about her question. It was an important tactical issue.

'No,' I said. 'If we fix it, it means we've seen it. If we've seen it, it means we know we're under attack. Better if they figure we don't know we're under attack. Because then they'll figure they don't need to be too careful next time. So we don't react at all. We make out we haven't been back here. We make out we haven't seen the door. We carry on acting dumb and innocent. If they think we're dumb and innocent, they'll get careless. Easier to spot them coming next time.'

'OK,' she said.

She didn't sound convinced, but she was agreeing.

'So throw what you need into a bag,' I said again.

She wasn't happy, but she went off to gather up some stuff. The game was starting. I didn't know exactly who the other players were. I didn't even know exactly what the game was. But I knew how to play. Opening move was I wanted them to feel like we were always one step behind.

'Should I go to work today?' Roscoe asked.

'Got to,' I said. 'Can't do anything different from normal. And we need to speak with Finlay. He's expecting the call from Washington. And we need what we can get on Sherman Stoller. But don't worry, they're not going to gun us down in the middle of the squad room. They'll go for somewhere quiet and isolated, probably at night. Teale's the only bad guy up there, so just don't be on your own with him. Stick around Finlay or Baker or Stevenson, OK?'

She nodded. Went to get showered and dressed for work. Within twenty minutes, she came out of the bedroom in her uniform. Patted herself down. Ready for the day. She looked at me.

'Promise?' she said.

The way she said it was like a question, an apology, a reassurance all in one word. I looked back at her.

'You bet your ass,' I said, and winked.

She nodded. Winked back. We were OK. We went out the front door and left it slightly open, just like we'd found it.

I hid the Bentley in her garage to maintain the illusion that we hadn't been back to her house. Then we got in her Chevy and decided to start with breakfast up at Eno's. She took off and gunned the car up the hill. It felt loose and low after the upright old Bentley. Coming down the hill toward us was a panel van. Smart dark green, very clean, brand-new. It looked like a utility van, but on the side was sign in fancy gold script. It said: Kliner Foundation. Same as I'd seen the gardeners using.

'What's that truck?' I said to Roscoe.

She wafted through the right at the coffee shop. Up onto Main Street.

'Foundation's got a lot of trucks,' she said.

'What is it they do?' I asked her.

'Big deal round here,' she said. 'Old man Kliner. The town sold him the land for his warehouses and part of the deal was he set up a community programme. Teale runs it out of the mayor's office.'

'Teale runs it?' I said. 'Teale's the enemy.'

'He runs it because he's the mayor,' she said. 'Not because he's Teale. The programme assigns a lot of money, spends it on public things, roads, gardens, the library, local business grants. Gives the police department a hell of a lot. Gives me a mortgage subsidy, just because I'm with the department.'

'Gives Teale a lot of power,' I said. 'And what's the story with the Kliner boy? He tried to warn me off you. Made out he had a prior claim.'

She shuddered.

'He's a jerk,' she said. 'I avoid him when I can. You should do the same.'

She drove on, looking edgy. Kept glancing around, startled. Like she felt under threat. Like someone was going to jump out in front of the car and gun us down. Her quiet life in the Georgia countryside was over. Four men in the night up at her house had shattered that.

We pulled into Eno's gravel lot and the big Chevy rocked gently on its soft springs. I slid out of the low seat and we crunched across the gravel together to Eno's door. It was a grey day. The night rain had chilled the air and left rags of cloud all over the sky. The siding on the diner reflected the dullness. It was cold. It felt like a new season.

We went in. The place was empty. We took a booth and the woman with glasses brought us coffee. We ordered eggs and bacon with all kinds of extras on the side. A black pickup was pulling into the lot outside. Same black pickup as I'd seen three times before. Different driver. Not the Kliner kid. This was an older guy. Maybe approaching sixty, but bone-hard and lean. Iron-grey hair shaved close to his scalp. He was dressed like a rancher in denim. Looked like he lived outdoors in the sun. Even through Eno's window I could sense his power and feel the glare in his eyes. Roscoe nudged me and nodded at the guy.

'That's Kliner,' she said. 'The old man himself.'

He pushed in through the door and stood for a moment. Looked left, looked right, and moved in to the lunch counter. Eno came around from the kitchen. The two of them talked quietly. Heads bent together. Then Kliner stood up again. Turned to the door. Stopped and looked left, looked right. Rested his gaze on Roscoe for a second. His face was lean and flat and hard. His mouth was a line carved into it. Then he moved his eyes onto me. I felt like I was being illuminated by a searchlight. His lips parted in a curious smile. He had amazing teeth. Long canines, canted inward, and flat square incisors. Yellow, like an old wolf. His lips closed again and he snapped his gaze away. Pulled the door and crunched over the gravel to his truck. Took off with the roar of a big motor and a spray of small stones.

I watched him go and turned to Roscoe.

'So tell me more about these Kliner people,' I said.

She still looked edgy.

237

'Why?' she said. 'We're fighting for our lives here and you want to talk about the Kliners?'

'I'm looking for information,' I said. 'Kliner's name crops up everywhere. He looks like an interesting guy. His son is a piece of work. And I saw his wife. She looked unhappy. I'm wondering if all that's got anything to do with anything.'

She shrugged and shook her head.

'I don't see how,' she said. 'They're newcomers, only been here five years. The family made a fortune in cotton processing, generations back, over in Mississippi. Invented some kind of a new chemical thing, some kind of a new formula. Chlorine or sodium something, I don't know for sure. Made a huge fortune, but they ran into trouble with the EPA over there, you know, about five years ago, pollution or something. There were fish dying all the way down to New Orleans because of dumping into the river.'

'So what happened?' I asked her.

'Kliner moved the whole plant,' she said. 'The company was his by then. He shut down the whole Mississippi operation and set it up again in Venezuela or somewhere. Then he tried to diversify. He turned up here in Georgia five years ago with this warehouse thing, consumer goods, electronics or something.'

'So they're not local?' I said.

'Never saw them before five years ago,' she said. 'Don't know much about them. But I never heard anything bad. Kliner's probably a tough guy, maybe even ruthless, but he's OK as long as you're not a fish, I guess.'

'So why is his wife so scared?' I said.

Roscoe made a face.

'She's not scared,' she said. 'She's sick. Maybe

she's scared because she's sick. She's going to die, right? That's not Kliner's fault.'

The waitress arrived with the food. We ate in silence. The portions were huge. The fried stuff was great. The eggs were delicious. This guy Eno had a way with eggs. I washed it all down with pints of coffee. I had the waitress running back and forth with the refill jug.

'Pluribus means nothing at all to you?' Roscoe asked. 'You guys never knew anything about some Pluribus thing? When you were kids?'

I thought hard and shook my head.

'Is it Latin?' she asked.

'It's part of the United States' motto, right?' I said. 'E Pluribus Unum. It means out of many, one. One nation built out of many former colonies.'

'So Pluribus means many?' she said. 'Did Joe know Latin?'

I shrugged.

'I've got no idea,' I said. 'Probably. He was a smart guy. He probably knew bits and pieces of Latin. I'm not sure.'

'OK,' she said. 'You got no other ideas at all why Joe was down here?'

'Money, maybe,' I said. 'That's all I can think of. Joe worked for the Treasury Department, as far as I know. Hubble worked for a bank. Their only thing in common would be money. Maybe we'll find out from Washington. If we don't, we're going to have to start from the beginning.'

'OK,' she said. 'You need anything?'

'I'll need that arrest report from Florida,' I said.

'For Sherman Stoller?' she said. 'That's two years old.'

'Got to start somewhere,' I said.

'OK, I'll ask for it,' she shrugged. 'I'll call Florida. Anything else?'

'I need a gun,' I said.

She didn't reply. I dropped a twenty on the laminate table top and we slid out and stood up. Walked out to the unmarked car.

'I need a gun,' I said again. 'This is a big deal, right? So I'll need a weapon. I can't just go to the store and buy one. No ID, no address.'

'OK,' she said. 'I'll get you one.'

'I've got no permit,' I said. 'You'll have to do it on the quiet, OK?'

She nodded.

'That's OK,' she said. 'There's one nobody else knows about.'

We kissed a long hard kiss in the station house lot. Then we got out of the car and went in through the heavy glass door. More or less bumped into Finlay rounding the reception counter on his way out.

'Got to go back to the morgue,' he said. 'You guys come with me, OK? We need to talk. Lot to talk about.'

So we went back out into the dull morning. Got back into Roscoe's Chevy. Same system as before. She drove. I sat across the back. Finlay sat in the front passenger seat, twisted around so he could look at the both of us at once. Roscoe started up and headed south.

'Long call from the Treasury Department,' Finlay said. 'Must have been twenty minutes, maybe a half-hour. I was nervous about Teale.'

'What did they say?' I asked him.

'Nothing,' he said. 'They took a half-hour to tell me nothing.'

240

'Nothing?' I said. 'What the hell does that mean?'

'They wouldn't tell me anything,' he said. 'They want a shitload of formal authorization from Teale before they say word one.'

'They confirmed Joe worked there, right?' I said.

'Sure, they went that far,' he said. 'He came from Military Intelligence ten years ago. They headhunted him. Recruited him specially.'

'What for?' I asked him.

Finlay just shrugged.

'They wouldn't tell me,' he said. 'He started some new project exactly a year ago, but the whole thing is a total secret. He was some kind of a very big deal up there, Reacher, that's for sure. You should have heard the way they were all talking about him. Like talking about God.'

I went quiet for a while. I had known nothing about Joe. Nothing at all.

'So that's it?' I said. 'Is that all you got?'

'No,' he said. 'I kept pushing until I got a woman called Molly Beth Gordon. You ever heard that name?'

'No,' I said. 'Should I have?'

'Sounds like she was very close to Joe,' Finlay said. 'Sounds like they may have had a thing going. She was very upset. Floods of tears.'

'So what did she tell you?' I asked him.

'Nothing,' Finlay said. 'Not authorized. But she promised to tell you what she can. She said she'll step out of line for you, because you're Joe's little brother.'

I nodded.

'OK,' I said. 'That's better. When do I speak to her?'

'Call her about one-thirty,' he said. 'Lunch break, when her office will be empty. She's taking a big risk, but she'll talk to you. That's what she said.'

'OK,' I said again. 'She say anything else?'

'She let one little thing slip,' Finlay said. 'Joe had a big debrief meeting scheduled. For next Monday morning.'

'Monday?' I said. 'As in the day after Sunday?'

'Correct,' he said. 'Looks like Hubble was right. Something is due to happen on or before Sunday. Whatever the hell he was doing, it looks like Joe knew he would have won or lost by then. But she wouldn't say anything more. She was out of line talking to me at all and she sounded like she was being overheard. So call her, but don't pin your hopes on her, Reacher. She may not know anything. Left hand doesn't know what the right hand is doing up there. Big-time secrecy, right?'

'Bureaucracy,' I said. 'Who the hell needs it? OK, we have to assume we're on our own here. At least for a while. We're going to need Picard again.'

Finlay nodded.

'He'll do what he can,' he said. 'He called me last night. The Hubbles are secure. Right now, he's sitting on it, but he'll stand up for us if we need him.'

'He should start tracing Joe,' I said. 'Joe must have used a car. Probably flew down from Washington, into Atlanta, got a hotel room, rented a car, right? We should look for the car. He must have driven it down here Thursday night. It must have been dumped somewhere in the area. It might lead us back to the hotel. Maybe there would be something in Joe's hotel room. Files, maybe.'

'Picard can't do that,' Finlay said. 'FBI isn't equipped to go looking for abandoned rental cars. And we can't do it ourselves, not with Teale around.'

I shrugged.

'We'll have to,' I said. 'No other way. You can sell Teale some story. You can double bluff him. Tell him you figure the escaped con who he says did the Morrison thing must have been in a rental car. Tell him you need to check it out. He can't say no to that, or else he's undermining his own cover story, right?'

'OK,' Finlay said. 'I'll try it. Might work, I guess.'

'Joe must have had phone numbers,' I said. 'The number you found in his shoe was torn off a computer printout, right? So where's the rest of the printout? I bet it's in his hotel room, just sitting there, covered with phone numbers, with Hubble's number torn off the top. So you find the car, then you twist Picard's arm to trace the hotel through the rental company, OK?'

'OK,' he said. 'I'll do my best.'

In Yellow Springs we slipped into the hospital entrance lane and slowed over the speed bumps. Nosed around to the lot in back. Parked near the morgue door. I didn't want to go inside. Joe was still in there. I started to think vaguely about funeral arrangements. I'd never had to do it before. The Marine Corps handled my father's. Joe arranged my mother's.

But I got out of the car with the two of them and we walked through the chill air to the door. Found our way back to the shabby office. The same doctor was at the desk. Still in a white coat.

Still looking tired. He waved us in and we sat down. I took one of the stools. I didn't want to sit next to the fax machine again. The doctor looked at all of us in turn. We looked back at him.

'What have you got for us?' Finlay said.

The tired man at the desk prepared to answer. Like preparing for a lecture. He picked up three files from his left and dropped them on his blotter. Opened the top one. Pulled out the second one and opened that, too.

'Morrison,' he said. 'Mr and Mrs.'

He glanced around the three of us again. Finlay nodded to him.

'Tortured and killed,' the pathologist said. 'The sequence is pretty clear. The woman was restrained. Two men, I'd say, one on each arm, gripping and twisting. Heavy bruising on the fore-arms and the upper arms, some ligament damage from twisting the arms up her back. Obviously the bruising continued to develop from the time she was first seized until the time she died. The bruis-ing stops developing when the circulation stops, you understand?'

We nodded. We understood.

'I'd put it at about ten minutes,' he said. 'Ten minutes, beginning to end. So the woman was being held. The man was being nailed to the wall. I'd guess both were naked by then. They were in nightwear before the attack, right?'

'Robes,' Finlay said. 'They were having break-fast.'

'OK, the robes came off early on,' the doctor said. 'The man was nailed to the wall, technically to the floor also, through the feet. His genital area was attacked. The scrotum was severed. Postmortem evidence suggests that the woman was persuaded to swallow the amputated testicles.'

The office was silent. Silent as a tomb. Roscoe looked at me. Stared at me for a while. Then she looked back at the doctor.

'I found them in her stomach,' the doctor said.

Roscoe was as white as the guy's coat. I thought she was going to pitch forward off her stool. She closed her eyes and hung on. She was hearing about what somebody had planned for us last night.

'And?' Finlay said.

'The woman was mutilated,' the doctor said. 'Breasts severed, genital area attacked, throat cut. Then the man's throat was cut. That was the last wound inflicted. You could see the arterial spray from his neck overlaying all the other bloodstains in the room.'

There was dead silence in the room. Lasted quite a while.

'Weapons?' I asked.

The guy at the desk swivelled his tired gaze towards me.

'Something sharp, obviously,' he said. A slight grin. 'Straight, maybe five inches long.'

'A razor?' I said.

'No,' he said. 'Certainly something as sharp as a razor, but rigid, not folding, and double-edged.'

'Why?' I said.

'There's evidence it was used back and forth,' the guy said. He swished his hand back and forth in a tiny arc. 'Like this. On the woman's breasts. Cutting both ways. Like filleting a salmon.'

I nodded. Roscoe and Finlay were silent.

'What about the other guy?' I said. 'Stoller?'

The pathologist pushed the two Morrison files

to one side and opened up the third. Glanced through it and looked across at me. The third file was thicker than the first two.

'His name was Stoller?' he said. 'We've got him down as John Doe.'

Roscoe looked up.

'We sent you a fax,' she said. 'Yesterday morning. We traced his prints.'

The pathologist rooted around on the messy desk. Found a curled-up fax. Read it and nodded. Crossed out 'John Doe' on the folder and wrote in 'Sherman Stoller'. Gave us his little grin again.

'I've had him since Sunday,' he said. 'Been able to do a more thorough job, you know? A bit chewed up by the rats, but not pulped like the first guy, and altogether a lot less mess than the Morrisons.'

'So what can you tell us?' I said.

'We've talked about the bullets, right?' he said. 'Nothing more to add about the exact cause of death.'

'So what else do you know?' I asked him.

The file was too thick for just the shooting and running and bleeding to death bits. This guy clearly had more to tell us. I saw him put his fingers on the pages and press lightly. Like he was trying to get vibrations or read the file in Braille.

'He was a truck driver,' he said.

'He was?' I said.

'I think so,' the guy said. Sounded confident.

Finlay looked up. He was interested. He loved the process of deduction. It fascinated him. Like when I'd scored with those long shots about Harvard, his divorce, quitting smoking.

'Go on,' he said.

'OK, briefly,' the pathologist said. 'I found

certain persuasive factors. A sedentary job, because his musculature was slack, his posture poor, flabby buttocks. Slightly rough hands, a fair bit of old diesel fuel ingrained in the skin. Also traces of old diesel fuel on the soles of his shoes. Internally, a poor diet, high in fat, plus a bit too much hydrogen sulphide in the blood gases and the tissues. This guy spent his life on the road, sniffing other people's catalytic converters. I make him a truck driver, because of the diesel fuel.'

Finlay nodded. I nodded. Stoller had come in with no ID, no history, nothing but his watch. This guy was pretty good. He watched us nod our approval. Looked pleased. Looked like he had more to say.

'But he's been out of work for a while,' he said.

'Why?' Finlay asked him.

'Because all that evidence is old,' the doctor said. 'Looks to me like he was driving a lot for a long period, but then he stopped. I think he's done very little driving for nine months, maybe a year. So I make him a truck driver, but an unemployed truck driver.'

'OK, doc, good work,' Finlay said. 'You got copies of all that for us?'

The doctor slid a large envelope across the desk. Finlay stepped over and picked it up. Then we all stood up. I wanted to get out. I didn't want to go back to the cold store again. I didn't want to see any more damage. Roscoe and Finlay sensed it and nodded. We hustled out like we were ten minutes late for something. The guy at the desk let us go. He'd seen lots of people rushing out of his office like they were ten minutes late for something.

We got into Roscoe's car. Finlay opened the big

envelope and pulled out the stuff on Sherman Stoller. Folded it into his pocket.

'That's ours, for the time being,' he said. 'It might get us somewhere.'

'I'll get the arrest report from Florida,' Roscoe said. 'And we'll find an address for him somewhere. Got to be a lot of paperwork on a trucker, right? Union, medical, licences. Should be easy enough to do.'

We rode the rest of the way back to Margrave in silence. The station house was deserted, apart from the desk guy. Lunch break in Margrave, lunch break in Washington DC. Same time zone. Finlay handed me a scrap of paper from his pocket and stood guard on the door to the rosewood office. I went inside to call the woman who may have been my brother's lover.

The number Finlay had handed me reached Molly Beth Gordon's private line. She answered on the first ring. I gave her my name. It made her cry.

'You sound so much like Joe,' she said.

I didn't reply. I didn't want to get into a whole lot of reminiscing. Neither should she, not if she was stepping out of line and was in danger of being overheard. She should just tell me what she had to tell me and get off the line.

'So what was Joe doing down here?' I asked her.

I heard her sniffing, and then her voice came back clear.

'He was running an investigation,' she said. 'Into what, I don't know specifically.'

'But what sort of a thing?' I asked her. 'What was his job?'

'Don't you know?' she said.

'No,' I said. 'We found it very hard to keep in touch, I'm afraid. You'll have to start from the beginning for me.'

There was a long pause on the line.

'OK,' she said. 'I shouldn't tell you this. Not without clearance. But I will. It was counterfeiting. He ran the Treasury's anticounterfeiting operation.'

'Counterfeiting?' I said. 'Counterfeit money?'

'Yes,' she said. 'He was head of the department. Ran the whole show. He was an amazing guy, Jack.'

'But why was he down here in Georgia?' I asked her.

'I don't know,' she said. 'I really don't. What I aim to do is find out for you. I can copy his files. I know his computer password.'

There was another pause. Now I knew something about Molly Beth Gordon. I'd spent a lot of time on computer passwords. Any military cop does. I'd studied the pyschology. Most users make bad choices. A lot of them write the damn word on a Post-It note and stick it on the monitor case. The ones who are too smart to do that use their spouse's name, or their dog's name, or their favourite car or ball player, or the name of the island where they took their honeymoon or balled their secretary. The ones who think they're really smart use figures, not words, but they choose their birthday or their wedding anniversary or something pretty obvious. If you can find something out about the user, you've normally got a better than even chance of figuring their password.

But that would never work with Joe. He was a professional. He'd spent important years in Military Intelligence. His password would be a random mixture of numbers, letters, punctuation marks, upper and lower case. His password would be unbreakable. If Molly Beth Gordon knew what it was, Joe must have told her. No other way. He had really trusted her. He had been really close to her. So I put some tenderness into my voice.

'Molly, that would be great,' I said. 'I really need that information.'

'I know you do,' she said. 'I hope to get it tomorrow. I'll call you again, soon as I can. Soon as I know something.'

'Is there counterfeiting going on down here?' I asked her. 'Is that what this could be all about?'

'No,' she said. 'It doesn't happen like that. Not inside the States. All that stuff about little guys with green eyeshades down in secret cellars printing dollar bills is all nonsense. Just doesn't happen. Joe stopped it. Your brother was a genius, Jack. He set up procedures years ago for the special paper sales and the inks, so if somebody starts up, he gets nailed within days. One hundred per cent foolproof. Printing money in the States just doesn't happen any more. Joe made sure of that. It all happens abroad. Any fakes we get here are shipped in. That's what Joe spent his time chasing. International stuff. Why he was in Georgia, I don't know. I really don't. But I'll find out tomorrow, I promise you that.'

I gave her the station house number and told her to speak to nobody except me or Roscoe or Finlay. Then she hung up in a hurry like somebody had just walked in on her. I sat for a moment and tried to imagine what she looked like.

Teale was back in the station house. And old man Kliner was inside with him. They were over by the reception counter, heads together. Kliner was talking to Teale like I'd seen him talking to Eno at the diner. Foundation business, maybe. Roscoe and Finlay were standing together by the cells. I walked over to them. Stood between them and talked low.

'Counterfeiting,' I said. 'This is about counterfeit money. Joe was running the Treasury Department's defence for them. You know anything about that sort of a thing down here? Either of you?'

They both shrugged and shook their heads. I heard the glass door suck open. Looked up. Kliner was on his way out. Teale was starting in toward us.

'I'm out of here,' I said.

I brushed past Teale and headed for the door. Kliner was standing in the lot, next to the black pickup. Waiting for me. He smiled. Wolf's teeth showing.

'Sorry for your loss,' he said.

His voice had a quiet, cultured tone. Educated. A slight hiss on the sibilants. Not the voice to go with his sunbaked appearance.

'You upset my son,' he said.

He looked at me. Something burning in his eyes. I shrugged.

'The kid upset me first,' I said.

'How?' Kliner asked. Sharply.

'He lived and breathed?' I said.

I moved on across the lot. Kliner slid into the black pickup. Fired it up and nosed out. He turned north. I turned south. Started the walk down to Roscoe's place. It was a half-mile through the new fall chill. Ten minutes at a brisk pace. I got the Bentley out of the garage. Drove it back up the slope to town. Made the right onto Main Street and cruised along. I was peering left and right in under the smart striped awnings, looking for the clothes store. Found it three doors north of the barbershop. Left the Bentley on the street and went in. Paid out some of Charlie Hubble's expenses cash to a sullen middle-aged guy for a pair of pants, a shirt and a jacket. A light fawn colour, pressed cotton, as near to formal as I was prepared to go. No tie. I put it all on in the changing cubicle in the back of the store. Bagged up the old stuff and threw it in the Bentley's trunk as I passed.

I walked the three doors south to the barbershop. The younger of the two old guys was on his way out of the door. He stopped and put his hand on my arm.

'What's your name, son?' he asked me.

No reason not to tell him. Not that I could see.

'Jack Reacher,' I said.

'You got any Hispanic friends in town?'

'No,' I said.

'Well, you got some now,' he said. 'Two guys, looking all over for you.'

I looked at him. He scanned the street.

'Who were they?' I asked him.

'Never saw them before,' the old guy said. 'Little guys, brown car, fancy shirts. Been all over, asking for Jack Reacher. We told them we never heard of no Jack Reacher.'

'When was this?' I said.

'This morning,' he said. 'After breakfast.'

I nodded.

'OK,' I said. 'Thanks.'

The guy held the door open for me.

'Go right in,' he said. 'My partner will take care

of you. But he's a bit skittish this morning. Getting old.'

'Thanks,' I said again. 'See you around.'

'Sure hope so, son,' he said.

He strolled off down Main Street and I went inside his shop. The older guy was in there. The gnarled old man whose sister had sung with Blind Blake. No other customers. I nodded to the old guy and sat down in his chair.

'Good morning, my friend,' he said.

'You remember me?' I said.

'Sure do,' he said. 'You were our last customer. Nobody in between to muddle me up.'

I asked him for a shave and he set about whipping up the lather.

'I was your last customer?' I said. 'That was Sunday. Today is Tuesday. Business always that bad?'

The old guy paused and gestured with the razor.

'Been that bad for years,' he said. 'Old Mayor Teale won't come in here, and what the old mayor won't do, nobody else white will do neither. Except old Mr Gray from the station house, came in here regular as clockwork three, four times a week, until he went and hung himself, God rest his soul. You're the first white face in here since last February, yes sir, that's for sure.'

'Why won't Teale come in here?' I asked him.

'Man's got a problem,' the old guy said. 'I figure he don't like to sit all swathed up in the towel while there's a black man standing next him with a razor. Maybe worried something bad might happen to him.'

'Might something bad happen to him?' I said.

He laughed a short laugh.

'I figure there's a serious risk,' he said. 'Asshole.'

'So you got enough black customers to make a living?' I asked him.

He put the towel around my shoulders and started brushing on the lather.

'Man, we don't need customers to make a living,' he said.

'You don't?' I said. 'Why not?'

'We got the community money,' he said.

'You do?' I said. 'What's that?'

'Thousand dollars,' he said.

'Who gives you that?' I asked him.

He started scraping my chin. His hand was shaking like old people do.

'Kliner Foundation,' he whispered. 'The community programme. It's a business grant. All the merchants get it. Been getting it five years.'

I nodded.

'That's good,' I said. 'But a thousand bucks a year won't keep you. It's better than a poke in the eye, but you need customers too, right?'

I was just making conversation, like you do with barbers. But it set the old guy off. He was shaking and cackling. Had a whole lot of trouble finishing the shave. I was staring into the mirror. After last night, it would be a hell of a thing to get my throat cut by accident.

'Man, I shouldn't tell you about it,' he whispered. 'But seeing as you're a friend of my sister's, I'm going to tell you a big secret.'

He was getting confused. I wasn't a friend of his sister's. Didn't even know her. He'd told me about her, was all. He was standing there with the razor. We were looking at each other in the mirror. Like with Finlay in the coffee shop.

'It's not a thousand dollars a year,' he whispered. Then he bent close to my ear. 'It's a thousand dollars a week.'

He started stomping around, chuckling like a demon. He filled the sink and dabbed off the spare lather. Patted my face down with a hot wet cloth. Then he whipped the towel off my shoulders like a conjurer doing a trick.

'That's why we don't need no customers,' he cackled.

I paid him and got out. The guy was crazy.

'Say hello to my sister,' he called after me.

SEVENTEEN

The trip to Atlanta was the best part of fifty miles. Took nearly an hour. The highway swept me right into the city. I headed for the tallest buildings. Soon as I started to see marble foyers I dumped the car and walked to the nearest corner and asked a cop for the commercial district.

He gave me a half-mile walk after which I found one bank after another. Sunrise International had its own building. It was a big glass tower set back behind a piazza with a fountain. That part looked like Milan, but the entranceway at the base of the tower was clad in heavy stone, trying to look like Frankfurt or London. Trying to look like a big heavy-duty bank. Foyer full of dark carpet and leather. Receptionist behind a mahogany counter. Could have been a quiet hotel.

I asked for Paul Hubble's office and the receptionist flipped through a directory. She said she was sorry, but she was new in the job and she didn't recognize me, so would I wait while she got clearance for my visit? She dialled a number and started a low conversation. Then she covered the phone with her hand.

'May I say what it's in connection with?'

'I'm a friend,' I said.

She resumed the phone call and then directed me to an elevator. I had to go to reception on the seventeenth floor. I got in the elevator and tapped the button. Stood there while it carried me up.

The seventeenth floor looked even more like a gentleman's club than the entrance foyer had. It was carpeted and panelled and dim. Full of glowing antiques and old pictures. As I waded across the thick pile a door opened and a suit stepped out to meet me. Shook my hand and fussed me back into a little anteroom. He introduced himself as some sort of a manager and we sat down.

'So how may I help you?' he asked.

'I'm looking for Paul Hubble,' I said.

'May I know why?'

'He's an old friend,' I said. 'I remembered him saying he works here, so I thought I'd look him up while I'm passing through.'

The guy in the suit nodded. Dropped his gaze.

'Thing is, you see,' he said, 'Mr Hubble doesn't work here any more. We had to let him go, I'm afraid, about eighteen months ago.'

I just nodded blankly. Then I sat there in the clubby little office and looked at the guy in the suit and waited. A bit of silence might set him talking. If I asked him questions straight out, he might clam up. He might go all confidential, like lawyers do. But I could see he was a chatty type of a guy. A lot of those managers are. They love to impress the hell out of you, given the chance. So I sat tight and waited. Then the guy started apologizing to me because I was Hubble's friend.

'No fault of his own, you understand,' he said. 'He did an excellent job, but it was in a field we moved out of. A strategic business decision, very unfortunate for the people concerned, but there you are.'

I nodded at him like I understood.

'I haven't been in touch for a long time,' I said. 'I didn't know. I didn't even really know what he did here.'

I smiled at him. Tried to look amiable and ignorant. Didn't take much effort, in a bank. I gave him my best receptive look. Guaranteed to set a chatty guy talking. It had worked for me plenty of times before.

'He was part of our retail operation,' the guy said. 'We closed it down.'

I looked enquiringly at him.

'Retail?' I said.

'Over-the-counter banking,' he said. 'You know, cash, cheques, loans, personal customers.'

'And you closed that down?' I said. 'Why?'

'Too expensive,' he said. 'Big overhead, small margin. It had to go.'

'And Hubble was a part of that?' I asked him.

He nodded.

'Mr Hubble was our currency manager,' he said. 'It was an important position. He was very good.'

'So what was his exact role?' I asked him.

The guy didn't know how to explain it. Didn't know where to start. He made a couple of attempts and gave them up.

'Do you understand cash?' he said.

'I've got some,' I said. 'I don't know if I understand it, exactly.'

He got to his feet and gave me a fussy gesture. Wanted me to join him at the window. We peered out together at the people on the street, seventeen floors down. He pointed at a guy in a suit, hurrying along the sidewalk.

'Take that gentleman,' he said. 'Let's make a few guesses, shall we? Probably lives in the outer suburbs, maybe has a vacation cabin somewhere, two big mortgages, two cars, half a dozen mutual funds, pension provision, some blue chip stock, college plans, five or six credit cards, store cards, charge cards. Net worth about a half-million, shall we say?'

'OK,' I said.

'But how much cash does he have?' the guy asked me.

'No idea,' I said.

'Probably about fifty dollars,' he said. 'About fifty dollars in a leather billfold which cost him a hundred and fifty dollars.'

I looked at him. I wasn't following his drift. The guy changed gear. Became very patient with me.

'The US economy is huge,' he said. 'Net assets and net liabilities are incalculably large. Trillions of dollars. But almost none of it is actually represented by cash. That gentleman had a net worth of a half-million dollars, but only fifty of it was in actual cash. All the rest of it is on paper or in computers. The fact is, there isn't much actual cash around. There's only about a hundred and thirty billion actual cash dollars inside the whole US.'

I shrugged at him again.

'Sounds like enough to me,' I said.

The guy looked at me severely.

'But how many people are there?' he asked me. 'Nearly three hundred million. That's only about four hundred and fifty actual cash dollars per head of population. That's the problem a retail bank has to deal with, day by day. Four hundred and fifty dollars is a very modest cash withdrawal, but if everybody chose to make such a withdrawal, the nation's banks would run out of cash in the blink of an eye.'

He stopped and looked at me. I nodded.

'OK,' I said. 'I see that.'

'And most of that cash isn't in banks,' he said. 'It's in Vegas or at the racetrack. It's concentrated in what we call cash-intensive areas of the economy. So a good currency manager, and Mr Hubble was one of the very best, has a constant battle just to keep enough paper dollars on hand in our part of the system. He has to reach out and find them. He has to know where to locate them. He has to sniff them out. It's not easy. In the end, it was one of the factors which made retail so expensive for us. One of the reasons why we pulled out. We kept it going as long as we could, but we had to close the operation eventually. We had to let Mr Hubble go. We were very sorry about it.'

'Any idea where he's working now?' I said.

He shook his head.

'I'm afraid not,' he said.

'Must be working somewhere, right?' I said.

The guy shook his head again.

'Professionally, he's dropped out of sight,' he said. 'He's not working in banking, I'm sure of that. His institute membership lapsed immediately, and we've never had an enquiry for a recommendation. I'm sorry, but I can't help you. If he was working anywhere in banking, I'd know it, I can assure you of that. He must be in something else now.'

I shrugged. Hubble's trail was stone cold. And the discussion with this guy was over. His body language indicated it. He was shifting forward, ready to get up and get on. I stood up with him. Thanked him for his time. Shook his hand. Stepped through the antique gloom to the elevator. Hit the button for the street and walked out into the dull grey weather.

My assumptions had been all wrong. I had seen Hubble as a banker, doing a straight job. Maybe turning a blind eye to some peripheral con, maybe with half a finger in some dirty pie. Maybe signing off on a few bogus figures. With his arm twisted way up his back. Involved, useful, tainted, but somehow not central. But he hadn't been a banker. Not for a year and a half. He had been a criminal. Full time. Right inside the scam. Right at the centre. Not peripheral at all.

I drove straight back to the Margrave station house. Parked up and went looking for Roscoe. Teale was stalking around in the open area, but the desk guy winked and nodded me back to a file room. Roscoe was in there. She looked weary. She had an armful of old files. She smiled.

'Hello, Reacher,' she said. 'Come to take me away from all this?'

'What's new?' I said.

She dumped the stack of paper onto a cabinet top. Dusted herself off and flicked her hair back. Glanced at the door.

'Couple of things,' she said. 'Teale's got a Foundation board meeting in ten minutes. I'm getting the fax from Florida soon as he's out of here. And we're due a call from the state police about abandoned cars.'

'Where's the gun you've got for me?' I asked her.

She paused. Bit her lip. She was remembering why I needed one.

'It's in a box,' she said. 'In my desk. We'll have to wait until Teale is gone. And don't open it here, OK? Nobody knows about it.'

We stepped out of the file room and walked over toward the rosewood office. The squad room was quiet. The two backup guys from Friday were paging through computer records. Neat stacks of files were everywhere. The bogus hunt was on for the chief's killer. I saw a big new bulletin board on the wall. It was marked: Morrison. It was empty. Not much progress was being made.

We waited in the rosewood office with Finlay. Five minutes. Ten. Then we heard a knock and Baker ducked his head around the door. He grinned in at us. I saw his gold tooth again.

'Teale's gone,' he said.

We went out into the open area. Roscoe turned on the fax machine and picked up the phone to call Florida. Finlay dialled the state police for news on abandoned rental cars. I sat down at the desk next to Roscoe's and called Charlie Hubble. I dialled the mobile number that Joe had printed out and hidden in his shoe. I got no answer. Just an electronic sound and a recorded voice telling me the phone I was calling was switched off.

I looked across at Roscoe.

'She's got the damn mobile switched off,' I said.

Roscoe shrugged and moved over to the fax machine. Finlay was still talking to the state police. I saw Baker hanging around on the fringe of the triangle the three of us were making. I got up and went to join Roscoe.

'Does Baker want in on this?' I asked her.

'He seems to,' she said. 'Finlay's got him acting as a kind of a lookout. Should we get him involved?'

I thought about it for a second, but shook my head.

'No,' I said. 'Smaller the better, a thing like this, right?'

I sat down again at the desk I was borrowing and tried the mobile number again. Same result. Same patient electronic voice telling me it was switched off.

'Damn,' I said to myself. 'Can you believe that?'

I needed to know where Hubble had spent his time for the last year and a half. Charlie might have given me some idea. The time he left home in the morning, the time he got home at night, toll receipts, restaurant bills, things like that. And she might have remembered something about Sunday or something about Pluribus. It was possible she might have come up with something useful. And I needed something useful. I needed it very badly. And she'd switched the damn phone off.

'Reacher?' Roscoe said. 'I got the stuff on Sherman Stoller.'

She was holding a couple of fax pages. Densely typed.

'Great,' I said. 'Let's take a look.'

Finlay got off the phone and stepped over.

'State guys are calling back,' he said. 'They may have something for us.'

'Great,' I said again. 'Maybe we're getting somewhere.'

We all went back into the rosewood office. Spread the Sherman Stoller stuff out on the desk and bent over it together. It was an arrest report from the police department in Jacksonville, Florida.

'Blind Blake was born in Jacksonville,' I said. 'Did you know that?'

'Who's Blind Blake?' Roscoe asked.

'Singer,' Finlay said.

'Guitar player, Finlay,' I said.

Sherman Stoller had been flagged down by a sector car for exceeding the speed limit on the river bridge between Jacksonville and Jacksonville Beach at a quarter to midnight on a September night, two years ago. He had been driving a small panel truck eleven miles an hour too fast. He had become extremely agitated and abusive toward the sector car crew. This had caused them to arrest him for suspected DUI. He had been printed and photographed at Jacksonville Central and both he and his vehicle had been searched. He had given an Atlanta address and stated his occupation as truck driver.

The search of his person produced a negative result. His truck was searched by hand and with dogs and produced a negative result. The truck contained nothing but a cargo of twenty new air conditioners boxed for export from Jacksonville Beach. The boxes were sealed and marked with the manufacturer's logo, and each box was marked with a serial number.

After being Mirandized, Stoller had made one phone call. Within twenty minutes of the call, a lawyer named Perez from the respected Jacksonville firm of Zacarias Perez was in attendance, and within a further ten minutes Stoller had been released. From being flagged down to walking out with the lawyer, fifty-five minutes had elapsed.

'Interesting,' Finlay said. 'The guy's three hundred miles from home, it's midnight, and he gets lawyered up within twenty minutes? With a partner from a respected firm? Stoller was some kind of a truck driver, that's for sure.'

'You recognize his address?' I asked Roscoe.

She shook her head.

'Not really,' she said. 'But I could find it.'

The door cracked open and Baker stuck his head in again.

'State police on the line,' he said. 'Sounds like they got a car for you.'

Finlay checked his watch. Decided there was time before Teale got back.

'OK,' he said. 'Punch it through here, Baker.'

Finlay picked up the phone on the big desk and listened. Scribbled some notes and grunted a thank-you. Hung the phone up and got out of his chair.

'OK,' he said. 'Let's go take a look.'

We all three filed out quickly. We needed to be well clear before Teale got back and started asking questions. Baker watched us go. Called out after us.

'What should I tell Teale?' he said.

'Tell him we traced the car,' Finlay said. 'The one the crazy ex-con used to get down to Morrison's place. Tell him we're making some real progress, OK?'

This time Finlay drove. He was using an unmarked Chevy, identical to Roscoe's issue. He bounced it out of the lot and turned south. Accelerated through the little town. The first few miles I recognized as the route down toward Yellow Springs, but then we swung off onto a track which struck out due east. It led out toward the highway and ended up in a kind of maintenance area, right below the roadway. There were piles of asphalt and tar barrels lying around. And a car. It had been rolled off the highway and it was lying on its roof. And it was burned out.

'They noticed it Friday morning,' Finlay said. 'Wasn't here Thursday, they're sure about that. It could have been Joe's.'

We looked it over very carefully. Wasn't much left to see. It was totally burned out. Everything that wasn't steel had gone. We couldn't even tell what make it had been. By the shape, Finlay thought it had been a General Motors product, but we couldn't tell which division. It had been a mid-size sedan, and once the plastic trim has gone, you can't tell a Buick from a Chevy from a Pontiac.

I got Finlay to support the front fender and I crawled under the upside-down hood. Looked for the number they stamp on the scuttle. I had to scrape off some scorched flakes, but I found the little aluminium strip and got most of the number. Crawled out again and recited it to Roscoe. She wrote it down.

'So what do you think?' Finlay asked.

'Could be the one,' I said. 'Say he rented it Thursday evening up at the airport in Atlanta, full tank of gas. Drove it to the warehouses at the Margrave cloverleaf, then somebody drove it on down here afterward. Couple of gallons gone, maybe two and a half. Plenty left to burn.'

Finlay nodded.

'Makes sense,' he said. 'But they'd have to be local guys. This is a great spot to dump a car, right? Pull onto the shoulder up there, wheels in the dirt, push the car off the edge, scramble down and torch it, then jump in with your buddy who's already down here in his own car waiting for you, and you're away. But only if you knew about this little maintenance track. And only a local guy would know about this little maintenance track, right?'

We left the wreck there. Drove back up to the station house. The desk sergeant was waiting for Finlay.

'Teale wants you in the office,' he said.

Finlay grunted and was heading back there, but I caught his arm.

'Keep him talking a while,' I said. 'Give Roscoe a chance to phone in that number from the car.'

He nodded and carried on to the back. Roscoe and I headed over to her desk. She picked up the phone, but I stopped her.

'Give me the gun,' I whispered. 'Before Teale is through with Finlay.'

She nodded and glanced around the room. Sat down and unclipped the keys from her belt. Unlocked her desk and rolled open a deep drawer. Nodded down to a shallow cardboard box. I picked it out. It was an office storage box, about two inches deep, for holding papers. The cardboard was printed with elaborate woodgrain. Someone had written a name across the top. Gray. I tucked it under my arm and nodded to Roscoe. She rolled the drawer shut and locked it again.

'Thanks,' I said. 'Now make those calls, OK?'

I walked down to the entrance and levered the heavy glass door open with my back. Carried the box over to the Bentley. I set the box on the roof of the car and unlocked the door. Dumped the box on the passenger seat and got in. Pulled the box over onto my lap. Saw a brown sedan slowing up on the road about a hundred yards to the north.

Two Hispanic men in it. The same car I'd seen outside Charlie Hubble's place the day before. The same guys. No doubt about that. Their car came to a stop about seventy-five yards from the station house. I saw it settle, like the engine had been turned off. Neither of the guys got out. They just sat there, seventy-five yards away, watching the station house parking lot. Seemed to me they were looking straight at the Bentley. Seemed to me my new friends had found me. They'd looked all morning. Now they didn't have to look any more. They didn't move. Just sat there, watching. I watched them back for more than five minutes. They weren't going to get out. I could see that. They were settled there. So I turned my attention back to the box.

It was empty apart from a box of bullets and a gun. A hell of a weapon. It was a Desert Eagle automatic. I'd used one before. They come from Israel. We used to get them in exchange for all kinds of stuff we sent over there. I picked it up. Very heavy, fourteen inch barrel, more than a foot and a half long, front to back. I clicked out the magazine. This was the eight-shot .44 version. Takes eight .44-Magnum shells. Not what you would call a subtle weapon. The bullet weighs about twice as much as the .38 in a police revolver. It leaves the barrel going way faster than the speed of sound. It hits the target with more force than anything this side of a train wreck. Not subtle at all. Ammunition is a problem. You've got a choice. If you load up with a hard-nose bullet, it goes right through the guy you're shooting and probably right on through some other guy a hundred yards away. So you use a soft-nose bullet and it blows a hole out of your guy about the size of a garbage can. Your choice.

The bullets in the box were all soft-nose. OK with me. I checked the weapon over. Brutal, but in fine condition. Everything worked. The grip was engraved with a name. Gray. Same as the file box. The dead detective, the guy before Finlay. Hanged himself last February. Must have been a gun collector. This wasn't his service piece. No police department in the world would authorize the use of a cannon like this on the job. Altogether too heavy.

I loaded the dead detective's big handgun with eight of his shells. Put the spares back in the box and left the box on the floor of the car. Cocked the gun and clicked the safety catch on. Cocked and locked, we used to call it. Saves you a split-second before your first shot. Saves your life, maybe. I put the gun in the Bentley's walnut glove compartment. It was a tight fit.

Then I sat for a moment and watched the two guys in their car. They were still watching me. We looked at each other from seventy-five yards away. They were relaxed and comfortable. But they were watching me. I got out of the Bentley and locked it up again. Stepped back to the entrance and pulled the door. Glanced back toward the brown sedan. Still there. Still watching.

Roscoe was at her desk, talking on the phone. She waved. Looked excited. Held her hand up to tell me to wait. I watched the door to the rosewood office. Hoped Teale wouldn't come out before she finished her call.

He came out just as she hung up. He was all red in the face. Looked mad. Started stamping around the squad room, banging his heavy stick on the floor. Glaring up at the big empty bulletin board. Finlay stuck his head out of the office and nodded me in. I shrugged at Roscoe and went to see what Finlay had to say.

'What was that all about?' I asked him.

He laughed.

'I was winding him up,' he said. 'He asked what we'd been doing, looking at a car. I said we weren't. Said we'd told Baker we weren't going far, but he'd misheard it as we're looking at a car.'

'Take care, Finlay,' I said. 'They're killing people. This is a big deal.'

He shrugged.

'It's driving me crazy,' he said. 'Got to have some fun, right?'

He'd survived twenty years in Boston. He might survive this.

'What's happening with Picard?' I asked him. 'You heard from him?'

'Nothing,' he said. 'Just standing by.'

'No possibility he might have put a couple of guys on surveillance?' I said.

Finlay shook his head. Looked definite about it.

'No way,' he said. 'Not without telling me first. Why?'

'There's a couple of guys watching this place,' I said. 'Got here about ten minutes ago. Plain brown sedan. They were at Hubble's yesterday and around town this morning, asking after me.'

He shook his head again.

'They're not Picard's,' he said. 'He'd have told me.'

Roscoe came in and shut the door. Held it shut with her hand like Teale might try to burst in after her.

'I called Detroit,' she said. 'It was a Pontiac. Delivered four months ago. Big fleet order for a rental company. DMV is tracing the registration. I told them to get back to Picard up in Atlanta. The rental people might be able to give him the story about where it was rented. We might be getting somewhere.'

I felt I was getting closer to Joe. Like I was hearing a faint echo.

'Great,' I said to her. 'Good work, Roscoe. I'm out of here. Meet you back here at six. You two

270

stick close together, OK? Watch your backs.'

'Where are you going?' Finlay said.

'I'm going for a drive in the country,' I said.

I left them there in the office and walked back to the entrance. Pushed the door open and stepped outside. Scanned north up the road. The plain sedan was still there, seventy-five yards away. The two guys were still in it. Still watching. I walked over to the Bentley. Unlocked the door and got in. Nosed out of the parking lot and pulled out onto the county road. Wide and slow. Drove slowly past the two guys and carried on north. In the mirror I saw the plain sedan start up. Saw it pull out and turn in the road. It accelerated north and fell in behind me. Like I was towing it on a long invisible rope. I slowed, it slowed. I sped up, it sped up. Like a game.

EIGHTEEN

I drove past Eno's diner and rolled on north away from town. The plain sedan followed. Forty yards back. No attempt to hide. The two guys just cruised behind me. Gazing forward. I swung west on the road to Warburton. Slowed to a cruise. The plain sedan followed. Still forty yards back. We cruised west. We were the only things moving in that vast landscape. I could see the two guys in the mirror. Gazing at me. They were spotlit by the low afternoon sun. The low, brassy light made them vivid. Young guys, Hispanic, loud shirts, black hair, very neat, very similar. Their car sat steadily in my wake.

I cruised seven or eight miles. I was looking for a place. There were bumpy earth tracks off to the left and right, every half-mile or so. They led into the fields. Looped around aimlessly. I didn't know what they were for. Maybe they led to gathering points where farmers parked machinery for the harvest. Whenever that was. I was looking for a particular track I'd seen before. It led around behind a small stand of trees on the right-hand side of the road. The only cover for miles. I'd seen it from the prison bus on Friday. Seen it again driving back in from Alabama. A sturdy stand of trees. This morning it had been floating on the mist. A little oval copse, next to the road, on the right, an earth track looping behind it, then joining up with the road again.

I saw it a couple of miles ahead. The trees were a smudge on the horizon. I drove on towards it. Snapped the glove compartment open and lifted the big automatic out. Wedged it between the squabs on the seat next to me. The two guys followed. Still forty yards back. A quarter-mile from the woods I slammed the selector into second and floored the pedal. The old car gulped and shot forwards. At the track I hauled the wheel around and bounced and slewed the Bentley off the road. Hurled it around to the back of the copse. Jammed it to a stop. Grabbed the gun and jumped. Left the driver's door swinging open like I'd tumbled out and dived straight left into the trees.

But I went the other way. I went to the right. I danced around the hood and hurled myself fifteen feet into the peanut field and flattened into the ground. Crawled through the bushes and put myself on a level with where their car would have to stop on the track behind the Bentley. Pressed myself up against the brawny stalks, low down under the leaves, on the damp red earth. Then I waited. I figured they'd dropped off maybe sixty or seventy yards. They hadn't tracked my sudden acceleration. I snicked the safety catch off. Then I heard their brown Buick. I caught the noise of the motor and the groan of the suspension. It bounced into view on the track in front of me. It stopped behind the Bentley, framed against the trees. It was about twenty feet away from me.

They were reasonably smart guys. Not at all the worst I'd ever seen. The passenger had gotten out on the road before they turned in. He thought I was in the woods. He thought he was going to come at me from behind. The driver scrambled across inside the car and rolled out of the passenger door on the far side from the trees. Right in front of me. He was holding a gun and he knelt down in the dirt, his back turned to me, hidden from where he thought I was by the Buick, looking through the car at the woods. I'd have to make him move. I didn't want him to stay next to the car. The car had to stay driveable. I didn't want it damaged.

They were wary of the copse. That had been the idea. Why would I drive all the way to the only woods for miles, and then hide in a field? A classic diversion. They'd fallen for it without even thinking. The guy by the car was staring through at the woods. I was staring at his back. I had the Desert Eagle lined up on him, breathing low. His partner was creeping slowly through the trees, looking for me. Pretty soon he'd come right out into view.

He arrived after about five minutes. He was holding a gun out in front of him. He dodged around the back of the Buick. Kept distance between himself and the Bentley. He crouched down next to his partner and they exchanged shrugs. Then they started peering at the Bentley. Worried that I was lying on the floor or crouching behind the stately chrome radiator. The guy who'd just come out of the woods crawled along in the dirt, keeping the Buick between himself and the trees, right in front of me, staring under the Bentley, looking for my feet.

He crawled the whole length of the Bentley. I could hear him grunting and gasping as he hauled himself along on his elbows. Then he crawled all the way back and knelt up again beside his partner. They both shuffled sideways and slowly stood up next to the Buick's hood. They stepped over and checked inside the Bentley. They walked together to the edge of the copse and peered into the darkness. They couldn't find me. Then they came back and stood together on the rough track, away from the cars, framed against the orange sky, staring at the trees, their backs to the field, their backs to me.

They didn't know what to do. They were city boys. Maybe from Miami. They wore Florida clothes. They were used to neon alleys and construction sites. They were used to action under raised highways, in the trash-filled lots the tourists never saw. They didn't know what to do about a small copse standing alone in a million acres of peanuts.

I shot them both in the back as they stood there. Two quick shots. Aimed high up between their shoulder blades. The big automatic made a sound like hand grenades going off. Birds wheeled into the air from all around. The twin crashes rolled over the countryside like thunder. The recoils pounded my hand. The two guys were hurled forward off their feet. Landed on their faces sprawled against the trees on the far side of the earth track. I raised my head and peered over. They had that slack, empty look that is left behind when life has departed.

I held onto the gun and stepped over to them. They were dead. I had seen a lot of dead people, and these two were as dead as any of them. The big Magnum shells had caught them high up on their backs. Where the big arteries and veins are, going on up into the head. The bullets had made quite a mess. I looked down at the two guys in the silence and thought about Joe.

Then I had things to do. I stepped back to the Bentley. Clicked the safety on and tossed the Desert Eagle back on the seat. Stepped over to their Buick and yanked the keys out. Popped the trunk. I guess I was hoping to find something in there. I didn't feel bad about the two boys. But I was going to feel better still if I found something in there. Like a silenced .22 automatic. Or like four pairs of rubber overshoes and four nylon body-suits. A few five-inch blades. Things like that. But I didn't find things like that. I found Spivey.

He'd been dead a few hours. He'd been shot through the forehead with a .38. From close range. The revolver barrel must have been about six inches from his head. I rubbed my thumb across the skin around the bullet hole. Looked at it. There was no soot, but there were tiny gunpowder particles blasted into the skin. They wouldn't rub off. That kind of tattooing means a fairly close range. Six inches will do it, maybe eight. Somebody had suddenly raised a gun and the slow heavy assistant warden hadn't been quick enough to duck.

There was a scab on his chin where I'd cut him with Morrison's blade. His small snake eyes were open. He was still in his greasy uniform. His white hairy belly showed through where I'd slashed at his shirt. He had been a big guy. To fit him in the trunk, they'd broken his legs. Probably with a shovel. They'd broken them and folded them sideways at the knee to get his body in. I gazed at him and felt angry. He'd known, and he hadn't told me. But they'd killed him anyway. The fact that he hadn't told me hadn't counted for anything. They were panicking. They were silencing everybody, while the clock ticked slowly around to Sunday. I gazed into Spivey's dead eyes, like there was information still in there.

Then I ran back to the bodies on the edge of the copse and searched them. Two wallets and a car rental agreement. A mobile phone. That was all. The rental agreement was for the Buick. Rented at the Atlanta airport, Monday morning at eight. An early flight in from somewhere. I went through the wallets. No airline tickets. Florida driver's licences, both with Jacksonville addresses. Bland photographs, meaningless names. Credit cards to match. Lots of cash in the wallets. I stole it all. They weren't going to spend it.

I took the battery out of the mobile phone and put the phone in one guy's pocket and the battery in the other's. Then I dragged the bodies over to the Buick and heaved them into the trunk with Spivey. Not easy. They weren't tall guys, but they were floppy and awkward. Made me sweat, despite the chill. I had to shove them around to get them both in the space Spivey was leaving. I scouted around and found their revolvers. Both .38 calibre. One had a full load. The other had fired once. Smelled recent. I pitched the guns into the trunk. Found the passenger's shoes. The Desert Eagle had blown him right out of them. I threw them in the trunk and slammed the lid. Walked back into the field and found my hiding place in the bushes. Where I'd shot them from. Scrabbled around and picked up the two shell cases. Put them in my pocket.

Then I locked up the Buick and left it. Popped the Bentley's trunk. Pulled out the bag with my old clothes in. My new gear was covered in red mud and streaked with the dead guys' blood. I put the old things back on. Balled up the muddy blood-stained stuff and shoved it in the bag. Threw the bag in the Bentley's trunk and closed the lid on it. Last thing I did was use a tree branch to sweep away all the footprints I could see.

I drove the Bentley slowly back east to Margrave and used the time to calm down. A straightforward ambush, no technical difficulty, no real danger. I had thirteen years of hard time behind me. I should be able to walk through a one-on-two against amateurs in my sleep. But my heart was thumping harder than it should have been and a cold blast of adrenalin was shaking me up. It was the sight of Spivey lying there with his legs folded sideways that had done it. I breathed hard and got myself under control. My right arm was sore. Like somebody had hit my palm with a hammer. It jarred all the way up to the shoulder. That Desert Eagle had a hell of a recoil. And it made a hell of a noise. My ears were still ringing from the twin explosions. But I felt good. It had been a job well done. Two tough guys had followed me out there. They weren't following me back.

I parked up in the station house lot, furthest slot from the door. Put my gun back in the glove compartment and got out of the car. It was getting late. The evening gloom was gathering. The huge Georgia sky was darkening. Turning a deep inky shade. The moon was coming up.

Roscoe was at her desk. She got up when she saw me and walked over. We went back out through the door. Walked a few paces. Kissed.

'Anything from the car rental people?' I asked her.

She shook her head.

'Tomorrow,' she said. 'Picard's dealing with it. He's doing his best.'

'OK,' I said. 'What hotels you got up at the airport?'

She reeled off a list of hotels. Pretty much the same list you got at any airport. I picked the first name she'd listed. Then I told her what had happened with the two Florida boys. Last week, she'd have arrested me for it. Sent me to the chair. Now, her reaction was different. Those four men who had padded through her place in their rubber shoes had changed her mind about a lot of things. So she just nodded and smiled a tight grim smile of satisfaction.

'Two down,' she said. 'Good work, Reacher. Were they the ones?'

'From last night?' I said. 'No. They weren't local. We can't count them in Hubble's ten. They were hired help from outside.'

'Were they any good?' she asked.

I shrugged at her. Rocked my hand from side to side, equivocally.

'Not really,' I said. 'Not good enough, anyway.'

Then I told her what I had found in the Buick's trunk. She shivered again.

'So is he one of the ten?' she asked. 'Spivey?'

I shook my head.

'No,' I said. 'I can't see it. He was outside help, too. Nobody would have a slug like that on the inside.'

She nodded. I opened up the Bentley and got the gun out of the glove box. It was too big to go in my pocket. I put it back in the old file box with the bullets. Roscoe put the whole thing in the trunk of her Chevy. I got the carrier bag of stained clothes out. Locked the Bentley up and left it there in the police lot.

'I'm going to call Molly again,' I said. 'I'm getting in pretty deep. I need some background. There are things I don't understand.'

The place was quiet so I used the rosewood office. I dialled the Washington number and got Molly on the second ring.

'Can you talk?' I asked her.

She told me to wait, and I heard her get up and close her office door.

'It's too soon, Jack,' she said. 'I can't get the stuff until tomorrow.'

'I need background,' I said. 'I need to understand this international stuff Joe was doing. I need to know why things are happening here, if the action is supposed to be overseas.'

I heard her figuring out where to start.

'OK, background,' she said. 'I guess Joe's assumption was it's maybe controlled from this country. And it's a very difficult problem to explain, but I'll try. The forging happens abroad, and the trick is most of it stays abroad. Only a few of the fake bills ever come back here, which is not a huge deal domestically, but obviously it's something we want to stop. But abroad, it presents a completely different type of problem. You know how much cash is inside the US, Jack?'

I thought back to what the bank guy had told me.

'A hundred and thirty billion dollars,' I said.

'Right,' she said. 'But exactly twice that much is held offshore. That's a fact. People all over the

280

world are holding onto two hundred and sixty billion dollars' worth of American cash. It's in safety deposits in London, Rome, Berlin, Moscow, stuffed into mattresses all over South America, Eastern Europe, hidden under floorboards, false walls, in banks, travel agencies, everywhere. And why is that?'

'Don't know,' I said.

'Because the dollar is the world's most trusted currency,' she said. 'People believe in it. They want it. And naturally, the government is very, very happy about that.'

'Good for the ego, right?' I said.

I heard her change the phone to the other hand.

'It's not an emotional thing,' she said. 'It's business. Think about it, Jack. If there's a hundred-dollar bill in somebody's bureau in Bucharest, that means somebody somewhere once exchanged a hundred dollars' worth of foreign assets for it. It means our government sold them a piece of paper with green and black ink on it for a hundred bucks. Good business. And because it's a trusted currency, chances are that hundred-dollar bill will probably stay in that bureau in Bucharest for many years. The US will never have to deliver the foreign assets back again. As long as the dollar stays trusted, we can't lose.'

'So what's the problem?' I asked her.

'Difficult to describe,' Molly said. 'It's all about trust and faith. It's almost metaphysical. If foreign markets are getting flooded with fake dollars, that doesn't really matter in itself. But if the people in those foreign markets find out, then it does matter. Because they panic. They lose their faith. They lose their trust. They don't want dollars any more. They'll turn to Japanese yen or German marks to

281

stuff their mattresses with. They'll get rid of their dollars. In effect, overnight, the government would have to repay a two-hundred-sixty-billion dollar foreign loan. Overnight. And we couldn't do that, Jack.'

'Big problem,' I said.

'That's the truth,' she said. 'And a remote problem. The fakes are all made abroad, and they're mostly distributed abroad. It makes sense that way. The factories are hidden away in some remote foreign region, where we don't know about them, and the fakes are distributed to foreigners who are happy as long as the stuff looks vaguely like real dollars are supposed to look. That's why not very many are imported. Only the very best fakes come back to the States.'

'How many come back?' I asked her.

I heard her shrug. A little breath sound, like she had pursed her lips.

'Not many,' she said. 'A few billion, now and then, I guess.'

'A few billion?' I said. 'That's not many?'

'A drop in the ocean,' she said. 'From a macro-economic point of view. Compared to the size of the economy, I mean.'

'And what exactly are we doing about it?' I asked her.

'Two things,' she said. 'First thing is Joe was trying like mad to stop it from happening. The reason behind that is obvious. Second thing is we're pretending like mad it isn't happening at all. So as to keep the faith.'

I nodded. Started to see some shape behind the big-time secrecy going on up there in Washington.

'OK,' I said. 'So if I were to call the Treasury and ask them about it?'

'We'd deny everything,' she said. 'We'd say, what counterfeiting?'

I walked through the silent squad room and joined Roscoe in her car. Told her to drive out toward Warburton. It was dark when we reached the little stand of trees. Just enough moonlight to pick it out. Roscoe pulled up where I showed her. I kissed her and got out. Told her I'd see her up at the hotel. Slapped lightly on the Chevy's roof and waved her off. She turned in the road. Drove slowly away.

I pushed directly through the copse. Didn't want to leave footprints on the track. The fat carrier bag made it awkward. It kept snagging in the brush. I came out right by the Buick. Still there. All quiet. I unlocked the driver's door with the key and got in. Started up and bounced down the track. The rear suspension kept bottoming out on the ruts. I wasn't too surprised about that. Must have been about five hundred pounds weight in the trunk.

I jounced out onto the road and drove east toward Margrave. But I turned left at the county road and headed north. Cruised the rest of the fourteen miles up to the highway. Passed by the warehouses and joined the stream north to Atlanta. I didn't drive fast, didn't drive slow. Didn't want to get noticed. The plain Buick was very anonymous. Very inconspicuous. That was how I wanted to keep it.

After an hour I followed the airport signs. Found my way round to the long-term parking. Took a ticket at the little automated barrier and nosed in. It was a huge lot. Couldn't be better. I found a slot near the middle, about a hundred yards from the nearest fence. Wiped off the wheel and the transmission. Got out with the carrier bag. Locked the Buick and walked away.

After a minute, I looked back. Couldn't pick out the car I'd just dumped. What's the best place to hide a car? In an airport long-term lot. Like where's the best place to hide a grain of sand? On the beach. The Buick could sit there for a month. Nobody would think twice.

I walked back toward the entrance barrier. At the first trash can I dumped the carrier bag. At the second I got rid of the parking ticket. At the barrier I caught the little courtesy bus and rode to the departure terminal. Walked in and found a bathroom. Wrapped the Buick keys in a paper towel and dropped them in the garbage. Then I slipped down to the arrivals hall and stepped out into the damp night again. Caught the hotel courtesy bus and rode off to meet Roscoe.

I found her in the neon glare of a hotel lobby. I paid cash for a room. Used a bill I'd taken from the Florida boys. We went up in the elevator. The room was a dingy, dark place. Big enough. Looked out over the airport sprawl. The window had three layers of glass against the jet noise. The place was airless.

'First, we eat,' I said.

'First, we shower,' Roscoe said.

So we showered. Put us in a better frame of mind. We soaped up and started fooling around. Ended up making love in the stall with the water beating down on us. Afterwards, I just wanted to curl up in the glow. But we were hungry. And we had things to do. Roscoe put on the clothes she'd brought from her place in the morning. Jeans, shirt, jacket. Looked wonderful. Very feminine, but very tough. She had a lot of spirit.

284

We rode up to a restaurant on the top floor. It was OK. A big panoramic view of the airport district. We sat in candlelight by a window. A cheerful foreign guy brought us food. I crammed it all down. I was starving. I had a beer and a pint of coffee. Started to feel halfway human again. Paid for the meal with more of the dead guys' money. Then we rode down to the lobby and picked up an Atlanta street map at the desk. Walked out to Roscoe's car.

The night air was cold and damp and stank of kerosene. Airport smell. We got in the Chevy and pored over the street map. Headed out northwest. Roscoe drove and I tried to direct her. We battled traffic and ended up roughly in the right place. It was a sprawl of low-rise housing. The sort of place you see from planes coming in to land. Small houses on small lots, hurricane fencing, above ground pools. Some nice yards, some dumps. Old cars up on blocks. Everything bathed in yellow sodium glare.

We found the right street. Found the right house. Decent place. Well looked after. Neat and clean. A tiny one-storey. Small yard, small single-car garage. Narrow gate in the wire fence. We went through. Rang the bell. An old woman cracked the door against the chain.

'Good evening,' Roscoe said. 'We're looking for Sherman Stoller.'

Roscoe looked at me after she said it. She should have said we were looking for his house. We knew where Sherman Stoller was. Sherman Stoller was in the Yellow Springs morgue, seventy miles away.

'Who are you?' the old woman asked, politely.

'Ma'am, we're police officers,' Roscoe said. Half true.

The old lady eased the door and took the chain off.

'You better come in,' she said. 'He's in the kitchen. Eating, I'm afraid.'

'Who is?' said Roscoe.

The old lady stopped and looked at her. Puzzled.

'Sherman,' she said. 'That's who you want, isn't it?'

We followed her into the kitchen. There was an old guy eating supper at the table. When he saw us, he stopped and dabbed at his lips with a napkin.

'Police officers, Sherman,' the old lady said.

The old guy looked up at us blankly.

'Is there another Sherman Stoller?' I asked him.

The old guy nodded. Looked worried.

'Our son,' he said.

'About thirty?' I asked him. 'Thirty-five?'

The old guy nodded again. The old lady moved behind him and put her hand on his arm. Parents.

'He don't live here,' the old man said.

'Is he in trouble?' the old lady asked.

'Could you give us his address?' Roscoe said.

They fussed around like old people do. Very deferential to authority. Very respectful. Wanted to ask us a lot of questions, but just gave us the address.

'He hasn't lived here for two years,' the old man said.

He was afraid. He was trying to distance himself from the trouble his son was in. We nodded to them and backed out. As we were shutting their front door, the old man called out after us.

'He moved out there two years ago,' he said.

We trooped out through the gate and got back in

the car. Looked on the street map again. The new address wasn't on it.

'What did you make of those two?' Roscoe asked me.

'The parents?' I said. 'They know their boy was up to no good. They know he was doing something bad. Probably don't know exactly what it was.'

'That's what I thought,' she said. 'Let's go find this new place.'

We drove off. Roscoe got gas and directions at the first place we saw.

'About five miles the other way,' she said. Pulled the car around and headed away from the city. 'New condominiums on a golf course.'

She was peering into the gloom, looking for the landmarks the gas station attendant had given her. After five miles she swung off the main drag. Nosed along a new road and pulled up by a developer's sign. It advertised condominiums, top quality, built right on the fairway. It boasted that only a few remained unsold. Beyond the billboard were rows of new buildings. Very pleasant, not huge, but nicely done. Balconies, garages, good details. Ambitious landscaping loomed up in the dark. Lighted pathways led over to a health club. On the other side was nothing. Must have been the golf course.

Roscoe killed the motor. We sat in the car. I stretched my arm along the back of her seat. Cupped her shoulder. I was tired. I'd been busy all day. I wanted to sit like this for a while. It was a quiet, dull night. Warm in the car. I wanted music. Something with an ache to it. But we had things to do. We had to find Judy. The woman who had bought Sherman Stoller's watch and had it engraved. To Sherman, love Judy. We had to find

Judy and tell her the man she'd loved had bled to death under a highway.

'What do you make of this?' Roscoe said. She was bright and awake.

'Don't know,' I said. 'They're for sale, not rental. They look expensive. Could a truck driver afford this?'

'Doubt it,' she said. 'These probably cost as much as my place, and I couldn't make my payments without the subsidy I get. And I make more than any truck driver, that's for sure.'

'OK,' I said. 'So our guess is old Sherman was getting some kind of a subsidy, too, right? Otherwise he couldn't afford to live here.'

'Sure,' she said. 'But what kind of a subsidy?'

'The kind that gets people killed,' I said.

Stoller's building was way in back. Probably the first phase to have been built. The old man in the poor part of town had said his son had moved out two years ago. That could be about right. This first block could be about two years old. We threaded through walkways and around raised up flowerbeds. Walked up a path to Sherman Stoller's door. The path was stepping stones set in the wiry lawn. Forced an unnatural gait on you. I had to step short. Roscoe had to stretch her stride from one flagstone to the next. We reached the door. It was blue. No shine on it. Old-fashioned paint.

'Are we going to tell her?' I said.

'We can't not tell her, can we?' Roscoe said. 'She's got to know.'

I knocked on the door. Waited. Knocked again. I heard the floor creaking inside. Someone was coming. The door opened. A woman stood there.

Maybe thirty, but she looked older. Short, nervous, tired. Blonde from a bottle. She looked out at us.

'We're police officers, ma'am,' Roscoe said. 'We're looking for the Sherman Stoller residence.'

There was silence for a moment.

'Well, you found it, I guess,' the woman said.

'May we come in?' Roscoe asked. Gently.

Again there was silence. No movement. Then the blonde woman turned and walked back down the hallway. Roscoe and I looked at each other. Roscoe followed the woman. I followed Roscoe. I shut the door behind us.

The woman led us into a living room. A decent-sized space. Expensive furniture and rugs. A big TV. No stereo, no books. It all looked a bit half-hearted. Like somebody had spent twenty minutes with a catalogue and ten thousand dollars. One of these, one of those, two of that. All delivered one morning and just kind of dumped in there.

'Are you Mrs Stoller?' Roscoe asked the woman. Still gentle.

'More or less,' the woman said. 'Not exactly Mrs, but as near as makes no difference anyhow.'

'Is your name Judy?' I asked her.

She nodded. Kept on nodding for a while. Thinking.

'He's dead, isn't he?' Judy said.

I didn't answer. This was the part I wasn't good at. This was Roscoe's part. She didn't say anything, either.

'He's dead, right?' Judy said again, louder.

'Yes, he is,' Roscoe said. 'I'm very sorry.'

Judy nodded to herself and looked around the hideous room. Nobody spoke. We just stood there.

Judy sat down. She waved us to sit as well. We sat, in separate chairs. We were all sitting in a neat triangle.

'We need to ask you some questions,' Roscoe said. She was sitting forward, leaning towards the blonde woman. 'May we do that?'

Judy nodded. Looked pretty blank.

'How long did you know Sherman?' Roscoe asked.

'About four years, I guess,' Judy said. 'Met him in Florida, where I lived. Came up here to be with him four years ago. Lived up here ever since.'

'What was Sherman's job?' Roscoe asked.

Judy shrugged miserably.

'He was a truck driver,' she said. 'He got some kind of a big driving contract up here. Supposed to be long term, you know? So we bought a little place. His folks moved in too. Lived with us for a while. Then we moved out here. Left his folks in the old house. He made good money for three years. Busy all the time. Then it stopped, a year ago. He hardly worked at all since. Just an odd day, now and then.'

'You own both the houses?' Roscoe said.

'I don't own a damn thing,' Judy said. 'Sherman owned the houses. Yes, both of them.'

'So he was doing well for the first three years?' Roscoe asked her.

Judy gave her a look.

'Doing well?' she said. 'Grow up, for God's sake. He was a thief. He was ripping somebody off.'

'You sure?' I said.

Judy swung her gaze my way. Like an artillery piece traversing.

'It don't need much brains to figure it out,' she said. 'In three years he paid cash for two houses,

290

two lots of furniture, cars, God knows what. And this place wasn't cheap, either. We got lawyers and doctors and all sorts living here. And he had enough saved so he didn't have to work at all since last September. If he did all that on the level, then I'm the First Lady, right?'

She was giving us a defiant stare. She'd known about it all along. She'd known what would happen when he was found out. She was challenging us to deny her the right to blame him.

'Who was his big contract with?' Roscoe asked her.

'Some outfit called Island Air-conditioning,' she said. 'He spent three years hauling air conditioners. Taking them down to Florida. Maybe they went on to the islands, I don't know. He used to steal them. There's two old boxes in the garage right now. Want to see?'

She didn't wait for a reply. Just jumped up and stalked out. We followed. We all went down some back stairs and through a basement door. Into a garage. It was empty except for a couple of old cartons dumped against a wall. Cardboard cartons, could have been a year or two old. Marked with a manufacturer's logo. Island Air-conditioning, Inc. This End Up. The sealing tape was torn and hanging off. Each box had a long serial number written on by hand. Each box must have held a single unit. The sort you jam in your window frame, makes a hell of a noise. Judy glared at the boxes and glared at us. It was a glare which said: I gave him a gold watch and he gave me a shitload of worry.

I walked over and looked at the cartons. They were empty. I smelled a faint, sour odour in them. Then we went back upstairs. Judy got an album out of a cupboard. Sat and looked at a photograph of Sherman.

'What happened to him?' she asked.

It was a simple question. Deserved a simple answer.

'He was shot in the head,' I lied. 'Died instantly.'

Judy nodded. Like she wasn't surprised.

'When?' she asked.

'On Thursday night,' Roscoe told her. 'At midnight. Did he say where he was going on Thursday night?'

Judy shook her head.

'He never told me much,' she said.

'Did he ever mention meeting an investigator?' Roscoe asked.

Judy shook her head again.

'What about Pluribus?' I asked her. 'Did he ever use that word?'

She looked blank.

'Is that a disease?' she said. 'Lungs or something?'

'What about Sunday?' I said. 'This Sunday coming? Did he ever say anything about that?'

'No,' Judy said. 'He never said much about anything.'

She sat and stared at the photographs in the album. The room was quiet.

'Did he know any lawyers in Florida?' Roscoe asked her.

'Lawyers?' Judy said. 'In Florida? Why should he?'

'He was arrested in Jacksonville,' Roscoe said. 'Two years ago. It was a traffic violation in his truck. A lawyer came to help him out.'

Judy shrugged, like two years ago was ancient history to her.

'There are lawyers sniffing everywhere, right?' she said. 'No big deal.'

'This guy wasn't an ambulance-chaser,' Roscoe said. 'He was a partner in a big firm down there. Any idea how Sherman could have gotten hold of him?'

Judy shrugged again.

'Maybe his employer did it,' she said. 'Island Air-conditioning. They gave us good medical insurance. Sherman let me go to the doctor, any old time I needed to.'

We all went quiet. Nothing more to say. Judy sat and gazed at the photographs in the album.

'Want to see his picture?' she said.

I walked around behind her chair and bent to look at the photograph. It showed a sandy, rat-faced man. Small, slight, with a grin. He was standing in front of a yellow panel van. Grinning and squinting at the camera. The grin gave it poignancy.

'That's the truck he drove,' Judy said.

But I wasn't looking at the truck or Sherman Stoller's poignant grin. I was looking at a figure in the background of the picture. It was out of focus and turned half away from the camera, but I could make out who it was. It was Paul Hubble.

I waved Roscoe over and she bent beside me and looked at the photograph. I saw a wave of surprise pass over her face as she recognized Hubble. Then she bent closer. Looked harder. I saw a second wave of surprise. She had recognized something else.

'When was this picture taken?' she asked.

Judy shrugged.

'Summer last year, I guess,' she said.

Roscoe touched the blurred image of Hubble with her fingernail.

'Did Sherman say who this guy was?'

'The new boss,' Judy said. 'He was there six months, then he fired Sherman's ass.'

'Island Air-conditioning's new boss?' Roscoe said. 'Was there a reason he laid Sherman off?'

'Sherman said they didn't need him no more,' Judy said. 'He never said much.'

'Is this where Island Air-conditioning is based?' Roscoe asked. 'Where this picture was taken?'

Judy shrugged and nodded her head, tentatively.

'I guess so,' she said. 'Sherman never told me much about it.'

'We need to keep this photograph,' Roscoe told her. 'We'll let you have it back later.'

Judy fished it out of the plastic. Handed it to her.

'Keep it,' she said. 'I don't want it.'

Roscoe took the picture and put it in her inside jacket pocket. She and I moved back to the middle of the room and stood there.

'Shot in the head,' Judy said. 'That's what happens when you mess around. I told him they'd catch up with him, sooner or later.'

Roscoe nodded sympathetically.

'We'll keep in touch,' she said to her. 'You know, the funeral arrangements, and we might want a statement.'

Judy glared at us again.

'Don't bother,' she said. 'I'm not going to his funeral. I wasn't his wife, so I'm not his widow. I'm going to forget I ever knew him. That man was trouble from beginning to end.'

She stood there glaring at us. We shuffled out,

down the hall, out through the door. Across the awkward path. We held hands as we walked back to the car.

'What?' I asked her. 'What's in the photograph?'
She was walking fast.
'Wait,' she said. 'I'll show you in the car.'

NINETEEN

We got in the Chevy and she snapped on the dome light. Pulled the photograph out of her pocket. Leaned over and tilted the picture so the light caught the shiny surface. Checked it carefully. Handed it to me.

'Look at the edge,' she said. 'On the left.'

The picture was of Sherman Stoller standing in front of a yellow truck. Paul Hubble was turned away, in the background. The two figures and the truck filled the whole frame apart from a wedge of blacktop at the bottom. And a thin margin of background to the left. The background slice was even more out of focus than Hubble was, but I could see the edge of a modern metal building, with silver siding. A tall tree beyond. The frame of a door. It was a big industrial door, rolled up. The frame was a dark red colour. Some kind of baked-on industrial coating. Partly decorative, partly preservative. Some kind of a shed door. There was gloom inside the shed.

'That's Kliner's warehouse,' she said. 'At the top of the county road.'

'Are you sure?' I said.

'I recognize the tree,' she said.

I looked again. It was a very distinctive tree. Dead on one side. Maybe split by lightning.

'That's Kliner's warehouse,' she said again. 'No doubt about that.'

Then she clicked her car phone on and took the photograph back. Dialled DMV in Atlanta and called in the number from the front of Stoller's truck. Waited a long moment, tapping her index finger on the steering wheel. I heard the crackle of the response in the earpiece. Then she clicked the phone off and turned to me.

'The truck is registered to Kliner Industries,' she said. 'And the registered address is Zacarias Perez, Attorneys-at-Law, Jacksonville, Florida.'

I nodded. She nodded back. Sherman Stoller's buddies. The ones who had got him out of Jacksonville Central in fifty-five minutes flat, two years ago.

'OK,' she said. 'Put it all together. Hubble, Stoller, Joe's investigation. They're printing counterfeit money down in Kliner's warehouse, right?'

I shook my head.

'Wrong,' I said. 'There's no printing going on inside the States. It all happens abroad. Molly Beth Gordon told me that, and she ought to know what she's talking about. She said Joe had made it impossible. And whatever Stoller was doing, Judy said he stopped doing it a year ago. And Finlay said Joe only started this whole thing a year ago. Around the same time Hubble fired Stoller.'

Roscoe nodded. Shrugged.

'We need Molly's help,' she said. 'We need a copy of Joe's file.'

'Or Picard's help,' I said. 'We might find Joe's hotel room and get hold of the original. It's a race to see who's going to call us first, Molly or Picard.'

Roscoe clicked off the dome light. Started the car for the ride back to the airport hotel. I just sprawled out beside her, yawning. I could sense she was getting uptight. She had run out of things to do. Run out of distractions. Now she had to face the quiet vulnerable hours of the night. The first night after last night. The prospect was making her agitated.

'You got that gun, Reacher?' she asked.

I squirmed around in the seat to face her.

'It's in the trunk,' I said. 'In that box. You put it in there, remember?'

'Bring it inside, OK?' she said. 'Makes me feel better.'

I grinned sleepily in the dark. Yawned.

'Makes me feel better too,' I said. 'It's a hell of a gun.'

Then we lapsed back into silence. Roscoe found the hotel lot. We got out of the car and stood stretching in the dark. I opened the trunk. Lifted the box out and slammed the lid. Went in through our lobby and up in the elevator.

In the room we just crashed out. Roscoe laid her shiny .38 on the carpet on her side of the bed. I reloaded my giant .44 and laid it on my side. Cocked and locked. We wedged a chair under the doorhandle. Roscoe felt safer that way.

I woke early and lay in bed, thinking about Joe. Wednesday morning. He'd been dead five days. Roscoe was already up. She was standing in the middle of the floor, stretching. Some kind of a yoga thing. She'd taken a shower and she was only half dressed. She had no trousers on. Just a shirt. She had her back to me. As she stretched, the shirt was riding way up. Suddenly I wasn't thinking about Joe any more.

'Roscoe?' I said.

'What?' she said.

'You've got the most wonderful ass on the planet,' I said.

She giggled. I jumped on her. Couldn't help it. Couldn't do anything else. She drove me crazy. It was the giggle that did it to me. It made me crazy. I hauled her back into the big hotel bed. The building could have fallen down and we wouldn't have noticed it. We finished in an exhausted tangle. Lay there for a while. Then Roscoe got up again and showered for the second time that morning. Got dressed again. Trousers and everything. Grinned at me as if to say she was sparing me from any further temptation.

'So did you mean it?' she said.

'Mean what?' I said, with a smile.

'You know what,' she smiled back. 'When you told me I had a cute ass.'

'I didn't say you had a cute ass,' I said. 'I've seen plenty of cute asses. I said yours was the most wonderful ass on the whole damn planet.'

'But did you mean it?' she said.

'You bet I meant it,' I said. 'Don't underestimate the attraction of your ass, Roscoe, whatever you do.'

I called room service for breakfast. Removed the chair from under the door handle ready for the little cart. Pulled the heavy drapes. It was a glorious morning. A bright blue sky, no clouds at all, brilliant fall sunshine. The room was flooded with light. We cracked the window and let in the air and the smells and the sounds of the day. The view was spectacular. Right over the airport and to the city beyond. The cars in the lots caught the sun and looked like jewels on beige velvet. The planes clawed their way into the air and wheeled slowly away like fat, important birds. The buildings downtown grew tall and straight in the sun. A glorious morning. But it was the sixth straight morning my brother wasn't alive to see.

Roscoe used the phone to call Finlay down in Margrave. She told him about the photograph of Hubble and Stoller standing in the sun on the warehouse forecourt. Then she gave him our room number and told him to call us if Molly got back to us from Washington. Or if Picard got back to us with information from the car rental people about the burned Pontiac. I figured we should stay in Atlanta in case Picard beat Molly and we got a hotel trace on Joe. Chances were he stayed in the city, maybe near the airport. No point in us driving all the way back down to Margrave and then having to drive all the way back up to Atlanta again. So we waited. I fiddled with the radio built into the nightstand thing. Came up with a station playing something halfway decent. Sounded like they were playing through an early Canned Heat album. Bouncy and sunny and just right for a bright empty morning.

Breakfast came and we ate it. The whole bit. Pancakes, syrup, bacon. Lots of coffee in a thick china jug. Afterward, I lay back on the bed. Pretty soon started feeling restless. Started feeling like it had been a mistake to wait around. It felt like we weren't doing anything. I could see Roscoe was feeling the same way. She propped the photograph of Hubble and Stoller and the yellow van on the nightstand and glared at it. I glared at the telephone. It wasn't ringing. We wandered around the room, waiting. Then I stooped to pick up the Desert Eagle off the floor by the bed. Hefted it in my hand. Traced the engraved name on the grip with my finger. Looked across at Roscoe. I was curious about the guy who'd bought that massive automatic.

'What was Gray like?' I asked.

'Gray?' she said. 'He was so thorough. You want to get Joe's files? You should see Gray's paperwork. There are twenty-five years of his files in the station house. All meticulous, all comprehensive. Gray was a good detective.'

'Why did he hang himself?' I asked her.

'I don't know,' she said. 'I never understood it.'

'Was he depressed?' I said.

'Not really,' she said. 'I mean, he was always sort of depressed. Lugubrious, you know? A very dour sort of guy. And bored. He was a good detective, and he was wasted in Margrave. But no worse in February than any other time. It was a total surprise to me. I was very upset.'

'Were you close?' I asked her.

She shrugged.

'Yes, we were,' she said. 'In a way, we were pretty close. He was a dour guy, you know, not really that close to anybody. Never married, always lived alone, no relatives. He was a teetotaller, so he would never come out for a beer or anything. He was quiet, messy, a little overweight. No hair and a big straggly beard. A very self-contained, comfortable type of a guy. A loner, really. But he was as close to me as he was ever going to get to anybody. We liked each other, in a quiet sort of a way.'

'And he never said anything?' I asked her. 'Just hanged himself one day?'

'That's how it was,' she said. 'A total shock. I'll never understand it.'

'Why did you have his gun in your desk?' I said.

'He asked if he could keep it in there,' she said. 'He had no space in his own desk. He generated a lot of paperwork. He just asked if I could keep a box for him with the gun hidden in it. It was his private weapon. He said he couldn't get it approved by the department because the calibre was too big. He made it feel like some kind of a big secret.'

I put the dead man's secret gun down on the carpet again and the silence was shattered by the phone ringing. I sprinted for the nightstand and answered it. Heard Finlay's voice. I gripped the phone and held my breath.

'Reacher?' Finlay said. 'Picard got what we need. He traced the car.'

I breathed out and nodded to Roscoe.

'Great, Finlay,' I said. 'So what's the story?'

'Go to his office,' he said. 'He'll give you the spread, face to face. I didn't want too much conversation on the phones down here.'

I closed my eyes for a second and felt a surge of energy.

'Thanks, Finlay,' I said. 'Speak to you later.'

'OK,' he said. 'Take care, right?'

Then he hung up and left me sitting there holding the phone, smiling.

'I thought he'd never call,' Roscoe laughed. 'But I guess eighteen hours isn't too bad, even for the Bureau, right?'

The Atlanta FBI was housed in a new federal building downtown. Roscoe parked at the kerb outside. The Bureau reception called upstairs and told us Special Agent Picard would come right down to meet with us. We waited for him in the lobby. It was a big hall, with a brave stab at decoration, but it still had the glum atmosphere government buildings have. Picard came out of an elevator within three minutes. He loped over. He seemed to fill the whole hall. He nodded to me and took Roscoe's hand.

'Heard a lot about you from Finlay,' he said to her.

His bear's voice rumbled. Roscoe nodded and smiled.

'The car Finlay found?' he said. 'Rental Pontiac. Booked out to Joe Reacher, Atlanta airport, Thursday night at eight.'

'Great, Picard,' I said. 'Any guess about where he was holed up?'

'Better than a guess, my friend,' Picard said. 'They had the exact location. It was a prebooked car. They delivered it right to his hotel.'

He mentioned a place a mile the other way from the hotel we were using.

'Thanks, Picard,' I said. 'I owe you.'

'No problem, my friend,' he said. 'You take care now, OK?'

He loped off back to the elevator and we raced back south to the airport. Roscoe swung onto the perimeter road and accelerated into the flow. Across the divider, a black pickup flashed by. Brand-new. I spun around and caught a glimpse of it disappearing behind a raft of trucks. Black. Brand-new. Probably nothing. They sell more pickups down here than anything else.

Roscoe pulled her badge at the desk where Picard said Joe had checked in on Thursday. The clerk did some keyboard work and told us he had been in 621, sixth floor, far end of the corridor. She said a manager would meet us up there. So we went up in the elevator and walked the length of a dark corridor. Stood waiting outside the door to Joe's room.

The manager came by more or less straight away and opened the room up with his pass key. We stepped in. The room was empty. It had been cleaned and tidied. It looked like it was ready for new occupants.

'What about his stuff?' I said. 'Where is it all?'

'We cleared it out Saturday,' the manager said. 'The guy was booked in Thursday night, supposed to vacate by eleven Friday morning. What we do is we give them an extra day, then if they don't show, we clear them out, down to house-keeping.'

'So his stuff is in a closet somewhere?' I asked.

'Downstairs,' the manager said. 'You should see the stuff we got down there. People leave things all the time.'

'So can we go take a look?' I said.

'Basement,' he said. 'Use the stairs from the lobby. You'll find it.'

The manager strolled off. Roscoe and I walked the length of the corridor again and rode back down in the elevator. We found the service staircase and went down to the basement. Housekeeping was a giant hall stacked with linens and towels. There were hampers and baskets full of soap and those free sachets you find in the showers. Maids were pulling in and out with the trolleys they use for servicing the rooms. There was a glassed-in office cubicle in the near corner with a woman at a small desk. We walked over and rapped on the glass. She looked up. Roscoe held out her badge.

'Help you?' the woman said.

'Room six-two-one,' Roscoe said. 'You cleared out some belongings, Saturday morning. You got them down here?'

I was holding my breath again.

'Six-two-one?' the woman said. 'He came by for them already. They're gone.'

I breathed out. We were too late. I went numb with disappointment.

'Who came by?' I asked. 'When?'

'The guest,' the woman said. 'This morning, maybe nine, nine-thirty.'

'Who was he?' I asked her.

She pulled a small book off a shelf and thumbed it open. Licked a stubby finger and pointed to a line.

'Joe Reacher,' she said. 'He signed the book and took the stuff.'

She reversed the book and slid it toward us. There was a scrawled signature on the line.

'What did this Reacher guy look like?' I asked her.

She shrugged.

'Foreign,' she said. 'Some kind of a Latino. Maybe from Cuba? Little dark guy, slender, nice smile. Very polite sort of a guy, as I recall.'

'You got a list of the stuff?' I said.

She slid the stubby finger further along the line. There was a small column filled with tight handwriting. It listed a garment bag, eight articles of clothing, a toilet bag, four shoes. The last item listed was: one briefcase.

We just walked away from her and found the stairs back to the lobby. Walked out into the morning sun. It didn't feel like such a great day any more.

We reached the car. Leaned side by side on the front fender. I was weighing up in my mind whether Joe would have been smart enough and careful enough to do what I would have done. I figured maybe he would have been. He'd spent a long time around smart and careful people.

'Roscoe?' I said. 'If you were the guy walking out of here with Joe's stuff, what would you do?'

She stopped with the car door half open. Thought about it.

'I'd keep the briefcase,' she said. 'Take it wherever I was supposed to take it. The rest of the stuff, I'd get rid of it.'

'That's what I would do as well,' I said. 'Where would you get rid of it?'

'First place I saw, I guess,' she said.

There was a service road running between the hotel and the next one in line. It looped behind the hotels and then out onto the perimeter road. There was a line of dumpsters along a twenty-yard stretch of it. I pointed.

'Suppose he drove out that way?' I said. 'Suppose he stopped and lobbed the garment bag straight into one of those dumpsters?'

'But he'd have kept the briefcase, right?' Roscoe said.

'Maybe we aren't looking for the briefcase,' I said. 'Yesterday, I drove miles and miles out to that stand of trees, but I hid in the field. A diversion, right? It's a habit. Maybe Joe had the same habit. Maybe he carried a briefcase but kept his important stuff in the garment bag.'

Roscoe shrugged. Wasn't convinced. We started walking down the service road. Up close, the dumpsters were huge. I had to lever myself up on the edge of each one and peer in. The first one was empty. Nothing in it at all, except the baked-on kitchen dirt from years of use. The second one was full. I found a length of studding from some demolished drywall and poked around with it. Couldn't see anything. I heaved myself down and walked to the next one.

There was a garment bag in it. Lying right on top of some old cartons. I fished for it with the length of wood. Hauled it out. Tossed it onto the ground at Roscoe's feet. Jumped down next to it. It was a battered, well-travelled bag. Scuffed and scratched. Lots of airline tags all over it. There was a little nameplate in the shape of a miniature gold credit card fastened to the handle. It said: Reacher.

'OK, Joe,' I said to myself. 'Let's see if you were a smart guy.'

I was looking for the shoes. They were in the outside pocket of the bag. Two pairs. Four shoes, just like it said on the housekeeper's list. I pulled the inner soles out of each one in turn. Under the third one, I found a tiny Ziplock bag. With a sheet of computer paper folded up inside it.

'Smart as a whip, Joe,' I said to myself, and laughed.

TWENTY

Roscoe and I danced around the service alley together like players in the dugout watching the winning run soar out of sight. Then we hustled over to the Chevy and raced the mile back to our hotel. Ran into the lobby, into the elevator. Unlocked our room and fell in. The telephone was ringing. It was Finlay, on the line from Margrave again. He sounded as excited as we were.

'Molly Beth Gordon just called,' he said. 'She did it. She's got the files we need. She's flying down here, right now. She told me it was amazing stuff. Sounded high as a kite. Atlanta arrivals, two o'clock. I'll meet you there. Delta, from Washington. Picard give you anything?'

'Sure did,' I said. 'He's quite a guy. I got the rest of the printout, I think.'

'You think?' Finlay said. 'You don't know?'

'Only just got back,' I said. 'Haven't looked at it yet.'

'So look at it, for Christ's sake,' he said. 'It's important, right?'

'See you later, Harvard guy,' I said.

We sat down at the table over by the window. Unzipped the little plastic bag and pulled out the paper. Unfolded it carefully. It was a sheet of computer paper. The top inch had been torn off the right-hand corner. Half the heading had been left behind. It said: Operation E Unum.

'Operation E Unum Pluribus,' Roscoe said.

Underneath was a triple-spaced list of initials with telephone numbers opposite. The first set of initials was P.H. The phone number was torn off.

'Paul Hubble,' Roscoe said. 'His number and the other half of the heading was what Finlay found.'

I nodded. Then there were four more sets of initials. The first two were W.B. and K.K. They had phone numbers alongside. I recognized a New York area code against K.K. The W.B. area code I figured I'd have to look up. The third set of initials was J.S. The code was 504. New Orleans area. I'd been there less than a month ago. The fourth set of initials was M.B.G. There was a phone number with a 202 area code. I pointed to it, so Roscoe could see it.

'Molly Beth Gordon,' she said. 'Washington DC.'

I nodded again. It wasn't the number I had called from the rosewood office. Maybe her home number. The final two items on the torn paper were not initials, and there were no corresponding phone numbers. The second-to-last item was just two words: Stollers' Garage. The last item was three words: Gray's Kliner File. I looked at the careful capital letters and I could just about feel my dead brother's neat, pedantic personality bursting off the page.

Paul Hubble we knew about. He was dead.

Molly Beth Gordon we knew about. She'd be here at two o'clock. We'd seen the garage up at Sherman Stoller's place on the golf course. It held nothing but two empty cartons. That left the underlined heading, three sets of initials with three phone numbers, and the three words: Gray's Kliner File. I checked the time. Just past noon. Too early to sit back and wait for Molly Beth to arrive. I figured we should make a start.

'First we think about the heading,' I said. 'E Unum Pluribus.'

Roscoe shrugged.

'That's the US motto, right?' she said. 'The Latin thing?'

'No,' I said. 'It's the motto backwards. This more or less means out of one comes many. Not out of many comes one.'

'Could Joe have written it down wrong?' she said.

I shook my head.

'I doubt it,' I said. 'I don't think Joe would make that kind of a mistake. It must mean something.'

Roscoe shrugged again.

'Doesn't mean anything to me,' she said. 'What else?'

'Gray's Kliner File,' I said. 'Did Gray have a file on Kliner?'

'Probably,' Roscoe said. 'He had a file on just about everything. Somebody spat on the sidewalk, he'd put it in a file.'

I nodded. Stepped back to the bed and picked up the phone. Called Finlay down in Margrave. Baker told me he'd already left. So I dialled the other numbers on Joe's printout. The W.B. number was in New Jersey. Princeton University. Faculty of modern history. I hung up straight away. Couldn't see the connection. The K.K. number was in New York City. Columbia University. Faculty of modern history. I hung up again. Then I dialled J.S. in New Orleans. I heard one ring tone and a busy voice.

'Fifteenth squad, detectives,' the voice said.

'Detectives?' I said. 'Is that the NOPD?'

'Fifteenth squad,' the voice said again. 'Can I help you?'

'You got somebody there with the initials J.S.?' I asked.

'J.S.?' the voice said. 'I got three of them. Which one do you want?'

'Don't know,' I said. 'Does the name Joe Reacher mean anything to you?'

'What the hell is this?' the voice said. 'Twenty Questions or something?'

'Ask them, will you?' I said. 'Ask each J.S. if they know Joe Reacher. Will you do that? I'll call back later, OK?'

Down in New Orleans, the fifteenth squad desk guy grunted and hung up. I shrugged at Roscoe and put the phone back on the nightstand.

'We wait for Molly?' she said.

I nodded. I was a little nervous about meeting Molly. It was going to be like meeting a ghost connected to another ghost.

We waited at the cramped table in the window. Watched the sun fall away from its noontime peak. Wasted time passing Joe's torn printout back and forth between us. I stared at the heading. E Unum Pluribus. Out of one comes many. That was Joe Reacher, in three words. Something important, all bound up in a wry little pun.

'Let's go,' Roscoe said.

We were early, but we were anxious. We gathered

311

up our things. Rode the elevator to the lobby and let the dead guys settle up for our phone calls. Then we walked over to Roscoe's Chevy. Started threading our way around to arrivals. It wasn't easy. The airport hotels were planned for people heading out of arrivals or heading into departures. Nobody had thought of people going our way.

'We don't know what Molly looks like,' Roscoe said.

'But she knows what I look like,' I said. 'I look like Joe.'

The airport was vast. We saw most of it as we crabbed over to the right quarter. It was bigger than some cities I'd been in. We drove for miles. Found the right terminal. Missed a lane change and passed the short-term parking. Came around again and lined up at the barrier. Roscoe snatched the ticket and eased into the lot.

'Go left,' I said.

The lot was packed. I was craning over, looking for spaces. Then I saw a vague black shape slide by in the line on my right. I caught it out of the corner of my eye.

'Go right, go right,' I said.

I thought it was the rear end of a black pickup. Brand-new. Sliding by on my right. Roscoe hauled the wheel over and we swung into the next aisle. Caught a flash of red brake lights in black sheet metal. A pickup swung out of sight. Roscoe howled down the aisle and cornered hard.

The next aisle was empty. Nothing moving. Just ranks of automobiles standing quiet in the sun. Same thing in the next aisle. Nothing on the move. No black pickup. We drove all over the lot. Took us a long time. We were held up by the cars moving in and out. But we covered the whole area. Couldn't find a black pickup anywhere.

But we did find Finlay. We parked up in an empty space and started the long walk to the terminal. Finlay had parked in a different quarter and was walking in on a different diagonal. He walked the rest of the way with us.

The terminal was very busy. And it was huge. Built low, but it spread horizontally over acres. The whole place was crowded. Flickering screens high up announced the arrivals. The two o'clock Delta from Washington was in and taxiing. We walked down toward the gate. Felt like a half-mile walk. We were in a long corridor with a ribbed rubber floor. A pair of moving walkways ran down the centre of the corridor. On the right was an endless row of bright gaudy advertisements about the attractions of the Sunbelt. Business or pleasure, it was all down here, that's for sure. On the left was a glass partition, floor to ceiling, with a white etched stripe at eye level to stop people trying to walk through the glass.

Behind the glass were the gates. There was an endless sequence of them. The passengers came out of the planes and walked along on their side of the glass. Half of them disappeared sideways into the baggage claim areas. Then they came out again and found exit doors in the glass partition which let them out into the main corridor. The other half were the short-haul fliers with no checked baggage. They went straight to the doors. Each set of doors was mobbed by big knots of meeters and greeters. We pushed our way through them as we headed down.

Passengers were spilling out of the doors, every thirty yards. Friends and relatives were moving in close and the two streams of people were colliding.

We fought through eight separate crowds before we got to the right gate. I just pushed my way through. I felt anxious. The glimpse of the black pickup in the lot had unsettled me.

We reached the gate. We walked on our side of the glass right past the doors. Right down to level with the end of the jetway. People were already coming off the plane. I watched them spilling out of the jetway and turning to walk up toward the baggage area and the exit doors. On our side of the glass, people were walking down to the gates farther on. They were pushing at us as they passed. We were being dragged down the corridor. Like swimming in a heavy sea. We were stepping backward all the time just to stay standing still.

There was a stream of people behind the glass. I saw a woman coming in who could have been Molly. She was about thirty-five, dressed well in a business suit, carrying a briefcase and a garment bag. I was standing there, trying to get recognized, but she suddenly saw somebody else and pointed and gave a silent shriek behind the glass and blew a kiss to a guy ten yards from me. He shouldered backwards towards the doors to wait for her.

Then it seemed like just about any of the women could be Molly. There must have been a couple of dozen candidates. There were blondes and brunettes, tall ones, short ones, pretty ones, homely ones. All dressed for business, all carrying efficient luggage, all striding in with the weary purposeful manner of tired executives in the middle of a busy day. I watched them all. They flowed with the tide behind the glass, some of them peering out for husbands, lovers, drivers, business contacts, some of them looking straight ahead. All of them carried along in the swarming crowd.

One of them had matching burgundy leather luggage, a heavy briefcase in one hand and a carry-on which she was wheeling on a long handle with the other. She was small, blonde, excited. She slowed as she turned out of the jetway and scanned the crowd through the glass. Her eyes flashed past me. Then they snapped back. She looked straight at me. Stopped. People piled up behind her. She was pushed forward. She fought her way over to the glass. I moved in close on my side. She stared at me. Smiled. Greeted her dead lover's brother with her eyes.

'Molly?' I mouthed through the glass at her.

She held up the heavy briefcase like a trophy. Nodded towards it. Smiled a big wide smile of excited triumph. She was pushed in the back. Borne along by the crowd towards the exit. She looked back to see if I was following. Roscoe and Finlay and I struggled after her.

On Molly's side of the glass, the flow was with her. Our side, it was against us. We were being separated at double speed. There was a solid mob of college kids bearing down on us. Aiming to fly out of a gate further down. Big, well-fed kids, clumsy luggage, rowdy. The three of us were shoved backwards five yards. Through the glass, Molly was way ahead. I saw her blonde head disappear. I fought sideways and vaulted over onto the moving walkway. It was going the wrong way. I was carried another five yards before I made it over the moving handgrip onto the other side.

Now I was going in the right direction, but the walkway was a solid mass of people just standing still on it. Content with the snail's pace the rubber floor was carrying them. They were standing three abreast. No way through at all. I climbed up onto the narrow handrail and tried to walk along it like a tightrope. I had to crouch because I couldn't balance. I fell heavily to my right. Got carried five yards the wrong way before I could struggle up. I looked around in panic. Through the glass, I could see Molly was being crowded into the baggage claim. I could see Roscoe and Finlay were way behind me. I was moving slowly the wrong way.

I didn't want Molly to go into the baggage claim. She'd flown down here in a hurry. She had urgent news. No way would she have packed a big valise. No way would she have checked any luggage. She shouldn't be going into the baggage claim. I put my head down and ran. Barged people out of the way. I was travelling against the pace of the walkway. The rubber floor was grabbing at my shoes. Each impact was costing me time. People were yelling in outrage. I didn't care. I tore through them and left them sprawling. Vaulted off the walkway and clawed through the crowd at the exit doors.

The baggage claim was a wide low hall, lit with dull yellow lights. I fought my way in through the exit lane. Looking everywhere for Molly. Couldn't find her. The hall was jammed with people. There must have been a hundred passengers standing around the carousel, three deep. The belt was grinding around under a heavy load of bags. There were ragged lines of luggage carts on the side wall. People were lining up to put quarters in a slot and pull them free. They were wheeling them away through the crowd. Carts were clashing and tangling. People were pushing and shoving.

I waded into the mass. Shouldered my way through and spun people around, searching for Molly. I'd seen her go in. I hadn't seen her come out. But she wasn't in there. I checked every face. I trawled through the whole hall. I let myself be carried outside on the relentless tide. Fought ahead to the exit door. Roscoe was holding tight to the doorframe, battling the flow.

'She come out?' I said.

'No,' she said. 'Finlay's gone to the end of the corridor. He's waiting there. I'm waiting here.'

We stood there with people pouring past us. Then the crowd coming towards us from the gate was suddenly thinning. The whole planeload was just about through. The last stragglers were strolling down. An old woman in a wheelchair was bringing up the rear. She was being pushed along by an airline employee. The guy had to pause and manoeuvre his way around something lying in the entrance to the baggage hall. It was a burgundy leather carry-on. It was lying on its side. Its extending handle was still pulled out. From fifteen feet away, I could read the fancy gold monogram on the front. It read: M.B.G.

Roscoe and I dived back into the baggage claim. In the few minutes I'd been out of there, the place had just about emptied. Not more than a dozen people still in there. Most of them were already hauling their bags off the belt and heading out as we headed in. Within a minute, the hall was deserted. The luggage belt was grinding round, empty. Then it stopped. The hall fell silent. Roscoe and I stood in the sudden quiet and looked at each other.

The hall had four walls and a floor and a ceiling. There was an entrance door and an exit door. The carousel snaked in through a hole a yard square and snaked out again through a hole a yard square. Both holes were draped with black rubber curtains cut into slats a few inches wide. Next to the carousel was a cargo door. On our side, it was blank. No handle. Locked.

Roscoe darted back and grabbed Molly Beth's carry-on. Opened it up. It held a change of clothes and a toilet bag. And a photograph. Eight by ten, in a brassed frame. It was Joe. He looked like me, but a little thinner. A shaved, tanned scalp. A wry, amused smile.

The hall was filled with the shriek of a warning siren. It sounded for a moment and then the luggage belt graunched back into motion. We stared at it. Stared at the shrouded hole it was coming through. The rubber curtains bellied. A briefcase came out. Burgundy leather. The straps were slashed through. The case was open. It was empty.

It wobbled mechanically around toward us. We stared at it. Stared at the cut straps. They had been severed with a sharp blade. Severed by somebody in too much of a hurry to click open the catches.

I leapt onto the moving carousel. Ran back against the belt's lurching motion and dived like a swimmer head first through the rubber slats shrouding the yard-square hole. I landed hard and the belt started to drag me back out. I scrambled and crawled like a kid on my hands and knees. Rolled off and jumped up. I was in a loading bay. Deserted. The afternoon blazed outside. There was a stink of kerosene and diesel fuel from the baggage trains hauling in from the planes on the tarmac.

All around me were tall piles of forlorn cargo and forgotten suitcases. They were all stacked in three-sided storage bays. The rubber floor was littered with old labels and long barcodes. The place was like a filthy maze. I dodged and skidded about, hopelessly looking for Molly. I ran behind one tall

318

pile after another. Into one bay and then the next. I grabbed at the metal racking and heaved myself around the tight corners. Glancing around desperately. Nobody there. Nobody anywhere. I ran on, sliding and skidding on the litter.

I found her left shoe. It was lying on its side at the entrance to a dark bay. I plunged in. Nothing there. I tried the next bay. Nothing there. I held onto the shelving, breathing hard. I had to organize. I ran to the far end of the corridor. Started ducking into each bay in turn. Left and right, left and right, working my way back as fast as I could, in a desperate breathless zigzag.

I found her right shoe three bays from the end. Then I found her blood. At the entry to the next bay, it was pooled on the floor, sticky, spreading. She was slumped at the back of the bay, on her back in the gloom, jammed between two towers of crates. Just sprawled there on the rubber floor. Blood was pouring out of her. Her gut was torn open. Somebody had jammed a knife in her and ripped it savagely upward under her ribs.

But she was alive. One pale hand was fluttering. Her lips were flecked with bright bubbles of blood. Her head was still, but her eyes were roving. I ran to her. Cradled her head. She gazed at me. Forced her mouth to work.

'Got to get in before Sunday,' she whispered.

Then she died in my arms.

TWENTY-ONE

I studied chemistry in maybe seven different high schools. Didn't learn much of it. Just came away with general impressions. One thing I remember is how you can throw some little extra thing into a glass tube and make everything blow up with a bang. Just some little powder, produces a result way bigger than it should.

That was how I felt about Molly. I'd never met her before. Never even heard of her. But I felt angry, way out of all proportion. I felt worse about her than I felt about Joe. What happened to Joe was in the line of his duty. Joe knew that. He would have accepted that. Joe and I knew about risk and duty right from the moment we first knew about anything at all. But Molly was different.

The other thing I remember from the chemistry lab is stuff about pressure. Pressure turns coal into diamonds. Pressure does things. It was doing things to me. I was angry and I was short of time. In my mind I was seeing Molly coming out of that jetway. Striding out, determined to find Joe's brother and help him. Smiling a wide smile of triumph. Holding up a briefcase of files she shouldn't have copied. Risking a lot. For me. For Joe. That image in my mind was building up like massive pressure on some old geological seam. I had to decide how to use that pressure. I had to decide whether it was going to crush me or turn me into a diamond.

We were leaning on the front fender of Roscoe's car in the airport short-term lot. Stunned and silent. Wednesday afternoon, nearly three o'clock. I had hold of Finlay's arm. He had wanted to stay inside and get involved. He had said it was his duty. I had screamed at him that we didn't have time. I had dragged him out of the terminal by force. I had marched him straight to the car, because I knew what we did in the next few moments was going to make the difference between winning and losing.

'We've got to go get Gray's file,' I said. 'It's the next best thing.'

Finlay shrugged. Gave up the struggle.

'It's all we got,' he said.

Roscoe nodded.

'Let's go,' she said.

She and I drove down together in her car. Finlay was in front of us all the way. She and I didn't speak a single word. But Finlay was talking to himself through the whole trip. He was shouting and cursing. I could see his head jerking back and forth in his car. Cursing and shouting and yelling at his windshield.

Teale was waiting just inside the station house doors. Back against the reception counter. Stick clutched in his spotty old hand. He saw the three of us coming in and limped away into the big open squad room. Sat down at a desk. The desk nearest to the file room door.

We walked past him into the rosewood office. Sat down to wait it out. I pulled Joe's torn printout from my pocket and passed it across the desk. Finlay scanned it through.

'Not much, is it?' he said. 'What does the heading mean? E Unum Pluribus? That's backwards, right?'

I nodded.

'Out of one comes many,' I said. 'I don't get the significance.'

He shrugged. Started reading it through again. I watched him study it. Then there was a loud knock on the office door and Baker came in.

'Teale's on his way out of the building,' he said. 'Talking to Stevenson in the parking lot. You guys need anything?'

Finlay handed him the torn printout.

'Get me a xerox of this, will you?' he said.

Baker stepped out to do it and Finlay drummed his fingers on the desk.

'Who are all those initials?' he said.

'We only know the dead ones,' I said. 'Hubble and Molly Beth. Two are college numbers. Princeton and Columbia. Last one is a detective down in New Orleans.'

'What about Stoller's garage?' he said. 'You get a look at that?'

'Nothing,' I said. 'Just a couple of empty air conditioner cartons from last year when he was hauling them to Florida and stealing them.'

Finlay grunted and Baker came back in. Handed me Joe's paper with a copy of it. I kept the original and gave the copy to Finlay.

'Teale's gone,' Baker said.

We hustled out of the office. Caught a glimpse of the white Cadillac easing out of the lot. Pushed open the file room door.

Margrave was a tiny town in the middle of nowhere but Gray had spent twenty-five years filling that file room with paper. There was more paper in there than I'd seen in a long time. All four walls had floor-to-ceiling cabinets with doors in crisp white enamel. We pulled open all the doors. Each cabinet was full of rows of files. There must have been a thousand letter-size boxes in there. Fibreboard boxes, labels on the spines, little plastic loops under the labels so you could pull the boxes out when you needed them. Left of the door, top shelf, was the A section. Right of the door, low down, the last Z. The K section was on the wall facing the door, left of centre, eye level.

We found a box labelled 'Kliner'. Right between three boxes labelled 'Klan' and one labelled 'Klipspringer v State of Georgia'. I put my finger in the little loop. Pulled the box out. It was heavy. I handed it to Finlay. We ran back to the rosewood office. Laid the box on the rosewood desk. Opened it up. It was full of old yellowing paper.

But it was the wrong paper. It had nothing to do with Kliner. Nothing at all. It was a three-inch pile of ancient police department memos. Operational stuff. Stuff that should have been junked decades ago. A slice of history. Procedures to be followed if the Soviet Union aimed a missile at Atlanta. Procedures to be followed if a black man wanted to ride in the front of the bus. A mass of stuff. But none of the headings began with the letter K. Not one word concerned Kliner. I gazed at the three-inch pile and felt the pressure build up.

'Somebody beat us to it,' Roscoe said. 'They took out the Kliner stuff and substituted this junk instead.'

Finlay nodded. But I shook my head.

'No,' I said. 'Doesn't make any sense. They'd have pulled the whole box and just thrown it in the trash. Gray did this himself. He needed to hide the stuff, but he couldn't bring himself to spoil his sequence in the file room. So he took the contents out of the box and put in this old stuff instead. Kept everything neat and tidy. You said he was a meticulous guy, right?'

Roscoe shrugged.

'Gray hid it?' she said. 'He could have done. He hid his gun in my desk. He didn't mind hiding things.'

I looked at her. Something she had said was ringing a warning bell.

'When did he give you the gun?' I asked her.

'After Christmas,' she said. 'Not long before he died.'

'There's something wrong with that,' I said. 'The guy was a detective with twenty-five years in the job, right? A good detective. A senior, respected guy. Why would a guy like that feel his choice of off-duty weapon should have to be a secret? That wasn't his problem. He gave you the box because it held something needed hiding.'

'He was hiding the gun,' Roscoe said. 'I told you that.'

'No,' I said. 'I don't believe that. The gun was a decoy, to make sure you kept the box in a locked drawer. He didn't need to hide the gun. Guy like that could have a nuclear warhead for an off-duty weapon if he wanted to. The gun wasn't the big secret. The big secret was something else in the box.'

'But there isn't anything else in the box,' Roscoe said. 'Certainly no files, right?'

We stood still for a second. Then we ran for the doors. Crashed through and ran over to Roscoe's Chevy in the lot. Pulled Gray's file box out of the trunk. Opened it up. I handed the Desert Eagle to Finlay. Examined the box of bullets. Nothing there. There was nothing else in the file box. I shook it out. Examined the lid. Nothing there. I tore the box apart. Forced the glued seams and flattened the cardboard out. Nothing there. Then I tore the lid apart. Hidden under the corner flap there was a key. Taped to the inside face. Where it could never be seen. Where it had been carefully hidden by a dead man.

We didn't know what the key fit. We discounted anything in the station house. Discounted anything in Gray's home. Felt those places were too obvious for a cautious man to choose. I stared at the key and felt the pressure building. Closed my eyes and built a picture of Gray easing back the corner of that lid and taping his key under it. Handing the box to his friend Roscoe. Watching her put it in her drawer. Watching the drawer roll shut. Watching her lock it. Relaxing. I built that picture into a movie and ran it in my head twice before it told me what the key fitted.

'Something in the barbershop,' I said.

I snatched the Desert Eagle back from Finlay and hustled him and Roscoe into the car. Roscoe drove. She fired it up and slewed out of the lot. Turned south toward town.

'Why?' she said.

'He used to go in there,' I said. 'Three, four times a week. The old guy told me that. He was the only white guy ever went in there. It felt like safe territory. Away from Teale and Kliner and everybody else. And he didn't need to go in there, did he? You said he had a big messy beard and no hair. He wasn't going in there to get barbered. He was going in there because he liked the old guys. He turned to them. Gave them the stuff to hide.'

Roscoe jammed the Chevy to a stop on the street outside the barbershop and we jumped out and ran in. There were no customers in there. Just the two old guys sitting in their own chairs, doing nothing. I held up the key.

'We've come for Gray's stuff,' I said.

The younger guy shook his head.

'Can't give it to you, my friend,' he said.

He walked over and took the key from me. Stepped over and pressed it into Roscoe's palm.

'Now we can,' he said. 'Old Mr Gray told us, give it up to nobody except his friend Miss Roscoe.'

He took the key back from her. Stepped back to the sink and stooped down to unlock a narrow mahogany drawer built in underneath. Pulled out three files. They were thick files, each in an old furred buff paper cover. He handed one to me, one to Finlay and one to Roscoe. Then he signalled his partner and they walked through to the back. Left us alone. Roscoe sat on the upholstered bench in the window. Finlay and I hitched ourselves into the barber chairs. Put our feet up on the chrome rests. Started reading.

My file was a thick stack of police reports. They had all been xeroxed and faxed. Doubly blurred. But I could read them. They formed a dossier put together by Detective James Spirenza, Fifteenth

326

Squad, New Orleans Police Department, Homicide Bureau. Spirenza had been assigned a homicide, eight years ago. Then he had been assigned seven more. He had ended up with a case involving eight homicides. He hadn't cleared any of them. Not one. A total failure.

But he'd tried hard. His investigation had been meticulous. Painstaking. The first victim had been the owner of a textile plant. A specialist, involved in some new chemical process for cotton. The second victim was the first guy's foreman. He'd left the first guy's operation and was trying to raise seed money to start up on his own.

The next six victims were government people. EPA employees. They had been running a case out of their New Orleans office. The case concerned pollution in the Mississippi Delta. Fish were dying. The cause was traced two hundred and fifty miles upriver. A textile processing plant in Mississippi State was pumping chemicals into the river, sodium hydroxide and sodium hypochlorite and chlorine, all mixing with the river water and forming a deadly acidic cocktail.

All eight victims had died the same way. Two shots to the head with a silenced automatic pistol. A .22 calibre. Neat and clinical. Spirenza had assumed they were professional hits. He went after the shooter two ways. He called in every favour he could and shook all the trees. Professional hit men are thin on the ground. Spirenza and his buddies talked to them all. None of them knew a thing.

Spirenza's second approach was the classic approach. Figure out who is benefiting. Didn't take him long to piece it together. The textile processor up in Mississippi State looked good. He was under attack from the eight who died. Two of them were attacking him commercially. The other six were threatening to close him down. Spirenza pulled him apart. Turned him inside out. He was on his back for a year. The paperwork in my hand was a testimony to that. Spirenza had pulled in the FBI and the IRS. They'd searched every cent in every account for unexplained cash payments to the elusive shooter.

They'd searched for a year and found nothing. On the way, they turned up a lot of unsavoury stuff. Spirenza was convinced the guy had killed his wife. Plain beat her to death was his verdict. The guy had married again and Spirenza had faxed the local police department with a warning. The guy's only son was a psychopath. Worse than his father, in Spirenza's view. A stone-cold psychopath. The textile processor had protected his son every step of the way. Covered for him. Paid his way out of trouble. The boy had records from a dozen different institutions.

But nothing would stick. New Orleans FBI had lost interest. Spirenza had closed the case. Forgotten all about it, until an old detective from an obscure Georgia jurisdiction had faxed him, asking for information on the Kliner family.

Finlay closed his file. Spun his barber chair to face mine.

'The Kliner Foundation is bogus,' he said. 'Totally bogus. It's a cover for something else. It's all here. Gray bust it wide open. Audited it from top to bottom. The Foundation is spending millions every year, but its audited income is zero. Precisely zero.'

He selected a sheet from the file. Leaned over. Passed it over to me. It was a sort of balance sheet, showing the Foundation's expenditures.

'See that?' he said. 'It's incredible. That's what they're spending.'

I looked at it. The sheet contained a huge figure. I nodded.

'Maybe a lot more than that,' I said. 'I've been down here five days, right? Prior to that I was all over the States for six months. Prior to that I was all over the world. Margrave is by far the cleanest, best maintained, most manicured place I've ever seen. It's better looked after than the Pentagon or the White House. Believe me, I've been there. Everything in Margrave is either brand-new or else perfectly renovated. It's completely perfect. It's so perfect it's frightening. That must cost an absolute fortune.'

He nodded.

'And Margrave is a very weird place,' I said. 'It's deserted most of the time. There's no life. There's practically no commercial activity in the whole town. Nothing ever goes on. Nobody is earning any money.'

He looked blank. Didn't follow.

'Think about it,' I said. 'Look at Eno's, for example. Brand-new place. Gleaming, state-of-the-art diner. But he never has any customers. I've been in there a couple of times. There were never more than a couple of people in the place. The waitresses outnumber the customers. So how is Eno paying the bills? The overhead? The mortgage? Same goes for everywhere in town. Have you ever seen lines of customers rushing in and out of any of the stores?'

Finlay thought about it. Shook his head.

'Same goes for this barbershop,' I said. 'I was in here Sunday morning and Tuesday morning. The old guy said they'd had no customers in between. No customers in forty-eight hours.'

I stopped talking then. I thought about what else the old guy had said. That gnarled old barber. I suddenly thought about it in a new light.

'The old barber,' I said. 'He told me something. It was pretty weird. I thought he was crazy. I asked him how they make a living with no customers. He said they don't need customers to make a living because of the money they get from the Kliner Foundation. So I said, what money? He said a thousand bucks. He said all the merchants get it. So I figured he meant some kind of a business grant, a thousand bucks a year, right?'

Finlay nodded. Seemed about right to him.

'I was just chatting,' I said. 'Like you do in the barber's chair. So I said a thousand bucks a year is OK, but it's not going to keep the wolf from the door, something like that, right? You know what he said then?'

He shook his head and waited. I concentrated on remembering the old guy's exact words. I wanted to see if he would dismiss it as easily as I had done.

'He made it sound like a big secret,' I said. 'Like he was way out on a limb even to mention it. He was whispering to me. He said he shouldn't tell me, but he would, because I knew his sister.'

'You know his sister?' Finlay asked. Surprised.

'No, I don't,' I said. 'He was acting very confused. On Sunday, I'd been asking him about Blind Blake, you know, the old guitar player, and he said his sister had known the guy, sixty years ago. From that, he'd got mixed up, must have thought I'd said I knew his sister.'

'So what was the big secret?' he said.

'He said it wasn't a thousand dollars a year,' I said. 'He said it was a thousand dollars a week.'

'A thousand dollars a week?' Finlay said. 'A week? Is that possible?'

'I don't know,' I said. 'At the time, I assumed the old guy was crazy. But now, I think he was just telling the truth.'

'A thousand a week?' he said again. 'That's a hell of a business grant. That's fifty-two thousand bucks a year. That's a hell of a lot of money, Reacher.'

I thought about it. Pointed at the total on Gray's audit.

'They'd need figures like that,' I said. 'If this is how much they're spending, they'd need figures like that just to get rid of it all.'

Finlay was pensive. Thinking it through.

'They've bought the whole town,' he said. 'Very slowly, very quietly. They've bought the whole town for a grand a week, here and there.'

'Right,' I said. 'The Kliner Foundation has become the golden goose. Nobody will run the risk of killing it. They all keep their mouths shut and look away from whatever needs looking away from.'

'Right,' he said. 'The Kliners could get away with murder.'

I looked at him.

'They have got away with murder,' I said.

'So what do we do about it?' Finlay said.

'First we figure out exactly what the hell they're doing,' I said.

He looked at me like I was crazy.

'We know what they're doing, right?' he said. 'They're printing a shitload of funny money up in that warehouse.'

I shook my head at him.

'No, they're not,' I said. 'There's no serious manufacture of counterfeit money in the US. Joe put a stop to all that. The only place it happens is abroad.'

'So what's going on?' Finlay asked. 'I thought this was all about counterfeit money. Why else would Joe be involved?'

Roscoe looked over at us from the bench in the window.

'It is all about counterfeit money,' she said. 'I know exactly what it's all about. Every last little detail.'

She held up Gray's file in one hand.

'Part of the answer is in here,' she said.

Then she picked up the barbers' daily news-paper with the other hand.

'And the rest of the answer is in here,' she said.

Finlay and I joined her on the bench. Studied the file she'd been reading. It was a surveillance report. Gray had hidden out under the highway cloverleaf and watched the truck traffic in and out of the warehouses. Thirty-two separate days. The results were carefully listed, in three parts. On the first eleven occasions, he'd seen one truck a day incoming from the south, arriving early in the morning. He'd seen outgoing trucks all day long, heading north and west. He'd listed the outgoing trucks by destination, according to their licence plates. He must have been using field glasses. The list of destinations was all over the place. A complete spread, from California all the way up and over to Massachusetts. Those first eleven days, he'd logged eleven incoming trucks and sixty-seven outgoing. An average of one truck a day coming in, six going out, small trucks, maybe a ton of cargo in a week.

The first section of Gray's log covered the first calendar year. The second section covered the second calendar year. He'd hid out on nine separate occasions. He'd seen fifty-three outgoing trucks, the same six a day as before, with a similar list of destinations. But the log of incoming trucks was different. In the first half of the year, one truck a day was coming in, like normal. But in the second half of the year, the deliveries picked up. They built up to two trucks a day incoming.

The final twelve days of his surveillance were different again. They were all from the final five months of his life. Between last fall and February, he was still logging about six trucks a day going out to the same wide spread of destinations. But there were no incoming trucks listed at all. None at all. From last fall, stuff was being moved out, but it wasn't coming in.

'So?' Finlay asked Roscoe.

She sat back and smiled. She had it all figured.

'It's obvious, right?' she said. 'They're bringing counterfeit money into the country. It's printed in Venezuela, some place Kliner set up alongside his new chemical place there. It comes in by boat and they're hauling it up from Florida to the warehouse in Margrave. Then they're trucking it north and west, up to the big cities, LA, Chicago, Detroit, New York, Boston. They're feeding it into the cash flows in the big cities. It's an international counterfeit money distribution network. It's obvious, Finlay.'

'Is it?' he said.

'Of course it is,' she said again. 'Think of Sherman Stoller. He drove up and down to Florida to meet the boat coming in from the sea, at

Jacksonville Beach. He was on his way out there to meet the boat when he got picked up for speeding on the bridge, right? That's why he was so agitated. That's why he got the fancy lawyer out so fast, right?'

Finlay nodded.

'It all fits,' she said. 'Think of a map of the States. The money is printed in South America, comes here by sea. Lands in Florida. Flows up the southeast, and then sort of branches out from Margrave. Flows on out to LA in the west, up to Chicago in the middle, New York and Boston in the east. Separate branches, right? It looks like a candelabra or a menorah. You know what a menorah is?'

'Sure,' Finlay said. 'It's that candlestick Jewish people use.'

'Right,' she said. 'That's how it looks on a map. Florida to Margrave is the stem. Then the individual arms lead out and up to the big cities, LA across to Chicago across to Boston. It's an import network, Finlay.'

She was giving him plenty of help. Her hands were tracing menorah shapes in the air. The geography sounded OK to me. It made sense. An import flow, rolling north in trucks, up from Florida. It would need to use that knot of highways around Atlanta to branch itself out and head for the big cities in the north and west. The menorah idea was good. The left-hand arm of the candlestick would have to be bent out horizontally, to reach LA. Like somebody had dropped the thing and somebody else had accidentally stepped on it. But the idea made sense. Almost certainly Margrave itself was the pivot. Almost certainly that warehouse was the actual distribution centre. The geography was right. Using a sleepy nowhere place like Margrave as the distribution centre would be smart. And they would have a huge amount of available cash. That was for sure. Forged cash, but it would spend just the same. And there was a lot of it. They were shipping a ton a week. It was an industrial-scale operation. Huge. It would explain the Kliner Foundation's massive spending. If they ever ran short, they could just print some more. But Finlay still wasn't convinced.

'What about the last twelve months?' he said. 'There's been no import flow at all. Look at Gray's list. The incoming deliveries didn't happen. They stopped exactly a year ago. Sherman Stoller got laid off, right? There's been nothing coming up for a year. But they're still distributing something. There were still six trucks a day going out. Nothing coming in, but six trucks a day going out? What does that mean? What kind of an import flow is that?'

Roscoe just grinned at him and picked up the newspaper.

'The answer's in here,' she said. 'It's been in the papers since Friday. The Coast Guard. Last September, they started their big operation against smuggling, right? There was a lot of advance publicity. Kliner must have known it was coming. So he built up a stockpile ahead of time. See Gray's list? For the six months before last September, he doubled the incoming deliveries. He was building up a stockpile in the warehouse. He's kept on distributing it all year. That's why they've been panicking about exposure. They've been sitting there on top of a massive stockpile of counterfeit money for a year. Now the Coast Guard is going to abandon its operation, right? So they can start importing again as usual. That's what's going to happen on Sunday. That's what poor Molly meant when she said we have to get in before Sunday. We have to get in the warehouse while the last of the stockpile is still in there.'

TWENTY-TWO

Finlay nodded. He was convinced. Then he smiled. He stood up from the bench in the barbershop window and took Roscoe's hand. Shook it very formally.

'Good work,' he said to her. 'A perfect analysis. I always said you were smart, Roscoe. Right, Reacher? Didn't I tell you she's the best we got?'

I nodded and smiled and Roscoe blushed. Finlay held on to her hand and kept on smiling. But I could see him combing backward and forward through her theory, looking for loose ends. He only found two.

'What about Hubble?' he asked. 'Where did he fit in? They wouldn't recruit a bank executive just to load trucks, would they?'

I shook my head.

'Hubble used to be a currency manager,' I said. 'He was there to get rid of the fake money. He was feeding it into the system. He knew where it could be slipped in. Where it was needed. Like his old job, but in reverse.'

He nodded.

'What about the air conditioners?' he asked. 'Sherman Stoller was hauling them to Florida. That woman told you. We know that's for real because you saw two old cartons in her garage. And his truck was full of them when the Jacksonville PD searched it. What was that all about?'

'Legitimate business, I guess,' I said. 'Like a decoy. It concealed the illegal part. Like camouflage. It explained the truck movements up and down to Florida. They would have had to run south empty otherwise.'

Finlay nodded.

'Smart move, I guess,' he said. 'No empty run. Makes sense. Sell a few air conditioners, it makes money both ways, right?'

He nodded again and let go of Roscoe's hand.

'We need samples of the money,' he said.

I smiled at him. I had suddenly realized something.

'I've got samples,' I said. I put my hand in my pocket and pulled out my thick roll of hundreds. Pulled one off the back of the roll and one off the front. Gave the two banknotes to Finlay.

'These are their counterfeits?' he said.

'Got to be,' I said. 'Charlie Hubble gave me a wad of hundreds for expense money. She probably got them from Hubble. Then I took another wad from those guys who were out looking for me Tuesday.'

'And that means they're counterfeit?' Finlay said. 'Why?'

'Think about it,' I said. 'Kliner needs operating cash, why should he use real money? I bet he paid Hubble in counterfeit money. And I bet he gave those Jacksonville boys counterfeit money for their operating expenses, too.'

Finlay held the two hundreds right up to the bright light in the window. Roscoe and I crowded him for a look.

'Are you sure?' Roscoe said. 'They look real to me.'

'They're fakes,' I said. 'Got to be. Stands to reason, right? Hundreds are what fakers like to print. Anything bigger is hard to pass, anything smaller isn't worth the effort. And why should they spend real bucks when they've got truckloads of forgeries available?'

We took a good look at them. Peered at them, felt them, smelled them, rubbed them between our fingers. Finlay opened up his billfold and pulled out a hundred of his own. We compared the three notes. Passed them back and forth. Couldn't see any difference at all.

'If these are fakes, they're damn good,' Finlay said. 'But what you said makes sense. Probably the whole of the Kliner Foundation is funded with fakes. Millions every year.'

He put his own hundred back in his billfold. Slid the fakes into his pocket.

'I'm going back to the station house,' he said. 'You two come in tomorrow, about noon. Teale will be gone for lunch. We'll take it from there.'

Roscoe and I drove fifty miles south, to Macon. I wanted to keep on the move. It's a basic rule for safety. Keep moving around. We chose an anonymous motel on the southeastern fringe. As far from Margrave as you can get in Macon, with the city sprawl between us and our enemies. Old Mayor Teale had said a motel in Macon would suit me. Tonight, he was right.

We showered in cold water and fell into bed. Fell

into a restless sleep. The room was warm. We tossed around fitfully most of the night. Gave it up and got up again with the dawn. Stood there yawning in the half-light. Thursday morning. Felt like we hadn't slept at all. We groped around and got dressed in the dark. Roscoe put her uniform on. I put my old things on. I figured I'd need to buy some new stuff soon. I'd do it with Kliner's forgeries.

'What are we going to do?' Roscoe said.

I didn't answer. I was thinking about something else.

'Reacher?' she said. 'What are we going to do about all this?'

'What did Gray do about it?' I said.

'He hung himself,' she said.

I thought some more.

'Did he?' I asked her.

There was a silence.

'Oh God,' Roscoe said. 'You think there's some doubt about that?'

'Maybe,' I said. 'Think about it. Suppose he confronted one of them? Suppose he was found poking around somewhere he shouldn't have been?'

'You think they killed him?' she asked. There was panic in her voice.

'Maybe,' I said again. 'I think they killed Joe and Stoller and the Morrisons and Hubble and Molly Beth Gordon. I think they tried to kill you and me. If somebody is a threat, they kill him. That's how Kliner operates.'

Roscoe was quiet for a while. Thinking about her old colleague. Gray, the dour and patient detective. Twenty-five years of meticulous work. A guy like that was a threat. A guy who took thirty-two patient days to cross-check a suspicion was a threat. Roscoe looked up and nodded.

'He must have made a wrong move,' she said.

I nodded gently at her.

'They lynched him,' I said. 'Made it look like suicide.'

'I can't believe it,' she said.

'Was there an autopsy?' I asked her.

'Guess so,' she said.

'Then we'll check it out,' I said. 'We'll have to speak to that doctor again. Down in Yellow Springs.'

'But he'd have said, right?' she asked me. 'If he'd had doubts, wouldn't he have raised them at the time?'

'He'd have raised them with Morrison,' I said. 'Morrison would have ignored them. Because his people had caused them in the first place. We'll have to check it out for ourselves.'

Roscoe shuddered.

'I was at his funeral,' she said. 'We were all there. Chief Morrison made a speech on the lawn outside the church. So did Mayor Teale. They said he was a fine officer. They said he was Margrave's finest. But they killed him.'

She said it with a lot of feeling. She'd liked Margrave. Her family had toiled there for generations. She was rooted. She'd liked her job. Enjoyed the sense of contribution. But the community she'd served was rotten. It was dirty and corrupted. It wasn't a community. It was a swamp, wallowing in dirty money and blood. I sat and watched her world crumble.

We drove north on the road between Macon and Margrave. Halfway home Roscoe hung a right and we headed for Yellow Springs down a back road.

Over toward the hospital. I was hungry. We hadn't eaten breakfast. Not the best state for revisiting the morgue. We swung into the hospital lot. Took the speed bumps slowly and nosed around to the back. Parked up a little way from the big metal roller door.

We got out of the car. Stretched our legs on a roundabout route to the office door. The sun was warming the day up. It would have been pleasant to stay outside. But we ducked in and went looking for the doctor. We found him in his shabby office. He was at his chipped desk. Still looking tired. Still in a white coat. He looked up and nodded us in.

'Morning, folks,' he said. 'What can I do for you?'

We sat down on the same stools as Tuesday. I stayed away from the fax machine. I let Roscoe do the talking. Better that way. I had no official standing.

'February this year,' she said. 'My chief of detectives up at the Margrave PD killed himself. Do you remember?'

'Was that some guy called Gray?' the doctor said.

Roscoe nodded and the doctor got up and walked around to a file cabinet. Pulled open a drawer. It was tight and made a screeching sound. The doctor ran his fingers backwards over the files.

'February,' he said. 'Gray.'

He pulled a file and carried it back to his desk. Dropped it on his blotter. Sat back down heavily and opened it up. It was a thin file. Not much in it.

'Gray,' he said again. 'Yes, I remember this guy. Hung himself, right? First time we had a Margrave case in thirty years. I was called up to his house. In the garage, wasn't it? From a rafter?'

'That's right,' Roscoe said. She went quiet.

'So how can I help you?' the doctor said.

'Anything wrong with it?' she asked.

The doctor looked at the file. Turned a page.

'Guy hangs himself, there's always something wrong with it,' he said.

'Anything specially wrong with it?' I said.

The doctor swung his tired gaze over from Roscoe to me.

'Suspicious?' he said.

He was nearly smiling the same little smile he'd used on Tuesday.

'Was there anything suspicious about it?' I asked him.

He shook his head.

'No,' he said. 'Suicide by hanging. Open and shut. He was on a kitchen stool in his garage. Made himself a noose, jumped off the stool. Everything was consistent. We got the background story from the local people up there. I couldn't see a problem.'

'What was the background story?' Roscoe asked him.

He swung his gaze back to her. Glanced through the file.

'He was depressed,' he said. 'Had been for a while. The night it happened he was out drinking with his chief, who was the Morrison guy we just had in here, and the town mayor up there, some guy called Teale. The three of them were drowning their sorrows over some case Gray had screwed up on. He got falling down drunk and they had to help him home. They got him in to his house and left him there. He must have felt bad. He made it to the garage and hung himself.'

'That was the story?' Roscoe said.

'Morrison signed a statement,' the doctor said. 'He was real upset. Felt he should have done

343

more, you know, stayed with him or something.'

'Did it sound right to you?' she asked him.

'I didn't know Gray at all,' he said. 'This facility deals with a dozen police departments. I'd never seen anybody from Margrave before then. Quiet sort of a place, right? At least, it used to be. But what happened with this guy is consistent with what usually happens. Drinking sets people off.'

'Any physical evidence?' I asked him.

The doctor looked back in the file. Looked over at me.

'Corpse stank of whisky,' he said. 'Some fresh bruising on the upper and lower arms. Consistent with him being walked home by two men while inebriated. I couldn't see a problem.'

'Did you do a postmortem?' Roscoe asked him.

The doctor shook his head.

'No need,' he said. 'It was open and shut, we were very busy. Like I say, we have more to worry about down here than suicides over in Margrave. February, we had cases all over the place. Up to our eyes. Your Chief Morrison asked for minimum fuss. I think he sent us a note. Said it was kind of sensitive. Didn't want Gray's family to know that the old guy had been blind drunk. Wanted to preserve some kind of dignity. It was OK with me. I couldn't see a problem and we were very busy, so I released the body for cremation right away.'

Roscoe and I sat looking at each other. The doctor stepped back to the cabinet and put the file away. Closed the drawer with a screech.

'OK, folks?' he said. 'If you'll excuse me, I've got things to do.'

We nodded and thanked him for his time. Then we shuffled out of the cramped office. Got back out into the warm fall sunshine. Stood around blinking. We didn't speak. Roscoe was too upset. She'd just heard about her old friend getting murdered.

'I'm sorry,' I said.

'A bullshit story from beginning to end,' she said. 'He hadn't just screwed up on a case. He never screwed up on any case. He wasn't especially depressed. And he didn't drink. Never touched a drop. So he certainly wasn't falling down drunk. And he would never socialize with Morrison. Or the damn mayor. He just wouldn't. He didn't like them. Never in a million years would he spend a social evening with them. And he had no family. So all that stuff about his family and sensitivity and dignity is total bullshit. They killed him and bullshitted the coroner so he wouldn't look too closely.'

I sat there in the car and let the rage pour out of her. Then she was quiet and still. She was figuring out how they'd done it.

'Do you think it was Morrison and Teale?' she asked me.

'And somebody else,' I said. 'There were three guys involved. I figure the three of them went around to his place and knocked on the door. Gray opened up and Teale pulled a gun. Morrison and the third guy grabbed him and held him by the arms. That explains the bruising. Teale maybe poured a bottle of whisky down his throat, or at least splashed it all over his clothes. They hustled him off to the garage and strung him up.'

Roscoe started the car and eased it out of the hospital lot. She drove slowly over the speed bumps. Then she swung the wheel and blasted up the road through the countryside toward Margrave.

'They killed him,' she said. Just a simple

statement. 'Like they killed Joe. I think I know how you must be feeling.'

I nodded.

'They'll pay for it,' I said. 'For both of them.'

'You bet your ass,' she said.

We fell silent. Sped north for a while, then merged with the county road. A straight twelve miles up to Margrave.

'Poor old Gray,' she said. 'I can't believe it. He was so smart, so cautious.'

'Not smart enough,' I said. 'Or cautious enough. We've got to remember that. You know the rules, right? Don't be on your own. If you see somebody coming, run like hell. Or shoot the bastard. Stick with Finlay if you can, OK?'

She was concentrating on driving. She was doing a hell of a speed up the straight road. Thinking about Finlay.

'Finlay,' she repeated. 'You know what I can't figure?'

'What?' I said.

'There's the two of them, right?' she said. 'Teale and Morrison. They run the town for Kliner. They run the police department. Between them, they run everything. Their chief of detectives is Gray. An old guy, a wise head, smart and stubborn. He's been there for twenty-five years, since well before any of this shit started up. They inherited him and they can't get rid of him. So sure enough, one day their smart and stubborn detective sniffs them out. He's found out that something is going on. And they find out that he's found out. So they put him out of the way. They murder him to keep it all safe. Then what do they do next?'

'Go on,' I said.

'They hire in a replacement,' she said. 'Finlay,

down from Boston. A guy who is even smarter and even more stubborn than Gray was. Why the hell would they do that? If Gray was a danger to them, then Finlay would be twice as dangerous. So why did they do that? Why did they hire somebody even smarter than the last guy?'

'That's easy,' I said. 'They thought Finlay was really dumb.'

'Dumb?' she said. 'How the hell could they think that?'

So I told her the story Finlay had told me on Monday over doughnuts at the convenience store counter. About his divorce. About his mental state at the time. What had he said? He was a basket case. An idiot. Couldn't string two words together.

'Chief Morrison and Mayor Teale interviewed him,' I told her. 'He thought it was the worst job application in history. He thought he had come across as an idiot. He was totally amazed they gave him the job. Now I understand why they did. They really were looking for an idiot.'

Roscoe laughed. That made me feel better.

'God,' she said. 'That's ironic. They must have sat down and planned it out. Gray was a problem, they said. Better replace him with a fool, they said. Better pick the worst candidate who applies, they said.'

'Right,' I said. 'And they did. They picked a shell-shocked idiot from Boston. But by the time he turns up to start work, he's calmed down and turned back into the cool and intelligent guy he always was.'

She smiled about that for two miles. Then we crested a slight rise and began the long sweep down into Margrave. We were tensed up. It was like entering the battle zone. We'd been out of it for a while. Sweeping back into it didn't feel good. I had expected to feel better when I had identified the opposing players. But it wasn't what I had expected. It wasn't me against them, played out against a neutral background. The background wasn't neutral. The background was the opposition. The whole town was in it. The whole place was bought and paid for. Nobody would be neutral. We were barrelling down the rise at seventy miles an hour toward a dangerous mess. More dangerous than I had expected.

Roscoe slowed up at the town limit. The big Chevy glided onto Margrave's glassy blacktop. The magnolia and dogwood scrub to the left and right was replaced by velvet lawns and ornamental cherries. Those trees with smooth shiny trunks. Like the bark was buffed by hand. In Margrave, it probably was. The Kliner Foundation was probably paying somebody a handsome salary to do it.

We passed the neat blocks of stores, all of them empty and complacent, floating on an unearned thousand a week. We jinked around the village green with the statue of Caspar Teale. Wafted past the turn down to Roscoe's house with its smashed front door. Past the coffee shop. Past the benches under the smart awnings. Past the parkland where the bars and rooming houses had been, back when Margrave was honest. Then up to the station house. We pulled off into the lot and parked up. Charlie Hubble's Bentley was still there where I'd left it.

Roscoe killed the motor and we sat for a minute. Didn't want to get out. We squeezed hands, her right, my left. A brief good luck gesture. We got out of the car. Into battle.

* * *

The station house was cool and deserted except for Baker at his desk and Finlay on his way out of the rosewood office in back. He saw us and hurried over.

'Teale's back in ten minutes,' he said. 'And we got a slight problem.'

He hustled us back to the office. We went in and he shut the door.

'Picard called,' he said.

'So what's the problem?' I said.

'It's the safe house,' he said. 'Where Charlie and the kids are hiding out? That situation has to stay unofficial, right?'

'He told me that,' I said. 'He's out on a limb up there.'

'Exactly,' he said. 'That's the problem. He can't staff it. He needs somebody to be up there with Charlie. He's been doing duty himself. But he can't do any more. Can't take any more time out. And he feels it's not appropriate, you know, Charlie being a woman, and the little girl and all. Kid's terrified of him.'

He looked over at Roscoe. She saw where the conversation was going.

'He wants me up there?' she asked.

'Just for twenty-four hours,' Finlay said. 'That's what he's asking for. Will you do it for him?'

Roscoe shrugged. Smiled.

'Of course I will,' she said. 'No problem. I can spare a day. As long as you promise to get me back when the fun starts, OK?'

'That's automatic,' Finlay said. 'Fun can't start until we've got the detail, and as soon as we've got the detail, Picard goes official and he puts his own agents into the safe house. You come back here.'

'OK,' Roscoe said. 'When do I go?'

'Right now,' Finlay said. 'He'll be here any minute.'

She grinned at him.

'So you already figured I'd agree to it?' she said.

He grinned back at her.

'Like I told Reacher,' he said, 'you're the best we got.'

She and I went back through the squad room and out through the glass doors. Roscoe took her valise out of the Chevy and set it on the kerb.

'See you tomorrow, I guess,' she said.

'You going to be OK?' I asked her.

'Sure,' she said. 'I'm going to be fine. Can't get much safer than an FBI safe house, right? But I'm going to miss you, Reacher. I didn't figure to spend time apart just yet.'

I squeezed her hand. She kissed me on the cheek. Just stretched up for a quick peck. Finlay pushed the station house door open. I heard the suck of the rubber seal. He stuck his head out and called over to Roscoe.

'You better give Picard an update, OK?' he said.

Roscoe nodded to him. Then we stood waiting in the sun. Didn't have to wait long. Picard's blue sedan squealed into the lot within a couple of minutes. Bounced to a stop right next to us. The big guy folded himself out of the seat and stood up. Just about blotted out the sun.

'I appreciate this, Roscoe,' he said to her. 'You're really helping me out.'

'No problem,' she said. 'You're helping us out, right? Where is this place I'm going?'

Picard grinned a harassed grin. Nodded toward me.

'I can't say where it is,' he told her. 'Not in front of civilians, right? I'm way out of line already. And

I'm going to have to ask you not to tell him afterward, OK? And Reacher, don't you press her about it, or Charlie, OK?'

'OK,' I said. I wouldn't press her about it. She'd tell me anyway.

'Good,' Picard said.

He nodded a busy goodbye and picked up Roscoe's bag. Threw it onto his rear seat. Then the two of them got into the blue sedan and drove off. Nosed out of the lot and headed north. I waved after them. Then the car was lost to sight.

TWENTY-THREE

Details. Evidence gathering. Surveillance. It's the basis of everything. You've got to settle down and watch long enough and hard enough to get what you need. While Roscoe made cups of coffee for Charlie Hubble and Finlay sat in the rosewood office, I was going to have to watch the warehouse operation. Long enough and hard enough until I got a feel for exactly how they did it. It could take me a full twenty-four hours. Could be Roscoe would get back before I did.

I got in the Bentley and cruised up the fourteen miles to the cloverleaf. Slowed down as I passed the warehouses. I needed to scout out a vantage point. The northbound on-ramp dived under the southbound off-ramp. There was a kind of low overpass. Short, wide concrete pillars hoisted the road overhead. I figured the thing to do would be to hole up behind one of those pillars. I would be well hidden in the gloom and the slight elevation would give me a good view of the whole warehouse area. That was my spot.

I accelerated the Bentley up the ramp and carried

on north to Atlanta. Took an hour. I was picking up a rough idea of the geography. I wanted the low-rent shopping area and I found it easily enough. Saw the sort of street I wanted. Automobile customizers, pool table wholesalers, repossessed office furniture. I parked on the street in front of a storefront mission. Opposite me were two survival shops. I picked the left-hand one and went in.

The door worked a bell. The guy at the counter looked up. He was the usual type of guy. White man, black beard, camouflage fatigues, boots. He had a huge gold hoop in one ear. Looked like some kind of a pirate. He might have been a veteran. Might just have wanted to be one. He nodded to me.

He had the stuff I needed. I picked up olive fatigue pants and a shirt. Found a camouflage jacket big enough to fit. Looked at the pockets carefully. I had to get the Desert Eagle in there. Then I found a water canteen and some decent field glasses. Humped the whole lot over to the cash desk and piled it up. Pulled out my wad of hundreds. The guy with the beard looked at me.

'I could use a blackjack,' I said.

He looked at me and looked at my wad of hundreds. Then he ducked down and hoisted a box up. Looked heavy. I chose a fat sap about nine inches long. It was a leather tube. Taped at one end for a grip. Built around a plumber's spring. The thing they put inside pipes before they bend them. It was packed around with lead shot. An efficient weapon. I nodded. Paid for everything and left. The bell rang again as I pushed open the door.

I moved the Bentley along a hundred yards and parked up in front of the first automobile shop I saw advertising window tinting. Leaned on the horn and got out to meet the guy coming out of the door.

'Can you put tints on this for me?' I asked him.

'On this thing?' he said. 'Sure I can. I can put tints on anything.'

'How long?' I said.

The guy stepped up to the car and ran his finger down the silky coachwork.

'Thing like this, you want a first-rate job,' he said. 'Take me a couple of days, maybe three.'

'How much?' I said.

He carried on feeling the paint and sucked air in through his teeth, like all car guys do when you ask them how much.

'Couple of hundred,' he said. 'That's for a first-rate job, and you don't want anything less on a thing like this.'

'I'll give you two fifty,' I said. 'That's for a better than first-rate job, and you loan me a car the two or three days it's going to take you to do it, OK?'

The guy sucked in some more air and then slapped lightly on the Bentley's hood.

'It's a done deal, my friend,' he said.

I took the Bentley key off Charlie's ring and exchanged it for an eight-year-old Cadillac the colour of an old avocado pear. It seemed to drive pretty well and it was about as anonymous as you could hope to get. The Bentley was a lovely automobile, but it was not what I needed if the surveillance went mobile. It was about as distinctive as the most distinctive thing you could ever think of.

I cleared the southern rim of the city and stopped at a gas station. Brimmed the old Cadillac's big tank and bought candy bars and nuts and bottles of water. Then I used their toilet cubicle to get changed. I put on the military surplus gear and threw my old stuff into the towel bin. Went back out to the car. Put the Desert Eagle in the long inside pocket of my new jacket. Cocked and locked. Poured the spare bullets into the outside top pocket. Morrison's switchblade was in the left side pocket and I put the blackjack in the right.

I shared the nuts and the candy bars around the other pockets. Poured a bottle of water into the canteen and went to work. Took me another hour to get back to Margrave. I drove the old Cadillac right around the cloverleaf. Up the on-ramp again, heading north. Backed up about a hundred yards along the shoulder and stopped right in the no-man's-land between the off-ramp and the on-ramp. Where nobody would pass either leaving or joining the highway. Nobody would see the car except people shooting right past Margrave. And they wouldn't care.

I popped the hood and propped it open. Locked up the car and left it like that. It made it invisible. Just a broken-down old sedan on the shoulder. A sight so ordinary, you don't see it. Then I climbed over the low concrete wall at the edge of the shoulder. Scrambled down the high bank. Ran south and sprinted across the on-ramp. Carried on running for the shelter of the low overpass. I ran under the width of the highway to the other side and holed up behind a broad pillar. Over my head, the trucks coming off the highway rumbled around to the old county road. Then they ground their gears and branched right for the warehouses.

I settled back and got comfortable behind the pillar. I had a pretty good vantage point. Maybe two hundred yards distant, maybe thirty feet of elevation. The whole place was laid out below me like a diagram. The field glasses I'd bought were clear and powerful. There were actually four separate warehouses. All identical, built in a tight line, running away from me at an oblique angle. The whole area was ringed by a serious fence. Plenty of razor wire at the top. Each of the four compounds had its own inner fence. Each inner fence had its own gate. The outer fence held the main gate, fronting onto the road. The whole place was swarming with activity.

The first compound was totally innocent. The big roller door stood open. I could see local farm trucks rattling in and out. People were loading and unloading in plain view. Sturdy burlap sacks bulging with something or other. Maybe produce, maybe seed or fertilizer. Whatever farmers use. I had no idea. But there was nothing secret. Nothing hidden. All the trucks were local. Georgia plates on all of them. No out-of-state vehicles. Nothing big enough to roll south to north along the height of the nation. The first compound was clean, no doubt about that.

Same went for the second and third. Their gates stood open, their doors were up. All their activity was a cheerful swarm on their forecourts. Nothing secret. All in plain view. Different type of trucks, but all local. Couldn't see what they were hauling. Wholesale stuff for the little country stores, maybe. Possibly manufactured goods going somewhere. Some kind of oil drums in the third shed. But nothing to get excited about.

The fourth warehouse was the one I was looking for. The one at the end of the row. No doubt about it. It was a smart location. Made a lot of sense. It was screened by the chaos on the first three forecourts. But because it was the last in line, none of the local farmers or merchants would ever need to pass it by. Nobody would get a look at it. A smart location. It was definitely the one. Beyond it, maybe seventy-five yards away in a field, was the blasted tree. The one Roscoe had picked out of the photograph of Stoller and Hubble and the yellow truck. A camera on the forecourt would pick up the tree just beyond the far corner of the structure. I could see that. This was the place, no doubt about it.

The big roller door across the front was closed. The gate was closed. There were two gatemen hanging around on the forecourt. Even from two hundred yards, the field glasses picked up their alert glances and the wary tension in their walks. Some kind of a security role. I watched them for a while. They strode around, but nothing was happening. So I shifted around to watch the road. Waited for a truck bound for the fourth compound.

It was a good long wait. I was uptight about the time ticking away, so I sang to myself. I went through every version of 'Rambling on My Mind' that I knew. Everybody has a version. It's always listed as a traditional song. Nobody knows whose it was. Nobody knows where it came from. Probably from way back in the Delta. It's a song for people who can't stay around. Even though maybe there's a good reason to. People like me. I'd been around Margrave practically a week. Longest I'd ever stayed anywhere voluntarily. I should stay for ever. With Roscoe, because she was good for me. I was beginning to imagine a future with her. It felt good.

But there were going to be problems. When Kliner's dirty money was taken out, the whole town was going to fall apart. There wouldn't be anyplace left to stay around in. And I had to wander. Like the song I was singing in my head. I had to ramble. A traditional song. A song that could have been written for me. In my heart, I believed Blind Blake had made it up. He had wandered. He had walked right by this place, when the concrete pillars were old shade trees. Sixty years ago, he had walked down the road I was watching, maybe singing the song I was singing.

Joe and I used to sing that old song. We'd sing it as an ironic comment on army family life. We'd stumble off a plane somewhere and ride to an airless empty base house. Twenty minutes after moving in, we'd start up singing that song. Like we'd been there long enough and we were ready to move on again. So I leaned back on the concrete pillar and sang it for him, as well as for me.

Took me thirty-five minutes to run through every version of that old song, once for me and once for Joe. During that time I saw maybe a half-dozen trucks pull into the warehouse approach. All local guys. All little dusty Georgia trucks. Nothing with long-haul grime blasted all over it. Nothing headed for the end building. I sang softly for thirty-five minutes and picked up no information at all.

But I did get some applause. I finished the last song and heard a slow ironic handclap coming out of the darkness behind me. I whipped around the broad concrete pillar and stared into the gloom. The clapping stopped and I heard a shuffling sound. Picked up the vague shape of a man crawling towards me. The shape firmed up. Some kind of a hobo. Long grey matted hair and layers of heavy clothing. Bright eyes burning in a seamed and dirty face. The guy stopped out of reach.

'Who the hell are you?' I asked him.

He swiped his curtain of hair aside and grinned at me.

'Who the hell are you?' he said. 'Coming to my place and bawling like that?'

'This is your place?' I said. 'You live under here?'

He settled on his haunches and shrugged at me.

'Temporarily,' he said. 'Been here a month. You got a problem with that?'

I shook my head. I had no problem with that. The guy had to live somewhere.

'Sorry to disturb you,' I said. 'I'll be out of here by tonight.'

His smell was drifting over to me. Wasn't pleasant. This guy smelled like he'd been on the road all his life.

'Stay as long as you like,' he said. 'We just decided to move on. We're vacating the premises.'

'We?' I said. 'There's somebody else here?'

The guy looked at me oddly. Turned and pointed to the air beside him. There was nobody there. My eyes had adjusted to the gloom. I could see all the way back to the concrete cantilever under the elevated road. Just empty space.

'My family,' he said. 'We're pleased to meet you. But we got to go. Time to move on.'

He reached behind him and dragged a canvas kit bag out of the gloom. Army issue. There was a faint stencil on it. Pfc something, with a serial number and a unit designation. He pulled it up close and shuffled away.

'Wait up,' I said. 'Were you here last week? Thursday?'

The guy stopped and half-turned back.

'Been here a month,' he said. 'Didn't see anything last Thursday.'

I looked at him and his kit bag. A soldier. Soldiers don't volunteer anything. Their basic rule. So I eased off the concrete and pulled a candy bar out of my pocket. Wrapped it in a hundred dollar bill. Tossed it over to him. He caught it and put it in his coat. Nodded to me, silently.

'So what didn't you see last Thursday?' I asked him.

He shrugged.

'I didn't see anything,' he said. 'That's the honest truth. But my wife did. She saw plenty of things.'

'OK,' I said, slowly. 'Will you ask her what things she saw?'

He nodded. Turned and had a whispered conversation with the air beside him. Turned back to me.

'She saw aliens,' he said. 'An enemy starship, disguised like a shiny black truck. Two aliens disguised like regular earth guys in it. She saw lights in the sky. Smoke. Spaceship comes down, turns into a big car, starfleet commander comes out dressed as a cop, short fat guy. Then a white car comes off the highway, but it's really a starfighter landing, two guys in it, earth guys, pilot and co-pilot. They all do a dance, right there by the gate, because they come from another galaxy. She said it was exciting. She loves that stuff. Sees it everywhere she goes.'

He nodded at me. He meant it.

'I missed the whole thing,' he said. Gestured to the air beside him. 'The baby needed her bath. But that's what my wife saw. She loves that stuff.'

'She hear anything?' I asked him.

He asked her. Got her reply and shook his head like I was crazy.

'Space beings don't make sound,' he said. 'But

the starfighter co-pilot got all shot up with stun phasers, crawled in here later. Bled to death right where you're sitting. We tried to help him, but there's really nothing you can do about stun phasers, right? The medics got him out Sunday.'

I nodded. He crawled off, dragging his kit bag. I watched him go and then slid back around the pillar. Watched the road. Picked through his wife's story. An eyewitness report. The guy wouldn't have convinced the Supreme Court, but he sure as hell convinced me. It wasn't the Supreme Court's brother who had flown down in a starfighter and done a dance at the warehouse gate.

It was another hour before anything showed up. I'd eaten a candy bar and sipped most of a pint of water. I was just sitting and waiting. A decent-sized panel truck rolled in, coming south. It slowed up at the warehouse approach. I saw New York commercial plates through the field glasses. Dirty white rectangles. The truck nosed along the tarmac and waited at the fourth gate. The guys in the compound swung open the gate and signalled the truck through. It stopped again and the two guys swung the gate shut behind it. Then the driver backed up to the roller door and stopped. Got out of the truck. One of the gatemen climbed into the truck and the other ducked into a side door and cranked the roller open. The truck backed into the dark and the roller came down again. The New York driver was left on the forecourt, stretching in the sun. That was it. About thirty seconds, beginning to end. Nothing on show.

I watched and waited. The truck was in there eighteen minutes. Then the roller door winched open again and the gateman drove the truck back out. As soon as it was clear, the roller came down again and the gateman jumped down from the cab. The New York guy hoisted himself back into the seat while the gateman ran ahead to swing the gates. The truck passed through and rattled out and back onto the county road. It turned north and passed by twenty yards from where I was leaning up on the concrete overpass pillar. It swung onto the on-ramp and roared up to join the northbound traffic stream.

Pretty much straight away another truck was rumbling down the off-ramp, leaving the traffic stream coming down from the north. It was a similar truck. Same make, same size, same highway grime. It lumbered and bounced into the warehouse approach. I squinted through the field glasses. Illinois plates. It went through the same ritual. Paused at the gates. Backed up to the roller door. The driver was replaced by the gateman. The roller came up just long enough to swallow the truck into the gloom inside. Quick and efficient. About thirty seconds again, beginning to end. And secret. The long-haul drivers weren't allowed into the warehouse. They had to wait outside.

The Illinois truck was out quicker. Sixteen minutes. The driver reclaimed his place at the wheel and headed out, back to the highway. I watched him pass by, twenty yards away.

Our theory said both trucks had been loaded up with some of the stockpile and were grinding their way north. Thundering their way back to the big cities up there, ready to unload. So far, our theory looked good. I couldn't fault it.

The next hour, nothing happened. The fourth compound stayed closed up tight. I started to get bored. I started to wish the hobo hadn't left. We could have chatted awhile. Then I saw the third truck of the day come heading in. I raised the field glasses and saw California plates. Same type of truck, dirty red colour, rumbling in off the highway, heading for the end compound. It went through a different routine from the first two. It went in through the gates, but there was no change of driver. The truck just reversed straight in through the roller door. This guy was obviously authorized to see inside the shed. Then a wait. I timed it at twenty-two minutes. Then the roller door winched up and the truck came back out. Drove straight back out through the gates and headed for the high-way.

I took a fast decision. Time to go. I wanted to see inside one of those trucks. So I scrambled to my feet and grabbed the field glasses and the water canteen. Ran under the overpass to the northbound side. Clawed my way up the steep bank and leapt the concrete wall. Back to the old Cadillac. I slammed the hood shut and got in. Started up and rolled along the shoulder. Waited for a gap and gunned the big motor. Nudged the wheel and accelerated north.

I figured the red truck might be three or four minutes ahead. Not much more than that. I hopped past bunches of vehicles and pushed the big old car on. Then settled back to a fast cruise. I figured I was gaining all the time. After a few miles I spotted the truck. Eased off and sat well back, maybe three hundred yards behind him. Kept a half-dozen vehicles between him and me. I settled back and relaxed. We were going to LA, according to Roscoe's menorah theory.

We cruised slowly north. Not much more than fifty miles an hour. The Cadillac's tank was near enough full. Might get me three hundred miles, maybe three-fifty. At this slow cruise, maybe more. Acceleration was the killer. Gunning the worn eight-year-old V-8 would use gas faster than coffee comes out of a pot. But a steady cruise would give me reasonable mileage. Might get me up to four hundred miles. Enough to get as far west as Memphis, maybe.

We rolled on. The dirty red truck sat up big and obvious, three hundred yards ahead. It bore left around the southern fringe of Atlanta. Setting itself to strike out west, across the country. The distribution theory was looking good. I slowed down and hung back through the interchange. Didn't want the driver to get suspicious about being followed. But I could see by the way he was handling his lane changes this was not a guy who made much use of his rear-view mirrors. I closed up a little tighter.

The red truck rolled on. I stayed eight cars behind it. Time rolled by. It got late in the afternoon. It got to be early evening. I ate candy and sipped water for dinner as I drove. I couldn't work the radio. It was some kind of a fancy Japanese make. The guy at the auto shop must have transplanted it. Maybe it was busted. I wondered how he was doing with tinting the Bentley's windows. I wondered what Charlie was going to say about getting her car back with black glass. I figured maybe that was going to be the least of her worries. We rolled on.

We rolled on for almost four hundred miles. Eight hours. We drove out of Georgia, right through Alabama, into the northeast corner of Mississippi. It got pitch-dark. The fall sun had dropped away up ahead. People had switched their lights on. We drove on through the dark for hours.

It felt like I had been following the guy all my life. Then, approaching midnight, the red truck slowed down. A half-mile ahead, I saw it pull off into a truck stop in the middle of nowhere. Near a place called Myrtle. Maybe sixty miles short of the Tennessee state line. Maybe seventy miles shy of Memphis. I followed the truck into the lot. Parked up well away from it.

I saw the driver get out. A tall, thickset type of a guy. Thick neck and wide, powerful shoulders. Dark, in his thirties. Long arms, like an ape. I knew who he was. He was Kliner's son. A stone-cold psychopath. I watched him. He did some stretching and yawning in the dark standing by his truck. I stared at him and pictured him Thursday night, at the warehouse gate, dancing.

The Kliner kid locked up the truck and ambled off toward the buildings. I waited a spell and followed him. I figured he would have gone straight for the bathroom, so I hung around the newsstand in the bright neon and watched the door. I saw him come out and watched him amble into the diner area. He settled at a table and stretched again. Picked up the menu with the expansive air of a guy who was taking his time. He was there for a late dinner. I figured he'd take twenty-five minutes. Maybe a half-hour.

I headed back out to the parking lot. I wanted to break into the red truck and get a look inside. But I saw there was no chance of doing it out there in the lot. No chance at all. People were walking around and a couple of police cruisers were loafing about. The whole place was lit up with bright lights. Breaking into that truck was going to have to wait.

I walked back to the buildings. Crammed myself into a phone booth and dialled the station house in Margrave. Finlay answered right away. I heard his deep Harvard tones. He'd been sitting by the phone, waiting for me to check in.

'Where are you?' he said.

'Not far from Memphis,' I said. 'I watched a truck load up and I'm sticking with it until I get a chance to look inside. The driver's the Kliner kid.'

'OK,' he said. 'I heard from Picard. Roscoe's safely installed. Fast asleep now, if she's got any sense. He said she sends her love.'

'Send mine back if you get the chance,' I said. 'Take care, Harvard guy.'

'Take care yourself,' he said. Hung up.

I strolled back to the Cadillac. Got in and waited. It was a half-hour before the Kliner kid came out again. I saw him walk back toward the red truck. He was wiping his mouth with the back of his hand. Looked like he'd had a good dinner. Certainly taken him long enough. He walked out of sight. A minute later the truck rattled by and lurched onto the exit road. But the kid didn't head back to the highway. He ducked a left onto a service road. He was going around to the motel. He was going to stay overnight.

He drove right up to the row of motel cabins. Parked the red truck up against the second cabin from the end. Right in the glow of a big amp on a pole. He got out and locked up. Took a key from his pocket and opened up the cabin. Went in and shut the door. I saw the light go on and the blind come down. He'd had the key in his pocket. He hadn't gone into the office. He must have booked the room when he was inside for dinner. He must have paid for it and picked up the key. That's what had taken him so damn long in there.

It gave me a problem. I needed to see inside the truck. I needed the evidence. I needed to know I was in the right. And I needed to know soon. Sunday was forty-eight hours away. I had things to do before Sunday. A lot of things. I was going to have to break into the truck, right there in the glare of the light on the pole. While the psychopathic Kliner kid was ten feet away in his motel room. Not the safest thing in the world to do. I was going to have to wait to do it. Until the kid was sound asleep and wouldn't hear the boom and scrape as I went to work.

I waited a half-hour. Couldn't wait any more. I started the old Cadillac and moved it through the stillness. The tappets were out and the pistons were slapping. The motor was making a hell of a noise in the silence. I parked the car tight up to the red truck. Nose in, facing the kid's motel room door. I climbed out across the passenger seat. Stood still and listened. Nothing.

I took Morrison's switchblade from my jacket pocket and stepped up onto the Cadillac's front fender. Stepped onto the hood and up over the windshield. Up onto the Cadillac's roof. Stood still, up high. Listened hard. Nothing. I leaned over to the truck and hauled myself upward onto its roof.

A panel truck like that has a translucent roof. It's some kind of a fibreglass sheet. They make the roof out of it, or at least a sort of skylight set into the sheet metal. It's there to let a dim light down into the cargo area. Helps with loading and unloading. Maybe it's lighter in weight. Maybe cheaper. Manufacturer will do anything to save a buck. The roof is the best way into a truck like that.

My upper body was flat on the fibreglass panel and my feet were scrabbling for the Cadillac's gutter. I reached out as far as I could and sprang the switchblade. Stabbed it down through the plastic panel, right in the centre of the roof. Used the blade to saw a flap about ten inches deep, eighteen inches wide. I could push it down and peer in. Like looking down through a shallow slot.

The light in the motel room snapped on. The window blind threw a yellow square of light out over the Cadillac. Over the side of the red truck. Over my legs. I grunted and pushed off. Swam out onto the truck's roof. Lay flat and silent. Held my breath.

The motel room door opened. The Kliner kid came out. Stared at the Cadillac. Stooped and looked inside. Walked around and checked the truck. Checked the cab doors. Tugged the handles. The vehicle shook and rocked under me. He walked around to the back and tried the rear doors. Tugged the handles. I heard the doors rattle against their locks.

He walked a circuit of the truck. I lay there and listened to the crack of his footsteps below. He checked the Cadillac again. Then he went back inside. The room door slammed. The light snapped off. The yellow square of light died.

I waited five minutes. Just lay there up on the roof and waited. Then I hauled myself up onto my elbows. Reached for the slot in the fibreglass that I'd just cut. Forced the flap down and hooked my fingers in. Dragged myself over and peered through.

The truck was empty. Totally empty. Nothing in it at all.

TWENTY-FOUR

It was over four hundred miles back to the Margrave station house. I drove all of them as fast as I dared. I needed to see Finlay. Needed to lay out a brand-new theory for him. I slotted the old Cadillac into a space right next to Teale's brand-new model. Went inside and nodded to the desk guy. He nodded back.

'Finlay here?' I asked him.

'In back,' he told me. 'The mayor's with him.'

I skirted the reception counter and ran through the squad room to the rosewood office. Finlay was in there with Teale. Finlay had bad news for me. I could see it in the slope of his shoulders. Teale looked at me, surprised.

'You back in the army, Mr Reacher?' he said.

Took me a second to catch on. He was talking about my fatigues and the camouflage jacket. I looked him up and down. He was in a shiny grey suit with embroidered patterns all over it. Bootlace tie with a silver clasp.

'Don't you be talking to me about clothes, asshole,' I said.

He looked down at himself in surprise. Brushed off a speck that hadn't been there. Glared up at me.

'I could have you arrested for language like that,' he said.

'And I could tear your head off,' I said to him. 'And then I could stick it up your ratty old ass.'

We stood and glared at each other for what seemed like a long time. Teale gripped his heavy cane like he wanted to raise it up and hit me with it. I could see his hand tightening around it and his glance darting towards my head. But in the end he just stalked out of the office and slammed the door. I reopened it a crack and peered out after him. He was picking up a phone at one of the squad room desks. He was going to call Kliner. He was going to ask him when the hell he was going to do something about me. I shut the door again and turned to Finlay.

'What's the problem?' I asked him.

'Serious shit,' he said. 'But did you get a look in the truck?'

'I'll get to that in a minute,' I said. 'What's the problem here?'

'You want the small problem first?' he said. 'Or the big problem?'

'Small first,' I said.

'Picard's keeping Roscoe another day,' he said. 'No option.'

'Shit,' I said. 'I wanted to see her. She happy with that?'

'According to Picard she is,' he said.

'Shit,' I said again. 'So what's the big problem?'

'Somebody's ahead of us,' he whispered.

'Ahead of us?' I asked him. 'What do you mean?'

'Your brother's list?' he said. 'The initials and the note about Sherman Stoller's garage? First thing is there's a telex in from the Atlanta PD this morning. Stoller's house burned down in the night. Out by the golf course, where you went with Roscoe? Totally destroyed, garage and all. Torched. Somebody threw gasoline all over the place.'

'Christ,' I said. 'What about Judy?'

'Neighbour says she bailed out Tuesday night,' he said. 'Right after you spoke to her. Hasn't been back. The house was empty.'

I nodded.

'Judy's a smart woman,' I said. 'But that doesn't put them ahead of us. We already saw the inside of the garage. If they were trying to hide something, they were too late. Nothing to hide anyway, right?'

'The initials?' he said. 'The colleges? I identified the Princeton guy this morning. W.B. was Walter Bartholomew. Professor. He was killed last night, outside his house.'

'Shit,' I said. 'Killed how?'

'Stabbed,' he said. 'Jersey police are calling it a mugging. But we know better than that, right?'

'Any more good news?' I asked him.

He shook his head.

'Gets worse,' he said. 'Bartholomew knew something. They got to him before he could talk to us. They're ahead of us, Reacher.'

'He knew something?' I said. 'What?'

'Don't know,' Finlay said. 'When I called the number, I got some research assistant guy, works for Bartholomew. Seems Bartholomew was excited about something, stayed at his office late last night, working. This assistant guy was ferrying him all kinds of old material. Bartholomew was checking it through. Late on, he packed up, e-mailed Joe's computer and went home. He ran into the mugger, and that was that.'

'What did the e-mail say?' I asked him.

'It said stand by for a call in the morning,' he told me. 'The assistant guy said it felt like Bartholomew had hit on something important.'

'Shit,' I said again. 'What about the New York initials? K.K.?'

'Don't know yet,' he said. 'I'm guessing it's another professor. If they haven't gotten to him yet.'

'OK,' I said. 'I'm going to New York to find him.'

'Why the panic?' Finlay asked. 'Was there a problem with the truck?'

'There was one major problem,' I said. 'The truck was empty.'

There was silence in the office for a long moment.

'It was going back empty?' Finlay said.

'I got a look inside just after I called you,' I said. 'It was empty. Nothing in it at all. Just fresh air.'

'Christ,' he said.

He looked upset. He couldn't believe it. He'd admired Roscoe's distribution theory. He'd congratulated her. Shook her hand. The menorah shape. It was a good theory. It was so good, he couldn't believe it was wrong.

'We've got to be right,' he said. 'It makes so much sense. Think of what Roscoe said. Think of the map. Think of Gray's figures. It all fits together. It's so obvious, I can just about feel it. I can just about see it. It's a traffic flow. It can't be anything else. I've been over it so many times.'

'Roscoe was right,' I agreed. 'And everything

you just said is right. The menorah shape is right. Margrave is the centre. It's a traffic flow. We only got one little detail wrong.'

'What detail?' he said.

'We got the direction wrong,' I said. 'We got it ass-backward. The flow goes exactly the opposite direction. Same shape, but it's flowing down here, not out of here.'

He nodded. He saw it.

'So they're not loading up here,' he said. 'They're unloading here. They're not dispersing a stockpile. They're building up a stockpile. Right here in Margrave. But a stockpile of what? You're certain they're not printing money somewhere and bringing it down here?'

I shook my head.

'Doesn't make any sense,' I said. 'Molly said there's no printing going on in the States. Joe stopped it.'

'So what are they bringing down here?' he said.

'We need to figure that out,' I said. 'But we know it adds up to about a ton a week. And we know it fits into air conditioner boxes.'

'We do?' Finlay said.

'That's what changed last year,' I said. 'Before last September, they were smuggling it out of the country. That's what Sherman Stoller was doing. The air conditioner runs weren't a decoy operation. They were the actual operation itself. They were exporting something boxed up in air conditioner cartons. Sherman Stoller was driving them down to Florida every day to meet a boat. That's why he got so uptight when he was flagged down for speeding. That's why the fancy lawyer came running over. Not because he was on his way to load up. Because he was on his way to unload.

He had the Jacksonville police sniffing around a full load for fifty-five minutes.'

'But a full load of what?' Finlay said.

'I don't know,' I said. 'The cops didn't think to look. They saw a load of sealed-up air conditioner cartons, brand-new, serial numbers and everything, and they just assumed it was kosher. The air conditioner cartons were damn good cover. Very plausible product to be hauling south. Nobody would be suspicious of brand-new air conditioners heading south, right?'

'But they stopped a year ago?' he said.

'Correct,' I said. 'They knew the Coast Guard thing was coming, so they got as much out as they could ahead of time. Remember the double runs in Gray's notes? Then they stopped altogether, a year ago. Because they felt just as vulnerable smuggling outward past the Coast Guard as we figured they'd feel smuggling inward.'

Finlay nodded. Looked displeased with himself.

'We missed that,' he said.

'We missed a lot of things,' I said. 'They fired Sherman Stoller because they didn't need him any more. They decided just to sit on the stuff and wait for the Coast Guard thing to stop. That's why they're vulnerable right now. That's why they're panicking, Finlay. It's not the last remains of a stockpile they've got in there until Sunday. It's the whole damn thing.'

Finlay stood guard at the office door. I sat at the rosewood desk and called Columbia University in New York. The number reached the modern history department. The early part of the call was very easy. I got a helpful woman in their administrative office. I asked if they had a professor with the initials K.K. Straight away she identified a guy called Kelvin Kelstein. Been there many years. Sounded like he was a very eminent type of a guy. Then the call got very difficult. I asked if he would come to the phone. The woman said no he wouldn't. He was very busy and could not be disturbed again.

'Again?' I said. 'Who's been disturbing him already?'

'Two detectives from Atlanta, Georgia,' she said.

'When was this?' I asked her.

'This morning,' she said. 'They came in here asking for him and they wouldn't take no for an answer.'

'Can you describe these two men to me?' I asked her.

There was a pause as she tried to remember.

'They were Hispanic,' she said. 'I don't recall any details. The one who did the talking was very neat, very polite. Unremarkable, really, I'm afraid.'

'Have they met with him yet?' I asked her.

'They made a one o'clock appointment,' she said. 'They're taking him to lunch somewhere, I believe.'

I held the phone tighter.

'OK,' I said. 'This is very important. Did they ask for him by name? Or by the initials K.K.? Like I just did?'

'They asked exactly the same question you did,' she said. 'They asked if we had any faculty with those initials.'

'Listen to me,' I said. 'Listen very carefully. I want you to go see Professor Kelstein. Right now. Interrupt him, whatever he's doing. Tell him this is life or death. Tell him those Atlanta detectives are bogus. They were at Princeton last night and they murdered Professor Walter Bartholomew.'

'Are you kidding?' the woman said. Almost a scream.

'This is for real,' I said. 'My name is Jack Reacher. I believe Kelstein had been in touch with my brother, Joe Reacher, from the Treasury Department. Tell him my brother was murdered also.'

The woman paused again. Swallowed. Then she came back, calm.

'What should I tell Professor Kelstein to do?' she said.

'Two things,' I said. 'First, he must not, repeat, must not meet with the two Hispanic men from Atlanta. At any time. Got that?'

'Yes,' she said.

'Good,' I said. 'Second, he must go right now to the campus security office. Right now, OK? He must wait there for me. I'll be there in about three hours. Kelstein must sit in the security office and wait for me with a guard right next to him until I get there. Can you make absolutely sure he does that?'

'Yes,' she said again.

'Tell him to call Princeton from the security office,' I said. 'Tell him to ask after Bartholomew. That should convince him.'

'Yes,' the woman said again. 'I'll make sure he does what you say.'

'And give my name to your security desk,' I said. 'I don't want any problem getting in when I arrive. Professor Kelstein can ID me. Tell him I look like my brother.'

I hung up. Shouted across the room to Finlay.

'They've got Joe's list,' I said. 'They've got two

376

guys up in New York. One of them is the same guy who got Joe's briefcase. Neat, polite guy. They've got the list.'

'But how?' he said. 'The list wasn't in the brief-case.'

A clang of fear hit me. I knew how. It was staring me in the face.

'Baker,' I said. 'Baker's inside the scam. He made an extra xerox copy. You sent him to copy Joe's list. He made two copies and gave one to Teale.'

'Christ,' Finlay said. 'Are you sure?'

I nodded.

'There were other indications,' I said. 'Teale's pulled a bluff. We figured everybody in the department was clean. But he was just keeping them hidden. So now we don't know who the hell is involved and who the hell isn't. We've got to get out of here, right now. Let's go.'

We ran out of the office. Through the squad room. Out through the big plate-glass doors and into Finlay's car.

'Where to?' he said.

'Atlanta,' I told him. 'The airport. I've got to get to New York.'

He started up and headed out north along the county road.

'Baker was in it from the start,' I said. 'It was staring me in the face.'

I went through it with him as he drove. Step by step. Last Friday I had been alone in the small white interview room at the station house with Baker. I had held out my wrists to him. He'd removed my handcuffs. He'd taken the cuffs off a guy he was supposed to believe was a murderer. A murderer who had pulped his victim's body. He was willing to put himself alone in a room with such a guy. Then later I had called him over and made him escort me to the bathroom. He had been sloppy and careless. I'd had opportunities to disarm him and escape. I'd taken it as a sign he'd listened to me answering Finlay's questions and slowly become convinced I was innocent.

But he'd always known I was innocent. He knew exactly who was innocent and exactly who wasn't. That's why he had been so casual. He knew I was just a convenient fall guy. He knew I was just an innocent passerby. Who worries about taking the cuffs off an innocent passerby? Who takes a whole lot of precautions escorting an innocent passerby to the bathroom?

And he had brought Hubble in for questioning. I'd noticed his body language. He was all twisted up with conflict. I had figured he was feeling awkward because Hubble was Stevenson's buddy and his relative by marriage. But it wasn't that. He was all twisted up because he was caught in a trap. He knew bringing Hubble in was a disaster. But he couldn't disobey Finlay without alerting him. He was trapped. Damned if he did, damned if he didn't.

And there had been a deliberate attempt to conceal Joe's identity. Baker had deliberately screwed up the prints thing with the computer so that Joe would remain unidentified. He knew Joe was a government investigator. He knew Joe's prints would be in the Washington database. So he tried to make damn sure they didn't get matched. But he had blown his cover by announcing the null result far too early. It was inexperience. He'd always left the technical work to Roscoe. So he didn't know the system. But I hadn't put two and two together. I had been too overwhelmed when the second attempt with the prints had brought back my brother's name.

Since then, he had been poking and prying, hovering around on the edge of our hidden investigation. He had wanted in and he had been a willing helper. Finlay had used him on lookout duty. And all the time he was running to Teale with the snippets he was getting from us.

Finlay was blasting north at a hell of a speed. He flung the Chevy around the cloverleaf and mashed the pedal. The big car hurtled forward up the highway.

'Could we try the Coast Guard?' he said. 'Get them to stand by Sunday for when they start shipping out? Some kind of an extra patrol?'

'You're joking,' I said. 'The political flak the President's taken over that, he's not going to reverse himself the very first day, just because you ask him to.'

'So what do we do?' he said.

'Call Princeton back,' I told him. 'Get hold of that research assistant again. He may be able to piece together what Bartholomew figured out last night. Hole up somewhere safe and get busy.'

He laughed.

'Where the hell's safe now?' he said.

I told him to use the Alabama motel we'd used Monday. It was in the middle of nowhere and it was as safe as he needed to get. I told him I'd find him there when I got back. Asked him to bring the Bentley to the airport and to leave the key and the parking claim at the arrivals information desk. He repeated all the arrangements back to me to confirm he was solid. He was doing more than ninety miles an hour, but he was turning his head to look at me every time he spoke.

'Watch the road, Finlay,' I said. 'No good to anybody if you kill us in a damn car.'

He grinned and faced forward. Jammed his foot down harder. The big police Chevy eased up over a hundred. Then he turned again and looked straight into my eyes for about three hundred yards.

'Coward,' he said.

TWENTY-FIVE

No easy way to get through the airport security hoops with a sap and a knife and a big metal gun, so I left my camouflage jacket in Finlay's car and told him to transfer it to the Bentley. He ducked into Departures with me and put the best part of seven hundred bucks on his credit card for my round trip ticket on Delta to New York. Then he took off to find the Alabama motel and I went through to the gate for the plane to La Guardia.

I was airborne for a shade over two hours and in a cab for thirty-five minutes. Arrived in Manhattan just after four-thirty. I'd been there in May and it looked pretty much the same in September. The summer heat was over and the city was back to work. The cab took me over the Triborough Bridge and headed west on 116th. Slid around Morningside Park and dropped me at Columbia University's main entrance. I went in and found my way to the campus security office. Knocked on the glass.

A campus policeman checked a clipboard and let

me in. Led me through to a room in back and pointed to Professor Kelvin Kelstein. I saw a very old guy, tiny, wizened with age, sporting a huge shock of white hair. He looked exactly like that cleaner I'd seen on the third floor at Warburton, except he was white.

'The two Hispanic guys been back?' I asked the college cop.

He shook his head.

'Haven't seen them,' he said. 'The old guy's office told them that the lunch date was cancelled. Maybe they went away.'

'I hope so,' I said. 'Meanwhile, you're going to have to watch over this guy for a spell. Give it until Sunday.'

'Why?' he said. 'What's going on?'

'Not sure, exactly,' I said. 'I'm hoping the old guy can tell me.'

The guard walked us back to Kelstein's own office and left us there. It was a small and untidy room crammed full to the ceiling with books and thick journals. Kelstein sat in an old armchair and gestured me to sit opposite him in another.

'What exactly happened to Bartholomew?' he asked.

'I don't know exactly,' I said. 'Jersey police say he got stabbed during a mugging outside his home.'

'But you remain sceptical?' Kelstein asked.

'My brother made a list of contacts,' I said. 'You're the only one of them still alive.'

'Your brother was Mr Joe Reacher?' he said.

I nodded.

'He was murdered last Thursday,' I said. 'I'm trying to find out why.'

Kelstein inclined his head and peered out of a grimy window.

'I'm sure you know why,' he said. 'He was an investigator. Clearly he was killed in the course of an investigation. What you need to know is what he was investigating.'

'Can you tell me what that was?' I said.

The old professor shook his head.

'Only in the most general terms,' he said. 'I can't help you with specifics.'

'Didn't he discuss specifics with you?' I said.

'He used me as a sounding board,' he said. 'We were speculating together. I enjoyed it tremendously. Your brother Joe was a stimulating companion. He had a keen mind and a very attractive precision about the manner in which he expressed himself. It was a pleasure to work with him.'

'But you didn't discuss specifics?' I said again.

Kelstein cupped his hands like a man holding an empty vessel.

'We discussed everything,' he said. 'But we came to no conclusions.'

'OK,' I said. 'Can we start at the beginning? The discussion was about counterfeit currency, right?'

Kelstein tilted his great head to one side. Looked amused.

'Obviously,' he said. 'What else would Mr Joe Reacher and I find to discuss?'

'Why you?' I asked him bluntly.

The old professor smiled a modest smile which faded into a frown. Then he came up with an ironic grin.

'Because I am the biggest counterfeiter in history,' he said. 'I was going to say I was one of the two biggest in history, but after the events of last night at Princeton, sadly now I alone remain.'

'You and Bartholomew?' I said. 'You were counterfeiters?'

The old guy smiled again.

'Not by choice,' he said. 'During the Second World War, young men like Walter and me ended up with strange occupations. He and I were considered more useful in an intelligence role than in combat. We were drafted into the SIS, which as you know was the very earliest incarnation of the CIA. Other people were responsible for attacking the enemy with guns and bombs. We were handed the job of attacking the enemy with economics. We derived a scheme for shattering the Nazi economy with an assault on the value of its paper currency. Our project manufactured hundreds of billions of counterfeit reichsmarks. Spare bombers littered Germany with them. They came down out of the sky like confetti.'

'Did it work?' I asked him.

'Yes and no,' he said. 'Certainly, their economy was shattered. Their currency was worthless very quickly. But of course, much of their production used slave labour. Slaves aren't interested one way or the other whether the content of somebody else's wage packet is worth anything. And of course, alternative currencies were found. Chocolate, cigarettes, anything. Altogether, it was only a partial success. But it left Walter and me two of history's greatest forgers. That is, if you use sheer volume as a measure. I can't claim any great talent for the inky end of the process.'

'So Joe was picking your brains?' I asked him.

'Walter and I became obsessed,' Kelstein said. 'We studied the history of money forging. It started the day after paper money was first introduced. It's never gone away. We became experts. We carried on the interest after the war. We developed a loose relationship with the government. Finally, some years ago, a Senate subcommittee commissioned a report from us. With all due modesty, I can claim that it became the Treasury's anticounterfeiting bible. Your brother was familiar with it, of course. That's why he was talking to Walter and me.'

'But what was he talking to you about?' I said.

'Joe was a new broom,' Kelstein said. 'He was brought in to solve problems. He was a very talented man indeed. His job was to eradicate counterfeiting. Now, that's an impossible job. Walter and I told him that. But he nearly succeeded. He thought hard, and he applied strokes of appealing simplicity. He just about halted all illicit printing within the United States.'

I sat in his crowded office and listened to the old guy. Kelstein had known Joe better than I had. He had shared Joe's hopes and plans. Celebrated his successes. Sympathized over his setbacks. They had talked at length, animatedly, sparking off each other. The last time I had spoken to Joe face to face was very briefly after our mother's funeral. I hadn't asked him what he was doing. I'd just seen him as my older brother. Just seen him as Joe. I hadn't seen the reality of his life as a senior agent, with hundreds of people under him, trusted by the White House to solve big problems, capable of impressing a smart old bird like Kelstein. I sat there in the armchair and felt bad. I'd lost something I never knew I'd had.

'His systems were brilliant,' Kelstein said. 'His analysis was acute. He targeted ink and paper. In the end, it all boils down to ink and paper, doesn't it? If anybody bought the sort of ink or paper that could be used to forge a banknote, Joe's people knew within hours. He swept people up within days. Inside the States, he reduced counterfeiting activity by ninety per cent. And he tracked the remaining ten per cent so vigorously he got almost all of them before they'd even distributed the fakes. He impressed me greatly.'

'So what was the problem?' I asked him.

Kelstein made a couple of precise little motions with his small white hands, like he was moving one scenario aside and introducing another.

'The problem lay abroad,' he said. 'Outside the United States. The situation there is very different. Did you know there are twice as many dollars outside the US as inside?'

I nodded. I summarized what Molly had told me about foreign holdings. The trust and the faith. The fear of a sudden collapse in the desirability of the dollar. Kelstein was nodding away like I was his student and he liked my thesis.

'Quite so,' he said. 'It's more about politics than crime. In the end, a government's primary duty is to defend the value of its currency. We have two hundred and sixty billion dollars abroad. The dollar is the unofficial currency of dozens of nations. In the new Russia, for instance, there are more dollars than rubles. In effect, it's like Washington has raised a massive foreign loan. Raised any other way, that loan would cost us twenty-six billion dollars a year in interest payments alone. But this way, it costs us nothing at all except what we spend on printing pictures of dead politicians on little pieces of paper. That's what it's all about, Mr Reacher. Printing currency for foreigners to buy is the best racket a government can get into. So Joe's job in reality was worth twenty-six billion dollars a year to this country. And he pursued it with an energy appropriate to those high stakes.'

'So where was the problem?' I said. 'Geographically?'

'Two main places,' Kelstein said. 'First, the Middle East. Joe believed there was a plant in the Bekaa Valley that turned out fake hundreds which were practically perfect. But there was very little he could do about it. Have you been there?'

I shook my head. I'd been stationed in Beirut for a while. I had known a few people who had gone out to the Bekaa Valley for one reason or another. Not too many of them had come back.

'Syrian-controlled Lebanon,' Kelstein said. 'Joe called it the badlands. They do everything there. Training camps for the world's terrorists, drug processing laboratories, you name it, they've got it. Including a pretty good replica of our own Bureau of Printing and Engraving.'

I thought about it. Thought about my time there.

'Protected by who?' I asked him.

Kelstein smiled at me again. Nodded.

'A perceptive question,' he said. 'You instinctively grasp that an operation of that size is so visible, so complex, that it must be in some way sponsored. Joe believed it was protected by, or maybe even owned by, the Syrian government. Therefore his involvement was marginal. His conclusion was that the only solution was diplomatic. Failing that, he was in favour of air strikes against it. We may live to see such a solution one day.'

'And the second place?' I asked him.

He pointed his finger at his grimy office window. Aiming south down Amsterdam Avenue.

'South America,' he said. 'The second source is Venezuela. Joe had located it. That is what he was working on. Absolutely outstanding counterfeit hundred dollar bills are coming out of Venezuela.

But strictly private enterprise. No suggestion of government involvement.'

I nodded.

'We got that far,' I said. 'A guy called Kliner, based down in Georgia where Joe was killed.'

'Quite so,' Kelstein said. 'The ingenious Mr Kliner. It's his operation. He's running the whole thing. We knew that for certain. How is he?'

'He's panicking,' I said. 'He's killing people.'

Kelstein nodded sadly.

'We thought Kliner might panic,' he said. 'He's protecting an outstanding operation. The very best we've ever seen.'

'The best?' I said.

Kelstein nodded enthusiastically.

'Outstanding,' he said again. 'How much do you know about counterfeiting?'

I shrugged at him.

'More than I did last week,' I said. 'But not enough, I guess.'

Kelstein nodded and shifted his frail weight forward in his chair. His eyes lit up. He was about to start a lecture on his favourite subject.

'There are two sorts of counterfeiters,' he said. 'The bad ones and the good ones. The good ones do it properly. Do you know the difference between intaglio and lithography?'

I shrugged and shook my head. Kelstein scooped up a magazine from a pile and handed it to me. It was a quarterly bulletin from a history society.

'Open it,' he said. 'Any page will do. Run your fingers over the paper. It's smooth, isn't it? That's lithographic printing. That's how virtually everything is printed. Books, magazines, newspapers, everything. An inked roller passes over the blank paper. But intaglio is different.'

He suddenly clapped his hands together. I jumped. The sound was very loud in his quiet office.

'That's intaglio,' he said. 'A metal plate is smashed into the paper with considerable force. It leaves a definite embossed feel to the product. The printed image looks three dimensional. It feels three dimensional. It's unmistakable.'

He eased himself up and took his wallet out of his hip pocket. Pulled out a ten dollar bill. Passed it over to me.

'Can you feel it?' he asked. 'The metal plates are nickel, coated with chromium. Fine lines are engraved into the chromium and the lines are filled with ink. The plate hits the paper and the ink is printed onto its topmost surface. Understand? The ink is in the valleys of the plate, so it's transferred to the ridges on the paper. Intaglio printing is the only way to get that raised image. The only way to make the forgery feel right. It's how the real thing is done.'

'What about the ink?' I said.

'There are three colours,' he said. 'Black, and two greens. The back of the bill is printed first, with the darker green. Then the paper is left to dry, and the next day the front is printed with the black ink. That dries, and the front is printed again, with the lighter green. That's the other stuff you see there on the front, including the serial number. But the lighter green is printed by a different process, called letterpress. It's a stamping action, the same as intaglio, but the ink is stamped into the valleys on the paper, not onto the peaks.'

I nodded and looked at the ten dollar bill, front and back. Ran my fingers over it carefully. I'd never really studied one before.

'So, four problems,' Kelstein said. 'The press, the plates, the inks, and the paper. The press can be bought, new or used, anywhere in the world. There are hundreds of sources. Most countries print money and securities and bonds on them. So the presses are obtainable abroad. They can even be improvised. Joe found one intaglio operation in Thailand which was using a converted squid-processing machine. Their hundreds were absolutely immaculate.'

'What about the plates?' I asked him.

'Plates are problem number two,' he said. 'But it's a matter of talent. There are people in the world who can forge Old Master paintings and there are people who can play a Mozart piano concerto after hearing it once. And certainly there are engravers who can reproduce banknotes. It's a perfectly logical proposition, isn't it? If a human being in Washington can engrave the original, certainly there's a human being somewhere else who can copy it. But they're rare. Really good copyists, rarer still. There are a few in Armenia. The Thai operation using the squid-processor got a Malaysian to make the plates.'

'OK,' I said. 'So Kliner has bought a press, and he's found an engraver. What about the inks?'

'The inks are problem number three,' he said. 'You can't buy anything vaguely like them in the US. Joe saw to that. But abroad, they're available. As I said, virtually every country in the world has its own banknote printing industry. And obviously, Joe couldn't enforce his systems in every country in the world. So the inks are easy enough to find. The greens are only a question of colour. They mix them and experiment until they get them right. The black ink is magnetic, did you know that?'

I shook my head again. Looked at the sawbuck closely. Kelstein smiled.

'You can't see it,' he said. 'A liquid ferrous chemical is mixed with the black ink. That's how electronic money counters work. They scan the engraving down the centre of the portrait, and the machine reads the signal it gives off, like a tape head reads the sounds on a music cassette.'

'And they can get that ink?' I said.

'Anywhere in the world,' he said. 'Everybody uses it. We lag behind other countries. We don't like to admit we worry about counterfeiting.'

I remembered what Molly had said. Faith and trust. I nodded.

'The currency must look stable,' Kelstein said. 'That's why we're so reluctant to change it. It's got to look reliable, solid, unchanging. Turn that ten over and take a look.'

I looked at the green picture on the back of the ten. The Treasury Building was standing in a deserted street. Only one car was driving past. It looked like a Model-T Ford.

'Hardly changed since 1929,' Kelstein said. 'Psychologically, it's very important. We choose to put the appearance of dependability before security. It made Joe's job very difficult.'

I nodded again.

'Right,' I said. 'So we've covered the press, the plates, and the inks. What about the paper?'

Kelstein brightened up and clasped his small hands like we'd reached the really interesting part.

'Paper is problem number four,' he said. 'Actually, we should really say it's problem number one. It's by far the biggest problem. It's the thing Joe and I couldn't understand about Kliner's operation.'

'Why not?' I asked him.

'Because their paper is perfect,' he said. 'It's one hundred per cent perfect. Their paper is better than their printing. And that is absolutely unheard of.'

He started shaking his great white head in wonderment. Like he was lost in admiration for Kliner's achievement. We sat there, knee to knee in the old armchairs in silence.

'Perfect?' I prompted him.

He nodded and started up with the lecture again.

'It's unheard of,' he said again. 'The paper is the hardest part of the whole process. Don't forget, we're not talking about some amateur thing here. We're talking about an industrial-scale operation. In a year, they're printing four billion dollars' worth of hundreds.'

'That many?' I said, surprised.

'Four billion,' he said again. 'About the same as the Lebanon operation. Those were Joe's figures. He was in a position to know. And that makes it inexplicable. Four billion in hundreds is forty million banknotes. That's a lot of paper. That's a completely inexplicable amount of paper, Mr Reacher. And their paper is perfect.'

'What sort of paper would they need?' I asked him.

He reached over and took the ten dollar bill back from me. Crumpled it and pulled it and snapped it.

'It's a blend of fibres,' he said. 'Very clever and entirely unique. About eighty per cent cotton, about twenty per cent linen. No wood pulp in it at all. It's got more in common with the shirt on your back than with a newspaper, for instance. It's got a very clever chemical colourant in it, to give it a unique cream tint. And it's got random red and blue polymer threads pulped in, as fine as silk.

Currency stock is wonderful paper. Durable, lasts for years, won't come apart in water, hot or cold. Absolutely precise absorbency, capable of accepting the finest engraving the platemakers can achieve.'

'So the paper would be difficult to copy?' I said.

'Virtually impossible,' he said. 'In a way, it's so difficult to copy that even the official government supplier can't copy it. They have tremendous difficulty just keeping it consistent, batch to batch, and they're by far the most sophisticated papermaker in the entire world.'

I ran it all through in my head. Press, plates, ink and paper.

'So the paper supply is really the key to all this?' I said.

Kelstein nodded ruefully.

'That was our conclusion,' he said. 'We agreed the paper supply was crucial, and we agreed we had no idea how they were managing it. That's why I can't really help you. I couldn't help Joe, and I can't help you. I'm terribly sorry.'

I looked at him.

'They've got a warehouse full of something,' I said. 'Could that be paper?'

He snorted in derision. Snapped his great head around towards me.

'Don't you listen?' he said. 'Currency stock is unobtainable. Completely unobtainable. You couldn't get forty sheets of currency stock, never mind forty million sheets. The whole thing is a total mystery. Joe and Walter and I racked our brains for a year and we came up with nothing.'

'I think Bartholomew came up with something,' I said.

Kelstein nodded sadly. He levered himself slowly

out of his chair and stepped to his desk. Pressed the replay button on his telephone answering machine. The room was filled with an electronic beep, then with the sound of a dead man's voice.

'Kelstein?' the voice said. 'Bartholomew here. It's Thursday night, late. I'm going to call you in the morning and I'm going to tell you the answer. I knew I'd beat you to it. Goodnight, old man.'

The voice had excitement in it. Kelstein stood there and gazed into space as if Bartholomew's spirit was hanging there in the still air. He looked upset. I couldn't tell if that was because his old colleague was dead, or because his old colleague had beaten him to the answer.

'Poor Walter,' he said. 'I knew him fifty-six years.'

I sat quietly for a spell. Then I stood up as well.

'I'll figure it out,' I said.

Kelstein put his head on one side and looked at me sharply.

'Do you really think you will?' he said. 'When Joe couldn't?'

I shrugged at the old guy.

'Maybe Joe did,' I said. 'We don't know what he'd figured out before they got him. Anyway, right now I'm going back to Georgia. Carry on the search.'

Kelstein nodded and sighed. He looked stressed.

'Good luck, Mr Reacher,' he said. 'I hope you finish your brother's business. Perhaps you will. He spoke of you often. He liked you, you know.'

'He spoke of me?' I said.

'Often,' the old guy said again. 'He was very fond of you. He was sorry your job kept you so far away.'

For a moment I couldn't speak. I felt unbearably

guilty. Years would pass, I wouldn't think about him. But he was thinking about me?

'He was older, but you looked after him,' he said. 'That's what Joe told me. He said you were very fierce. Very tough. I guess if Joe wanted anybody to take care of the Kliners, he'd have nominated you.'

I nodded.

'I'm out of here,' I said.

I shook his frail hand and left him with the cops in the security office.

I was trying to figure where Kliner was getting his perfect paper, and I was trying to figure if I could get the six o'clock flight back to Atlanta if I hurried, and I was trying to ignore what Kelstein had told me about Joe speaking fondly of me. The streets were clogged and I was busy thinking about it all and scanning for an empty cab, which was why I didn't notice two Hispanic guys strolling up to me. But what I did notice was the gun the leading guy showed me. It was a small automatic held in a small hand, concealed under one of those khaki raincoats city people carry on their arms in September.

He showed me the weapon and his partner signalled to a car waiting twenty yards away at the kerb. The car lurched forward and the partner stood ready to open a door like the top-hatted guys do outside the expensive apartment houses up there. I was looking at the gun and looking at the car, making choices.

'Get into the car,' the guy with the gun said softly. 'Or I'll shoot you.'

I stood there and all that was passing through my mind was that I might miss my flight. I was trying to remember when the next non-stop left. Seven o'clock, I thought.

'In the car,' the guy said again.

I was pretty sure he wouldn't fire the gun on the street. It was a small gun, but there was no silencer on it. It would make a hell of a noise, and it was a crowded street. The other guy's hands were empty. He maybe had a gun in his pocket. There was just the driver in the car. Probably a gun on the seat beside him. I was unarmed. My jacket with the blackjack and the knife and the Desert Eagle was eight hundred miles away in Atlanta. Choices.

I chose not to get into the car. I just stood there in the street, gambling with my life that the guy wouldn't shoot in public. He stood there, holding the raincoat out towards me. The car stopped next to us. His partner stood on the other side of me. They were small guys. The both of them wouldn't have made one of me. The car waited, idling at the kerb. Nobody moved. We were just frozen there like some kind of a display in a store window. Like new fashions for the fall, old army fatigues put with Burberry raincoats.

It gave the two guys a big problem. In a situation like that, there's a split-second opportunity to carry out your threat. If you say you're going to shoot, you've got to shoot. If you don't, you're a spent force. Your bluff is called. If you don't shoot, you're nothing. And the guy didn't shoot. He just stood there, twisted up with indecision. People swirled around us on the busy sidewalk. Cars were blasting their horns at the guy stopped at the kerb.

They were smart guys. Smart enough not to shoot me on a busy New York street. Smart enough to know I'd called their bluff. Smart enough to never again make a threat they weren't going to keep. But not smart enough to walk away. They just stood there.

So I swayed backwards, as if I was going to take a step away. The gun under the raincoat prodded forwards at me. I tracked the movement and grabbed the little guy's wrist with my left hand. Pulled the gun around behind me and hugged the guy close with my right arm around his shoulders. We looked like we were dancing the waltz together or we were lovers at a train station. Then I fell forward and crushed him against the car. All the time I was squeezing his wrist as hard as I could, with my nails dug in. Left-handed, but it was hurting him. My weight leaning up on him was giving him a struggle to breathe.

His partner still had his hand on the car door. His glance was darting back and forth. Then his other hand was going for his pocket. So I jackknifed my weight back and rolled around my guy's gun hand and threw him against the car. And then I ran like hell. In five strides I was lost in the crowd. I dodged and barged my way through the mass of people. Ducked in and out of doorways and ran through shrieking and honking traffic across the streets. The two guys stayed with me for a spell, but the traffic eventually stopped them. They weren't taking the risks I was taking.

I got a cab eight blocks away from where I had started and made the six o'clock non-stop, La Guardia to Atlanta. Going back it took longer, for some reason. I was sitting there for two and a half hours. I thought about Joe all the way through the airspace above Jersey, Maryland and Virginia. Above the Carolinas and into Georgia, I thought about Roscoe. I wanted her back. I missed her like crazy.

We came down through storm clouds ten miles thick. The Atlanta evening gloom was turned to pitch-black by the clouds. Looked like an enormous weather system was rolling in from somewhere. When we got off the plane, the air in the little tunnel was thick and heavy, and smelled of storm as well as kerosene.

I picked up the Bentley key from the information counter in the arrivals hall. It was in an envelope with a parking claim. I walked out to find the car. Felt a warm wind blowing out of the north. The storm was going to be a big one. I could feel the voltage building up for the lightning. I found the car in the short-term lot. The rear windows were all tinted black. The guy hadn't gotten around to doing the front side glass or the windshield. It made the car look like something royalty might use, with a chauffeur driving them. My jacket was laid out in the trunk. I put it on and felt the reassuring weight of the weaponry in the pockets again. I got in the driver's seat and nosed out of the lot and headed south down the highway in the dark. It was nine o'clock, Friday evening. Maybe thirty-six hours before they could start shipping the stockpile out on Sunday.

It was ten o'clock when I got back to Margrave. Thirty-five hours to go. I had spent the hour thinking about some stuff we had learned back in Staff College. We'd studied military philosophies, mostly written by those old Krauts who loved all that stuff. I hadn't paid much attention, but I remember some big thing which said sooner or later, you've got to engage the enemy's main force. You don't win the war unless you do that. Sooner or later, you seek out their main force, and you take it on, and you destroy it.

I knew their main force had started with ten

people. Hubble had told me that. Then there were nine, after they ditched Morrison. I knew about the two Kliners, Teale, and Baker. That left me five more names to find. I smiled to myself. Pulled off the county road into Eno's gravel lot. Parked up on the far end of the row and got out. Stretched and yawned in the night air. The storm was holding off, but it was going to break. The air was still thick and heavy. I could still feel the voltage in the clouds. I could still feel the warm wind on my back. I got into the back of the car. Stretched out on the leather bench and went to sleep. I wanted to get an hour, hour and a half.

I started dreaming about John Lee Hooker. In the old days, before he got famous again. He had an old steel-strung guitar, played it sitting on a little stool. The stool was placed on a square of wooden board. He used to press old beer bottle caps into the soles of his shoes to make them noisy. Like homemade tap shoes. He'd sit on his stool and play that guitar with his bold, choppy style. All the while pounding on the wooden board with his noisy shoes. I was dreaming of him pounding out the rhythm with his shoes on that old board.

But it wasn't John Lee's shoes making the noise. It was somebody knocking on the Bentley's windshield. I snapped awake and struggled up. Sergeant Baker was looking in at me. The big chrome clock on the dash showed ten-thirty. I'd slept a half-hour. That was all I was going to get.

First thing I did was to change my plan. A much better one had fallen right into my lap. The old Krauts would have approved. Tactical flexibility was big with them. Second thing I did was to put my hand in my pocket and snick the safety off the Desert Eagle. Then I got out of the opposite door and looked along the car roof at Baker. He was using his friendly grin, gold tooth and all.

'How you doing?' he said. 'Sleeping in a public place, around here you could get arrested for vagrancy.'

I grinned a friendly grin right back at him.

'Highway safety,' I said. 'They tell you don't drive if you're tired. Pull off and take a nap, right?'

'Come on in and I'll buy you a cup of coffee,' he said. 'You want to wake up, Eno's coffee should do it for you.'

I locked the car. Kept my hand in my pocket. We crunched over the gravel and into the diner. Slid into the end booth. The woman with the glasses brought us coffee. We hadn't asked. She just seemed to know.

'So how you doing?' Baker said. 'Feeling bad about your brother?'

I shrugged at him. Drank my coffee left-handed. My right hand was wrapped around the Desert Eagle in my pocket.

'We weren't close,' I said.

Baker nodded.

'Roscoe still helping the Bureau out?' he said.

'Guess so,' I said.

'And where's old Finlay tonight?' he asked.

'Jacksonville,' I said. 'He had to go to Florida, check something out.'

'Jacksonville?' he said. 'What does he need to check out in Jacksonville?'

I shrugged again. Sipped my coffee.

'Search me,' I said. 'He doesn't tell me anything. I'm not on the payroll. I'm just an errand boy. Now he's got me running up to Hubble's place to fetch him something.'

'Hubble's place?' Baker said. 'What you got to fetch from there?'

'Some old papers,' I said. 'Anything I can find, I guess.'

'Then what?' he said. 'You going to Florida too?'

I shook my head. Sipped more coffee.

'Finlay told me to stick them in the mail,' I said. 'Some Washington address. I'm going to sleep up at Hubble's place and mail them in the morning.'

Baker nodded slowly. Then he flashed his friendly grin again. But it was forced. We finished up our coffee. Baker dropped a couple of bucks on the table and we slid out and left. He got into his patrol car. Waved at me as he drove off. I let him go ahead and strolled over the gravel to the Bentley. I rolled south to the end of the dark little town and made the right turn up Beckman Drive.

TWENTY-SIX

I had to be very careful about where I put the Bentley. I wanted it to look like it was just casually dumped. But it had to be left so nobody could get past it. I inched it back and forth for a while. Left it at the top of Hubble's driveway with the wheels turned away. It looked like I'd driven up in a hurry and just slewed to a stop.

I wanted the house to look like I was in there. Nothing is more obvious than an empty building. That quiet, abandoned look is a giveaway. There's a stillness. No human vibrations. So I opened the front door with the key from the big bunch Charlie had given me. Walked through and turned on some random lights. In the den, I switched the television set on and left it at a low murmur. Same thing with the radio in the kitchen. Pulled a few drapes. Went back outside. It looked pretty good. Looked like there might be someone in there.

Then the first stop was the coat closet off the main hallway. I was looking for gloves. Not easy to find in the Sunbelt. Not much call for them. But

Hubble had some. Two pairs, lying neatly on a shelf. One was a pair of ski gloves. Lime green and lilac. Not much good to me. I wanted something dark. The other pair was what I wanted. Dressy things in thin black leather. Banker's gloves. Very soft. Like a second skin.

The ski gloves made me look for a hat. If the Hubbles had taken trips up to Colorado, they'd have had all the gear. I found a box of hats. There was a kind of watch cap in there, some sort of a synthetic fibre. The bottom part rolled down to make earflaps. The hat was printed up in a dark green pattern. It would do.

Next stop was the master bedroom. I found Charlie's vanity table. It was bigger than some of the rooms I'd lived in. She had a mass of cosmetics. All kinds of things. I took a tube of waterproof mascara into the bathroom. Smeared it all over my face. Then I fastened the jacket, put on the hat, put on the gloves. I walked back into the bedroom and checked the result in the full-length mirrors on the closet doors. Not bad. Just about right for night work.

I went back outside. Locked up the front door again. I could feel the huge storm clouds clamping down overhead. It was very dark. I stood by the front door and checked myself over. Put the pistol in the inside jacket pocket. Moved the zip down and checked the draw. Came out OK. Loaded, cocked. Safety on. Spare shells in the outside top right pocket. Switchblade in the left side pocket. Blackjack in the right side pocket. Shoes tightly laced.

I walked down the driveway, away from the house, past the parked Bentley, twelve or fifteen yards. Pushed through the greenery and settled in a spot where I could just about see up and down the drive. I sat on the cold earth and got ready to wait. In an ambush situation, waiting is what wins the battle. If the other guy is wary, he'll come early or late. When he figures you won't be expecting him. So however early he might make it, you've got to be ready earlier. However late he might leave it, you've got to wait it out. You wait in a kind of trance. You need infinite patience. No use fretting or worrying. You just wait. Doing nothing, thinking nothing, burning no energy. Then you burst into action. After an hour, five hours, a day, a week. Waiting is a skill like anything else.

It was a quarter to midnight when I settled in for the wait. I could feel the storm boiling up overhead. The air was like soup. It was pitch-dark. About midnight, the storm broke. Heavy drops the size of quarters spattered the leaves around me. They built into a deluge within seconds. It was like sitting in a shower stall. Awesome thunderclaps crashed about. They ripped and banged and the lightning blazed in sheets. The garden around me was lit up like day for seconds at a time. I sat under the lashing rain and waited. Ten minutes. Fifteen.

They came for me at twenty minutes past midnight. The rain was still bad and the thunder was still crashing and rolling. I didn't hear their truck until it was well up the driveway. I heard it crunching over the gravel about forty feet away. It was a dark green panel truck. Gold lettering. Kliner Foundation. Like the one I'd seen near Roscoe's place on Tuesday morning. It crunched past me, about six feet away. Wide tyres on the gravel. That's what Finlay had seen up at the Morrison place. Marks in the gravel made by wide tyres.

404

The truck stopped a few yards beyond me. It pulled up sharp just behind the Bentley. Couldn't get past. Just where I wanted it. I heard the engine stop and the parking brake ratchet on.

First guy out was the driver. He was wearing a white nylon bodysuit. It had a hood pulled tight around his face. Over his face was a surgical mask. He was wearing thin rubber gloves. On his feet, rubber overshoes. He vaulted out of the driver's seat and walked around to the rear doors. I knew that walk. I knew that tall, heavy build. I knew those long powerful arms. It was the Kliner kid. The Kliner kid himself had come to kill me.

He slapped his palm on the rear door. It made a hollow boom. Then he turned the handle and opened up. Four men came out. All dressed the same. White nylon bodysuits, hoods pulled tight, masks, gloves, rubber overshoes. Two were carrying bags. Two had long fat shotguns. A total of five men. I'd expected four. Five was going to be harder. But more productive.

The rain was lashing down on them. I could hear the brittle spatter as it hit their stiff nylon suits. I could hear the metallic clang as the heavy drops bounced off the roof of their truck. I saw them caught by a lightning flash. They looked like banshees. Like something escaped from hell. They were a terrifying sight. For the first time, I doubted if I would have beaten them on Monday night. But I was going to beat them tonight. Tonight, I would have the advantage of surprise. I would be an invisible nightmare figure let loose among them.

The Kliner kid was organizing them. He reached into the back of the truck and pulled out a crowbar. Pointed to three of his soldiers and walked off with them through the downpour to the house. The fifth guy was going to wait with the truck. Because of the rain, he was going to get back in the cab. I saw him glance up at the black sky and glance forward at the driver's seat. I pulled out the sap. Forced my way through the bushes. The guy couldn't hear me. The rain was roaring in his ears.

He turned his back and took a step toward the driver's door. I shut my eyes for a second and pictured Joe lying on the slab at the morgue with no face. Pictured Roscoe shaking with horror as she stared at the footprints on her hallway floor. Then I crashed out of the bushes. Skipped up behind the guy. Smashed the sap across the back of his skull. It was a big sap and I gave it all I had. I felt the bone explode under it. The guy went down on the gravel like a tree. He lay face down and the rain hammered on his nylon suit. I broke his neck with a single mighty kick. One down.

I dragged the body across the gravel and left it at the back of the truck. Walked around and pulled the keys out of the ignition. Crept on up to the house. I put the sap back in my pocket. Popped the switchblade and carried it in my right hand. I didn't want to use the gun in the house. Too noisy, even with the thunder crashing outside. I stopped inside the front door. The lock was forced and the wood was splintered. I saw the crowbar on the hallway floor.

It was a big house. It was going to take them some time to search it. My guess was they'd stick together as a group of four. They'd search together. Then they'd split up. I could hear them tramping through the upper floor. I stepped back outside to wait for one of them to come down into the hallway. I waited, pressed against the wall, next to the broken door. I was sheltered by the overhang of the roof. The rain was still torrential. It was as bad as a tropical storm.

I waited nearly five minutes before the first one came downstairs. I heard the creak of his tread in the hallway. Heard him open the coat closet door. I stepped inside the house. His back was to me. He was one of the shotgun carriers, tall, lighter than me. I fell in behind him. Reached over the top of his head with my left hand. Stuck my fingers in his eyes. He dropped the shotgun. It thudded onto the carpet. I pulled him backward and turned him and ran him out through the door. Into the downpour. Dug my fingers deeper into his eyes. Hauled his head back. Cut his throat. You don't do it with one elegant swipe. Not like in the movies. No knife is sharp enough for that. There's all kinds of tough gristle in the human throat. You have to saw back and forth with a lot of strength. Takes a while. But it works. It works well. By the time you've sawed back to the bone, the guy is dead. This guy was no exception. His blood hosed out and mixed with the rain. He sagged against my grip. Two down.

I dragged the body over to the lawn by the top of his hood. No good picking him up under the knees and shoulders. His head would have lolled back and fallen off. I left him on the grass. Ran back inside. Picked up the shotgun and grimaced. It was a serious weapon. An Ithaca Mag-10. I'd seen them in the army. They fire an enormous cartridge. People call them the Roadblocker. There's enough power in them to kill people through the side of a soft-skinned vehicle. Face to face, they're devastating. They only hold three cartridges, but like we used to say, by the time you've fired three rounds, the battle is definitely over.

I kept the blade out as my weapon of choice.

Silent. But the shotgun would be better than the Desert Eagle as backup. Thing is with a shotgun, aiming is a luxury. A shotgun sprays a wide cone of lead. With a Mag-10, as long as it's pointed vaguely in the right direction, you're going to score.

I stepped back out through the splintered door and pressed against the wall, out of the deluge. I waited. Now my guess was they'd start coming out of the house. They wouldn't find me in there and they'd miss the guy I'd just dropped. So they'd start coming out. It was inevitable. They couldn't stay in there for ever. I waited. Ten minutes. I could hear creaking from the floor inside. Ignored it. Sooner or later, they'd come out.

They came out. Two guys together. They came as a pair. That made me hesitate a fraction. They stepped out into the downpour and I heard the rain start roaring against their nylon hoods. I pulled out the sap again. Swapped it into my right hand. The first guy went down easily enough. I caught him square on the back of his neck with the heavy sap and his head nearly came off. But the second guy reacted and twisted away so that I missed with the next swing. The sap just smashed his collar bone and dropped him to his knees. I stabbed him left-handed in the face. Lined up for another shot with the sap. Took me two more blows to break his neck. He was a wiry guy. But not wiry enough. Four down.

I dragged the two bodies through the lashing rain to the lawn at the edge of the gravel drive. Piled them with the other guy. I had four down and one shotgun captured. The truck keys in my pocket. The Kliner kid with a shotgun still on the loose.

I couldn't find him. I didn't know where he was. I stepped into the house, out of the rain, and listened. Couldn't hear a thing. The roar of the rain on the roof and on the gravel outside was too much. It was putting up a mask of white noise over everything else. If the kid was alerted and creeping around, I wouldn't hear him. It was going to be a problem.

I crept into the garden room. The rain was hammering on the roof. I stood still and listened hard. Heard the kid in the hallway. He was on his way out. He was going out the front door. If he turned right, he was going to trip over his three dead grunts piled on the lawn. But he turned left. He walked past the garden room windows. He was headed across the soaking lawn to the patio area. I watched him walk by, through the deluge, maybe eight feet away. Looked like a ghost from hell. A ghost from hell holding a long black shotgun out in front of him.

I had the garden room key in my pocket, on the Bentley ring. I unlocked the door and stepped out. The rain hit me like a drenching from a fire hose. I crept around to the patio. The Kliner kid was standing there, looking down towards the big swimming pool. I crouched in the rain, and watched him. From twenty feet, I could hear the downpour thrashing against his white nylon body-suit. Lightning was searing the sky and the thunder was a continuous crashing.

I didn't want to shoot him with the Mag-10 I was holding. I had to dispose of the bodies. I had to leave old man Kliner unsettled. I had to keep him guessing about what had happened. About where his boy had disappeared to. It would unbalance him. And it was crucial to my own safety. I couldn't afford to leave the slightest shred of evidence behind. Using the big Ithaca against the kid would make a hell of a mess. Disposing of his body would be a severe problem. Finding all of it would be difficult. I waited.

The kid set off down the long sloping lawn to the pool. I looped around, staying on the wet grass. The kid walked slowly. He was worried. He was on his own. His vision wasn't good. The tight hood around his face was limiting his field of view. He kept turning his head from side to side, stiff-necked, like a mechanical thing. He stopped at the edge of the pool. I was a yard behind him. I was swaying left and right, left and right, staying out of the edge of his vision as he swung his gaze from side to side. His massive shotgun was traversing left and right over the teeming pool.

The books I used to read, the movies people see, I should have fought him nobly. I was here to stand up for my brother. And right in front of me was the guy who'd kicked his body around like a bundle of rags. We should have duked it out, face to face. He should have been made aware of who his opponent was. He should have been made aware of why he had to die. All that noble, man-to-man stuff. But real life wasn't like that. Joe would have laughed at all that.

I swung the sap with all my strength at his head. Just as he turned to walk back to the house. The sap glanced off the slick nylon and the momentum of the heavy lead-filled tube pulled me hopelessly off balance. I was falling like a man on ice. The kid spun and raised the shotgun. Pumped a shell into the chamber. I flung my arm up and knocked the barrel aside. Rolled right under his field of fire. He squeezed the trigger and there was an enormous explosion, louder than the worst of the thunder. I heard leaves tearing and ripping as the shot smashed into the trees beyond us.

The ferocious recoil rocked him back, but he pumped the second shell. I heard the menacing double crunch-crunch of the mechanism. I was on my back on the poolside tiles, but I lunged up and grabbed the gun with both hands. Forced the barrel up and the stock down and he fired into the air again. Another terrifying explosion. This time I pulled with the recoil and tore the gun out of his hands. Thrust up and jabbed the stock at his face. It was a poor blow. The Ithaca has a big rubber pad on the stock. It protects the shooter's shoulder from the savage recoil. Now it protected the kid's head from my jab. He just rocked back. I dived at his legs and slammed him backward. Swiped at his feet and tripped him into the pool. He splashed in on his back. I jumped in on top of him.

We were in the deep end of the pool, thrashing about for the winning hold. The rain was hammering. Chlorine was burning my eyes and nose. I fought on until I got his throat. Tore the nylon hood back and got my hands right on his neck. Locked my arms and thrust the kid's head far under the water. I was crushing his throat with all my strength. That biker in Warburton had thought he was doing a job on me, but that had been like a lover's caress compared to what I was doing to the Kliner kid. I was tearing his head off. I squeezed and wrenched and held him a yard underwater until he died. Didn't take long. Never does, in that situation. The first guy under stays under. It could have been me.

I was treading water and gasping through the chlorine stink. The rain was chopping up the surface. It was impossible to tell where the water ended and the air began. I let his body float off and swam to the side. Clung on and got my breath. The weather was a nightmare. The thunder was now a continuous roar and the lightning blazed in sheets. The rain was a relentless downpour. It would have kept me drier to stay in the pool. But I had things to do.

I swam back to fetch the kid's body. It was floating a yard down. I towed it back to the side. Hauled myself out. Grabbed a bunch of nylon in each hand and dragged the body out after me. It weighed a ton. It lay on the poolside with water gushing out of the suit at the wrists and ankles. I left it there and staggered back up toward the garage.

Walking was not easy. My clothes were soaking wet and cold. It was like walking in chain-mail. But I made it to the garage and found the key. Unlocked the door and hit the light. It was a three-car garage. Just the other Bentley in there. Hubble's own car, same vintage as Charlie's. Gorgeous dark green, lovingly polished to a deep gloss. I could see my reflection in the paint as I moved about. I was looking for a wheelbarrow or a garden truck. Whatever gardeners use. The garage was full of garden gear. A big ride-on mower, hoses, tools. In the far corner, a sort of a barrow thing with big spoke wheels like a bicycle.

I wheeled it out into the storm and down to the pool. Scrabbled around and found the two shotguns and the wet sap. Dropped the shotguns in the barrow and put the sap back in my pocket. Checked the kid's corpse still had its shoes on and heaved it into the barrow. Wheeled it up to the house and down the driveway. Squeezed it past the Bentley and rolled it around to the back of the truck. I opened the rear doors and heaved the corpse inside. Scrambled up and dragged it well in. The rain was clattering on the roof. Then I lifted the first guy's body in and dragged it up next to the Kliner kid. Threw the shotguns in on top of them. Two stowed.

Then I took the barrow up to where I'd piled the other three. They were sprawled on the soaking lawn with the rain roaring on their hideous suits. I wheeled them back to the truck they'd come in. Got all five laid out inside.

Then I ran the barrow back through the deluge to the garage. Put it back in the corner where I'd found it. Took a flashlight from the workbench. I wanted to get a look at the four boys young Kliner had brought with him. I ran back through the rain to the truck and stepped up inside. Switched on the flashlight and crouched over the forlorn row of corpses.

The Kliner kid, I knew. The other four, I pulled back their hoods and tore away their masks. Played the flashlight beam over their faces. Two of them were the gatemen from the warehouse. I'd watched them through the field glasses on Thursday and I was sure of it. Maybe I wouldn't have sworn to it in a court-martial, but I wasn't interested in that kind of a judicial procedure tonight.

The other two, I did know for sure. No doubt about it. They were police. They were the backup crew from Friday. They'd come with Baker and Stevenson to the diner to arrest me. I'd seen them around the station house a few times since. They had been inside the scam. More of Mayor Teale's concealed troops.

I scrambled out of the truck again and took the flashlight back to the garage. Locked up the doors and ran through the rain to the front of the house. Scooped up the two bags they'd brought. Dumped them inside Hubble's hallway and hit the light. Looked through the bags. Spare gloves and masks. A box of 10-gauge shotgun shells. A hammer. A bag of six-inch nails. And four knives. Medical type of thing. They could cut you just looking at them.

I picked up the crowbar from where they'd dropped it after breaking the lock. Put it in one of the bags. Carried the bags down to the truck and hurled them in on top of the five bodies. Then I shut and locked the rear doors and ran through the lashing rain up to the house again.

I ran through and locked up the garden room. Ran back to the kitchen. I opened the oven door and emptied my pockets. Laid everything out on the floor. Found a couple of baking sheets in the next cupboard. I stripped down the Desert Eagle and laid the parts carefully on one of the trays. Piled the spare bullets next to them. Put the knife, the sap, the Bentley keys and my money and papers on the other tray. I put the trays in the oven and turned the heat on very low.

I went out the front and pulled the splintered door as far shut as it would go. Ran past the Bentley and got into the Kliner Foundation truck. Fiddled with the unfamiliar key and started it up. Reversed carefully down the driveway and swung backward out onto Beckman Drive. Rolled down the slope to town. The windshield wipers beat furiously against the rain. I skirted the big square with the church. Made the right turn at the bottom and headed south. The place was deserted. Nobody else on the road.

Three hundred yards south of the village green, I turned into Morrison's driveway. Drove the truck up to the house and parked it next to his abandoned Lincoln. Locked the door. Ran over to

Morrison's boundary fence and hurled the keys far into the field beyond. Shrugged my jacket tight around me and started walking back through the rain. Started thinking hard.

Saturday was already more than an hour old. Therefore Sunday was less than a day away. The shape of the thing was clear. I had three facts, for sure. Fact one, Kliner needed special paper. Fact two, it wasn't obtainable in the States. But fact three, the warehouse was jammed with something.

And the writing on those air conditioner boxes was bothering me. Not the Island Air-conditioning, Inc. Not the printed bit. The other writing. The serial numbers. The boxes I'd seen had handwritten serial numbers in printed rectangles. I'd seen them quite clearly. The Jacksonville cops had described the same thing on the boxes in Stoller's speeding truck. Long handwritten serial numbers. But why? The boxes themselves were good cover. Good camouflage. Hauling something secret to Florida and beyond in air conditioner boxes was a smart move. No product was more plausible for the markets down there. The boxes had fooled the Jacksonville cops. They hadn't thought twice about it. But the serial numbers bothered me. If there were no electrical appliances in the boxes, why write serial numbers on them? That was taking camouflage to absurd lengths. So what the hell did the serial numbers mean? What the hell had been in those damn boxes?

That was the question I was asking myself. In the end, it was Joe who answered it for me. I was walking along in the rain thinking about what Kelstein had said about precision. He had said Joe had a very attractive precision about the manner in which

415

he expressed himself. I knew that. I was thinking about the neat little list he'd printed out for himself. The proud capital letters. The rows of initials. The column of telephone numbers. The two notes at the bottom. Stollers' Garage. Gray's Kliner File. I needed to check the list again. But I was suddenly sure Joe was telling me if I wanted to know what Kliner had been putting into those boxes, it might be worth going up to the Stollers' garage and taking a look.

TWENTY-SEVEN

First thing I did back at the house was root around in Charlie Hubble's expensive kitchen for coffee. Started the machine burbling away. Then I opened up the oven. Got all my things out. They had been warmed for the best part of an hour and they were bone dry. The leather on the sap and the key ring had stiffened up some. Other than that, no damage. I put the gun back together and loaded it. Left it on the kitchen table. Cocked and locked.

Then I checked Joe's computer printout for the confirmation I thought was there. But there was a problem. A major problem. The paper was bone dry and crisp, but the writing had gone. The paper was completely blank. The swimming pool water had washed all the ink off. There were very faint blurred smudges, but I couldn't make out the words. I shrugged to myself. I'd read it through a hundred times. I'd rely on my memory of what it had said.

Next stop was the basement. I fiddled around with the furnace until it kicked in. Then I stripped off and shoved all my clothes in Charlie's electric dryer. Set it on low for an hour. I had no idea what I was doing. In the army, some corporal had done my laundry. Took it away, brought it back clean and folded. Since then, I always bought cheap stuff and just junked it.

I walked upstairs naked and went into Hubble's bathroom. Took a long hot shower and scrubbed the mascara off my face. Stood for a long time in the hot water. Wrapped myself up in a towel and went down for the coffee.

I couldn't go up to Atlanta that night. I couldn't get there before maybe three-thirty in the morning. That was the wrong time to be sure of talking my way inside. I had no ID to show and no proper status. A night visit could turn into a problem. I would have to leave it until tomorrow, first thing. No choice.

So I thought about sleeping. I turned the kitchen radio off and wandered through to Hubble's den. Turned the television off. Looked around. It was a dark, snug room. Lots of wood panelling and big leather chairs. Next to the television was a stereo. Some kind of a Japanese thing. Rows of compact discs and cassette tapes. Big emphasis on the Beatles. Hubble had said he'd been interested in John Lennon. He'd been to the Dakota in New York City and to Liverpool in England. He had just about everything. All the albums, a few bootlegs, that singles collection on CD they sold in a wooden box.

Over the desk was a bookshelf. Stacks of professional periodicals and a row of heavy books. Technical banking journals and reports. The professional periodicals took up a couple of feet of shelf space. They looked pretty deadly. Random copies of something calling itself the *Banking Journal*. A couple of issues of a solid magazine called *Bank Management*. One called *Banker*. *Banker's Magazine*, *Banker's Monthly*, *Business Journal*, *Business Week*, *Cash Management Bulletin*, *The Economist*, *The Financial Post*. All filed in line with the alphabet, all in neat date order. Just random copies, ranging back over the last few years. No complete sets. At the end of the row were some US Treasury Department dispatches and a couple of issues of something calling itself *World of Banking*. A curious collection. Seemed very selective. Maybe they were especially heavy issues. Maybe Hubble had read them through when he couldn't sleep.

I wasn't going to have any trouble sleeping. I was on my way out of the den, off to find a bed to borrow, when something occurred to me. I stepped back to the desk and peered at the bookshelf again. Ran my finger along the row of magazines and journals. Checked the dates printed on the spines, under the pompous titles. Some of them were recent issues. The random sequence continued right up to the latest issue of a couple of them. More than a dozen were from this year. Fully a third of them were published after Hubble had left his job at the bank. After he had been let go. They were published for bankers, but by then Hubble hadn't been a banker any more. But he had still been ordering up these heavy professional journals. He had still been getting them. Still reading all this complicated stuff. Why?

I pulled out a couple of the periodicals. Looked at the covers. They were thick, glossy magazines. I held them in my fingers at the top and bottom of the spines. They fell open at the pages Hubble had consulted. I looked at those pages. Pulled out some more issues. Let them fall open. I sat down in Hubble's leather chair. I sat there wrapped in his towel, reading. I read right through the shelf. From left to right, from beginning to end. All the periodicals. It took me an hour.

Then I started in on the books. I ran my finger along the dusty row. Stopped with a little shock when I spotted a couple of names I knew. Kelstein and Bartholomew. A big old volume. Bound in red leather. Their Senate subcommittee report. I pulled it out and started flicking through. It was an amazing publication. Kelstein had modestly described it as the anticounterfeiter's bible. And it was. He'd been too modest. It was totally exhaustive. It was a painstaking history of every known forging technique. Copious examples and instances were taken from every racket ever discovered. I hefted the heavy volume onto my lap. Read for another solid hour.

At first I concentrated on paper problems. Kelstein had said that paper was the key. He and Bartholomew had provided a long appendix about paper. It expanded on what he'd told me face to face. The cotton and linen fibres, the chemical colourant, the introduction of the red and blue polymer threads. The paper was produced in Dalton, Massachusetts, by an outfit called Crane and Company. I nodded to myself. I'd heard of them. Seemed to me I'd bought some Christmas cards made by them. I remembered the thick heavy card and the creamy rag envelopes. I'd liked them. The company had been making currency stock for the Treasury since 1879. For over a century, it had been trucked down to Washington under heavy guard in armoured cars. None had ever been stolen. Not a single sheet.

Then I flipped backward from the appendix and started looking at the main text. I piled Hubble's little library on his desk. Trawled through it all again. Some things I read twice, three times. I kept diving back into the untidy sprawl of dense articles and reports. Checking, cross-referencing, trying to understand the arcane language. I kept going back to the big red Senate report. There were three paragraphs I read over and over again. The first was about an old counterfeiting ring in Bogotá, Colombia. The second was about a much earlier Lebanese operation. The Christian Phalangists had teamed up with some Armenian engravers during an old civil war. The third was some basic stuff about chemistry. Lots of complicated formulas, but there were a few words I recognized. I read the three paragraphs time and time again. I wandered through to the kitchen. Picked up Joe's blank list. Stared at it for a long time. Wandered back to the dark quiet den and sat in a pool of light and thought and read halfway through the night.

It didn't put me to sleep. It had exactly the opposite effect. It woke me up. It gave me a hell of a buzz. It left me shaking with shock and excitement. Because by the time I had finished, I knew exactly how they were getting their paper. I knew exactly where they were getting it from. I knew what had been in those air conditioner boxes last year. I didn't need to go up to Atlanta and look. I knew. I knew what Kliner was stockpiling at his warehouse. I knew what all those trucks were bringing in every day. I knew what Joe's heading had meant. E Unum Pluribus. I knew why he'd chosen that reversed motto. I knew everything, with twenty-four hours still to go. The whole thing, from beginning to end. From top to bottom. From the inside out. And it was one hell of a clever operation. Old Professor Kelstein had said the paper was unobtainable. But Kliner had proved him wrong. Kliner had found a way of obtaining it. A very simple way.

I jumped up from the desk and ran down to the basement. Wrenched open the dryer door and pulled my clothes out. Dressed hopping from foot to foot on the concrete floor. Left the towel where it fell. Ran back up to the kitchen. Loaded up my jacket with the things I was going to need. Ran outside, leaving the splintered door swinging. Ran over the gravel to the Bentley. Started it up and threaded it backward down the drive. Roared off down Beckman and squealed a left onto Main Street. Gunned it through the silent town and out beyond the diner. Howled another left onto the Warburton road and pushed the stately old car along as fast as I dared.

The Bentley's headlights were dim. Twenty-year-old design. The night was patchy. Dawn was hours away and the last of the trailing storm clouds were scudding across the moon. The road was never quite straight. The camber was off and the surface was lumpy. And slick with storm water. The old car was sliding and wallowing. So I cut the speed back to a cruise. Figured it was smarter to take an extra ten minutes than to go ploughing off into a field. I didn't want to join Joe. I didn't want to be another Reacher brother who knew, but who was dead.

I passed the copse of trees. It was just a darker patch against the dark sky. Miles away, I could see the perimeter lights of the prison. They were blazing out over the night landscape. I cruised past.

Then for miles I could see their glow in the mirror, behind me. Then I was over the bridge, through Franklin, out of Georgia, into Alabama. I rushed past the old roadhouse Roscoe and I had been in. The Pond. It was closed up and dark. Another mile, I was at the motel. I left the motor running and ducked into the office to rouse the night guy.

'You got a guest called Finlay here?' I asked him.

He rubbed his eyes and looked at the register.

'Eleven,' he said.

The whole place had that night look on it. Slowed down and silent and asleep. I found Finlay's cabin. Number eleven. His police Chevy was parked up outside. I made a lot of noise banging on his door. Had to keep banging for a while. Then I heard an irritated groan. Couldn't make out any words. I banged some more.

'Come on, Finlay,' I called.

'Who's there?' I heard him shout.

'It's Reacher,' I said. 'Open the damn door.'

There was a pause. Then the door opened. Finlay was standing there. I'd woken him up. He was wearing a grey sweatshirt and boxer shorts. I was amazed. I realized I had expected him to be sleeping in his tweed suit. With the moleskin vest.

'What the hell do you want?' he said.

'Something to show you,' I told him.

He stood yawning and blinking.

'What the hell time is it?' he said.

'I don't know,' I said. 'Five o'clock, six, maybe. Get dressed. We're going somewhere.'

'Going where?' he said.

'Atlanta,' I said. 'Something to show you.'

'What something?' he said. 'Just tell me, can't you?'

'Get dressed, Finlay,' I said again. 'Got to go.'

He grunted, but he went to get dressed. Took him a while. Fifteen minutes, maybe. He disappeared into the bathroom. Went in there looking like a normal sort of a guy, just woken up. Came out looking like Finlay. Tweed suit and all.

'OK,' he said. 'This better be damn good, Reacher.'

We went out into the night. I walked over to the car while he locked his cabin door. Then he joined me.

'You driving?' he said.

'Why?' I said. 'You got a problem with that?'

He looked irritable as hell. Glared at the gleaming Bentley.

'Don't like people driving me,' he said. 'You want to let me drive?'

'I don't care who drives,' I said. 'Just get in the damn car, will you?'

He got in the driver's side and I handed him the keys. I was happy enough to do that. I was very tired. He started the Bentley up and backed it out of the lot. Swung east. Settled in for the drive. He went fast. Faster than I had. He was a hell of a good driver.

'So what's going on?' he said to me.

I looked across at him. I could see his eyes in the glow from the dash.

'I figured it out,' I said. 'I know what it's all about.'

He glanced back again.

'So are you going to tell me?' he said.

'Did you call Princeton?' I asked him.

He grunted and slapped the Bentley's wheel in irritation.

'I was on the phone for an hour,' he said. 'The

guy knew a hell of a lot, but in the end he knew nothing at all.'

'What did he tell you?' I asked him.

'He gave me the whole thing,' he said. 'He was a smart guy. History postgrad, working for Bartholomew. Turns out Bartholomew and the other guy, Kelstein, were the big noises in counterfeiting research. Joe had been using them for background.'

I nodded across at him.

'I got all that from Kelstein,' I said.

He glanced over again. Still irritable.

'So why are you asking me about it?' he said.

'I want your conclusions,' I told him. 'I want to see where you got to.'

'We didn't get to anywhere,' he said. 'They all talked for a year and decided there was no way Kliner could be getting so much good paper.'

'That's exactly what Kelstein said,' I told him. 'But I figured it out.'

He glanced over at me again. Surprise on his face. In the far distance I could see the glow of the prison lights at Warburton.

'So tell me about it,' he said.

'Wake up and figure it out for yourself, Harvard guy,' I said.

He grunted again. Still irritable. We drove on. We hurtled into the pool of light spilling from the prison fence. Passed by the prison approach. Then the fierce yellow glare was behind us.

'So start me off with a clue, will you?' he said.

'I'll give you two clues,' I said. 'The heading Joe used on his list. E Unum Pluribus. And then think about what's unique about American currency.'

He nodded. Thought about it. Drummed his long fingers on the wheel.

'E Unum Pluribus,' he said. 'It's a reversal of the US motto. So we can assume it means out of one comes many, right?'

'Correct,' I said. 'And what's unique about American banknotes, compared to any other country in the world?'

He thought about it. He was thinking about something so familiar he wasn't spotting it. We drove on. Shot past the stand of trees on the left. Up ahead, a faint glimmer of dawn in the east.

'What?' he said.

'I've lived all over the world,' I said. 'Six continents, if you count a brief spell in an air force weather hut in Antarctica. Dozens of countries. I've had lots of different sorts of paper money in my pocket. Yen, deutschmarks, pounds, lire, pesos, wons, francs, shekels, rupees. Now I've got dollars. What do I notice?'

Finlay shrugged.

'What?' he said.

'Dollars are all the same size,' I said. 'Fifties, hundreds, tens, twenties, fives and ones. All the same size. No other country I've seen does that. Anywhere else, the high-value notes are bigger than the small-value notes. There's a progression, right? Anywhere else, the one is a small bill, the five is bigger, the ten is bigger and so on. The biggest value bills are usually great big sheets of paper. But American dollars are all the same size. The hundred-dollar bill is the same size as the one-dollar bill.'

'So?' he asked.

'So where are they getting their paper from?' I asked him.

I waited. He glanced out of his window. Away

from me. He wasn't getting it and that was irritating him.

'They're buying it,' I said. 'They're buying the paper for a buck a sheet.'

He sighed and gave me a look.

'They're not buying it, for God's sake,' he said. 'Bartholomew's guy made that clear. It's manufactured up in Dalton and the whole operation is as tight as a fish's asshole. They haven't lost a single sheet in a hundred and twenty years. Nobody's selling it off on the side, Reacher.'

'Wrong, Finlay,' I said. 'It's for sale on the open market.'

He grunted again. We drove on. Came to the turn onto the county road. Finlay slowed and swung left. Headed north toward the highway. Now the glimmer of dawn was on our right. It was getting stronger.

'They're scouring the country for one-dollar bills,' I said. 'That was the role Hubble took over a year and a half ago. That used to be his job at the bank, cash management. He knew how to get hold of cash. So he arranged to obtain one-dollar bills from banks, malls, retail chains, supermarkets, racetracks, casinos, anywhere he could. It was a big job. They needed a lot of them. They're using bank cheques and wire transfers and bogus hundreds and they're buying in genuine one-dollar bills from all over the US. About a ton a week.'

Finlay stared across at me. Nodded. He was beginning to understand.

'A ton a week?' he said. 'How many is that?'

'A ton in singles is a million dollars,' I said. 'They need forty tons a year. Forty million dollars in singles.'

'Go on,' he said.

'The trucks bring them down to Margrave,' I said. 'From wherever Hubble sourced them. They come in to the warehouse.'

Finlay nodded. He was catching on. He could see it.

'Then they got shipped out again in the air conditioner cartons,' he said.

'Correct,' I said. 'Until a year ago. Until the Coast Guard stopped them. Nice new fresh boxes, probably ordered from some cardboard box factory two thousand miles away. They packed them up, sealed them with tape, shipped them out. But they used to count them first, before shipping them.'

He nodded again.

'To keep the books straight,' he said. 'But how the hell do you count a ton of dollar bills a week?'

'They weighed them,' I said. 'Every time they filled a box, they stuck it on a scale and weighed it. With singles, an ounce is worth thirty bucks. A pound is worth four hundred and eighty. I read about all that last night. They weighed it, they calculated the value, then they wrote the amount on the side of the box.'

'How do you know?' he said.

'The serial numbers,' I said. 'Showed how much money was in the box.'

Finlay smiled a rueful smile.

'OK,' he said. 'Then the boxes went to Jacksonville Beach, right?'

I nodded.

'Got put on a boat,' I said. 'Got taken down to Venezuela.'

Then we fell silent. We were approaching the warehouse complex up at the top of the old county road. It loomed up on our left like the centre of our universe. The metal siding reflected the pale dawn.

Finlay slowed. We looked over at the place. Our heads swivelled around as we drove past. Then we swung up the ramp onto the highway. Headed north for Atlanta. Finlay mashed the pedal and the stately old car hummed along faster.

'What's in Venezuela?' I asked him.

He shrugged across at me.

'Lots of things, right?' he said.

'Kliner's chemical works,' I said. 'It relocated there after the EPA problem.'

'So?' he said.

'So what does it do?' I asked him. 'What's that chemical plant for?'

'Something to do with cotton,' he said.

'Right,' I said. 'Involving sodium hydroxide, sodium hypochlorite, chlorine and water. What do you get when you mix all those chemicals together?'

He shrugged. The guy was a cop, not a chemist.

'Bleach,' I said. 'Bleach, pretty strong, specially for cotton fibre.'

'So?' he said again.

'What did Bartholomew's guy tell you about currency paper?' I asked him.

Finlay inhaled sharply. It was practically a gasp.

'Christ,' he said. 'Currency paper is mostly cotton fibre. With a bit of linen. They're bleaching the dollar bills. My God, Reacher, they're bleaching the ink off. I don't believe it. They're bleaching the ink off the singles and giving themselves forty million sheets of genuine blank paper to play with.'

I grinned at him and he held out his right hand. We smacked a high five and whooped at each other, alone in the speeding car.

'You got it, Harvard guy,' I said. 'That's how they're doing it. No doubt about that. They've figured out the chemistry and they're reprinting the blank bills as hundreds. That's what Joe meant. E Unum Pluribus. Out of one comes many. Out of one dollar comes a hundred dollars.'

'Christ,' Finlay said again. 'They're bleaching the ink off. This is something else, Reacher. And you know what this all means? Right now, that warehouse is stuffed full to the ceiling with forty tons of genuine dollar bills. There's forty million dollars in there. Forty tons, all piled up, waiting for the Coast Guard to pull back. We've caught them with their pants down, right?'

I laughed, happily.

'Right,' I said. 'Their pants are down around their ankles. Their asses are hanging out in the breeze. That's what they were so worried about. That's why they're panicking.'

Finlay shook his head. Grinned at the windshield.

'How the hell did you figure this out?' he asked.

I didn't answer right away. We drove on. The highway was hoisting us through the gathering sprawl of Atlanta's southern edge. Blocks were filling up. Construction and commerce were busy confirming the Sunbelt's growing strength. Cranes stood ready to shore up the city's southern wall against the rural emptiness outside.

'We're going to take this one step at a time,' I said. 'First of all, I'm going to prove it to you. I'm going to show you an air conditioner box stuffed with genuine one dollar bills.'

'You are?' he said. 'Where?'

I glanced across at him.

'In the Stollers' garage,' I said.

'Christ's sake, Reacher,' he said. 'It got burned down. And there was nothing in it, right? Even if

430

there was, now it's got the Atlanta PD and fire chiefs swarming all over it.'

'I've got no information says it got burned down,' I said.

'What the hell are you talking about?' he said. 'I told you, it was on the telex.'

'Where did you go to school?' I asked him.

'What's that got to do with anything?' he said.

'Precision,' I said. 'It's a habit of mind. It can get reinforced by good schooling. You saw Joe's computer printout, right?'

Finlay nodded.

'You recall the second-to-last item?' I asked him.

'Stollers' garage,' he said.

'Right,' I said. 'But think about the punctuation. If the apostrophe was before the final letter, it would mean the garage belonging to one person called Stoller. The singular possessive, they call it in school, right?'

'But?' he said.

'It wasn't written like that,' I said. 'The apostrophe came after the final letter. It meant the garage belonging to the Stollers. The plural possessive. The garage belonging to two people called Stoller. And there weren't two people called Stoller living at the house out by the golf course. Judy and Sherman weren't married. The only place we're going to find two people called Stoller is the little old house where Sherman's parents live. And they've got a garage.'

Finlay drove on in silence. Trawled back to his grade-school grammar.

'You think he stashed a box with his folks?' he said.

'It's logical,' I said. 'The boxes we saw in his own place were empty. But Sherman didn't know he

431

was going to die last Thursday. So it's reasonable to assume he had more savings stashed away somewhere else. He thought he was going to live for years without working.'

We were just about into Atlanta. The big interchange was coming up.

'Loop around past the airport,' I told him.

We skirted the city on a raised ribbon of concrete. We passed near the airport. I found my way back to the poor part of town. It was nearly seven-thirty in the morning. The place looked pretty good in the soft morning light. The low sun gave it a spurious glow. I found the right street, and the right house, crouching inoffensively behind its hurricane fencing.

We got out of the car and I led Finlay through the gate in the wire fence. Along the straight path to the door. I nodded to him. He pulled his badge and pounded on the door. We heard the hallway floor creak. We heard bolts and chains snapping and clinking. Then the door opened. Sherman Stoller's mother stood there. She looked awake. Didn't look like we'd got her out of bed. She didn't speak. Just stared out at us.

'Morning, Mrs Stoller,' I said. 'Remember me?'

'You're a police officer,' she said.

Finlay held his badge out toward her. She nodded.

'Better come in,' she said.

We followed her down the hall into the cramped kitchen.

'What can I do for you?' the old lady asked.

'We'd like to see the inside of your garage, ma'am,' Finlay said. 'We have reason to believe your son may have placed some stolen property there.'

The woman stood silently in her kitchen for a moment. Then she turned and took a key off a nail on the wall. Handed it to us without a word. Walked off down the narrow hallway and disappeared into another room. Finlay shrugged at me and we went back out the front door and walked around to the garage.

It was a small tumble-down structure, barely big enough for a single car. Finlay used the key on the lock and swung the door open. The garage was empty except for two tall cartons. They were stacked side by side against the end wall. Identical to the empty boxes I'd seen at Sherman Stoller's new house. Island Air-conditioning, Inc. But these were still sealed with tape. They had long hand-written serial numbers. I took a good look at them. According to those numbers, there was a hundred thousand dollars in each box.

Finlay and I stood there looking at the boxes. Just staring at them. Then I walked over and rocked one out from the wall. Took out Morrison's knife and popped the blade. Pushed the point under the sealing tape and slit the top open. Pulled up the flaps on the top and pushed the box over.

It landed with a dusty thump on the concrete floor. An avalanche of paper money poured out. Cash fluttered over the floor. A mass of paper money. Thousands and thousands of dollar bills. A river of singles, some new, some crumpled, some in thick rolls, some in wide bricks, some loose and fluttering. The carton spilled its contents and the flood tide of cash reached Finlay's polished shoes. He crouched down and plunged his hands into the lake of money. He grabbed two random fistfuls of cash and held them up. The tiny garage was dim. Just a small dirty windowpane letting in the pale morning light. Finlay stayed down on the floor with his big hands full of dollar bills. We looked at the money and we looked at each other.

'How much was in there?' Finlay asked.

I kicked the box over to find the handwritten number. More cash spilled out and fluttered over the floor.

'Nearly a hundred thousand,' I told him.

'What about the other one?' he said.

I looked over at the other box. Read the long handwritten number.

'A hundred grand plus change,' I said. 'Must be packed tighter.'

He shook his head. Dropped the dollar bills and started swishing his hands through the pile. Then he got up and started kicking it around. Like a kid does with fall leaves. I joined him. We were laughing and kicking great sprays of cash all over the place. The air was thick with it. We were whooping and slapping each other on the back. We were smacking high tens and dancing around in a hundred thousand dollars on a garage floor.

Finlay reversed the Bentley up to the garage door. I kicked the cash into piles and started stuffing it back into the air conditioner box. It wouldn't all go in. Problem was the tight rolls and bricks had sprung apart. It was just a mess of loose dollar bills. I stood the box upright and crushed the money down as far as I could, but it was hopeless. I must have left about thirty grand on the garage floor.

'We'll take the sealed box,' Finlay said. 'Come back for the rest later.'

'It's a drop in the bucket,' I said. 'We should leave it for the old folks. Like a pension fund. An inheritance from their boy.'

434

He thought about it. Shrugged, like it didn't matter. The cash was just lying around like litter. There was so much of it, it didn't seem like anything at all.

'OK,' he said.

We dragged the sealed box out into the morning light. Heaved it into the Bentley's trunk. It wasn't easy. The box was very heavy. A hundred thousand dollars weighs about two hundred pounds. We rested up for a moment, panting. Then we shut the garage door. Left the other hundred grand in there.

'I'm going to call Picard,' Finlay said.

He went back into the old couple's house to borrow their phone. I leaned against the Bentley's warm hood and enjoyed the morning sun. Two minutes, he was back out again.

'Got to go to his office,' he said. 'Strategy conference.'

He drove. He threaded his way out of the untidy maze of little streets toward the centre. Spun the big Bakelite wheel and headed for the towers.

'OK,' he said. 'You proved it to me. Tell me how you figured it.'

I squirmed around in the big leather seat to face him.

'I wanted to check Joe's list,' I said. 'That punctuation thing with the Stollers' garage. But the list had gotten soaked in chlorinated water. All the writing had bleached off.'

He glanced across.

'You put it together from that?' he said.

I shook my head.

'I got it from the Senate report,' I said. 'There were a couple of little paragraphs. One was about an old scam in Bogotá. There was another about an operation in the Lebanon years ago. They were doing the same thing, bleaching real dollar bills so they could reprint the blank paper.'

Finlay ran a red light. Glanced over at me.

'So Kliner's idea isn't original?' he asked.

'Not original at all,' I said. 'But those other guys were very small scale. Very low-level stuff. Kliner built it up to a huge scale. Sort of industrial. He's the Henry Ford of counterfeiting. Henry Ford didn't invent the automobile, right? But he invented mass production.'

He stopped at the next red light. There was traffic on the cross street.

'The bleaching thing was in the Senate report?' he said. 'So how come Bartholomew or Kelstein didn't get it? They wrote the damn thing, right?'

'I think Bartholomew did get it,' I said. 'I think that's what he finally figured out. That's what the e-mail was about. He'd just remembered it. It was a very long report. Thousands of pages, written a long time ago. The bleaching thing was just one tiny footnote in a mass of other stuff. And it referred to very small-scale operations. No comparison at all with the volume Kliner's into. Can't blame Bartholomew or Kelstein. They're old guys. No imagination.'

Finlay shrugged. Parked up next to a hydrant in a tow zone.

TWENTY-EIGHT

Picard met us in his dour lobby and took us off into a side room. We ran through what we knew. He nodded and his eyes gleamed. He was looking at a big case.

'Excellent work, my friends,' he said. 'But who are we dealing with now? I think we got to say all these little Hispanic guys are outsiders. They're the hired help. They're not concealed. But locally, we still got five out of the original ten hidden away. We haven't identified them. That could make things very tricky for us. We know about Morrison, Teale, Baker and the two Kliners, right? But who are the other five? Could be anybody down there, right?'

I shook my head at him.

'We only need to ID one more,' I said. 'I sniffed out four more last night. There's only the tenth guy we don't know.'

Picard and Finlay both sat up.

'Who are they?' Picard said.

'The two gatemen from the warehouse,' I said.

'And two more cops. The backup crew from last Friday.'

'More cops?' Finlay said. 'Shit.'

Picard nodded. Laid his giant hands palm down on the table.

'OK,' he said. 'You guys head back to Margrave right now. Try to stay out of trouble, but if you can't, then make the arrests. But be very careful of this tenth guy. Could be anybody at all. I'll be right behind you. Give me twenty minutes to go get Roscoe back, and I'll see you down there.'

We all stood up. Shook hands all round. Picard headed upstairs and Finlay and I headed back out to the Bentley.

'How?' he asked me.

'Baker,' I said. 'He bumped into me last night. I spun him a yarn about going up to Hubble's place looking for some documentation, then I went up there and waited to see what would happen. Along came the Kliner kid and four of his pals. They came to nail me to Hubble's bedroom wall.'

'Christ,' he said. 'So what happened?'

'I took them out,' I said.

He did his thing of staring sideways at me at ninety miles an hour.

'You took them out?' he said. 'You took the Kliner kid out?'

I nodded. He was quiet for a while. Slowed to eighty-five.

'How did it go down?' he asked.

'I ambushed them,' I said. 'Three of them, I hit on the head. One of them, I cut his throat. The Kliner kid, I drowned in the swimming pool. That's how Joe's list got soaked. Washed all the writing off.'

'Christ,' he said again. 'You killed five men.

That's a hell of a thing, Reacher. How do you feel about that?'

I shrugged. Thought about my brother Joe. Thought about him as a tall gawky eighteen-year-old, just off to West Point. Thought about Molly Beth Gordon, holding up her heavy burgundy leather briefcase, smiling at me. I glanced across at Finlay and answered his question with one of my own.

'How do you feel when you put roach powder down?' I asked him.

He shook his head in a spasm like a dog clearing its coat of cold water.

'Only four left,' he said.

He started kneading the old car's steering wheel like he was a baker making a pastry twist. He looked through the windshield and blew a huge sigh.

'Any feeling for this tenth guy?' he said.

'Doesn't really matter who it is,' I said. 'Right now he's up at the warehouse with the other three. They're short of staff now, right? They'll all be on guard duty overnight. Loading duty tomorrow. All four of them.'

I flicked on the Bentley's radio. Some big chrome thing. Some kind of a twenty-year-old English make. But it worked. It pulled in a decent station. I sat listening to the music, trying not to fall asleep.

'Unbelievable,' Finlay said. 'How the hell did a place like Margrave start up with a thing like this?'

'How did it start?' I said. 'It started with Eisenhower. It's his fault.'

'Eisenhower?' he said. 'What's he got to do with it?'

'He built the interstates,' I said. 'He killed Margrave. Way back, that old county road was the only road. Everybody and everything had to pass through Margrave. The place was full of rooming houses and bars, people were passing through, spending money. Then the highways got built, and air travel got cheap, and suddenly the town died. It withered away to a dot on the map because the highway missed it by fourteen miles.'

'So it's the highway's fault?' he said.

'It's Mayor Teale's fault,' I said. 'The town sold the land for the warehouses to earn itself some new money, right? Old Teale brokered the deal. But he didn't have the courage to say no when the new money turned out to be bad money. Kliner was fixing to use it for the scam he was setting up, and old Teale jumped straight into bed with him.'

'He's a politician,' Finlay said. 'They never say no to money. And it was a hell of a lot of money. Teale rebuilt the whole town with it.'

'He drowned the whole town with it,' I said. 'The place is a cesspool. They're all floating around in it. From the mayor right down to the guy who polishes the cherry trees.'

We stopped talking again. I fiddled with the radio dial and heard Albert King tell me if it wasn't for bad luck, he wouldn't have no luck at all.

'But why Margrave?' Finlay said again.

Old Albert told me bad luck and trouble's been his only friend.

'Geography and opportunity,' I said. 'It's in the right place. All kinds of highways meet down here and it's a straight run on down to the boatyards in Florida. It's a quiet place and the people who run the town were greedy scumbags who'd do what they were told.'

He went quiet. Thinking about the torrent of dollar bills rushing south and east. Like a storm drain after a flood. A little tidal wave. A small and harassed workforce in Margrave keeping it rolling on. The slightest hitch and tens of thousands of dollars would back up and jam. Like a sewer. Enough money to drown a whole town in. He drummed his long fingers on the wheel. Drove the rest of the way in silence.

We parked up in the slot nearest the station house door. The car was reflected in the plate glass. An antique black Bentley, worth a hundred grand on its own. With another hundred grand in the trunk. The most valuable vehicle in the State of Georgia. I popped the trunk lid. Laid my jacket on top of the air conditioner box. Waited for Finlay and walked up to the door.

The place was deserted apart from the desk sergeant. He nodded to us. We skirted the reception counter. Walked through the big quiet squad room to the rosewood office in back. Stepped in and closed the door. Finlay looked uneasy.

'I want to know who the tenth guy is,' he said. 'It could be anybody. Could be the desk sergeant. There's been four cops in this already.'

'It's not him,' I said. 'He never does anything. Just parks his fat ass on that stool. Could be Stevenson, though. He was connected to Hubble.'

He shook his head.

'No,' he said. 'Teale pulled him in off the road when he took over. He wanted him where he could see him. So it's not Stevenson. I guess it could be anybody. Could be Eno. Up at the diner? He's a bad-tempered type of a guy.'

I looked at him.

'You're a bad-tempered type of a guy, Finlay,' I

441

said. 'Bad temper never made anybody a criminal.'

He shrugged. Ignored the jibe.

'So what do we do?' he said.

'We wait for Roscoe and Picard,' I said. 'We take it from there.'

I sat on the edge of the big rosewood desk, swinging my leg. Finlay paced up and down on the expensive carpet. We waited like that for about twenty minutes and then the door opened. Picard stood there. He was so big, he filled the whole doorway. I saw Finlay staring at him, like there was something wrong with him. I followed his gaze.

There were two things wrong with Picard. First, he didn't have Roscoe with him. Second, he was holding a government-issue .38 in his giant hand. He was holding it rock steady, and he was pointing it straight at Finlay.

TWENTY-NINE

'You?' Finlay gasped.

Picard smiled a cold smile at him.

'None other,' he said. 'The pleasure's all mine, believe me. You've been very helpful, both of you. Very considerate. You've kept me in touch every step of the way. You've given me the Hubbles, and you've given me Officer Roscoe. I really couldn't have asked for anything more.'

Finlay was rooted to the spot. Shaking.

'You?' he said again.

'Should have spotted it Wednesday, asshole,' Picard said. 'I sent the little guy to Joe's hotel two hours before I told you about it. You disappointed me. I expected to be doing this scene way before now.'

He looked at us and smiled. Finlay turned away. Looked at me. I couldn't think of anything to say to him. I couldn't think about anything at all. I just looked at Picard's huge bulk in the doorway and had a strong feeling that this was going to be the last day of my life. Today, it would end.

'Get over there,' Picard said to me. 'Next to Finlay.'

He had taken two giant strides into the room and he was pointing the gun straight at me. I noticed mechanically that it was a new .38 with a short barrel. I calculated automatically that it would be accurate over such a short distance. But that a .38 couldn't be relied on to put a target down. And there were two of us and one of him. And that Finlay had a weapon in a shoulder holster under the tweed jacket. I spent a fraction of a second weighing up the odds. Then I abandoned the calculation because Mayor Teale stepped through the open door behind Picard. He had his heavy cane in his left hand. But in his right hand he was carrying a police-issue shotgun. It was an Ithaca Mag-10. Didn't really matter where he was pointing it.

'Get over there,' Picard said to me again.

'Where's Roscoe?' I said to him.

He laughed at me. Just laughed and gestured with the gun barrel that I should stand up and move over next to Finlay. I heaved myself off the desk and stepped over. I felt like I was weighted down with lead. I clamped my lips and moved with the grim determination of a cripple trying to walk.

I stood next to Finlay. Teale covered us with the giant scatter gun. Picard darted his hand up under Finlay's jacket. Took the revolver out of his holster. Slipped it into the pocket of his own enormous jacket. The jacket flapped open under the weight. It was the size of a tent. He stepped sideways and patted me down. I was unarmed. My jacket was outside in the Bentley's trunk. Then he stepped back and stood side by side with Teale. Finlay stared at Picard like his heart was breaking.

'What's this all about?' Finlay said. 'We go back a long way, right?'

Picard just shrugged at him.

'I told you to stay away,' he said. 'Back in March, I tried to stop you coming down here. I warned you off. That's true, right? But you wouldn't listen, would you, you stubborn asshole? So you get what you get, my friend.'

I listened to Picard's growl and felt worse for Finlay than I did for myself. But then Kliner stepped in through the door. His bone-hard face was cracked into a grin. His feral teeth glittered. His eyes bored into me. He was carrying another Ithaca Mag-10 in his left hand. In his right hand, he was carrying the gun that had killed Joe. It was pointed straight at me.

It was a Ruger Mark II. A sneaky little .22-calibre automatic. Fitted with a fat silencer. It was a gun for a killer who enjoys getting close. I stared at it. Nine days ago, the end of that silencer had touched my brother's temple. There was no doubt about that. I could feel it.

Picard and Teale moved around behind the desk. Teale sat in the chair. Picard towered over his shoulder. Kliner was gesturing Finlay and me to sit. He was using his shotgun barrel as a baton. Short jerky movements to move us around. We sat. We were side by side in front of the big rosewood desk. We stared straight at Teale. Kliner closed the office door and leaned on it. He held the shotgun one-handed, at his hip. Pointed at the side of my head. The silenced .22 was pointing at the floor.

I looked hard at the three of them in turn. Old Teale was staring at me with all kinds of hate showing in his leathery old face. He was shaken up. He looked like a man under terrible stress. He looked desperate. Like he was near collapse. He looked twenty years older than the smooth old guy I'd met on Monday. Picard looked better. He had the calm of a great athlete. Like a football star or an Olympic champion on a visit to his old high school. But there was a tightening around his eyes. And he was rattling his thumb against his thigh. There was some strain there.

I stared sideways at Kliner. Looked hard at him. But there was nothing on show. He was lean and hard and dried out. He didn't move. He was absolutely still. His face and body betrayed nothing. He was like a statue hewn from teak. But his eyes burned with a kind of cruel energy. They sneered at me out of his blank, bone-hard face.

Teale rattled open a drawer in the rosewood desk. Pulled out the cassette recorder Finlay had used on me. Handed it to Picard, behind him. Picard put his revolver down on the desk and fiddled with the stiff cords. He plugged in the power. Didn't bother with the microphone. They weren't going to record anything. They were going to play us something. Teale leaned forward and thumbed the intercom button on the desk. In the stillness, I heard the buzzer sound faintly outside in the squad room.

'Baker?' Teale said. 'In here, please.'

Kliner moved off the door and Baker came in. He was in his uniform. A .38 in his holster. He looked at me. Didn't grin. He was carrying two cassettes. Teale took them from him. Selected the second one.

'A tape,' he said. 'Listen up. You're going to find this interesting.'

He fiddled the cassette in and clicked the little door shut. Pressed play. The motor whirred and the speaker hissed. Underneath the hiss, I could hear a boomy acoustic. Then we heard Roscoe's voice. It was loud with panic. It filled the silent office.

'Reacher?' Roscoe's voice said. 'This is a message for you, OK? The message is you better do what they tell you, or I'm in trouble. The message is if you're in any doubt about what kind of trouble, you should go back down to the morgue and pull Mrs Morrison's autopsy report. That's the kind of trouble I'm going to be in. So help me out, OK? End of message, Reacher.'

Her voice tailed off into the boomy hiss. I heard a faint gasp of pain as if she'd been roughly dragged away from the microphone. Then Teale snapped the recorder off. I stared at him. My temperature had dropped away to nothing. I didn't feel human any more.

Picard and Baker were looking at me. Beaming in satisfaction. Like they were holding the winning hole card. Teale clicked the little door open and took the tape out. Laid it on one side on the desk. Held up the other tape for me to see and then put it in the machine. Closed the little door again and pressed play.

'Another one,' he said. 'Listen up.'

We heard the same hiss. The same boomy acoustic. Then we heard Charlie Hubble's voice. She sounded hysterical. Like she had on Monday morning, standing out on her bright gravel drive-way.

'Hub?' Charlie's voice said. 'This is Charlie. I've got the children with me. I'm not at home, you understand what that means? I've got to give you a message. If you don't come back, something will happen to the children. They tell me you know what that something is. It's the same thing they said would happen to you and me, but it'll be the children instead. So you have to come back straight away, OK?'

The voice ended on a rising note of panic and then died away in the boomy hiss. Teale stabbed the stop button. Took the tape out and placed it carefully on the edge of the desk. Right in front of me. Then Kliner walked around into my field of vision and spoke.

'You're going to take that with you,' he said to me. 'You're going to take it to wherever you've hidden Hubble and you're going to play it to him.'

Finlay and I looked at each other. Just stared at each other in blank astonishment. Then I snapped back and stared at Kliner.

'You killed Hubble already,' I said.

Kliner hesitated for a second.

'Don't try that shit,' he said. 'We were going to, but you got him out of the way. You're hiding him. Charlie told us.'

'Charlie told you?' I said.

'We asked her where he was,' he said. 'She promised us you'd be able to find him. She was most insistent about it. We had a knife between her little girl's legs at the time. She became very anxious to convince us that her husband was not beyond our reach. She said you'd given him all sorts of advice and guidance. She said you'd given him all sorts of help. She said you'd be able to find him. I hope for everybody's sake she wasn't lying.'

'You killed him,' I said again. 'I don't know anything about it.'

Kliner nodded and sighed. His voice was low.

'Let's cut the crap,' he said. 'You're hiding him, and we need him back. We need him back right away. It's a matter of urgency to us. We've got a business to run. So we've got a number of options. We could beat it out of you. We discussed that. It's a tactical problem, right? But we figured you might send us off in the wrong direction, because time is tight right now. You might figure that was your best option, right?'

He waited for some kind of a comment from me. He didn't get one.

'So what we're going to do is this,' he said. 'Picard is going to go with you to pick him up. When you get wherever he is, Picard is going to call me. On my mobile. He knows the number. Then you all three come on back here. OK?'

I didn't respond.

'Where is he?' Kliner asked suddenly.

I started to speak, but he held up his hand and stopped me.

'Like I told you, let's cut the crap,' he said. 'For instance, you've been sitting there thinking as hard as you can. No doubt you were trying to figure some way you might be able to take Picard out. But you won't be able to do that.'

I shrugged. Said nothing.

'Two problems,' Kliner said. 'I doubt if you could take Picard out. I doubt if anybody could. Nobody ever has. And my mobile number isn't written down. It's in Picard's head.'

I shrugged again. Kliner was a smart guy. The worst sort.

'Let me add a couple of factors,' he said. 'We don't know exactly how far away Hubble is. And you're not going to tell us the truth about that. So I'll tell you what we're going to do. We're going to give you a time limit.'

He stopped talking and walked around to where

Finlay was sitting. He raised the .22 and put the tip of the silencer in Finlay's ear. Pushed it in hard until Finlay was tilting over in his chair.

'The detective here is going in a cell,' he said. 'He's going to be handcuffed to the bars. If Picard hasn't called me by one hour before dawn tomorrow, I'm going to aim my shotgun into the detective's cell and blow him apart. Then I'm going to make the delightful Officer Roscoe clean his guts off the back wall with a sponge. Then I'm going to give you another hour. If Picard hasn't called me by the time the sun comes up, I'm going to start in on the delightful Officer Roscoe herself. She'll end up in a lot of pain, Reacher. But first there will be a great deal of sexual interference. A great deal. You have my word on that, Reacher. It'll be very messy. Very messy indeed. Mayor Teale and I have spent a pleasant hour discussing just exactly what we're going to do to her.'

Kliner was forcing Finlay practically out of the chair with the pressure of the automatic in his ear. Finlay's lips were clamped. Kliner was sneering at me. I smiled at him. Kliner was a dead man. He was as dead as a man who has just jumped off a high building. He hadn't hit the ground yet. But he'd jumped.

'Understand?' Kliner said to me. 'Call it six o'clock tomorrow morning to save Mr Finlay's life, seven o'clock to save Miss Roscoe's life. And don't go messing with Picard. Nobody else knows my phone number.'

I shrugged at him again.

'Do you understand?' he repeated.

'I think so,' I said. 'Hubble's run away and you don't know how to find him, right? Is that what you're telling me?'

Nobody spoke.

'You can't find him, can you?' I said. 'You're useless, Kliner. You're a useless piece of shit. You think you're some kind of a smart guy, but you can't find Hubble. You couldn't find your asshole if I gave you a mirror on a stick.'

I could hear that Finlay wasn't breathing. He thought I was playing with his life. But old man Kliner left him alone. Moved across into my field of vision again. He had gone pale. I could smell his stress. I was just about getting used to the idea that Hubble was still alive. He'd been dead all week, and now he was alive again. He was alive, and hiding out somewhere. He'd been hiding out somewhere all week, while they looked for him. He was on the run. He hadn't been dragged out of his house on Monday morning. He'd walked out by himself. He'd taken that stay-at-home call and smelled a rat and run for his life. And they couldn't find him. Paul Hubble had given me the tiny edge I was going to need.

'What's Hubble got that you want so much?' I said.

Kliner shrugged at me.

'He's the only loose end left,' he said. 'I've taken care of everything else. And I'm not going out of business just because an asshole like Hubble is running around somewhere shooting his stupid mouth off. So I need him at home. Where he belongs. So you're going to get him for me.'

I leaned forward and stared right into his eyes.

'Can't your son get him for you?' I said, quietly.

Nobody spoke. I leaned forward some more.

'Tell your boy to go pick him up,' I said.

Kliner was silent.

'Where's your son, Kliner?' I asked him.

He didn't say anything.

'What happened to him?' I said. 'Do you know?'

He knew, but he didn't know. I could see that. He hadn't accepted it. He'd sent his boy after me, and his boy hadn't come back. So he knew, but he hadn't admitted it to himself. His hard face went slack. He wanted to know. But he couldn't ask me. He wanted to hate me for killing his boy. But he couldn't do that either. Because to do that would be to admit it was true.

I stared at him. He wanted to raise that big shotgun and blow me into a red dew. But he couldn't. Because he needed me to get Hubble back. He was churning away inside. He wanted to shoot me right then. But forty tons of money was more important to him than his son's life.

I stared into his dead eyes. Unblinking. Spoke softly.

'Where's your son, Kliner?' I said.

There was silence in the office for a long time.

'Get him out of here,' Kliner said. 'If you're not out of here in one minute, Reacher, I'll shoot the detective right now.'

I stood up. Looked around the five of them. Nodded to Finlay. Headed out. Picard followed me and closed the door quietly.

THIRTY

Picard and I walked out together through the squad room. It was deserted. Quiet. The desk sergeant was gone. Teale must have sent him away. The coffee machine was on. I could smell it. I saw Roscoe's desk. I saw the big bulletin board. The Morrison investigation. It was still empty. No progress. I dodged around the reception counter. Pushed open the heavy glass door against its stiff rubber seal. Stepped out into the bright afternoon.

Picard signalled with the stubby gun barrel that I should get in the Bentley and drive. I didn't argue with the guy. Just headed across the lot to the car. I was closer to panic than I'd ever been in my whole life. My heart was thumping and I was taking little short breaths. I was putting one foot in front of the other and using every ounce of everything I had just to stay in control. I was telling myself that when I arrived at that driver's door, I better have some damn good idea about what the hell I was going to do next.

I got into the Bentley and drove up to Eno's

diner. Reached around to the seat pocket and found the map. Walked over through the bright afternoon sun and pushed in through Eno's door. Slid into an empty booth. Ordered coffee and eggs.

I was screaming at myself to listen to what I'd learned through thirteen hard years. The shorter the time, the cooler you've got to be. If you've only got one shot, you've got to make it count. You can't afford to miss because you screwed up the planning. Or because you ran out of blood sugar and got sick and dizzy in the small hours of the morning. So I forced the eggs down and drank the coffee. Then I pushed the empty mug and the plate aside and spread the map on the table. Started looking for Hubble. He could be anywhere. But I had to find him. I had one shot at it. I couldn't rush around from place to place. I had to find him inside my head. It had to be a thought process. I had to find him inside my head first and then go straight to him. So I bent over Eno's table. Stared at the map. Stared at it for a long time.

I spent the best part of an hour with the map. Then I folded it up and squared it on the table. Picked up the knife and the fork from the egg plate. Palmed them into my trouser pocket. Looked around me. The waitress walked over. The one with glasses.

'Planning a trip, honey?' she asked me.

I looked up at her. I could see myself reflected in her glasses. I could see Picard's huge bulk glowering in the booth behind me. I could just about feel his hand wrapping tight around the butt of his .38. I nodded at the woman.

'That's the idea,' I said. 'A hell of a trip. The trip of a lifetime.'

She didn't know what to say to that.

'Well, you take care, OK?' she said.

I got up and left one of Charlie's hundreds on the table for her. Maybe it was real, maybe it wasn't. It would spend just the same. And I wanted to leave her a big tip. Eno was getting a dirty grand a week, but I didn't know if he was passing much of it on. Probably not, looking at the guy.

'See you again, mister,' the one with glasses said.

'Maybe,' I said.

Picard pushed me out through the door. It was four o'clock. I hustled over the gravel to the Bentley. Picard followed me with his hand in his pocket. I slid in and fired it up. Eased out of the lot and scooted north up the old county road. Blasted the fourteen miles away in about twelve minutes.

Picard had made me use the Bentley. Not his own car. Had to be a reason for that. Not just because he wanted the extra leg-room. Because it was a very distinctive car. Which meant there was going to be extra insurance. I looked in the mirror and picked up a plain sedan. About a hundred yards behind. Two guys in it. I shrugged to myself. Slowed and glanced left at the warehouses at the top of the county road. Swooped up the ramp and round the cloverleaf. Hit the highway going as fast as I dared. Time was crucial.

The road skirted us around the southeast corner of the Atlanta sprawl. I threaded through the interchanges. Headed due east on I-20. Cruised on, with the two guys in their plain sedan a hundred yards back, mile after mile.

'So where is he?' Picard asked me.

It was the first time he'd spoken since leaving the station house. I glanced across at him and shrugged.

'No idea,' I said. 'Best I can do is go find a friend of his in Augusta.'

'Who's this friend?' he said.

'Guy called Lennon,' I said.

'In Augusta?' he said.

'Augusta,' I said. 'That's where we're going.'

Picard grunted. We cruised on. The two guys stayed behind us.

'So who is this guy in Augusta?' Picard said. 'Lennon?'

'Friend of Hubble's,' I said. 'Like I told you.'

'He doesn't have a friend in Augusta,' he said. 'Don't you think we check things like that?'

I shrugged. Didn't reply.

'You better not be bullshitting, my friend,' Picard said. 'Kliner wouldn't like that. It'll make it worse for the woman. He's got a cruel streak in him a mile wide. Believe me, I've seen him in action.'

'Like when?' I said.

'Lots of times,' he said. 'Like Wednesday, at the airport. That woman, Molly Beth. Screamer, he enjoys that. Like Sunday. Up at the Morrison place.'

'Kliner was there Sunday?' I said.

'He loved it,' Picard said. 'Him and his damn son. You did the world a favour, taking that kid out. You should have seen him on Sunday. We gave those two cops the day off. Didn't seem right they should off their own chief. The Kliners and I stood in for them. The old man loved every minute of it. Cruel streak, a mile wide, like I said. You better make sure I get to make that call on time, or your woman friend's in a lot of trouble.'

I went quiet for a moment. I'd seen the Kliner kid on Sunday. He'd picked his stepmother up from the coffee shop. About ten thirty. He'd been staring at me. He'd been on his way back from dismembering the Morrisons.

'Did old man Kliner shoot my brother?' I asked Picard.

'Thursday night?' he said. 'Sure. That's his weapon, the .22 with the suppressor.'

'And then the kid kicked him around?' I said.

Picard shrugged.

'The kid was berserk,' he said. 'Wrong in the head.'

'And then Morrison was supposed to clean up?' I said.

'Supposed to,' Picard grunted. 'Asshole was supposed to burn the bodies in the car. But he couldn't find Stoller's body. So he just left both of them there.'

'And Kliner killed eight guys in Louisiana, right?' I said.

Picard laughed.

'Eight they know about,' he said. 'That asshole Spirenza was on his back for a year. Looking for payments to a shooter. But there never was a shooter. Kliner did it all himself. Like a hobby, right?'

'You knew Kliner back then?' I said.

'I've always known Kliner,' he said. 'Got myself assigned as Spirenza's Bureau liaison. Kept everything neat and tidy.'

We drove on in silence for a mile or two. The two guys in the plain sedan kept station a hundred yards behind the Bentley. Then Picard looked at me.

'This guy Lennon?' he said. 'He's not another damn Treasury spook working for your brother, right?'

'Friend of Hubble's,' I said.

'Like hell,' he said. 'We checked, he's got no friends in Augusta. Hell, he's got no friends any-where. He thought Kliner was his damn friend, giving him a job and all.'

Picard started chuckling to himself in the passenger seat. His giant frame was shaking with mirth.

'Like Finlay thought you were his friend, right?' I said.

He shrugged.

'I tried to keep him away,' he said. 'I tried to warn him off. So what should I do? Get myself killed on his behalf?'

I didn't answer that. We cruised on in silence. The plain sedan sat steady, a hundred yards back.

'We need gas,' I said.

Picard craned over and peered at the needle. It was nudging the red.

'Pull over at the next place,' he said.

I saw a sign for gas near a place called Madison. I pulled off and drove the Bentley over to the pumps. Chose the furthest island and eased to a stop.

'Are you going to do this for me?' I asked Picard.

He looked at me in surprise.

'No,' he said. 'What the hell do you think I am? A damn pump jockey? Do it yourself.'

That was the answer I wanted to hear. I got out of the car. Picard got out on the other side. The plain sedan pulled up close by and the two guys got out. I looked them over. They were the same two I'd scuffled with in New York, on that crowded sidewalk outside Kelstein's college. The smaller guy had his khaki raincoat on. I nodded amiably to the two of them. I figured they had less than an hour to live. They strolled over and stood with

Picard in a knot of three. I unhooked the nozzle and shoved it in the Bentley's tank.

It was a big tank. Well over twenty gallons. I trapped my finger under the trigger on the nozzle so that it wouldn't pump at full speed. I held it in a casual backhand grip and leaned against the car as the gas trickled in. I wondered whether I should start whistling. Picard and the two Hispanics lost interest. There was a breeze coming up and they shuffled about in the slight evening chill.

I slipped Eno's flatware out of my pocket and pressed the tip of the knife into the tyre tread next to my right knee. From where Picard was standing, it looked like I was maybe rubbing my leg. Then I took the fork and bent one of the tines outward. Pressed it into the cut I'd made and snapped it off. Left a half inch sticking into the tyre. Then I finished up pumping the gas and latched the nozzle back into the pump.

'You paying for this?' I called to Picard.

He looked around and shrugged. Peeled a bill off his roll and sent the guy in the raincoat off to pay. Then we got back into the car.

'Wait,' Picard said.

I waited until the plain sedan had started up behind me and flashed its headlights twice. Then I moved out and accelerated gently back onto the highway and settled into the same steady cruise. Kept on going and the signs started flashing past. Augusta, seventy miles. Augusta, sixty miles. Augusta, forty miles. The old Bentley hummed along. Rock steady. The two guys followed. The setting sun behind me was red in the mirror. The horizon up ahead was black. It was already night far out over the Atlantic Ocean. We drove on.

The rear tyre went flat about twenty miles out

from Augusta. It was past seven thirty and it was getting dark. We both felt the rumbling from the wheel and the car wouldn't track straight.

'Shit,' I said. 'Flat tyre.'

'Pull over,' Picard said.

I slewed to a stop well over on the shoulder. The plain sedan pulled over and stopped behind us. We all four got out. The breeze had freshened up to a cold wind blowing in from the east. I shivered and popped the trunk. Picked up my jacket and put it on, like I was grateful for the warmth.

'Spare wheel's under the trunk floor,' I said to Picard. 'Want to help me get this box out?'

Picard stepped over and looked at the box of dollar bills.

'We burned the wrong house,' he said, and laughed.

He and I heaved the heavy box out and set it on its end on the highway shoulder. Then he pulled his gun out and showed it to me. His huge jacket was flapping in the wind.

'We'll let the little guys change the wheel,' he said. 'You stand still, right there, next to the box.'

He waved the two Hispanics over and told them to do the work. They found the jack and the wrench for the bolts. Jacked up the car and took the wheel off. Then they lined up the spare and lifted it into place. Bolted it carefully on. I was standing there next to the carton of money, shivering in the wind, wrapping my coat tight around me. Thrusting my hands deep in the pockets and stamping from foot to foot, trying to look like a guy who was getting cold standing around doing nothing.

I waited until Picard stepped around to check the bolts were tight. He put his weight on the lever and

I could hear the metal graunching. I came out with Morrison's switchblade already open and sliced up one side of the air conditioner box. Then across the top. Then down the other side. Before Picard could line up his gun, the box fell open like a steamer trunk and the wind caught a hundred thousand dollar bills and blew them all over the highway like a blizzard.

Then I dived over the concrete wall at the edge of the shoulder and rolled down the shallow bank. Pulled out the Desert Eagle. Shot at the guy with the raincoat as he came over the wall after me, but I missed my aim and just blew his leg away. Beyond him I saw a truck with dollar bills plastered all over its windshield run off the road and smash into the plain sedan behind the Bentley. Picard was batting away the snowstorm of cash and dancing over to the wall. I could hear tyres shrieking as cars on the highway braked and swerved to avoid the wreckage of the truck. I rolled over and aimed up the bank and shot the second Hispanic guy. Caught him through the chest and he came crashing down toward me. The guy with the raincoat was rolling around at the top of the slope, screaming, clutching his shattered leg, trying to free the small automatic he'd shown me in New York. I fired a third time and shot him through the head. I could see Picard aiming his .38 down at me. All the time the wind was howling and cars were sliding to a stop on the highway. I could see drivers getting out and jumping around, snatching at the money swirling in the air. It was chaos.

'Don't shoot me, Picard,' I yelled. 'You won't get Hubble if you do.'

He knew that. And he knew he was a dead man if he didn't get Hubble. Kliner wouldn't tolerate failure. He stood there with his .38 aimed at my head. But he didn't shoot. I ran up the bank and circled the car, forcing him out toward the traffic with the Desert Eagle.

'You don't shoot me, either,' Picard screamed. 'My phone call is the only way you're going to save that woman. That's for sure. You better believe it.'

'I know that, Picard,' I yelled back. 'I believe it. I'm not going to shoot you. Are you going to shoot me?'

He shook his head over the .38.

'I'm not going to shoot you, Reacher,' he said.

It looked like a stalemate. We circled the Bentley with our fingers white on the triggers, telling each other we weren't going to shoot.

He was telling the truth. But I was lying. I waited until he was lined up with the wreckage of the truck and I was next to the Bentley. Then I pulled the trigger. The .44 shell caught him and smashed his huge bulk backwards into the tangled metal. I didn't wait around for a second shot. I slammed the trunk lid and jumped for the driver's seat. Fired the car up and burned rubber. I peeled away from the shoulder and dodged the people running around after the dollar bills. Jammed my foot down and hurtled east.

Twenty miles to go. Took me twenty minutes. I was gasping and shaky with adrenalin. I forced my heartbeat down and took big gulps of air. Then I yelled to myself in triumph. Screamed and yelled out loud. Picard was gone.

THIRTY-ONE

It was dark when I hit the outlying Augusta suburbs. I pulled off the highway as soon as the taller buildings started to thicken up. Drove down the city streets and stopped at the first motel I saw. Locked the Bentley up and dodged into the office. Stepped over to the desk. The clerk looked up.

'Got a room?' I asked him.

'Thirty-six bucks,' the guy said.

'Phone in the room?' I asked him.

'Sure,' he said. 'Air conditioning and cable TV.'

'Yellow Pages in the room?' I asked him.

He nodded.

'Got a map of Augusta?' I said.

He jerked his thumb over to a rack next to a cigarette machine. It was stuffed with maps and brochures. I peeled off thirty-six bucks from the roll in my trouser pocket. Dropped the cash on the desk. Filled in the register. I put my name down as Roscoe Finlay.

'Room twelve,' the guy said. Slid me the key.

I stopped to grab a map and hustled out. Ran

down the row to room twelve. Let myself in and locked the door. I didn't look at the room. Just looked for the phone and the Yellow Pages. I lay on the bed and unfolded the map. Opened up the Yellow Pages to H for hotels.

There was a huge list. In Augusta, there were hundreds of places where you could pay for a bed for the night. Literally hundreds. Pages and pages of them. So I looked at the map. Concentrated on a wedge a half-mile long and four blocks deep, either side of the main drag in from the west. That was my target area. I downgraded the places right on the main drag. I upgraded the places a block or two off. Prioritized the places between a quarter-mile and a half-mile out. I was looking at a rough square, a quarter-mile long and a quarter-mile deep. I put the map and the phone book side by side and made a hit list.

Eighteen hotels. One of them was the place I was lying there in. So I picked up the phone and dialled zero for the desk. The clerk answered.

'You got a guy called Paul Lennon registered?' I asked him.

There was a pause. He was checking the book.

'Lennon?' he said. 'No, sir.'

'OK,' I said. Put the phone down.

I took a deep breath and started at the top of my list. Dialled the first place.

'You got a guy called Paul Lennon registered?' I asked the guy who answered.

There was a pause.

'No, sir,' the guy said.

I worked down the list. Dialled one place after another.

'You got a guy called Paul Lennon registered?' I asked each clerk.

There was always a pause while they checked their registers. Sometimes I could hear the pages turning. Some of them had computers. I could hear keyboards pattering.

'No, sir,' they all said. One after the other.

I lay there on the bed with the phone balanced on my chest. I was down to number thirteen out of the eighteen on my list.

'You got a guy called Paul Lennon registered?' I asked.

There was a pause. I could hear pages turning.

'No, sir,' the thirteenth clerk said.

'OK,' I said. Put the phone down.

I picked it up again and stabbed out the four-teenth number. Got a busy signal. So I dabbed the cradle and stabbed out the fifteenth number.

'You got a guy called Paul Lennon registered?' I asked.

There was a pause.

'Room one twenty,' the fifteenth clerk said.

'Thank you,' I said. Put the phone down.

I lay there. Closed my eyes. Breathed out. I put the phone back on the nightstand thing and checked the map. The fifteenth hotel was three blocks away. North of the main drag. I left the room key on the bed and went back out to the car. The engine was still warm. I'd been in there about twenty-five minutes.

I had to drive three blocks east before I could make a left. Then three blocks north before I could make another. I went around a kind of jagged spiral. I found the fifteenth hotel and parked at the door. Went into the lobby. It was a dingy sort of a place. Not clean, not well lit. It looked like a cave.

'Can I help you?' the desk guy asked.

'No,' I said.

I followed an arrow down a warren of corridors. Found room one twenty. Rapped on the door. I heard the rattle of the chain going on. I stood there. The door cracked open.

'Hello, Reacher,' he said.

'Hello, Hubble,' I said.

He was spilling over with questions for me, but I just hustled him out to the car. We had four hours on the road for all that stuff. We had to get going. I was over two hours ahead of schedule. I wanted to keep it that way. I wanted to put those two hours in the bank. I figured I might need them later.

He looked OK. He wasn't a wreck. He'd been running for six days and it had done him good. It had burned off that complacent gloss he'd had. Left him looking a little more tight and rangy. A bit tougher. More like my type of a guy. He was dressed up in cheap chainstore clothes and he was wearing socks. He was using an old pair of spectacles made from stainless steel. A seven-dollar digital watch covered the band of pale skin where the Rolex had been. He looked like a plumber or the guy who runs your local muffler franchise.

He had no bags. He was travelling light. He just glanced around his room and walked out with me. Like he couldn't believe his life on the road was over. Like he might be going to miss it to a degree. We stepped through the dark lobby and out into the night. He stopped when he saw the car parked at the door.

'You came in Charlie's car?' he said.

'She was worried about you,' I told him. 'She asked me to find you.'

He nodded. Looked blank.

'What's with the tinted glass?' he said.

I grinned at him and shrugged.

'Don't ask,' I said. 'Long story.'

I started up and eased away from the hotel. He should have asked me right away how Charlie was, but something was bothering him. I had seen when he cracked the hotel room door that a tidal wave of relief had hit him. But he had a tiny reservation. It was a pride thing. He'd been running and hiding. He'd thought he'd been doing it well. But he hadn't been, because I had found him. He was thinking about that. He was relieved and disappointed all at the same time.

'How the hell did you find me?' he asked.

I shrugged at him again.

'Easy,' I said. 'I've had a lot of practice. I've found a lot of guys. Spent years picking up deserters for the army.'

I was threading through the grids, working my way back to the highway. I could see the line of lights streaming west, but the on-ramp was like the prize at the centre of a maze. I was unwinding the same jagged spiral I'd been forced around on the way in.

'But how did you do it?' he said. 'I could have been anywhere.'

'No, you couldn't,' I said. 'That was the exact point. That's what made it easy. You had no credit cards, no driver's licence, no ID. All you had was cash. So you weren't using planes or rental cars. You were stuck with the bus.'

I found the on-ramp. Concentrated on the lane-change and nudged the wheel. Accelerated up the ramp and merged with the flow back toward Atlanta.

'That gave me a start,' I said to him. 'Then I put myself in your shoes, psychologically. You were

467

terrified for your family. So I figured you'd circle around Margrave at a distance. You'd want to feel you were still connected, consciously or subconsciously. You took the taxi up to the Atlanta bus depot, right?'

'Right,' he said. 'First bus out of there was to Memphis, but I waited for the next one. Memphis was too far. I didn't want to go that far away.'

'That's what made it easy,' I said. 'You were circling Margrave. Not too close, not too far. And counterclockwise. Give people a free choice, they always go counterclockwise. It's a universal truth, Hubble. All I had to do was to count the days and study the map and predict the hop you'd take each time. I figure Monday you were in Birmingham, Alabama. Tuesday was Montgomery, Wednesday was Columbus. I had a problem with Thursday. I gambled on Macon, but I thought it was maybe too close to Margrave.'

He nodded.

'Thursday was a nightmare,' he said. 'I was in Macon, some terrible dive, didn't sleep a wink.'

'So Friday morning you came out here to Augusta,' I said. 'My other big gamble was you stayed here two nights. I figured you were shaken up after Macon, maybe running out of energy. I really wasn't sure. I nearly went up to Greenville tonight, up in South Carolina. But I guessed right.'

Hubble went quiet. He'd thought he'd been invisible, but he'd been circling Margrave like a beacon flashing away in the night sky.

'But I used a false name,' he said. Defiantly.

'You used five false names,' I said. 'Five nights, five hotels, five names. The fifth name was the same as the first name, right?'

He was amazed. He thought back and nodded.

'How the hell did you know that?' he said again.

'I've hunted a lot of guys,' I said. 'And I knew a little about you.'

'Knew what?' he said.

'You're a Beatles guy,' I said. 'You told me about visiting the Dakota building and going to Liverpool in England. You've got just about every Beatles CD ever made in your den. So the first night, you were at some hotel desk and you signed Paul Lennon, right?'

'Right,' he said.

'Not John Lennon,' I said. 'People usually stick with their own first name. I don't know why, but they usually do. So you were Paul Lennon. Tuesday, you were Paul McCartney. Wednesday, you were Paul Harrison. Thursday, you were Paul Starr. Friday in Augusta, you started over again with Paul Lennon, right?'

'Right,' he said. 'But there's a million hotels in Augusta. Conventions, golf. How the hell did you know where to look?'

'I thought about it,' I said. 'You got in Friday, late morning, coming in from the west. Guy like you walks back the way he's already seen. Feels safer that way. You'd been on the bus four hours, you were cramped up, you wanted the air, so you walked a spell, maybe a quarter-mile. Then you got panicky and dived off the main drag a block or two. So I had a pretty small target area. Eighteen places. You were in number fifteen.'

He shook his head. Mixed feelings. We barrelled on down the road in the dark. The big old Bentley loped along, a hair over the legal limit.

'How are things in Margrave now?' he asked me.

That was the big question. He asked it tentatively, like he was nervous about it. I was nervous about answering it. I backed off the gas a little and slowed down. Just in case he got so upset that he grabbed at me. I didn't want to wreck the car. Didn't have time for that.

'We're in deep shit,' I told him. 'We've got about seven hours to fix it.'

I saved the worst part for last. I told him Charlie and the kids had gone with an FBI agent back on Monday. Because of the danger. And then I told him the FBI agent had been Picard.

There was silence in the car. I drove on three, four miles in the silence. It was more than a silence. It was a crushing vacuum of stillness. Like all the atmosphere had been sucked off the planet. It was a silence that roared and buzzed in my ears.

He started clenching and unclenching his hands. Started rocking back and forth on the big leather chair beside me. But then he went quiet. His re-action never really got going. Never really took hold. His brain just shut down and refused to react any more. Like a circuit-breaker clicking open. It was too big and too awful to react to. He just looked at me.

'OK,' he said. 'Then you'll have to get them back, won't you?'

I sped up again. Charged on toward Atlanta.

'I'll get them back,' I said. 'But I'll need your help. That's why I picked you up first.'

He nodded again. He had crashed through the barrier. He had stopped worrying and started relax-ing. He was up on that plateau where you just did whatever needed doing. I knew that place. I lived there.

Twenty miles out from Augusta we saw flashing lights up ahead and guys waving danger flares.

There was an accident on the other side of the divider. A truck had ploughed into a parked sedan. A gaggle of other vehicles were slewed all over the place. There were drifts of what looked like litter lying around. A big crowd of people was milling about, collecting it up. We crawled past in a slow line of traffic. Hubble watched out the window.

'I'm very sorry about your brother,' he said. 'I had no idea. I guess I got him killed, didn't I?'

He slumped down in the seat. But I wanted to keep him talking. He had to stay on the ball. So I asked him the question I'd been waiting a week to ask.

'How the hell did you get into all this?' I said.

He shrugged. Blew a big sigh at the windshield. Like it was impossible to imagine any way of getting into it. Like it was impossible to imagine any way of staying out of it.

'I lost my job,' he said. A simple statement. 'I was devastated. I felt angry and upset. And scared, Reacher. We'd been living a dream, you know? A golden dream. It was a perfect, idyllic life. I was earning a fortune and I was spending a fortune. It was totally fabulous. But then I started hearing things. The retail operation was under threat. My department was under review. I suddenly realized I was just one pay cheque away from disaster. Then the department got shut down. I got canned. And the pay cheques stopped.'

'And?' I said.

'I was out of my head,' he said. 'I was so angry. I had worked my butt off for those bastards. I was good at my job. I had made them a fortune. And they just slung me out like suddenly I was shit on their shoe. And I was scared. I was going to lose it all, right? And I was tired. I couldn't start again at

471

the bottom of something else. I was too old and I had no energy. I just didn't know what to do.'

'And then Kliner turned up?' I said.

He nodded. Looked pale.

'He had heard about it,' he said. 'I guess Teale told him. Teale knows everything about everybody. Kliner called me within a couple of days. I hadn't even told Charlie at that point. I couldn't face it. He called me and asked me to meet him up at the airport. He was in a private jet, on his way back from Venezuela. He flew me out to the Bahamas for lunch, and we talked. I was flattered, to be honest.'

'And?' I said.

'He gave me a lot of crap,' Hubble said. 'He was telling me to look at it as an opportunity to get out. He was saying I should dump the corporate thing, I should come and do a real job, make some real money, with him. I didn't know much about him. I knew about the family fortune and the Foundation, obviously, but I'd never met him face to face. But he was clearly a very rich and successful guy. And very, very smart. And there he was, sitting in a private jet, asking me to work with him. Not for him, with him. I was flattered and I was desperate and I was worried and I said yes.'

'And then?' I said.

'He called me again the next day,' Hubble said. 'He was sending the plane for me. I had to fly down to the Kliner plant in Venezuela to meet with him. So I did. I was only there one day. Didn't get to see anything. Then he flew me to Jacksonville. I was in the lawyer's office for a week. After that, it was too late. I couldn't get out.'

'Why not?' I asked him.

'It was a hell of a week,' he said. 'It sounds like a

short time, right? Just a week. But he did a real job on me. First day, it was all flattery. All temptation. He signed me up to a huge salary, bonuses, whatever I wanted. We went to clubs and hotels and he was spending money like it was out of a faucet. Tuesday, I started work. The actual job was a challenge. It was very difficult after what I'd been doing at the bank. It was so specialized. He wanted cash, of course, but he wanted dollars only. Nothing but singles. I had no idea why. And he wanted records. Very tight books. But I could handle it. And he was a relaxed boss. No pressures, no problems. The problems started Wednesday.'

'How?' I said.

'Wednesday, I asked him what was going on,' he said. 'And he told me. He just told me exactly what he was doing. But he said now I was doing it too. I was involved. I had to stay quiet. Thursday, I was getting really unhappy. I couldn't believe it. I told him I wanted out. So he drove me down to some awful place. His son was there. He had two Hispanic guys there with him. There was this other guy chained up in a back room. Kliner said this was a guy who had stepped out of line. He told me to watch carefully. His son just kicked the guy to a pulp. All over the room, right in front of me. Then the Hispanic guys got their knives out and just hacked the poor guy apart. There was blood everywhere. It was horrible. I couldn't believe it. I threw up all over the place.'

'Go on,' I said.

'It was a nightmare,' Hubble said. 'I couldn't sleep that night. I thought I'd never sleep again, any night. Friday morning, we flew home. We sat together on the little jet and he told me what would happen. He said it wouldn't be just me who got cut up. It would be Charlie too. He was discussing it with me. Which of her nipples would he slice off first? Left or right? Then after we were dead, which of the children would he start with? Lucy or Ben? It was a nightmare. He said they'd nail me to the wall. I was shitting myself. Then we landed and he called Charlie and insisted we go to dinner with him. He told her we were doing business together. Charlie was delighted because Kliner is such a big deal in the county. It was a total nightmare because I had to pretend there was nothing wrong. I hadn't even told Charlie I'd lost my job. I had to pretend I was still at the bank. And the whole evening that bastard was asking politely after Charlie and the children and smiling at me.'

We went quiet. I skirted around the southeast corner of Atlanta again, looking for the highway south. The big city glowed and glittered on the right. To the left was the dark empty mass of the rural southeast. I found the highway and accelerated south. Down toward one little dot in that dark empty mass.

'Then what?' I asked him.

'I started work at the warehouse,' he said. 'That's where he wanted me.'

'Doing what?' I said.

'Managing the supply,' he said. 'I had a little office in there, and I had to arrange to get the dollars, and then I'd supervise the loading and shipping.'

'Sherman Stoller was the driver?' I asked him.

'Right,' he said. 'He was trusted to do the Florida run. I'd send him out with a million dollar bills a week. Sometimes the gatemen did it if Sherman had a day off. But it was usually him. He helped me with the boxes and the loading. We had to work like crazy. A million dollars in singles is a hell of a sight. You've got no idea. It was like trying to empty a swimming pool with a shovel.'

'But Sherman was stealing, right?' I said.

He nodded. I saw the flash of his steel glasses in the glow from the dash.

'The money got counted properly in Venezuela,' he said. 'I used to get accurate totals back after about a month or so. I used them to cross-check my weighing formula. Many times, we were about a hundred grand down. No way had I made that kind of mistake. It was a trivial amount, because we were generating four billion in excellent fakes at the other end, so who cared? But it was about a boxful every time. That would be a large margin of error, so I figured Sherman was stealing the occasional box.'

'And?' I said.

'I warned him off,' Hubble said. 'I mean, I wasn't going to tell anybody about it. I just told him to take care, because Kliner would kill him if he found out. Might get me into trouble as well. I was already worried enough about what I was doing. The whole thing was insane. Kliner was importing a lot of the fakes. He couldn't resist it. I thought it made the whole thing way too visible. Teale was spending the fakes like confetti, prettying up the town.'

'And what about the last twelve months?' I asked him.

He shrugged and shook his head.

'We had to stop the shipping,' he said. 'The Coast Guard thing made it impossible. Kliner decided to stockpile instead. He figured the interdiction couldn't last. He knew the Coast Guard budget wouldn't stand it for long. But it just lasted and lasted. It was a hell of a year. The tension was awful. And now the Coast Guard's finally pulling back, it's caught us by surprise. Kliner figured it's lasted this long, it would last until after the election in November. We're not ready to ship. Not ready at all. It's all just piled up in there. It's not boxed yet.'

'When did you contact Joe?' I asked him.

'Joe?' he said. 'Was that your brother's name? I knew him as Polo.'

I nodded.

'Palo,' I said. 'It's where he was born. It's a town on Leyte. Philippine Islands. The hospital was converted from an old cathedral. I had malaria shots there when I was seven.'

He went quiet for a mile, like he was paying his respects.

'I called Treasury a year ago,' he said. 'I didn't know who else to call. Couldn't call the police because of Morrison, couldn't call the FBI because of Picard. So I called Washington and tipped off this guy who called himself Polo. He was a smart guy. I thought he'd get away with it. I knew his best chance was to strike while they were stockpiling. While there was evidence in there.'

I saw a sign for gas and took a last-minute decision to pull off. Hubble filled the tank. I found a plastic bottle in a trash can and got him to fill that, too.

'What's that for?' he asked me.

I shrugged at him.

'Emergencies?' I said.

He didn't come back on that. We just paid at the window and pulled back onto the highway. Carried on driving south. We were a half-hour from Margrave. It was approaching midnight.

'So what made you take off on Monday?' I asked him.

'Kliner called me,' he said. 'He told me to stay home. He said two guys would be coming by. I asked him why, and he said there was a problem at the Florida end and I had to go sort it out.'

'But?' I said.

'I didn't believe him,' he said. 'Soon as he mentioned two guys, it flashed into my mind what had happened down in Jacksonville that first week. I panicked. I called the taxi and ran.'

'You did good, Hubble,' I said. 'You saved your life.'

'You know what?' he said.

I glanced a question at him.

'If he'd said one guy, I wouldn't have noticed,' he said. 'You know, if he'd said stay home, a guy is coming by, I'd have fallen for it. But he said two guys.'

'He made a mistake,' I said.

'I know,' Hubble said. 'I can't believe it. He never makes mistakes.'

I shook my head. Smiled in the dark.

'He made a mistake last Thursday.'

The big chrome clock on the Bentley's dash said midnight. I needed this whole deal over and done by five in the morning. So I had five hours. If all went well, that was way more than I needed. If I screwed up, it didn't matter if I had five hours or five days or five years. This was a once-only thing. In and out. In the service we used to say: do it once and do it right. Tonight I was going to add: and do it quickly.

'Hubble?' I said. 'I need your help.'

He roused himself and looked over at me.

'How?' he asked.

I spent the last ten minutes of the highway cruise

going over it. Over and over it, until he was totally solid. I swung off the highway where it met the county road. Blasted past the warehouses and on down the fourteen miles to town. Slowed as I passed the station house. It was quiet, lights off. No cars in the lot. The fire house next door looked OK. The town was silent and deserted. The only light showing in the whole place was in the barbershop.

I made the right onto Beckman and drove up the rise to Hubble's place. Turned in at the familiar white mailbox and spun the wheel through the curves up the driveway. Pulled up at the door.

'My car keys are in the house,' Hubble said.

'It's open,' I said.

He went to check it out. Pushed at the splintered door gingerly, with one finger, like it might be booby-trapped. I saw him go in. A minute later, he was back out. He had his keys, but he didn't walk round to the garage. He came back over to me and leaned into the car.

'It's a hell of a mess in there,' he said. 'What's been going on?'

'I used this place for an ambush,' I said. 'Four guys were tramping all over the place looking for me. It was raining at the time.'

He leaned down and looked in at me.

'Were they the ones?' he said. 'You know, the ones Kliner would have sent if I'd talked?'

I nodded.

'They had all their gear with them,' I said.

I could see his face in the dim glow from the old dials on the dash. His eyes were wide open, but he wasn't seeing me. He was seeing what he'd seen in his nightmares. He nodded slowly. Then he reached in and put his hand on my arm. Squeezed it. Didn't speak. Then he ducked back out and was gone. I was left sitting there, wondering how the hell I'd ever hated the guy a week ago.

I used the time to reload the Desert Eagle. I replaced the four shells I'd used out there on the highway near Augusta. Then I saw Hubble drive his old green Bentley around from the garage. The engine was cold and he was trailing a cloud of white vapour. He gave me a thumbs-up as he passed and I followed the white cloud down the driveway and down Beckman. We passed by the church and turned left onto Main Street in stately procession. Two fine old cars, nose to tail through the sleeping town, ready to do battle.

Hubble pulled up forty yards shy of the station house. Pulled in to the kerb just where I'd told him to. Killed his lights and waited, motor running. I wafted past him and nosed into the police department lot. Parked up in the end slot and got out. Left all four doors unlocked. Pulled the big automatic out of my pocket. The night air was cold and the silence was crushing. I could hear Hubble's motor idling from forty yards away. I unlatched the Desert Eagle's safety and the click sounded deafening in the stillness.

I ran to the station house wall and dropped to the ground. Slid forward until I could see in through the bottom of the heavy glass door. Watched and listened. Held my breath. I watched and listened long enough to be sure.

I stood up and clicked the safety back on. Put the gun back in my pocket. Stood there and made a calculation. The fire house and the station house stood together three hundred yards from the north end of Main Street. Further on up the road, Eno's was eight hundred yards away. I figured the earliest anybody could get to us would be maybe three minutes. Two minutes to react, and a minute for a fast jog up from Main Street. So we had three minutes. Halve that for a margin of safety, call it ninety seconds, beginning to end.

I ran out to the middle of the county road and waved a signal to Hubble. I saw his car pull away from the kerb and I ran over to the fire house entrance. Stood to the side of the big red door and waited.

Hubble drove up and slewed his old Bentley in a tight turn across the road. Ended up at a right angle, just about lined up with the fire house entrance, facing away from me. I saw the car lurch as he slammed the shift into reverse. Then he hit the gas and the big old sedan shot backward toward me.

It accelerated all the way and smashed backwards into the fire house door. That old Bentley must have weighed two tons and it tore the metal door right off its mountings with no trouble at all. There was a tremendous crashing and tearing of metal and I heard the rear lights smash and the clang of the fender as it fell off and bounced on the concrete. I was through the gap between the door and the frame before Hubble slammed into drive and dragged clear of the wreckage. It was dark in there, but I found what I was looking for. It was clipped to the side of the fire truck, horizontally, at head height. A bolt cutter, a huge thing, must have been four feet long. I wrenched it out of its mountings and ran for the door.

Soon as Hubble saw me come out, he pulled a wide circle across the road. The back end of his Bentley was wrecked. The trunk lid was flapping and the sheet metal was crunched and screeching.

But he did his job. He made the wide turn and lined up with the station house entrance. Paused for a second and floored the gas. Accelerated straight towards the heavy glass doors. This time head on.

The old Bentley smashed through the doors in a shower of glass and demolished the reception desk. Ploughed on into the squad room and stopped. I ran in right behind it. Finlay was standing in the middle cell. Frozen in shock. He was handcuffed by his left wrist to the bars separating him from the end cell. Well to the back. Couldn't have been better.

I tore and shoved at the wreckage of the reception counter and cleared a path behind Hubble. Waved him back. He spun the wheel and reversed into the space I'd cleared. I hauled and shoved the squad room desks out of the way to give him a clear run in front. Turned and gave him the signal.

The front end of his car was as bad as the back. The hood was buckled and the radiator was smashed. Green water was pouring out of the bottom and steam was hissing out of the top. The headlights were smashed and the fender was rubbing the tyre. But Hubble was doing his job. He was holding the car on the brake and speeding the motor. Just like I'd told him to.

I could see the car shuddering against the brake. Then it shot forward and hurtled toward Finlay in the middle cell. Smashed into the titanium bars at an angle and ripped them open like a swung axe on a picket fence. The Bentley's hood flew up and the windshield exploded. Torn metal clanged and screeched. Hubble came to a stop a yard short of where Finlay was standing. The wrecked car settled in a loud hiss of steam. The air was thick with dust.

I dived through the gap into the cell and clamped the bolt cutter on the link fixing Finlay's wrist to the bars. Leaned on the four-foot levers until the handcuffs sheared through. I gave Finlay the bolt cutter and hauled him through the gap and out of the cell. Hubble was climbing out of the Bentley's window. The impact had distorted the door and it wouldn't open. I pulled him out and leaned in and yanked the keys. Then we all three ran through the shattered squad room and crunched over the shards of plate glass where the big doors had been. Ran over to the car and dived in. I started it up and howled backward out of the lot. Slammed into drive and took off down the road towards town.

Finlay was out. Ninety seconds, beginning to end.

THIRTY-TWO

I slowed down at the north end of Main Street and rolled gently south through the sleeping town. Nobody spoke. Hubble was lying on the rear bench, shaken up. Finlay was beside me in the front passenger seat. Just sitting there, rigid, staring out through the windshield. We were all breathing heavily. We were all in that quiet zone which follows an intense blast of danger.

The clock on the dash showed one in the morning. I wanted to hole up until four. I had a superstitious thing about four o'clock in the morning. We used to call it KGB time. Story was it was the time they chose to go knocking on doors. Four o'clock in the morning. Story was it had always worked well for them. Their victims were at a low ebb at that hour. Progress was easy. We had tried it ourselves, time to time. It had always worked well for me. So I wanted to wait until four, one last time.

I jinked the car left and right, down the service alleys behind the last block of stores. Switched the running lights off and pulled up in the dark behind the barbershop. Killed the motor. Finlay glanced around and shrugged. Going to the barber at one in the morning was no more crazy than driving a hundred-thousand-dollar Bentley into a building. No more crazy than getting locked in a cell for ten hours by a madman. After twenty years in Boston and six months in Margrave, there wasn't a whole lot left that Finlay was ever going to raise an eyebrow at.

Hubble leaned forward from the back seat. He was pretty shaken up. He'd deliberately driven into three separate crashes. The three impacts had left him battered and jarred. And drained. It had taken a lot to keep his foot jammed down on the gas, heading for one solid object after another. But he'd done it. Not everybody would have. But he was suffering for it now. I slid out of the seat and stood in the alley. Gestured Hubble out of the car. He joined me in the dark. Stood there, a bit unsteady.

'You OK?' I asked him.

He shrugged.

'I guess,' he said. 'I banged my knee and my neck hurts like hell.'

'Walk up and down,' I said. 'Don't stiffen up.'

I walked him up and down the dark alley. Ten paces up and back, a couple of times. He was pecking his stride on the left. Maybe the door had caved in and hit his left knee. He was rolling his head around, loosening the jarred muscles in his neck.

'OK?' I said.

He smiled. Changed it to a grimace as a tendon graunched.

'I'll live,' he said.

Finlay got out and joined us in the alley. He was coming round. He was stretching like he was waking up. Getting excited. He smiled at me in the dark.

'Good job, Reacher,' he said. 'I was wondering how the hell you were going to get me out. What happened to Picard?'

I made a gun with my fingers, like a child's mime. He nodded a sort of partner's nod to me. Too reserved to go any further. I shook his hand. Seemed like the right thing to do. Then I turned and rapped softly on the service door at the back of the barbershop. It opened up straight away. The older guy was standing there like he'd been waiting for us to knock. He held the door like some kind of an old butler. Gestured us in. We trooped single file down a passage into a storeroom. Waited next to shelves piled high with barber stuff. The gnarled old man caught up to us.

'We need your help,' I said.

The old guy shrugged. Held up his mahogany palm in a wait gesture. Shuffled through to the front and came back with his partner. The younger old guy. They discussed my request in loud rasping whispers.

'Upstairs,' the younger guy said.

We filed up a narrow staircase. Came out in an apartment above the shop. The two old barbers showed us through to the living room. They pulled the blinds and switched on a couple of dim lamps. Waved us to sit. The room was small and threadbare, but clean. It had a cosy feel. I figured if I had a room, I'd want it to look like that. We sat down. The younger guy sat with us and the older guy shuffled out again. Closed the door. The four of us sat there looking at each other. Then the barber leaned forward.

'You boys ain't the first to hide out with us,' he said.

Finlay glanced around. Appointed himself spokesman.

'We're not?' he said.

'No sir, you're not,' the barber said. 'We've had lots of boys hiding out with us. And girls too, tell the truth.'

'Like who?' Finlay asked.

'You name it, we had it,' the old guy said. 'We've had farmworkers' union boys from the peanut farms. We've had farmworkers' union boys from the peach growers. We've had civil rights girls from the voter registration. We've had boys who didn't want their ass sent to Vietnam. You name it, we had it.'

Finlay nodded.

'And now you've got us,' he said.

'Local trouble?' the barber asked.

Finlay nodded again.

'Big trouble,' he said. 'Big changes coming.'

'Been expecting it,' the old guy said. 'Been expecting it for years.'

'You have?' Finlay said.

The barber nodded and stood up. Stepped over to a large closet. Opened the door and waved us over to take a look. It was a big closet, fitted with deep shelves. The shelves were stacked with money. Bricks and bricks of cash held together with rubber bands. It filled the closet from floor to ceiling. Must have been a couple of hundred thousand dollars in there.

'Kliner Foundation's money,' the old guy said. 'They just keep on throwing it at us. Something wrong with it. I'm seventy-four years old. Seventy years, people are pissing all over me. Now people are throwing money all over me. Something wrong with that, right?'

He closed the door on the cash.

'We don't spend it,' he said. 'We don't spend a cent we don't earn. We just put it in the closet. You boys going after the Kliner Foundation?'

'Tomorrow there won't be any Kliner Foundation,' I said.

The old guy just nodded. Glanced at the closet door as he passed by and shook his head. Closed the door on us and left us alone in the small cosy room.

'Not going to be easy,' Finlay said. 'Three of us and three of them. They hold four hostages. Two of the hostages are children. We're not even certain where they're holding them.'

'They're at the warehouse,' I said. 'That's for sure. Where else would they be? No manpower available to hold them anyplace else. And you heard that tape. That boomy echo? That was the warehouse, for sure.'

'What tape?' Hubble asked.

Finlay looked at him.

'They had Roscoe make a tape for Reacher,' he said. 'A message. To prove they were holding her.'

'Roscoe?' Hubble said. 'What about Charlie?'

Finlay shook his head.

'Just Roscoe,' he lied. 'Nothing from Charlie.'

Hubble nodded. Smart move, Harvard guy, I thought. The image of Charlie being held down at a microphone with a sharp knife at her throat would have tipped Hubble right over the edge. Right off the plateau, back down to where panic would make him useless.

'The warehouse is where they are,' I said again. 'No doubt about it.'

Hubble knew the warehouse well. He'd been

working up there most days for a year and a half. So we got him to go over and over it, describing the layout. We found paper and pencil and got him to draw plans. We went over and over the plans, putting in all the doors, the stairs, the distances, the details. We ended up with the sort of drawing an architect would have been proud of.

The warehouse stood in its own compound at the end of the row of four. It was very close in line with the third shed, which was a farmers' operation. There was a fence running between the two with just a path's width between it and the metal siding. The other three sides were ringed by the main fence running around the whole complex. That fence ran close to the warehouse across the back and down the far end, but there was plenty of space in front for trucks to turn.

The big roller door covered just about the whole of the front wall. There was a small staff door just around the far corner which gave on to the main floor. There was a cage just inside the staff door where the roller door winch was sited. Go in the staff door and turn left, there was an open metal staircase running up to an office. The office was cantilevered way up into the top back corner of the huge shed, hanging there about forty feet above the main floor. The office had big windows and a railed balcony looking down into the shed for supervision. In back, the office had a door leading out to an external fire escape which was another open metal staircase bolted to the outside back wall.

'OK,' I said. 'Clear enough, right?'

Finlay shrugged.

'I'm worried about reinforcements,' he said. 'Guards on the exterior.'

I shrugged back.

'There won't be reinforcements,' I said. 'I'm more worried about the shotguns. It's a big space. And there are two kids in there.'

Finlay nodded. Looked grim. He knew what I was saying. Shotguns spray a cone of lead over a big wide angle. Shotguns and children don't mix. We went quiet. It was nearly two in the morning. An hour and a half to wait. We would leave at three-thirty. Get up there at four. My favourite attack time.

The waiting period. Like soldiers in a dugout. Like pilots before a raid. It was silent. Finlay dozed. He had done this before. Probably many times. He sprawled in his chair. His left arm hung over the side. Half of the shattered handcuff dangled from his wrist. Like a silver bracelet.

Hubble sat upright. He hadn't done this before. He just fidgeted around, burning energy. Couldn't blame him. He kept looking over at me. Questions in his eyes. I just kept on shrugging back at him.

Two-thirty, there was a knock on the door. Just a soft tap. The door opened a foot. The older of the two old barbers was there. He pointed a gnarled and trembling finger into the room. Aimed straight at me.

'Someone to see you, son,' he said.

Finlay sat up and Hubble looked scared. I signalled them both to stay put. Stood up and pulled the big automatic out of my pocket. Clicked the safety off. The old guy flapped his hand at me and fussed.

'You don't need that, son,' he said. 'Don't need that at all.'

He was impatient, beckoning me out to join him. I put the gun away again. Shrugged at the other two and went with the old guy. He led me into a tiny kitchen. There was a very old woman in there, sitting on a stool. Same mahogany colour as the old guy, stick thin. She looked like an old tree in winter.

'This is my sister,' the old barber said. 'You boys woke her up, chattering.'

Then he stepped over to her. Bent down and spoke right in her ear.

'This is the boy I told you about,' he said.

She looked up and smiled at me. It was like the sun coming out. I caught a flash of the beauty she must have had, long ago. She held out her hand and I took it. Felt like thin wires in a soft dry glove. The old barber left us alone together in the kitchen. Stopped as he passed me.

'Ask her about him,' he said.

The old guy shuffled out. I still had the old lady's hand in mine. I squatted down next to her. She didn't try to pull her hand away. Just left it nestled there, like a brown twig in my huge paw.

'I don't hear so good,' she said. 'You got to lean close.'

I spoke in her ear. She smelled like an old flower. Like a faded bloom.

'How's this?' I said.

'That's good, son,' she said. 'I can hear that OK.'

'I was asking your brother about Blind Blake,' I said.

'I know that, son,' she said. 'He told me all about it.'

'He told me you knew him,' I said, in her ear.

'I sure did,' she said. 'I knew him real well.'

'Will you tell me about him?' I asked her.

She turned her head and gazed at me sadly.

'What's to tell?' she said. 'He's been gone a real long time.'

'What was he like?' I said.

She was still gazing at me. Her eyes were misting over as she trawled backwards sixty, seventy years.

'He was blind,' she said.

She didn't say anything more for a while. Her lips fluttered soundlessly and I could feel a strong pulse hammering in her bony wrist. She moved her head as if she was trying to hear something from far away.

'He was blind,' she said again. 'And he was a sweet boy.'

She was more than ninety years old. She was as old as the twentieth century. So she was remembering back to her twenties and thirties. Not to her childhood or her teens. She was remembering back to her womanhood. And she was calling Blake a sweet boy.

'I was a singer,' she said. 'And he played the guitar. You know that old expression, he could play the guitar just like ringing a bell? That's what I used to say about Blake. He would pick up that old instrument of his and the notes would just come tumbling out, faster than you could sing them. But each note was just a perfect little silver bell, floating off into the air. We'd sing and play all night long, then in the morning I'd lead him out into a meadow, and we'd sit under some old shade tree, and we'd sing and play some more. Just for the joy of it. Just because I could sing and he could play.'

She hummed a couple of bars of something under her breath. Her voice was about a fifth lower pitched than it ought to have been. She was so thin and fragile, you'd have expected a high, faltering soprano. But she was singing with a low, breathy contralto. I thought back with her and put the two of them in an old Georgia meadow. The heavy

491

smell of wildflower blossom, the buzz of lazy noon-time insects, the two of them backs against a tree, singing and playing for the joy of it. Belting out the wry, defiant songs that Blake had made up and that I loved so much.

'What happened to him?' I asked her. 'Do you know?'

She nodded.

'Two people on this earth know that,' she whispered. 'I'm one of them.'

'Will you tell me?' I said. 'I sort of came down here to find out.'

'Sixty-two years,' she said. 'I never told a soul in sixty-two years.'

'Will you tell me?' I asked her again.

She nodded. Sadly. Tears in her misty old eyes.

'Sixty-two years,' she said. 'You're the first person ever asked me.'

I held my breath. Her lips fluttered and her hand scrabbled in my palm.

'He was blind,' she said. 'But he was sporty. You know that word? Sporty? It means kind of uppity. Uppity with a smile and a grin is sporty. Blake was sporty. Had a lot of spirit and energy. Walked fast and talked fast, always moving, always smiling his sweet fool head off. But one time, we came out of a place in town here, walking down the sidewalk, laughing. Nobody else around but for two white folks coming towards us on the sidewalk. A man and a boy. I saw them and ducked off the sidewalk, like we were supposed to. Stood in the dirt to let them pass. But poor Blake was blind. Didn't see them. Just crashed into the white boy. A white boy, maybe ten years old, maybe twelve. Blake sent him flying into the dirt. White boy cut his head on a stone, set up such a hollering like you never heard. The white boy's daddy was there with him. I knew him. He was a big important man in this town. His boy was screaming fit to burst. Screaming at his daddy to punish the nigger. So the daddy lost his temper and set about Blake with his cane. Big silver knob on the top. He beat poor Blake with that cane until his head was just split open like a burst watermelon. Killed him stone dead. Picked up the boy and turned to me. Sent me over to the horse trough to wash poor Blake's hair and blood and brains off from the end of his cane. Told me never to say a word about it, or he'd kill me too. So I just hid out and waited until somebody else found poor Blake there on the sidewalk. Then I ran out screaming and hollering with the rest of them all. Never said a word about it to another living soul, that day to this.'

Big wet tears were welling out of her eyes and rolling slowly down her thin cheeks. I reached over and smudged them dry with the back of my finger. Took her other hand in mine.

'Who was the boy?' I asked her.

'Somebody I seen around ever since,' she said. 'Somebody I seen sneering around just about every day since, reminding me of my poor Blake lying there with his head split open.'

'Who was he?' I said.

'It was an accident,' she said. 'Anybody could have seen that. Poor Blake was a blind man. Boy didn't have to set up such a hollering. He wasn't hurt so bad. He was old enough to know better. It was his fault for hollering and screaming like he did.'

'Who was the boy?' I asked her again.

She turned to me and stared into my eyes. Told me the sixty-two-year-old secret.

'Grover Teale,' she said. 'Grew up to be mayor, just like his old daddy. Thinks he's king of the damn world, but he's just a screaming brat who got my poor Blake killed for no reason at all except he was blind and he was black.'

THIRTY-THREE

We piled back into Charlie's black Bentley in the
alley behind the barbershop. Nobody spoke. I fired
it up. Swung out and rolled north. Kept the lights
off and drove slow. The big dark sedan rolled north
through the night like a stealthy animal leaving its
lair. Like a big black submarine slipping its moor-
ing and gliding out into icy water. I drove through
the town and pulled up shy of the station house.
Quiet as a tomb.

'I want to get a weapon,' Finlay said.

We picked our way through the shattered wreckage of the entrance. Hubble's own Bentley was
sitting in the squad room, inert in the gloom. The
front tyres had blown and it had settled nose-down,
buried in the wreckage of the cells. There was a
stink of gasoline. The tank must have split. The
trunk lid was up because of the way the rear end
was smashed in. Hubble didn't even glance at it.

Finlay picked his way past the wrecked car to the
big office in back. Disappeared inside. I waited with
Hubble in the heap of shards that had been the

entrance doors. Finlay came back out of the dark with a stainless-steel revolver and a book of matches. And a grin. He waved the two of us out to the car and struck a match. Threw it under the rear of the wrecked green Bentley and crunched on out to join us.

'Diversion, right?' he said.

We saw the fire start as we nosed out of the lot. Bright blue flames were rolling across the carpet like a wave on the beach. The fire took hold of the splintered wood and rolled outward, feeding itself on the huge gasoline stain. The flames changed to yellow and orange and the air started sucking in through the hole where the entrance had been. Within a minute, the whole place was burning. I smiled and took off up the county road.

I used headlights for most of the fourteen miles. Drove fast. Took maybe twelve minutes. Doused the lights and pulled up a quarter-mile short of the target. Turned around in the road and backed up a little way. Left the car facing south. Down towards town. Doors unlocked. Keys in.

Hubble carried the big bolt cutter. Finlay checked the revolver he'd taken from the office. I reached under the seat and pulled out the plastic bottle we'd filled with gas. Slipped it into my pocket with the blackjack. It was heavy. Pulled my jacket down on the right and brought the Desert Eagle up high on my chest. Finlay gave me the matches. I put them in the other pocket.

We stood together in the dark in the dirt on the side of the road. Exchanged tight nods. Struck out over the field to the blasted tree. It was silhouetted against the moon. Took us a couple of minutes to get there. We slogged over the soft earth. Paused against the distorted tree trunk. I took the bolt cutter from Hubble and we nodded again and headed for the fence where it ran close to the back of the warehouse. It was ten to four in the morning. Nobody had spoken since leaving the burning police building.

It was seventy-five yards from the tree to the fence. Took us a minute. We kept on going until we were opposite the bottom of the fire escape. Right where it was bolted down to the concrete path which ran around the whole building. Finlay and Hubble grabbed the chain link to put some tension on it and I bit through each strand in turn with the bolt cutter. Went through it like it was liquorice. I cut a big piece out, seven feet high, right up to where the razor wire started, maybe eight feet wide.

We stepped through the gap. Walked over to the bottom of the stairs. Waited. I could hear sounds inside. Movement and scraping, muffled to a dull boom by the huge space. I took a deep breath. Motioned the others to flatten themselves against the metal siding. I still wasn't sure about exterior guards. My gut said there wouldn't be any reinforcements. But Finlay was worried about it. And I'd learned a long time ago to take account of what people like Finlay worried about.

So I motioned the others to stay put and I crept around to the corner of the massive building. Crouched down and dropped the bolt cutter onto the concrete path from a height of about a foot. It made just about the right amount of noise. It sounded like somebody trying to break into the compound. I flattened myself against the wall and waited with the blackjack in my right hand.

Finlay was right. There was an exterior guard. And I was right. There were no reinforcements. The exterior guard was Sergeant Baker. He was on duty patrolling outside the shed. I heard him before I saw him. I heard his tense breathing and his feet on the concrete. He came around the corner of the building and stopped a yard away from me. He stood and stared at the bolt cutter. He had his .38 in his hand. He looked at the bolt cutter and then swung his gaze along the fence as far as the missing panel. Then he started to run towards it.

Then he died. I swung the sap and hit him. But he didn't go down. He dropped his revolver. Danced a circle on rubber legs. Finlay came up behind me. Caught him by the throat. Looked like a country boy wringing a chicken's neck. Made a fine job of it. Baker was still wearing his acetate nameplate above his uniform pocket. First thing I'd noticed, nine days ago. We left his body on the path. Waited five minutes. Listened hard. Nobody else came.

We went back to where Hubble was waiting. I took another deep breath. Stepped onto the fire escape. Went up. Planted each foot carefully and silently on each step. Eased my way up. The staircase was cast from some kind of iron or steel. Open treads. The whole thing would ring like a damn bell if we were clumsy. Finlay was behind me, gripping the handrail with his right hand, gun in his left. Behind him came Hubble, too scared to breathe.

We crept up. Took us minutes to do the forty feet. We were very cautious. We stood on the little platform at the top. I pressed my ear to the door. Quiet. No sound. Hubble pulled out his office keys. Clenched in his hand to stop them jingling. He selected the right one, slowly, carefully. Inched it into the lock. We held our breath. He turned the key. The lock clicked back. The door sagged open. We held our breath. No sound. No reaction. Quiet.

Hubble eased the door back, slowly, carefully. Finlay took it from him and eased it further. Passed it to me. I eased it back flat against the wall. Propped it all the way open with the bottle of gasoline from my pocket.

Light was flooding out of the office, spilling over the fire escape and laying a bright bar down on the fence and the field forty feet below. Arc lamps were lit inside the body of the warehouse and they were flooding in through the big office windows. I could see everything in the office. And what I saw made my heart stop.

I'd never believed in luck. Never had any cause to. Never relied on it, because I never could. But now I was lucky in a big way. Thirty-six years of bad luck and trouble were wiped away in one single bright glance. The gods were sitting on my shoulder, whooping and driving me on. In that one single bright glance, I knew that I had won.

Because the children were asleep on the office floor. Hubble's kids. Ben and Lucy. Sprawled out on a pile of empty burlap sacks. Fast asleep, wide open and innocent like only sleeping children can be. They were filthy and ragged. Still dressed in their school clothes from Monday. They looked like ragamuffins in a sepia picture of old New York. Sprawled out, fast asleep. Four o'clock in the morning. My lucky time.

The children had been worrying the hell out of me. They were what made this whole damn thing just about impossible. I'd thought it through a thousand times. I'd run war-games through my head, trying to find one that would work. I hadn't found one. I'd always come up with some kind of a bad outcome. What the staff colleges call unsatisfactory results. I'd always come up with the children splattered all over the place by the big shotguns. Children and shotguns don't mix. And I'd always visualized the four hostages and the two shotguns in the same place at the same time. I'd visualized panicking children and Charlie screaming and the big Ithacas booming. All in the same place. I hadn't come up with any kind of a solution. If I could have given anything I ever had or ever would have, I'd have given it to have the children fast asleep somewhere else on their own. And it had happened. It had happened. The elation roared in my ears like a hysterical crowd in a huge stadium.

I turned to the other two. Cupped a hand behind each of their heads and pulled them close to mine. Spoke in the faintest of whispers.

'Hubble, take the girl,' I whispered. 'Finlay, take the boy. Put a hand over their mouths. No sound at all. Carry them back to the tree. Hubble, take them on back to the car. Stay there with them and wait. Finlay, come back here. Do it now. Do it quietly.'

I pulled out the Desert Eagle and clicked the safety off. Clamped my wrist against the door frame and aimed across the office at the inner door. Finlay and Hubble crept into the office. They did it right. They kept low. They kept quiet. They clamped their palms over the little mouths. Scooped the children up. Crept back out. Straightened up and looped past the barrel of my big .44. The children woke up and struggled. Their wide eyes stared at me. Hubble and Finlay carried them to the top of the long staircase. Eased their way quietly down. I backed out of the doorway to the far corner of the metal platform. Found an angle to cover them all the way. Watched them pick their way slowly down the fire escape, to the ground, to the fence, through the gap and away.

They stepped through the bright bar of light spilling over the field, forty feet below me, and vanished into the night.

I relaxed. Lowered the gun. Listened hard. Heard nothing but the faint noises scraping up from inside the huge metal shed. I crept into the office. Crawled over the floor to the windows. Slowly raised my head up and looked out and down. Saw a sight I would never ever forget.

There were a hundred arc lights bolted up inside the roof of the warehouse. They lit the place up brighter than day. It was a big space. Must have been a hundred feet long, maybe eighty deep. Maybe sixty feet high. And it was full of dollar bills. A gigantic dune of money filled the whole shed. It was piled maybe fifty feet high into the back far corner. It sloped down to the floor like a mountainside. It was a mountain of cash. It reared up like a gigantic green iceberg. It was huge.

I saw Teale at the far end of the shed. He was sitting on the lower slope of the mountain, maybe ten feet up. Shotgun across his knees. He was dwarfed by the huge green pile rearing above him. Fifty feet closer to me, I saw old man Kliner. Sitting higher up on the slope. Sitting on forty tons of money. Shotgun across his knees.

The two shotguns were triangulated on Roscoe and Charlie Hubble. They were tiny figures forty feet below me. They were being made to work. Roscoe had a snow shovel. One of those curved things they use in the snow states to clear their driveways. She was pushing drifts of dollars toward Charlie. Charlie was scooping them into air conditioner cartons and tamping them in firmly with a garden rake. There was a line of sealed boxes behind the two women. In front of them was the huge stockpile. They toiled away far below me, dwarfed like two ants below the mountain of dollar bills.

I held my breath. I was transfixed. It was an utterly unbelievable sight. I could see Kliner's black pickup truck. It was backed in, just inside the roller door. Next to it was Teale's white Cadillac. Both were big automobiles. But they were nothing next to the mountain of cash. They were just like toys on the beach. It was awesome. It was a fantastic scene from a fairy tale. Like a huge underground cavern in an emerald mine from some glittering fable. All brightly lit by the hundred arc lights. Tiny figures far below. I couldn't believe it. Hubble had said a million dollars in singles was a hell of a sight. I was looking at forty million. It was the height of the drift that did it to me. It towered way up. Ten times higher than the two tiny figures working at floor level. Higher than a house. Higher than two houses. It was incredible. It was a huge warehouse. And it was full of a solid mass of money. Full of forty million genuine one-dollar bills.

The two women were moving with the dullness of extreme fatigue, like exhausted troopers at the end of some cruel manoeuvre. Asleep on their feet, moving about automatically while their minds screamed for rest. They were packing armful after armful of dollars from the gigantic stockpile into the boxes. It was a hopeless task. The Coast Guard retreat had caught Kliner by surprise. He wasn't ready. The warehouse was hopelessly jammed. Roscoe and Charlie were being worked like exhausted slaves. Teale and Kliner were watching them like overseers, listlessly, like they knew they were at the end of the road. The enormous drift of cash was going to bury them. It was going to engulf them and choke them to death.

I heard the faint clang of Finlay's feet on the fire escape. I crawled back out of the office and met him on the metal platform outside.

'They're back at the car,' he whispered to me. 'How we doing here?'

'Two shotguns out and ready,' I whispered. 'Roscoe and Charlie look OK.'

He glanced in towards the bright light and the faint noises.

'What are they all doing in there?' he asked me in a whisper.

'Come take a look,' I said softly. 'But hold your breath.'

We crawled in together. Crawled over the floor to the windows. Slowly popped our heads up. Finlay looked down at the fantastic scene below. He stared down for a long time. His eyes flicked all over the place. Ended up staring at me. Holding his breath.

'Christ,' he whispered.

I nodded him back out. We crawled to the fire escape platform.

'Christ,' he whispered again. 'Can you believe that?'

I shook my head.

'No,' I whispered back to him. 'I can't believe it.'

'What are we going to do?' he asked me.

I held my hand up to make Finlay wait on the platform. Crawled back inside and peered down through the window. I looked all over the place. Looked at where Teale was sitting, looked at the office inner door, checked Kliner's field of fire, guessed where Roscoe and Charlie might end up. I calculated angles and estimated distances. I came up with one definite conclusion. It was a hell of a problem.

Old man Kliner was the nearest person to us. Roscoe and Charlie were working between him and Teale. Teale was the dangerous one because he was at the far end of the warehouse. When I came out at the top of the inside stairs, they were all four going to look up at me. Kliner was going to raise his shotgun. Teale was going to raise his shotgun. They were both going to shoot at me.

Kliner had a straight shot, sixty degrees upward, like a duck hunter. But Roscoe and Charlie were down there between Teale and me. Teale was going to be shooting on a fairly shallow angle. He was already perched ten feet up the slope. He would be looking for another thirty feet of elevation from a distance of a hundred feet. A shallow angle. Maybe fifteen or twenty degrees. His big Ithaca was designed to cover a much wider spread than fifteen or twenty degrees. His shot was going to catch the women in a murderous spray. His shot was going to kill them. When Teale looked up at me and fired, Roscoe and Charlie were going to die.

I crawled back out of the office and joined Finlay on the fire escape. Bent down and picked up the plastic bottle of gasoline. Handed it to him with the matchbook. Leaned close and told him what to do. We whispered together and he set off slowly back down the long flight of metal steps. I crawled through the office and laid the Desert Eagle carefully on the floor by the inner door. Safety off. Crawled back under the window. Eased my head up and waited.

Three minutes went by. I was staring at the far end of the roller door. Staring and waiting.

Watching the crack between the bottom of the door and the concrete, right at the far end, diagonally opposite me across the whole huge space. I stared and waited. Four minutes had gone by. The tiny figures below toiled on. Roscoe and Charlie stuffing boxes, under Teale's careful gaze. Kliner clambering his way over the mountainside to kick a new river of dollars down the slope toward the women. Five minutes had gone by. Kliner had put his shotgun down. He was thirty feet away from it, scrabbling in the pile, starting a small avalanche which rolled down to Roscoe's feet. Six minutes had gone by. Seven.

Then I saw the dark wet stain of gasoline seeping under the roller door. It flowed into a semicircular pool. It kept coming. It reached the bottom of the enormous dune of dollars, ten feet below where Teale was sprawled on the lower slopes. It kept growing outward. A dark stain on the concrete. Kliner was still working, forty feet across the mountain from Teale. Still thirty feet away from his weapon.

I crawled back to the inner door. Eased the handle down. The door came free of the catch. I picked up my gun. Eased the door halfway open. Crawled back to the window. Watched the growing pool of gasoline.

I had been afraid Teale would smell it straight away. That was the weak part of the plan. But he couldn't smell it. Because the whole shed was full of a powerful, appalling stink. It had hit me like a hammer as soon as I opened the door. A heavy, sour, greasy smell. The smell of money. Millions and millions of crumpled and greasy dollar bills were seeping out the stink of sweaty hands and sour pockets. The smell hung in the air. It was the same smell I had noticed in the empty boxes in Sherman Stoller's garage. The sour smell of used money.

Then I saw the flame bloom under the door. Finlay had dropped the match. It was a low blue flame. It raced in under the door and bloomed out over the wide stain like a flower opening. It reached the bottom of the huge green mountain. I saw Teale snap his head around and stare at it, frozen in horror.

I stepped to the door and squeezed out. Aimed the gun. Braced my wrist against the balcony railing. Pulled the trigger and blew Teale's head off, a hundred feet away. The big bullet caught him in the temple and exploded his skull all over the metal siding behind him.

Then everything went wrong. I saw it happen in that terrible slow motion you get when your mind is racing faster than you can move. My gun hand was drifting left to track Kliner on his way back to his own weapon. But Kliner dived to the right. He launched himself in a desperate leap down the mountainside to the spot where Teale had dropped his shotgun. He wasn't going back for his own gun. He was going to use Teale's weapon. He was going to use the same lethal geometry that Teale would have used. I saw my hand reverse its direction. It was cutting a graceful smooth arc through the air just behind Kliner tumbling and sliding down in a great spray of dollars. Then I heard the crash of the staff door bursting open below. The crash of the door fought with the echo of the roar of the shot which had killed Teale and I saw Picard stagger onto the warehouse floor.

His jacket was gone and I saw blood soaking his enormous white shirt. I saw him taking giant lurching strides towards the women. His head was turning and his right arm was windmilling upward to point at me. I saw his .38 dwarfed in his hand. A hundred feet from him I saw Kliner reach Teale's shotgun where it had fallen and buried itself in the cash pile.

I saw the blue flames bursting upward at the bottom of the huge dune of dollars. I saw Roscoe spinning slowly to look up at me. I saw Charlie Hubble spinning slowly the other way to look at Teale. I saw her start to scream. Her hands were slowly moving up to her face and her mouth was opening and her eyes were closing. The sound of her screaming drifted gently up to me and fought the dying echo of the Desert Eagle's bullet and the crash of the door.

I grasped the balcony railing in front of me and hauled myself one-handed toward it. Swung my gun hand vertically down and fired and hit Picard through the right shoulder a tiny fraction before his .38 came to rest on me. I saw him hit the floor in an explosion of blood as I hauled my aim back over to Kliner.

My mind was detached. Just treating it like a purely mechanical problem. I had locked my shoulder so that the big automatic's recoil would kick it upwards. That won me a tiny fraction as I hauled the sights over to the other end of the warehouse. I felt the smack in my palm as the burnt gases hurled the spent shell case out and crashed the next bullet in. Kliner had the Ithaca barrel on the way up in a slow motion flurry of dollar bills and he was pumping the shell. I heard the double crunch-crunch of the mechanism over the roar of the shot that had stopped Picard.

My detached mind computed that Kliner would fire just slightly above the horizontal to hit me with the top of the spray and that the bottom of the spray would decapitate Roscoe and Charlie. It told me my bullet would take a hair over seven hundredths of a second to cover the length of the warehouse and that I should aim high up on his right side to rotate the shotgun away from the women.

After that, my brain just shut down. Handed me all that information and sat back to mock my attempt to haul my arm up faster than Kliner could haul the Ithaca's barrel up. It was a race in agonizing slow motion. I was leaning half off the balcony slowly bringing my arm up as if I was lifting an enormous weight. A hundred feet away Kliner was slowly raising the shotgun barrel as if it was mired in molasses. They came up together, slowly, inch by inch, degree by degree. Up and up. It took for ever. It took the whole of my lifetime. Flames were bursting and exploding at the bottom of the mountain. They were spreading upward and outward through the money. Kliner's yellow teeth were parting in a wolfish smile. Charlie was screaming. Roscoe was slowly floating down toward the concrete floor like gossamer. My arm and Kliner's shotgun were travelling slowly upward together, inch by ghastly inch.

My arm got there first. I fired and hit Kliner in the right upper chest and the huge .44 slug hurled him off his feet. The Ithaca barrel whipped sideways as he pulled the trigger. The shotgun boomed and fired point-blank into the enormous mountain of money. The air was instantly thick with tiny scraps of paper. Shreds and fragments of dollar bills were blasted all over the place. They swirled like a thick blizzard and burst into flames as they settled into the fire.

Then time restarted and I was racing down the stairs to the warehouse floor. Flames were ripping through the greasy mountain faster than a man could run. I fought through the smoke and caught Roscoe under one arm and Charlie under the other. Spun them off their feet and carried them back towards the staircase. I could feel a gale of oxygen sucking in under the roller door to feed the fire. The whole huge shed was bursting into flame. The enormous dune of money was exploding. I was running flat out for the stairs, dragging the two women with me.

I ran straight into Picard. He reared up off the floor in front of me and the impact sent me sprawling. He stood there like a wounded giant bellowing in fury. His right shoulder was shattered and pumping blood. His shirt was soaked an appalling crimson. I staggered up off the floor and he hit me with his left hand. It was a shuddering impact and it rocked me back. He followed it up with another swinging left that hit me on the arm and sent the Desert Eagle clattering over the concrete. The fire was billowing around us and my lungs were burning and I could hear Charlie Hubble screaming hysterically.

Picard had lost his revolver. He stood unsteadily in front of me, rocking back and forth, swinging his massive left arm ready for another blow. I threw myself inside the swing and hit him in the throat with my elbow. I hit him harder than I had ever hit anything before in my life. But he just shook himself and stepped nearer. Swung his enormous left fist and knocked me sideways into the fire.

I was breathing pure smoke as I rolled out. Picard stepped nearer. He was standing in a burning drift of money. He leaned forward and kicked

me in the chest. Like being hit by a truck. My
jacket caught fire. I tore it off and hurled it at him.
But he just swatted it aside and swung his leg back
for the kick that was going to kill me. Then his
body started jerking like somebody was behind
him, hitting him with a hammer. I saw Finlay
standing there shooting Picard with the handgun
he'd got from the station house. He fired six shots
into Picard's back. Picard turned and looked at
him. Took a step towards him. Finlay's gun clicked
empty.

I scrabbled for my big Israeli automatic. Swept it
up off the hot concrete and shot Picard through the
back of the head. His skull exploded under
the impact of the huge bullet. His legs crumpled
and he started falling. I fired my last four shells into
him before he hit the floor.

Finlay grabbed Charlie and raced away through
the flames. I hauled Roscoe off the floor and hurled
myself at the stairs and dragged her up and out
through the office. Out and down the fire escape as
the flames boiled out through the door after us. We
hurled ourselves through the gap in the fence. I
hoisted Roscoe high into my arms and ran across
the field to the tree.

Behind us the superheated air blew the roof off
the shed and flames burst a hundred feet into the
night sky. All around us burning fragments of
dollar bills were drifting down. The warehouse was
blasting like a furnace. I could feel the heat on my
back and Roscoe was beating away the flaming
paper that was landing on us. We raced for the tree.
Didn't stop. Raced on to the road. Two hundred
yards. A hundred yards. Behind me I could hear
screeching and tearing as the metal shed distorted
and burst. Up ahead Hubble was standing next to

510

the Bentley. He flung open the rear doors and raced for the driver's seat.

The four of us crammed into the back and Hubble stamped on the gas. The car shot forward and the doors slammed shut. The children were in the front. Both screaming. Charlie was screaming. Roscoe was screaming. I noticed with a kind of detached curiosity that I was screaming, too.

Hubble blasted a mile down the road. Then he jammed to a stop and we untangled ourselves and fell out of the car. Stumbled about. Hugged and kissed and cried, staggering about in the dirt at the side of the old county road. The four Hubbles clung together. Roscoe and Finlay and I clung together. Then Finlay was dancing around, yelling and laughing like a madman. All his old Boston reserve was gone. Roscoe was huddled in my arms. I was watching the fire, a mile away. It was getting worse. It was getting higher. It was spreading to the farmers' sheds next in line. Bags of nitrogen fertilizer and drums of tractor oil were exploding like bombs.

We all turned to watch the inferno and the explosions. Seven of us, in a ragged line on the road. From a mile away, we watched the firestorm. Great spouts of flame were leaping a thousand feet. Exploding oil drums were blowing up like mortar shells. The night sky was full of burning banknotes like a million orange stars. It looked like hell on earth.

'Christ,' Finlay said. 'Did we do that?'

'You did that, Finlay,' I said. 'You dropped the match.'

We laughed and hugged. We danced and laughed and slapped each other's backs. We swung the children up in the air and hugged them and kissed them. Hubble hugged me and pounded me on the back. Charlie hugged me and kissed me. I lifted Roscoe off her feet and kissed her long and hard. On and on. She wrapped her legs around my waist and locked her arms behind my head. We kissed like we would die if we stopped.

Then I drove slowly and quietly back to town. Finlay and Roscoe squeezed together with me in the front. The four Hubbles squeezed into the back. Soon as we lost the glow of the fire behind us, we picked up the glow of the station house burning in front of us. I slowed as we drove past. Burning fiercely. It was going to burn to the ground. Hundreds of people were milling about in a ragged circle, watching it. Nobody was doing anything about it.

I picked up speed again and we rolled through the silent town. Made the right up Beckman opposite the statue of old Caspar Teale. Jinked around the silent white church. Drove the mile up to the familiar white mailbox at number twenty-five. I turned in and wound my way up the driveway. Stopped at the door just long enough for the Hubbles to spill out. Hauled the old car around and back down the driveway. Rolled down Beckman again and stopped at the bottom.

'Out, Finlay,' I said.

He grinned and got out. Walked off into the night. I drove across the bottom of Main Street and coasted down to Roscoe's place. Stopped on her drive. We stumbled into the house. Dragged a chest of drawers down the hallway and shoved it up against the splintered door. Sealed ourselves off from the world.

THIRTY-FOUR

It didn't work out for Roscoe and me. It never really stood a chance. There were too many problems. It lasted a hair over twenty-four hours, and then it was over. I was back on the road.

It was five o'clock Sunday morning when we hauled that chest of drawers over and shoved it up against the broken door. We were both exhausted. But the adrenalin was still boiling through us. So we couldn't sleep. Instead, we talked. And the more we talked, the worse it got.

Roscoe had been a prisoner the best part of sixty-four hours. She hadn't been mistreated. She told me they hadn't touched her. She'd been terrified, but they'd just worked her like a slave. Thursday, Picard had driven her off in his car. I had watched them go. I'd waved them off. She'd updated him with our progress. A mile up the county road, he'd pulled his gun on her. Disarmed her, handcuffed her, driven her up to the warehouse. He'd driven right in through the roller door and she'd been put straight to work with Charlie Hubble. The two of

513

them had been in there working the whole time I'd been sitting under the highway, watching the place. Roscoe herself had unloaded the red truck the Kliner kid had brought in. Then I'd followed it out to that truck stop near Memphis and wondered why the hell it was empty.

Charlie Hubble had been in there working five and a half days. Since Monday evening. Kliner had already started panicking by then. The Coast Guard retreat was coming too soon for him. He knew he had to work fast to clear the stockpile. So Picard had brought the Hubbles straight to the warehouse. Kliner had made the hostages work. They'd slept just a few hours a night, lying down on the dune of dollars, handcuffed to the bottom of the office stairs.

Saturday morning, when his son and the two gatemen hadn't come back, Kliner had gone crazy. Now he had no staff at all. So he worked the hostages around the clock. They didn't sleep at all Saturday night. Just ploughed on with the hopeless task of trying to box up the huge pile. They were falling further and further behind. Every time an incoming truck spilled a new load out on the warehouse floor, Kliner had become more and more frantic.

So Roscoe had been a slave the best part of three days. In fear for her life, in danger, exhausted and humiliated for three long days. And it was my fault. I told her that. The more I told her, the more she said she didn't blame me. It was my fault, I was saying. It wasn't your fault, she was saying. I'm sorry, I was saying. Don't be, she was telling me.

We listened to each other. We accepted what was being said. But I still thought it was my fault.

Wasn't a 100 per cent sure she didn't think so, too. Despite what she was saying. We didn't fall out about it. But it was the first faint sign of a problem between us.

We showered together in her tiny stall. Stayed in there the best part of an hour. We were soaping off the stink of the money and the sweat and the fire. And we were still talking. I was telling her about Friday night. The ambush in the storm up at Hubble's place. I told her all about it. I told her about the bags with the knives and the hammer and the nails. I told her what I'd done to the five of them. I thought she'd be happy about it.

And that was the second problem. Not a big deal as we stood there with the hot water beating down on us. But I heard something in her voice. Just a tiny tremor. Not shock or disapproval. Just a hint of a question. That maybe I had gone too far. I could hear it in her voice.

I felt somehow I'd done it all for her and Joe. I hadn't done it because I had wanted to do it. It was Joe's business and it was her town and these were her people. I'd done it because I'd seen her trying to melt into her kitchen wall, crying like her heart was breaking. I'd done it for Joe and Molly. At the same time as feeling I needed no justification at all, I had been justifying it to myself like that.

It didn't feel like a problem at the time. The shower loosened us up. Steamed some glow back into us. We went to bed. Left the drapes open. It was a glorious day. The sun was up in a bright blue sky and the air looked fresh and clean. It looked like it should look. Like a new day.

We made love with great tenderness, great energy, great joy. If somebody had told me then that I'd be back on the road the next morning, I'd have thought they were crazy. I told myself there were no problems. I was imagining them. And if there were problems, there were good reasons for them. Maybe the after-effects of the stress and the adrenalin. Maybe the deep fatigue. Maybe because Roscoe had been a hostage. Maybe she was reacting like a lot of hostages do. They feel some kind of a faint jealousy against anybody who hadn't been a hostage with them. Some kind of a faint resentment. Maybe that was feeding the guilt I was carrying for letting her get captured in the first place. Maybe a lot of things. I fell asleep certain we'd wake up happy and I'd stay there for ever.

We did wake up happy. We slept through until late afternoon. Then we spent a gorgeous couple of hours with the afternoon sun streaming in the window, dozing and stretching, kissing and laughing. We made love again. We were fuelled up with the joy of being safe and alive and alone together. It was the best lovemaking we ever had. It was also the last. But we didn't know that at the time.

Roscoe took the Bentley up to Eno's for some food. She was gone an hour and came back with news. She'd seen Finlay. She was talking about what was going to happen next. That was the big problem. It made the other tiny problems look like nothing at all.

'You should see the station house,' she said. 'Nothing left more than a foot high.'

She put the food on a tray and we ate it sitting on the bed. Fried chicken.

'All four warehouses burned down,' she said. 'There was debris exploding all over the highway. The state police got involved. They had to get fire trucks all the way from Atlanta and Macon.'

'State police are involved?' I said.

She laughed.

'Everybody's involved,' she said. 'It sort of snow-balled. The Atlanta fire chief called in the bomb squad because of the explosions, because he didn't know for sure what they were. The bomb squad can't go anywhere without notifying the FBI, in case it's terrorism, so the Bureau is interested. Then the National Guard got involved this morning.'

'The National Guard?' I said. 'Why?'

'This is the best part,' she said. 'Finlay says when the roof blew off the warehouse last night, the sudden updraft of air blew the money all over the place. Remember those burning pieces that kept landing on us? There are millions of dollar bills all over the place. Miles around. The wind blew them everywhere, in the fields, all over the highway. Most of them are partially burned, of course, but some of them aren't. Soon as the sun came up, thousands of people came out of nowhere, swarming around all over the place, picking all the money up. So the National Guard was ordered in to disperse the crowds.'

I ate some food. Thought about it.

'Governor calls in the Guard, right?' I asked her.

She nodded. Mouth full of chicken wing.

'The governor's involved,' she said. 'He's in town right now. And Finlay called the Treasury Department, because of Joe. They're sending a team down here. I told you, it sort of snowballed.'

'What the hell else?' I said.

'Big problems here, of course,' she said. 'Rumours are flying around. Everybody seems to know the Foundation is finished. Finlay says half of them are pretending they never knew what was going on, and the other half are mad as hell their thousand dollars a week is going to stop. You should have seen old Eno, when I picked up the food. Looked like he's furious.'

'Finlay worried?' I said.

'He's OK,' she said. 'Busy, of course. We're down to a four-person police department. Finlay, me, Stevenson and the desk man. Finlay says that's half of what we need, because of the crisis, but twice as many as we can afford, because the Foundation subsidy is going to stop. But anyway, there's nothing anybody can do about hiring and firing without the mayor's approval, and we haven't got a mayor any more, have we?'

I sat there on the bed, eating. The problems started bearing down on me. I hadn't really seen them clearly before. But I was seeing them now. A huge question was forming in my mind. It was a question for Roscoe. I wanted to ask it straight away and get her honest, spontaneous response. I didn't want to give her any time to think about her answer.

'Roscoe?' I said.

She looked up at me. Waited.

'What are you going to do?' I asked her.

She looked at me like it was an odd question.

'Work my butt off, I guess,' she said. 'There's going to be a lot to do. We're going to have to rebuild this whole town. Maybe we can make something better out of it, create something worth-while. And I can play a big part in it. I'll move up the totem pole a couple of notches. I'm really excited. I'm looking forward to it. This is my town and I'm going to be really involved in it. Maybe I'll get on the town board. Maybe I'll even run for mayor. That would be a hell of a thing, wouldn't it? After all these years, a Roscoe for mayor, instead of a Teale?'

I looked at her. It was a great answer, but it was the wrong answer. Wrong for me. I didn't want to try to change her mind. I didn't want to put any kind of pressure on her at all. That's why I had asked her straight out, before I told her what I was going to have to do. I had wanted her honest, natural response. And I had got it. It was right for her. This was her town. If anybody could fix it, she could. If anybody should stick around, working her butt off, she should.

But it was the wrong answer for me. Because I knew by then I had to go. I knew by then that I had to get out fast. The problem was what was going to happen next. The whole thing had got out of hand. Before, it had all been about Joe. It had been private. Now it was public. It was like those half-burnt dollar bills. It was scattered all over the damn place.

Roscoe had mentioned the governor, the Treasury Department, the National Guard, the state police, the FBI, Atlanta fire investigators. A half-dozen competent agencies, all looking at what had gone on in Margrave. And they'd be looking hard. They'd be calling Kliner the counterfeiter of the century. They'd find out the mayor had disappeared. They'd find out that four police officers had been involved. The FBI would be looking for Picard. Interpol would get involved because of the Venezuela connection. The heat would be tremendous. There would be six agencies competing like mad to get a result. They'd tear the place apart.

And one or other of them would snarl me up. I

was a stranger in the wrong place at the wrong time. It would take about a minute and a half to realize I was the brother of the dead government investigator who had started the whole thing off. They'd look at my agenda. Somebody would think: revenge. I would be hauled in, and they would go to work on me.

I wouldn't be convicted. There was no risk of that. There was no evidence hanging around. I'd been careful every step of the way. And I knew how to bullshit. They could talk to me until I grew a long white beard and they wouldn't get anything from me. That was for sure. But they'd try. They'd try like crazy. They'd keep me two years in Warburton. Two years up there on the holding floor. Two years of my life. That was the problem. No way could I stand still for that. I'd only just got my life back. I'd had six months of freedom in thirty-six years. Those six months had been the happiest months I'd ever had.

So I was getting out. Before any of them ever knew I'd been there in the first place. My mind was made up. I had to become invisible again. I had to get far away from the Margrave spotlight, where those diligent agencies would never look. It meant my dreams of a future with Roscoe were going to be snuffed out before they were even started. It meant I had to tell Roscoe she wasn't worth gambling two years of my life for. I had to tell her that.

We talked about it all night. We didn't fall out over it. Just talked about it. She knew what I was going to do was right for me. I knew what she was going to do was right for her. She asked me to stay. I thought hard, but said no. I asked her to come with me. She thought hard, but said no. Nothing more to say.

Then we talked about other things. We talked about what I would be doing, and what she would be doing. And I slowly realized that staying there would tear me apart just as much as leaving was going to. Because I didn't want the stuff she was talking about. I didn't want elections and mayors and votes and boards and committees. I didn't want property taxes and maintenance and chambers of commerce and strategies. I didn't want to be sitting there all bored and chafing. Not with the tiny resentments and guilts and disapprovals growing bigger and bigger until they choked us. I wanted what I was talking about. I wanted the open road and a new place every day. I wanted miles to travel and absolutely no idea where I was going. I wanted to ramble. I had rambling on my mind.

We sat around talking, miserable, until dawn. I asked her to do one last thing for me. I asked her to arrange a funeral for Joe. I told her I wanted Finlay to be there, and the Hubbles, and the two old barbers, and her. I told her to ask the old guy's sister to be there and sing a sad song for Joe. I told her to ask the old lady where the meadow was where she'd sung along with Blind Blake's guitar, sixty-two years ago. I asked her to scatter Joe's ashes on the grass there.

Roscoe drove me down to Macon in the Bentley. Seven in the morning. We hadn't slept at all. The trip took us an hour. I sat in the back, behind the new black glass. I didn't want anybody to see me. We drove up the rise from her place and threaded through traffic. The whole town was getting packed. Even before we got up to Main Street, I could see the place was swarming. There were dozens of cars parked up everywhere. There were television trucks from the networks and CNN. I hunched down in the back of the car. People were crowding everywhere, even at seven in the morning. There were ranks of dark blue government sedans all over. We turned at the corner where the coffee shop was. People were lining up on the sidewalk, waiting to get in for breakfast.

We drove through the sunny town. Main Street was parked solid. There were vehicles up on the sidewalks. I saw fire chiefs' cars and state police cruisers. I glanced into the barbershop as we crawled past, but the old guys weren't there. I would miss them. I would miss old Finlay. I would always wonder how things turned out for him. Good luck, Harvard guy, I thought. Good luck, too, to the Hubbles. This morning was the start of a long road for them. They were going to need a lot of luck. Good luck, too, to Roscoe. I sat there, silently wishing her the best of everything. She deserved it. She really did.

She drove me all the way south to Macon. She found the bus depot. Parked up. Handed me a small envelope. Told me not to open it right away. I put it in my pocket. Kissed her goodbye. Got out of the car. Didn't look back. I heard the sound of the big tyres on the pavement and I knew she was gone. I walked into the depot. Bought a ticket. Then I crossed the street to a cheap store and bought new clothes. Changed in their cubicle, left the filthy old fatigues in their garbage can. Then I strolled back and got on a bus for California.

I had tears in my eyes for more than a hundred miles. Then the old bus rattled over the state line. I looked out at the southeast corner of Alabama. Opened Roscoe's envelope. It was the photograph of Joe. She'd taken it from Molly Beth's valise. Taken it out of the frame. Trimmed it with scissors to fit my pocket. On the back she had written her telephone number. But I didn't need that. I had already committed it to memory.

DIE TRYING
by Lee Child

The powerful bestseller from the author of *Killing Floor*.

A Chicago street in bright sunshine. Jack Reacher, strolling nowhere, meets an attractive young woman, limping, struggling with her crutches, alone. Naturally he stops to offer her a steadying arm, and then they turn together – to face twin handguns held level and motionless and aimed straight at their stomachs.

Chained to the woman, locked in a dark, stifling van racing 2,000 miles across America, Reacher needs to know who he's dealing with. The kidnappers are saying nothing and his companion claims to be Holly Johnson, FBI agent. She's fierce enough and tough enough, but he knows there must be more to her than that. And at their remote, hostile destination, they will need to act as a team and trust each other, pitting raw courage and cunning against insane violence and seemingly hopeless odds, with their own lives and hundreds more at stake.

Filled with non-stop action and gritty suspense, *Die Trying* is a tightly plotted thriller from one of the most exciting British talents writing today.

'Cunning and explosive. . . A thumping good read'
Time Out

A Bantam Paperback
0553 505416

TRIPWIRE
by Lee Child

'A slickly effective thriller which confirms Child's ability to keep the reader guessing – and sweating'
The Times

Digging a swimming pool by hand in Key West, former military policeman Jack Reacher is not pleased when Costello, a private detective, comes nosing around asking questions about him. Determined to keep out of trouble, Reacher conceals his identity. But when he finds Costello dead with his fingertips sliced off, he realizes it is time to move on – and move on fast. Yet two questions worry him: who was Costello's employer, the mysterious Mrs Jacobs? And why is she determined to find Reacher?

Moreover, who is Hook Hobie, the vicious and amoral manipulator in a Wall Street office who preys on other people's assets? As Reacher follows the trail, it becomes clear that the stakes are high: the livelihood of a whole community; the fate of the soldiers missing in action in Vietnam; and, not least, the reappearance of a woman from Reacher's own troubled past with a key to his destiny.

'Fast-moving, violent and gripping'
Daily Telegraph

A Bantam Paperback
0553 811851

THE VISITOR
by Lee Child

'Once again, terrific stuff'
Independent on Sunday

Sergeant Amy Callan and Lieutenant Caroline Cook have a lot in common. High-flying army career women, both are victims of sexual harassment from their superiors; both are forced to resign from the service.

And now they're both dead.

Their unmarked bodies are discovered in their own homes, naked, in baths filled with army-issue camouflage paint. Expert FBI psychological profilers start to hunt for a serial murderer, a smart guy with a score to settle, a loner, an army man, a ruthless vigilante known to both of them.

Jack Reacher, a former US military cop, is a smart guy, a loner and a drifter, as tough as they come. He knew both victims. For Agent-in-Charge Nelson Blake and his team he's the perfect match. They're sure only Reacher has the answers to their burning questions: how did these women die? And why?

'Relentlessly fast-paced and beautifully structured . . . Amply fulfils the promise of its predecessors. Reacher is the sort of hero no woman could help falling for, and he looks destined to have a very long life'
Daily Mail

A Bantam Paperback
0553 81188 6

A SELECTED LIST OF CRIME AND MYSTERY NOVELS AVAILABLE FROM BANTAM BOOKS

THE PRICES SHOWN BELOW WERE CORRECT AT THE TIME OF GOING TO PRESS. HOWEVER TRANSWORLD PUBLISHERS RESERVE THE RIGHT TO SHOW NEW RETAIL PRICES ON COVERS WHICH MAY DIFFER FROM THOSE PREVIOUSLY ADVERTISED IN THE TEXT OR ELSEWHERE.

☐	81187 8	SANCTUARY	*Lisa Appignanesi*	£5.99
☐	50329 4	DANGER ZONES	*Sally Beauman*	£5.99
☐	50630 7	DARK ANGEL	*Sally Beauman*	£6.99
☐	50631 5	DESTINY	*Sally Beauman*	£6.99
☐	50326 X	SEXTET	*Sally Beauman*	£6.99
☐	50541 6	DIE TRYING	*Lee Child*	£6.99
☐	81185 1	TRIPWIRE	*Lee Child*	£6.99
☐	81188 6	THE VISITOR	*Lee Child*	£5.99
☐	81330 7	ECHO BURNING	*Lee Child*	£5.99
☐	17510 6	A GREAT DELIVERANCE	*Elizabeth George*	£6.99
☐	40168 8	A SUITABLE VENGEANCE	*Elizabeth George*	£6.99
☐	40237 4	FOR THE SAKE OF ELENA	*Elizabeth George*	£6.99
☐	40846 1	IN THE PRESENCE OF THE ENEMY	*Elizabeth George*	£6.99
☐	40238 2	MISSING JOSEPH	*Elizabeth George*	£6.99
☐	17511 4	PAYMENT IN BLOOD	*Elizabeth George*	£6.99
☐	40845 3	PLAYING FOR THE ASHES	*Elizabeth George*	£6.99
☐	40167 X	WELL-SCHOOLED IN MURDER	*Elizabeth George*	£6.99
☐	50385 5	A DRINK BEFORE THE WAR	*Dennis Lehane*	£5.99
☐	50584 X	DARKNESS, TAKE MY HAND	*Dennis Lehane*	£5.99
☐	81220 3	GONE, BABY, GONE	*Dennis Lehane*	£6.99
☐	50585 8	SACRED	*Dennis Lehane*	£6.99
☐	81221 1	PRAYERS FOR RAIN	*Dennis Lehane*	£5.99
☐	81222 X	MYSTIC RIVER	*Dennis Lehane*	£6.99
☐	50694 3	GARNETHILL	*Denise Mina*	£5.99
☐	81327 7	EXILE	*Denise Mina*	£5.99
☐	81328 5	RESOLUTION	*Denise Mina*	£5.99
☐	50586 6	FAREWELL TO THE FLESH	*Gemma O'Connor*	£5.99
☐	50587 4	TIME TO REMEMBER	*Gemma O'Connor*	£5.99
☐	81263 7	SINS OF OMISSION	*Gemma O'Connor*	£5.99
☐	81262 9	FALLS THE SHADOW	*Gemma O'Connor*	£5.99
☐	81258 0	WALKING ON WATER	*Gemma O'Connor*	£5.99
☐	81215 7	EVERYBODY SMOKES IN HELL	*John Ridley*	£5.99
☐	50542 4	THE POISON TREE	*Tony Strong*	£5.99
☐	50543 2	THE DEATH PIT	*Tony Strong*	£5.99
☐	81365 X	THE DECOY	*Tony Strong*	£5.99

All Transworld titles are available by post from:

Bookpost, P.O. Box 29, Douglas, Isle of Man IM99 1BQ

Credit cards accepted. Please telephone 01624 836000,
fax 01624 837033, Internet http://www.bookpost.co.uk or
e-mail: bookshop@enterprise.net for details.

Free postage and packing in the UK. Overseas customers allow
£1 per book (paperbacks) and £3 per book (hardbacks).